Consciên

By Alex Buzz

Table of Contents

Part 1 - An unexpected journey

1

Damnation! The attention of an unknown biting insect promised to add yet
another itchy red swelling to those left by its comrades. Jessica's love for nature
was being sorely tested today by some of the less endearing inhabitants of the
forest. She had been trekking through the forest now for two days and the heat,
humidity and the attention of some of the smaller denizens who lived beneath
the canopy was starting to take its toll on Jessica's humour.

So why was she here? She had tried to rationalise this many times over the last
few days and was still far from convinced she had a satisfactory explanation.
The only thing she did know was that something in her life was missing; there
was this strange emptiness inside that never quite seemed to go away.

She had first become conscious of this feeling after the death of her older sister
Natasha who had been tragically killed in a car collision when Jessica was just
seventeen. Her sister, whom Jessica loved and idolised, was twenty at the time
and had been out clubbing with her boyfriend Peter one late summer's evening.
Nobody in the family had any concerns before they had gone to bed, they were
used to Natasha staying out late and she often stopped over at Peter's parents'
house after they had been to the clubs.

Jessica could still remember the knock on the door from the police at about 2.30
in the morning. She had sat with her parents in disbelief as a traffic officer had
explained what the police believed to be the events that had led that night to
her sister's death. A drunk driver had fallen asleep at the wheel of his car and
careered across the central reservation on the dual carriageway. The police
estimated that the two vehicles had collided head on at a combined speed of
over 100 mph. Natasha was killed instantly and Peter suffered a severe
concussion and had lost the use of his left leg through irreparable damage to his
spinal cord.

At first Jessica couldn't accept that her sister was no longer with them. The
rational part of her brain understood that Natasha was no longer alive but her
heart, her emotions, still refuted this incontrovertible evidence. Sometimes she
would wake up in the morning having momentarily forgotten, only for the

emotions and hurt to come flooding back when she realised that her sister was no longer there for her.

She remembered the funeral at the crematorium as if it was some kind of play, the whole occasion somehow surreal and artificial. It had been a dismal day with grey overcast skies and a persistent drizzle. They had all filed into the chapel of rest and had listened whilst a vicar, who had never even met Natasha, said a few words about God's love. Natasha had never had any time for God and Jessica thought it was somehow disingenuous to her memory to bring God in at the end of her life without her consent.

For several months after her sister's death, the emotional aftermath left Jessica feeling adrift. Her grades at school started to slip and even her closest friends found it increasingly difficult to engage with her. It was as if Jessica was deliberately keeping a safe emotional distance from anyone she had previously cared for. Maybe this was subconsciously a way of protecting herself from the possibility of further emotional pain. Invitations to go out with her old friends started to dry up and part of her welcomed this as she sought to be alone, just her own thoughts and the memories of her sister for company.

One night, about nine months after Natasha's death, Jessica had a very vivid dream. She was stood on a small beach lit only by the silver light of a full moon. She heard the booming sound of waves hurling themselves to destruction upon black rocky outcrops which rose up each side of the narrow band of sand. The dark sky had a strange luminescent greenish hue and Jessica was looking out into the white foamy crests of the waves which were captured by the light of the moon as they collapsed against the rising slope of the beach. She was desperately searching for something in the swirling water but she had no idea what it was she was looking for.

As she peered intently into the rolling waves she saw a waif like figure emerge from the surf and glide across the sand towards her. The figure had a haunted and sad expression and she soon realised it was her sister Natasha. Jessica' heart leapt and she ran out to meet her sister with a cry of delight. As she went to fling her arms around her sister, the substance of Natasha's figure melted away and instead she clasped empty air. Above the sound of the crashing waves she heard Natasha's fading voice repeating the same words again and again; 'let me go Jessica, please let me go' until all that was left was the sound of the waves hurling themselves against the rocks.

Jessica awoke with a start; the dream had seemed so real that she felt that she had just lost Natasha for a second time. Despite an overwhelming feeling of grief at her renewed sense of loss, she realised that the dream was sending her a clear message that she had to somehow move on and re-engage with her life. She knew she had to let her sister go and focus on the future, not dwell in the memories of the past. The loss of her sister had left an emotional wound within her that would never completely heal. This would ache in her breast when something like a favourite song on the radio triggered a memory of a special moment they had once shared together.

Jessica returned to her life with renewed enthusiasm, determined to somehow make up for another life that had been so tragically and pointlessly cut short. Her school grades rapidly improved to the extent that she was soon in the top ten percent of students in most of her subjects. She actively renewed her old friendships and had her fill of partying, willingly succumbing to the amorous attentions of various suitors. This left her with memories that brought both smiles and grimaces in equal measure. She had travelled widely, had bungee jumped off a bridge in Australia and white water canoed in Wales. Despite her frenetic re-engagement with life, when the adrenalin rushes had subsided Jessica was still left with a profound feeling that something deep within her still remained unfulfilled. Life had to be more substantial than a number of hedonistic experiences followed by the inevitability of death. Surely there had to be a more fundamental purpose to existence?

It was her search to find a meaning for her life that had led her to take up the course on philosophy at the University of Bath. This ultimately proved to be a vain attempt to identify what it was that was missing. Nearly three years of study and copious reading of the works of Plato, Kant, Heidegger and Descartes had failed to provide a satisfactory answer. She could now rationalise about the nature of existence but she couldn't emotionally engage with any of the theories she had studied and a sense that something important was missing remained.

It was halfway through her third year of her undergraduate studies in philosophy at the University of Bath that the seeds of her current adventure were sown. She had been having a rare tutorial with Professor Brian Henderson. They were discussing her studies and the progress that she was making on her final dissertation on the relevance of philosophy for society in the 21st Century. The professor was quite satisfied with the work that she had produced but noticed a hint of dissatisfaction in her demeanour.

"What's the problem Jessica?" the professor enquired "you will almost certainly get a first if you keep up this standard of work."

"I'm not worried about the degree as such; it's just that the course hasn't provided the answers I was hoping to find about the purpose of my life. This was my motivation for taking up the philosophy course in the first place and I almost feel that all this time and effort has been wasted. Despite all my studies, human existence still seems rather purposeless and arbitrary. All the reading and discussions on the nature of humanity that I have undertaken during the last two and a half years have still left my fundamental questions unanswered."

The professor chuckled, "so you were expecting to understand the meaning of life after completing your studies with us? If we could genuinely answer that question I am sure that our University would be positively brimming with budding philosophy students and I would be happily retired on the huge royalties my research would have attracted. Are you sure that you shouldn't have chosen a course on theology instead?"

Jessica looked at her professor in disdain, "I don't believe there is some petulant all powerful supernatural God directing my future" she snorted in derision. "I think that most religions have only been created to provide a convenient excuse for men to suppress the rights and freedom of women. I also don't want to believe that the only purpose of life is to replicate yet another generation of the species or indulge in a meaningless hedonistic orgy of self-indulgence. Surely there must be more to life than this?"

"Have you considered that there may be no higher purpose in life except to just exist?" her professor replied.

"That is my greatest fear" replied Jessica, "what if there really is no greater purpose. Will I just have to spend the rest of my life seeking distractions to avoid having to face up to the truth that our lives are essentially pointless?"

"So what is the question you want me to answer Jessica?"

"That's just it; I don't even know the question, let alone the answer. I just have this conviction that I am missing out on something important. I look at our frenetic society whose values seem to be based on the worship of greed and celebrity and often feel like a complete outsider. What's the point of striving to become a multi-millionaire if underneath you realise that all this ambition for wealth and materialism is just a distraction? Perhaps we have to face up to the awful truth that we are all intrinsically worthless in any true sense of the meaning. Are we really just temporary specks on a small planet going around a very mediocre sun in one arm of a small spiral galaxy in the company of billions of other galaxies?"

"Oh my goodness Jessica, is this really how you feel about your life?"

"Not most of the time Brian." Jessica's professor was not particularly keen on formality and preferred to be on first name terms with his students. "Normally just like most of the other students I am sufficiently distracted by the day to day realities of student living; dating, partying, listening to music and of course studying!" The professor smiled at this. "It's when the noise has died down and my friends have gone and I am left to my own thoughts that the same old questions keep coming back to me. What's the purpose of my life, what am I going to do with it and, at the end, will I have made any difference at all?"

"So basically you want me to answer a question you don't know and that hasn't been answered by studying the world's greatest philosophers for two and a half years. Pity, I was hoping that you might ask me something a bit more challenging." The professor smiled but he was actually concerned about this highly intelligent yet emotionally vulnerable young woman sat in front of him. Deep down he also knew the truth that this was a question that had also tormented him at certain points in his life and that he had studiously tried to avoid it. Fortunately his three marriages, the demands of the university for new research, and the prevarications and excuses for not studying from most of his students usually kept his mind sufficiently occupied. He inwardly smiled at the thought of his first wife Alison whom he had met when she was a student on a master's degree and he was a junior lecturer. There was something about Jessica that reminded him of Alison, maybe it was the same restless spirit that ultimately drew Alison away from their marriage. It had been many years since he had last had any contact with her and he sometimes wondered what had become of her.

"I don't think I am the best person to help you with this Jessica. I think that you are on more of a spiritual quest and it is unlikely to be fulfilled by further rational reasoning on the nature of humanity and society. There is perhaps someone whom you might try but I can offer no guarantees that she will be able to help you any more than I can."

"I really am prepared to explore any avenue" said Jessica, "how do I make contact with this person?"

"Her name is Ellen MacDonald. My wife has an interest in Wicca and witchcraft and Ellen has sometimes helped her to find some of the more obscure manuscripts that can't be conjured up on Amazon and similar mainstream sources. She runs a small bookshop called Alternative Reality that is located in Trim Street. You could try her to see if she has any material that she thinks could be of use to you in your search. In the meantime, let's get back to your dissertation shall we?"

The following morning at 9.00 a.m. sharp Jessica was outside Alternative Reality waiting for the bookshop to open. After about ten minutes there seemed to be no sign of life and she started to look for clues on the door and window about opening times. There was nothing obvious but as she looked at another door which obviously led to a flat above the shop she saw Ellen MacDonald on a small nameplate next to a bell.

Slightly nervously Jessica rang the doorbell and she heard a faint ringing from inside. After a considerable pause, just before Jessica was considering giving up, she heard some footsteps coming down a flight of stairs. The door opened to reveal a grey haired woman, who Jessica estimated must have been about sixty years old, cradling a small black cat in crux of her left arm. The woman had startling blue eyes, similar in colour and alertness to those that might belong to a Malamute Husky. These looked keenly into Jessica's and raising a quizzical eyebrow she said "well?"

"Oh, um I'm sorry to disturb you" spluttered Jessica, "I was just wondering if you can tell me when your bookshop will be open?"

"What do you want it to be open for?" said the woman.

Jessica was completely taken aback by this response. She had never expected a shop owner to question why their shop should be opened to a prospective customer.

"I'm looking for a book" said Jessica.

"Which book?" said the woman who Jessica guessed by now must be Ellen MacDonald.

"I don't know" said Jessica sheepishly, "that's my problem."

"Well I suggest you come back again when you do know" said Ellen and with that she closed the door leaving an utterly bemused and slightly angry Jessica standing outside on the street. What a completely unreasonable and rude woman she thought.

Completely nonplussed, Jessica went for a walk to Parade Gardens nearby to collect her thoughts. What should she do now? If her professor couldn't answer her questions and this Ellen woman wouldn't even talk to her what was she going to do next?

She went to a nearby coffee shop and had a hot chocolate with whipped cream on top, "naughty but nice" she thought to herself as she savoured the hot chocolate through the cold cream that caressed her lips. Maybe hot chocolate and whipped cream is the true meaning of life she considered and the ridiculous thought cheered her up a bit.

She decided that she would keep trying the shop until it was open. Even if Ellen wasn't going to help her directly she might still find something on the bookshelves that would help her take the next step on her 'spiritual quest' as Brian had called it. What on earth is a spiritual quest anyway she mused.

To her satisfaction the shop was open and Ellen was at the back chatting to a rather attractive woman who had dyed flaming red hair and who looked about ten years her junior. They were talking in the familiar manner of friends and Jessica guessed that this was probably more of a social visit by the woman than one from a customer.

Jessica avoided making eye contact and started to look at the shelves. There were books on religion, witchcraft, crystals, astrology, philosophy, anthropology and archaeology, many of them obviously second hand. There was also a set of shelves that seemed to contain journals and articles, some of which seemed to be actually handwritten originals.

"Ah, the young lady who doesn't know what book she is looking for" came a voice from the back of the shop.

"Don't be so horrid Ellen" said the red haired woman. "Please don't worry my dear, Ellen is actually a far nicer person than she would have you believe, how can we help you?" Ellen gave the red haired lady a sharp look but despite her gruff expression her eyes were smiling. Jessica's suspicions were right; the two ladies were obviously close friends.

"That's really the problem; I was advised to come here by my Professor, Brian Henderson at the University. He felt that you might be able to steer me towards some books or texts that might assist me but the trouble is I really don't know what I am looking for."

Ellen now looked at Jessica with considerably more interest. "Brian suggested that you came to see me? I wonder what was on his mind. Tell me the conversation that you had with Brian that led to you coming here."

Jessica repeated as best she could the conversation that she had had during her tutorial.

"Well I am not remotely surprised that your philosophical studies haven't helped you much with the answers that you are seeking" said the red haired woman.

"Forgive Roxie, she's from London and is under some strange illusion that residing in the great metropolis gives her more insight than us primitive West Country folk" said Ellen using an appalling attempt at a Somerset accent.

"You know I am right" said Roxie showing no sign of offence at her friend's deliberate provocation. She turned to Jessica, "tell me the one thing that all the philosophical texts that you have been encouraged to read have in common?"

Jessica wracked her brains but couldn't think what all these authors had in common. Although their works were collectively called philosophy, many of the writers through the ages had very different views and theories on the nature of humanity.

"It's you that is being horrid to the girl now" said Ellen. "By the way, what is your name young lady?"

"Jessica."

"Well Jessica," said Ellen "I suspect that the fundamental flaw in your studies is that all the books and texts you have been recommended to read were written by men."

Jessica immediately realised that they were completely right. When she had started her course she had been given a list of the top twenty philosophers whose works she should consider and they were all men, from Aquinas and Aristotle to Nietzsche and Wittgenstein. There were absolutely no female perspectives at all in any of the works that she had read.

"Men, embedded in the patriarchal societies that have dominated most prevailing cultures over the last three millennia, are convinced of the ultimate power of logical reasoning" continued Ellen. "In reality, the most powerful influences in our lives originate in the human unconscious, in the realm of the instincts and the emotions. It is therefore no surprise that has led to the world being in the perilous state that it is in today and we are in the midst of yet another global financial crisis. It is also the reason why the models used by most economists are so fundamentally flawed. Economists try to predict what is going to happen through rational predictive models when so much of human activity is subject to the whims of irrational human impulses. The main influences on economics are the insecurities, fears, greed and ambitions of those human beings who act upon the world's markets. Make one senior trader emotionally insecure and you can end up creating a run on the markets that has nothing whatever to do with the relative values of the commodities and shares being traded. Women are far more attuned to their emotions and the value of intuition. If we had had three millennia of matriarchal politics and religion instead of dysfunctional patriarchal models I am convinced that the world would not now be on the verge of ecological and financial collapse."

Jessica was captivated by these two eccentric women in this small nondescript bookshop in Bath. In the space of five minutes she felt that she had already been exposed to a very different perspective on the world and her head was already working on the possible implications of what she had heard.

"Where do I look next?" asked Jessica. "I think I understand what you have said about the importance of emotions and instincts but how will this understanding help me towards finding a sense of purpose in my life?"

"You want to know the meaning of life?" laughed Roxie. "Well I can answer that for you but I am sure that you will not understand the answer. I have spent a lifetime trying to understand the answer and there are still parts that remain obscure to me despite all my efforts."

"Please tell me the answer" pleaded Jessica earnestly.

"Why should she?" replied Ellen. "The answer will be completely meaningless unless you have the appetite to try to unravel it and you may spend a lifetime on such a journey without success. Are you really determined enough to spend a lifetime searching for an essential purpose to your life? You will have to make huge sacrifices in rejecting what the majority of your peers mistakenly consider to be of greater value if you are to do this. Perhaps you should consider finding a decently paid job, settle down with a nice boy or girl and have a happy contented life like everyone else?"

"You are obviously an intelligent and competent young lady" continued Ellen "and I am sure you will succeed very well in the generally understood way that contemporary society defines success. There are many distractions in the world that can help take your mind off such a fundamental question as the meaning of life. For most people the meaning of life is their new house, the next car, the new release for their Xbox, a promotion, or children and the responsibilities of parenthood."

"I wish I could convince myself that this was true" said Jessica, "life would be so much simpler but I know that none of these will stop the nagging questions and my restlessness. I am often jealous of fellow students and friends who seem to bob quite happily along the surface of life with absolutely no interest in whether there is any greater or more significant meaning to life than just existing."

"What you seek can also be dangerous Jessica; it's not a journey of enquiry that should be taken lightly" interposed Roxie. "You may well not find what you are looking for, but your journey will almost certainly shatter many of the illusions that now provide some comfort and reassurance. One example of such an illusion which is held by very many people is the belief in the existence of a personal God that knows and loves them. They believe this God will be waiting for them in a heaven devoid of all the suffering, misery and cruelty that you find in our world. It would be very unkind to shatter the illusions of one who held such a belief. Fortunately the emotional attachments of many 'believers' are so strong they can readily defy the mountain of logic and evidence that would shatter their belief, protected by minds that are firmly closed."

"For goodness sake don't read Roxie's book if you harbour any such comforting illusions" said Ellen.

"That will not be a problem for me" said Jessica, "I have never felt any affinity with such an implausible notion. Please help me. Today is probably the first day that I have had any real indication that there are people who have some understanding of what it is I am seeking and may be able to help me. Please don't turn me away, I beg you to at least point me in the right direction for the next step on my journey."

"Before we agree to help you I will set you a small task. Take this copy of the Bhagavad Gita and tell us what you think it is about. Roxie and I are visiting the stone circle Avebury on Friday. It has a wonderfully calming aura which provides an escape from the madness of the world around us and helps to put things in a different perspective. This gives you three days to read the book and come up with an answer. You could do far worse than reading the Bhagavad Gita. Those who fully understand its meaning are already well on the path to self-understanding and this is ultimately the purpose of your quest. Any attempt to understand the nature of reality must start with trying to understand your own nature. We will be in Molly's tearoom in Avebury at 9.30 a.m. If you are genuine you will be there, if not you have saved us wasting any more precious time on you."

With that the two women re-joined their conversation as if their exchange with Jessica had never happened.

2

It was 10.00 a.m. and Jessica was still sat alone in Molly's teashop in Avebury. She had ridden the thirty miles to Avebury on her much loved 125cc pink Honda scooter and had arrived outside Molly's tearoom at about quarter past eight. Fortunately the weather was untypically sunny and dry that morning so she had not had to climb into all her waterproofs for the journey. Being early she had taken the opportunity to walk amongst some of the ancient stones in the 4500 year old stone circle before returning to Molly's.

She was starting to believe that she had been deliberately sent on a wild goose chase when the bell sounded on the opening door and she saw the familiar figures of Roxie and Ellen.

"My you are a persistent one aren't you?" said Ellen as her starkly blue eyes alighted on the figure of Jessica sat in the corner. Roxie smiled and Jessica was slightly taken aback by the warm hug she received from Roxie as she rose to greet the two women.

Ellen and Roxie ordered tea and toasted teacakes; Jessica was already on her second coffee whilst she had been waiting and declined the invitation for another.

"So what did you make of the Bhagavad Gita" asked Ellen inquisitorially.

"On the surface it appeared to be a conversation between Prince Arjuna and Krishna about a great battle that was to take place three thousand years ago and Arjuna's worries and insecurities."

"And beneath the surface?"

"It seemed more about Arjuna's battle to understand his own nature and through that understanding to gain insight into the universal nature of God or Brahman."

"I'm impressed Jessica, you are on the right track. Isn't this the path that you also seek?" asked Ellen. "A true understanding of the Bhagavad Gita could take you a long way towards your goal but first you too will need to gain the self-knowledge that will enable you to better understand what has been written."

Jessica held out the book to return it to Ellen but she gestured for Jessica to keep it.

"Will acquiring such knowledge give me a sense of purpose and meaning?" asked Jessica.

"There are no guarantees that you will gain the knowledge that you need, the only guarantee is that if you don't commit yourself to seek the knowledge you desire, you may never find the inner peace you are looking for. On the other hand you might easily fall madly in love with someone and come to the realisation that you really don't care about finding an objective meaning or purpose for life as your love and hopes give you purpose enough."

"The most important thing for me at this time is to discover some sense of purpose and meaning for my existence" said Jessica firmly. "If I don't do this I don't believe I will ever find peace of mind."

"You must realise that many people through the generations have also searched for the meaning of life and it is uncertain that any could have claimed to have found it" said Roxie. "You do realise that you may be embarking on an impossible task? If you seriously embark on this journey you have to realise that there is no going back to life as it was. You will soon become aware that many of the drivers of society amount to no more than self-deception and you will begin to see beneath the layers of illusion. This will make you look at the world around you in a very different way and this enhanced perception will almost certainly cause you considerable distress."

"What I have already understood from my studies and observations is already distressing enough" replied Jessica. "Are you able to help me?"

"The answer to your question is yes. The more important question is whether we are prepared to offer you such help? People place a high value on material trinkets that are utterly worthless in any true sense of the word and yet they expect to gain something as priceless as wisdom for nothing. So what would you be prepared to sacrifice for the knowledge that you seek?" asked Ellen.

This was a completely unexpected question that rather nonplussed Jessica. After a considerable pause for thought she sadly replied "I afraid I have virtually nothing to offer you except a few clothes, my scooter and a pile of student debt. I could probably sell the scooter for a few hundred pounds if that would be enough to secure your help?"

"Ellen is not looking for any material reward Jessica" said Roxie kindly.

"What about your degree?" said Ellen. "Would you be prepared to give up your studies, even though you are so close to completing them, if that was the price to secure our further assistance in continuing your quest?"

Jessica looked at Ellen in shock. Was this enigmatic lady with whom she was hardly even acquainted asking her to give up on the university education that she had aspired to for most of her life? On top of that she would have accrued nearly thirty thousand pounds of student debt by the end of this academic year with nothing to show for it. Without her qualification, how would she ever be able to pay this money back? She was being asked to sacrifice everything she had strived so hard to obtain through her education and for what? A vague offer to set out on an improbable quest for wisdom that she may never attain, and that might not even exist? How did she know that she could even trust these women whom she knew so little about?

Ellen smiled at the expression on the young woman in front of her. She could just imagine Jessica's mind working through all the implications of what had just been said.

"Wisdom is the most precious thing that anyone can possess and it is completely hidden from the vast majority of people. This is not through any deliberate artifice but through the many layers of illusion and deception that envelope them. Is it really such a high price to ask that you discard that which has already demonstrably failed to give you the inner peace that you seek?"

"I don't know" said Jessica "is there really no other way?"

"There may be, but not with our help" replied Ellen. "Your emotional attachment to material considerations will be a serious impediment if you genuinely wish to be able to take on a new understanding of yourself and the universe in which you are embedded. I have prepared something for you and you will need to sign it if you wish us to help you. You have ten minutes whist

Roxie and I have another cup of tea so I suggest you go for a short walk and think it over."

Ellen passed over a short letter addressed to Professor Brian Henderson. The letter informed the professor that Jessica had decided to terminate her studies immediately and that this decision was irrevocable. There was a place to print, sign and date the letter at the bottom.

Jessica left her crash helmet on the table and walked out of the tearoom with the letter in her hand. She had just ten minutes to decide whether to sacrifice her whole life's work for a vague promise of limited assistance from two women who were virtual strangers to her. She walked up to one of the stones and placed her hands on its cracked and weathered surface. She wondered what had been going through the minds of these ancient people as they had struggled with their monumental task. What personal sacrifices had they had to make in order to build this ancient monument? What was it that they thought they were creating through their labours and had this provided meaning and purpose in their lives?

Jessica came to a sudden decision; she could not go back to a path that had already proved so fruitless. It was a bit like throwing herself off that bridge in Australia with the bungee ropes attached to her ankles. She would never know what the experience was like without taking the plunge and once she had taken the plunge there could be no turning back.

She pulled a pen out of the pocket of her motorcycle jacket, knelt down with Ellen's letter resting on her thigh and signed her name at the bottom.

Ellen and Roxie looked up as the bell to the teashop rang and Jessica reappeared. Jessica placed the signed letter in front of Ellen.

"Sit down Jessica" said Ellen kindly, "you really are quite a remarkable young lady. I believe less than one in a thousand people would have been prepared to do what you have done today. It is a privilege to be sat here with you at this moment as you start a new direction in your life."

Jessica couldn't believe the change in demeanour that had come over Ellen. The eyes that had been so harsh and unforgiving during their previous encounters and her curt dismissive manner had completely changed. In their place was a face transformed with kindness and the eyes were now glistening with tears as she reached across the table and grasped Jessica by the hands.

"What happens now?" asked Jessica.

"Well one of the first tasks is that when you get back to your room you will frame that letter and put it on the wall. This will act as a constant reminder of the sacrifices you were prepared to make in the pursuit of wisdom. There will be many difficult moments ahead when you will have the gravest of doubts and it is at such times that you will need the same conviction and determination that you have shown today."

"You mean that you don't want me to hand this letter in to Professor Henderson!" exclaimed Jessica.

"Oh goodness no Jessica, we would never do that to you," said Roxie "but we had to be absolutely convinced of your sincerity before we could agree to help you further. Ellen was completely right about the dangers of following such a path and it should not be undertaken lightly. We belong to an international movement that is trying to create a very different world than the one we are living in, but the obstacles are immense and time for our fragile world is so terribly short. We live in a world that is dominated by greed and ignorance and humanity seems determined to follow a path to self-destruction. The only small hope is to try to spread a different kind of knowledge and through the application of wisdom to try and create an alternative future from the one that seems to be predestined."

"There are many people who profess an interest in acquiring knowledge but for most this is just to provide another distraction in their lives. Such people are easily deterred by the obstacles we deliberately place before them. I thought Ellen had happily seen you off at her doorstep but you have proved to be a very determined and remarkable young lady."

"Time may be short" interjected Ellen, "but there is still plenty of time for you to finish your studies with Brian Henderson. I was also slightly cruel to the philosophers through the ages. Despite the fact that they all had the handicap of being locked into a male psyche, there is still much that can be usefully gained through studying their work."

Jessica was completely taken aback by the change in events that had happened so quickly and the associated rollercoaster in her emotions that had accompanied them. She did still have the presence of mind to remind Roxie of something she had said in the bookshop. "Roxie, the last time we met I asked you if you could give me the answer to the meaning of life and you told me that you could."

"You will also recall that I said the answer would be useless because you would not understand it" teased Roxie.

"Nevertheless I would still like to know the answer."

"The answer to the meaning of life is love Jessica."

"What do you mean by love?" replied Jessica.

"You see Roxie" exclaimed Ellen, "I told you she was an intelligent girl."

"The path to understanding love is to be found by seeking the truth" said Roxie.

"Where can one find the truth" asked Jessica.

"The truth is a concept, it exists but to know the complete truth you would need to have universal knowledge of everything and that will always be out of the reach of humans. We are surrounded by ignorance, much of this deliberately created by those amongst us who seek to manipulate and control us. To approach the truth it is first necessary to strip away the layers of illusion that mask it. It is only when we have stripped away illusion that we can let the light of love into our lives" replied Roxie. "Fortunately in our current world we can make rapid initial progress because we are surrounded with such blatant stupidity and obvious absurdities. I think the term 'low hanging fruit' is appropriate. Now I have answered your question, Ellen and I have a desire to wander around this amazing place and absorb its atmosphere. Would you care to join us?"

The three women spent the next hour walking amongst the ancient stones of Avebury, letting their imaginations speculate on the motives of the ancient people who had gone to such extraordinary effort for purposes unknown.

3

Four months later a package arrived through Jessica's door. With it was a letter from Roxie with a series of instructions, a thousand pounds in traveller's cheques, and an airline ticket to Lima in Peru. Roxie said that Ellen sent her love, that she hoped Brian Henderson was pleased with her dissertation, and that it was now time for Jessica to start her search for a purpose to her life.

Jessica was asked to find her way to a guest house run by a woman called Dominga in a small village called Lamas near the town of Tarapoto. How she got there was left to her own initiative but she had ten days to get there after her arrival in Lima. On the evening of the 25th September she would be met by a guide called Sensatez. She was to put her complete trust in her guide and Ellen and Roxie were looking forward to reading her account of her trip and what she had learned. This was the price she had to pay back for those who were financing her trip.

It was this extraordinarily improbable chain of events that had led this naïve student from the streets of Bath to a rigorous trek through the Amazon forest in Peru, heading towards a mysterious destination in the foothills of the Andes.

Sensatez, the enigmatic guide on her journey signalled a halt. Sensi, as she liked to be called was a woman of few words, but somehow this didn't seem to matter. Perhaps it was the majestic beauty of the forest or the background chorus of the birds and animals but Jessica did not miss the conversation. In the few days that they had been together Jessica had come to completely trust Sensi's judgement. She had developed an empathy that now seemed completely natural with this person who the strange hand of fate had drawn into her life.

To Jessica's mild frustration Sensi had insisted that her tired legs climb a further ten metres up the bank from the side of the burbling stream that snaked between the trees. She asked Sensi why they couldn't just camp next to the stream which would seem to be far more convenient.

Sensi answered patiently. "For the last two days the humidity in the forest has been building and we have heard the distant rumble of thunder in the far hills. We do not have to hear the sound of the rain falling to predict that the mood of the stream will change. The building tensions in the forest will be released onto the foothills of the mountains and this gentle stream will become an unstoppable torrent. It is an important lesson to know that all actions played out on our Earth are interconnected and that they will have their consequences."

Jessica awoke just after the first light of dawn to the sound of a thunderous roar in the valley just below them. The gentle inviting stream had become hostile overnight and would have certainly brought disaster to the unwary traveller. Jessica looked with renewed respect upon Sensi who was packing up their things for the day's journey ahead.

Within a few hours the track started to climb more steeply, and soon the vegetation was changing as they started to climb into the lower montane rainforest. Jessica looked back over her shoulder and saw the forest canopy of the Amazon basin spread out below, a magnificent testament to the extraordinary diversity of nature.

For the rest of the day they continued to climb out of the forest, Jessica's legs complaining about the unaccustomed exertion. She looked at Sensi enviously as she climbed ahead of her, the muscles of her toned legs flexing effortlessly as they worked. Jessica estimated that Sensi must have been in her late-twenties with beautiful olive skin and long black hair which she kept tied back to stop it getting snagged as she forged a path through the surrounding foliage. She was slim but athletic, her body showing a life used to physical activity. She was wearing shorts that hugged a muscular rounded bottom and a singlet which revealed a well-developed cleavage that glistened with moisture as a result of her exertion.

Jessica had never been particularly attracted to women but she had to acknowledge that there was something quite exotic and sensuous about her mysterious guide that stirred some inner passion within her. She had to admit to herself that she wasn't entirely indifferent to Sensi's physical charms. On occasion she had caught Sensi appraising her and smiling flirtatiously as she had caught her eye. It seemed to Jessica that here was a woman who was quite aware of her own sexuality and entirely comfortable with it.

Late in the afternoon they climbed over a ridge and came across the panorama of a hidden valley cut into the low foothills of the eastern slope of the Andes as they emerged from the jungle below. Jessica had no idea of their location except a vague notion that they were somewhere in northern Peru not far from the border with Ecuador. Sensi led Jessica down a barely traceable path until they came into a clearing in the vegetation around which Jessica could just make out the remains of some ancient stonework.

"We will camp here tonight and tomorrow we will reach our destination" said Sensi. They erected their tent under the shelter of an ancient stone wall. Whilst Sensi started to prepare their food, Jessica went up to examine the ruins in more detail. It was obvious that at some point in history this had been quite a substantial settlement. Although nature had taken its toll over the years some of the walls were still fully three metres high in places. What particularly impressed Jessica was the incredible quality and precision of the ancient stonework.

The stones were so well dressed that you could not have fitted a sheet of paper between them despite the fact that some of the stones must have easily weighed half a tonne. Jessica couldn't contemplate how these ancient people produced such perfect joints from the hard rock with the tools they had available to them. Modern masons would have been hard pushed to replicate such precision with all of today's technology available to them. We know so little about our history and the nature of these ancient civilisations, she thought to herself as she ran her hand over the smooth surface of the wall. She felt quite humbled and somewhat inadequate in the presence of the skilful work of these ancient craftsmen.

As the long shadows from the hills above spread over the valley, the two women sat down to eat a supper of corn humitas that Sensi had prepared for them. Night had now fallen and they sat in the light of a flickering fire that gave some warmth against the chill of the night and which created strange flickering shadows on the stonework behind them.

Jessica felt that she could almost feel the presence of the ancient people who had once laboured and farmed there. What was their life like all those centuries ago? What were their hopes and dreams? She asked Sensi about the people who had created the ruins that surrounded them.

"We don't really know but we think that these ruins belonged to a culture called the Tiwanaku who flourished between about one thousand and three hundred CE" said Sensi. "It is thought that the Tiwanaku civilisation ended because of a rapid and dramatic change of climate but nobody knows for sure. It is known that they made human sacrifices to their gods but this seems to have failed to stop the demise of their civilisation at the hands of nature. Modern civilisation may also find the reality of this as they worship at their contemporary temples of mammon and disregard their impact on greater nature with ignorance and contempt."

Sensi's words fuelled Jessica's imagination about the lost civilisation that had left such a presence on the side of the valley. A sudden chill made her shudder at the thought of the sacrifices that were made in a vain attempt to gain the blessings of their gods, maybe close to the very spot where they had made their camp. She pulled on the poncho she had bought in a market just three days before and listened to the cry of some unknown nocturnal animal in the valley below them. It was all a world away from her cosy home in Cheltenham and her studies at the University of Bath. Despite this Jessica felt a heightened sense of awareness as she sat by the fire surrounded by these ancient ruins in the company of her beautiful enigmatic guide.

"Would you like to join me in a meditation?" asked Sensi "I have made a preparation from local plants that helps to open the mind the influences of the natural world that act upon us. So often we are blocked from such awareness by a lifetime of conditioning in our modern materialistic world and this inhibits us from getting to know our true natures."

Jessica had like many students experimented with cannabis but had resisted the temptation to try harder drugs and a part of her was cautious about accepting Sensi's offer. Sensi, detecting Jessica's concern, smiled at her reassuringly. She explained that the drugs in her potion had been used by her family for generations to enhance the senses and to tune into the natural world. She assured Jessica that she would come to no harm. She explained to Jessica that the experience might help her to open her mind to new feelings and perceptions. Wasn't this part of the reason she had decided to undertake her journey in the first place?

"You would never have set out on this adventure if your mind wasn't searching for a different reality to the one that you have left behind" she said. "The first step to receiving new ideas is the realisation that the contemporary world around you has failed to answer some of the most fundamental questions about life and human existence. You would not have journeyed so far if you had not felt this to be true. You will learn nothing from your journey if your mind remains closed to alternative ideas to the ones you have previously known. The questions to which you wish to have an answer are as yet unknown to you. They originate as much in your emotions and instincts as in the rational part of your mind and therefore they cannot be simply explained to you. The answers to such questions need to be felt as well as understood. An important first step is to open yourself up to influences that living in contemporary society has closed to you."

Jessica looked intently at this woman who had guided her to a world so distant from the one that she had left behind. She couldn't explain why, but she felt a complete trust in her guide and as their eyes met she gently nodded her acquiescence to Sensi. She noticed that Sensi had hung a small copper pot over the fire and after a few moments she poured the contents into two small ceramic cups that she had taken out of her rucksack.

The potion was initially quite bitter tasting with a slightly citrus aftertaste. Sensi encouraged Jessica to close her eyes and to relax. After a few minutes she heard Sensi start to quietly recite some sounds. It was obviously some language but it was definitely not Portuguese or Spanish so she assumed it was an indigenous native language. Sensi's voice was somewhere between speaking and singing. It had a poetic musical quality and Jessica let herself succumb to its seductive tones. As she came further under the influence of Sensi's preparation she gained the impression that other voices had joined in with Sensi's voice. She imagined voices from the people who had performed the rituals in the distant past, reawakened by Sensi's chanting and summoned to join her in the present.

Jessica felt the coolness of a sudden breeze on her face and noticed that she could feel her heart pumping and the pulse of her blood as it passed through her veins. She felt her lungs working and noticed the strong smell of the vegetation in the night air around her as she breathed. She heard the sounds of the forest at night, the crackling of the fire became more intense and she felt that she could actually feel the presence of nocturnal animals passing nearby.

As she let herself fall under the influence of Sensi's potion, the difference between the functions of her own body and the world outside became blurred to her. She felt that the world of nature, the trees and animals around her were not separate, but at one with her. It was almost as if she could feel the pulses and breathing of the natural world around her, just as she had felt the dynamics of her own body moments earlier. She sensed herself rising up and found herself looking down upon her own form lying on her back in her poncho. She saw Sensi on the other side of the fire sitting cross legged with her eyes shut and with only her lips moving. She thought she could see the movement of strange figures dancing in the flickering shadows beyond the light of the fire.

At this point she must have succumbed to sleep because the next thing she knew it was daylight and she was being woken up in her tent by a smiling Sensi holding a mug of steaming tea for her.

"How do you feel this morning?" asked Sensi.

Jessica climbed out of the tent into the cool morning air and sat on a rock. She sipped her tea, as she looked out across the valley below her. There was a mist rising up from the stream that ran along the bottom of the valley which looked like smoke rising up through the lush vegetation that clung to either side. She felt absolutely fine, no, better than fine, she felt as if she had awoken from a long sleep. Not the sleep of the night before, but a sleep that had seemed to have encompassed most of her life.

She had no previous perception of having been previously asleep until she experienced this new awakening and could compare the experience. The only similar feelings of being truly awake she could recollect had been as she sat listening to the policeman tell her the news of her sister's death or the rush of adrenalin during her dangerous sports phase.

"I feel alive" said Jessica in reply to Sensi's questioning, "more alive than I have felt for such a long time." She realised that much of the noise that had usually filled her head, the clutter of the concerns of everyday life, the petty desires and attachments that fill every waking hour were strangely absent. Sitting on this rock above the valley sipping the mug of hot tea she felt a complete sense of inner calm and contentment.

"I'm afraid the experience will not last long" said Sensi, "the desires, attachments and frustrations of the day will soon fill your mind again. You have experienced an altered state of awareness. With a lot of practice, concentration and effort, you may learn the skill to reach such a state of consciousness without the assistance of the natural herbs and drugs you took in my potion. It is through this interconnectedness and an understanding of our relationship with the natural world that the path to wisdom lays."

The truth of Sensi's words about the brevity of her inner peace became only too apparent as Jessica tore a fingernail trying to pull out a tent peg. She cursed as she sucked it in a vain attempt to stop the throbbing pain. How quickly the realities of the physical world had already returned to her!

After packing up camp and hoisting up their rucksacks the two women followed the faint path down the side of the valley which ran parallel to the burbling stream to the left of them. After walking for about an hour Jessica noticed that the vegetation was clearing. As the valley began to flatten out fields began to appear on either side. About a kilometre later the valley opened up on the left hand side and she saw a large array of solar panels glinting in the morning sunshine. There were also about ten wind turbines slowly turning in the breeze on the hillside above.

The path had now become a metalled road and she saw three small electric vehicles, similar in size to a golf buggy which could seat four people. One vehicle had a small trailer attached to the back which she assumed was for carrying produce back from the fields. Sensi took off her rucksack and threw it into a luggage space behind the seats in the first vehicle, inviting Jessica to sit next to her in the front of the vehicle. Sensi pressed down on the pedal in the front with her right foot and the buggy leapt forward with surprising urgency for such a small vehicle.

"Won't the owners mind us taking their vehicle?" inquired Jessica.

"Oh no, these vehicles belong to the community and their guests, they are for everyone to use" replied Sensi. They sped past traditionally built farm houses and barns. As they progressed further down the valley Jessica noticed a large building on the left hand side. This was situated at the base of a substantial dam with what looked to be some kind of chemical plant next to it.

She asked Sensi the purpose of the infrastructure and it was explained that the first building was a hydro-electric power station and that the plant next to it produced hydrogen and oxygen gas. Sensi explained that most of the larger vehicles used by the community used hydrogen fuel cells and hydrogen was also used as a backup fuel for generating electricity when necessary.

She told Jessica that two years ago they had managed to start creating and storing their own hydrogen and oxygen at the plant. The plant was still in development and they were getting more proficient all the time as they continued to learn about the challenges of safe production, storage and distribution. She explained that the problem with electricity was that it was impossible to store except in the form of large arrays of capacitors or batteries. By its very nature, the amount of electricity produced as renewable energy from the wind turbines, solar electric and hydro-electric power varied greatly depending on the weather. By using the excess electricity to produce hydrogen they could effectively store this excess capacity in the form of a highly versatile fuel. Surplus hydrogen and the associated oxygen were sold to industrial and medical customers as part of the community's ongoing funding.

They were now entering a small village; the buildings were completely different to the traditional dwellings they had passed as they had driven up the valley. Most of the buildings were very modern looking. Although they differed in individual style and building materials, most of them incorporated solar panels and some had strange looking cones on the roofs that Jessica assumed were for ventilation purposes.

Jessica pulled up outside a modern looking café with three large rectangular windows revealing a number of round white tables, comfortable looking round backed blue chairs, and a long service bar faced with terracotta brickwork. The two women entered and they sat down at a table next to a window that had been slid half open to let in a gentle morning breeze. Sensi pulled out a mobile phone and was soon speaking excitedly in English. They ordered three coffees and about five minutes later another of the communal electric buggies pulled up outside. A woman entered and rushed over to the table to embrace Sensi who had leapt up to meet her. The women hugged and kissed and laughed with an intimacy reminiscent of long lost lovers in a sudden reunion. When they finally drew apart Sensi apologised to Jessica.

"I would like you to meet a very special friend of mine, this is Vanessa."

Sensi saw a woman that she would have estimated to be approximately forty years old. She had dark brunette hair which had been cut into a smart bob that was just below her chin at the front and slightly tapered upwards towards the back. She was wearing a peach coloured trouser suit which seemed to Jessica to be rather out of keeping for a small village nestled in the Andean foothills. The woman had an attractive elegance about her, not strikingly beautiful but captivating and she would have secured a few admiring glances at some of the bars and clubs that Jessica frequented. She had slight laughter lines around the corner of her eyes which were filled with humour and warmth. Jessica took an instant liking to this woman and was suddenly very aware that, apart from the rudimentary application of soap in the stream this morning, she hadn't had a proper shower or a bath for three days. She must have looked quite a sight and be none too fragrant.

Vanessa kissed Jessica on each cheek, "welcome to Consciência" she said. She then pretended to scold Sensi for not looking after Jessica properly. "Just look at the poor girl, she's covered in scratches and bites and she hasn't even had a chance to have a shower or a change of clothes yet. Really Sensi you are so negligent of the needs of your guests at times, I just can't imagine what you have put this poor girl through over the last few days."

Sensi was quite immune to the scolding and just smiled affectionately at Vanessa as she was being verbally chastised. The three women sat down at the table and drank their coffee whilst they chatted. Jessica said she was completely surprised with the village of Consciência. After their long trek she had expected to come to a tribal community in mud brick huts located in a jungle clearing. Yet here she was, sitting in a sparkling clean modern café sipping an Americano with a smart English lady in a trouser suit. She looked at Sensi and quizzed her as to why they had trekked through the jungle and climbed up through the hills when it was now obvious that they could have simply driven here?

"Don't be deceived," said Sensi, "Consciência may seem a bit familiar to you at first glance but you have entered a community with a totally different set of ideas and values. If we had just driven here you would not be properly prepared to think differently and therefore you would gain little from your experience here. The trek we have undertaken and last night's experience has allowed your mind to open up to new emotions and ideas that would not have been possible otherwise. It is also a useful allegory for what lies ahead of you. If you really want to understand your nature and develop a sense of purpose you will have to strive hard to achieve your goal and there is no guarantee that you will get there. Your physical journey to get here was nowhere near as difficult as the internal journey your mind must take to reveal to you what you are looking for. Self-realisation is not easily obtained and the obstacles that must be overcome are considerable and daunting."

"Be that as it may" interrupted Vanessa, "I think it is time for you to take Jessica to her lodgings to get changed and refreshed. Then you can show her around a bit."

Jessica was taken to a house which reminded her of the Italian villas she had once seen on holiday in Rimini. It had brightly painted shutters and was surrounded by a garden which sloped gently down to a small stream that twinkled in the sunlight as it flowed towards the main river at the bottom of the valley. The villa had five guest suites, each with a bedroom, bathroom, a seating area with a desk and a video monitor for television or internet browsing, and a small kitchenette.

Sensi explained that there were two such guest buildings in Consciência that were directly funded by the community. She left Jessica to refresh herself and arranged to meet in an hour's time at the base of a majestic Kapok tree in the middle of a pentagram shaped area that marked the centre of the community. Jessica's suitcase had been separately brought by prior arrangement from Lima and she found it laid out for her on the bed. She had a steaming hot shower that washed away the accumulated sweat and grime of her days of trekking in the forest.

As Jessica towelled herself in front of the bathroom mirror she grimaced at the red blotches where various biting creatures had taken their toll on her fair skin. Even more annoyingly some of them were starting to unbearably itch and she liberally applied some 'jungle formula' after-bite cream she had prudently picked up before leaving England. She had noted with considerable jealously that none of these creatures seemed to have had the audacity to bite Sensi's beautiful olive skin which remained as pristine as it had looked when they started their trek. Jessica decided on a long sleeved top and her blue dungarees which would cover up the worst evidence of the attentions of the various feasting fiends.

At the appointed hour she met Sensi at the huge Kapok and they sat together for a snack outside a taverna. All around the edges of the roads that met at the central area were beautiful flowers that gave a blaze of colour.

Sensi then escorted Jessica around some of the main features of the community, there was a substantial two storey building which Sensi explained was the community centre where the day to day running of the community was administered. Vanessa worked at the centre and she gave Jessica a big wave as Sensi guided her through the building. There was a large IT suite and library in the centre which was open to all. Sensi explained that they had satellite broadband access at   Consciência. Jessica had already discovered this to her complete surprise in her apartment when her iPad linked automatically to the Wi-Fi at a speed that put the link on the campus at her university to shame.

There was a small hospital and pharmacy and Sensi asked Jessica if she would mind taking a few minutes to pop in and have a quick swab and blood test. Jessica was quite intrigued by this and asked Sensi the purpose of the tests. Sensi explained to Jessica that for most of the population of Consciência, having sex with someone to whom you were attracted was thought of as a beautiful thing. Sex was considered a gift from nature that should be celebrated, not some shameful act that should be hidden away or some kind of mortal sin to be condemned. It was quite common for residents to have more than one lover. It was also surprisingly common for visitors to quickly discover that the special atmosphere of the community enhanced their own libido and freed previously suppressed desires.

"We ask visitors that will be staying with us for a while to take a few precautionary tests because we have managed to eliminate sexually transmitted disease in Consciência apart from two residents who sadly contracted HIV before joining us. Such progress could happen in much of the rest of the world if there was a will to do so. Unfortunately the shame that many societies associate with sexual activity, largely through institutionalised religious intolerance, has the consequence that many societies fail to effectively contain such diseases. This can lead to terrible consequences for the victims. We also stock a comprehensive range of free contraceptives at the hospital because sexual relations for many in the community are about sharing mutual joy, not producing children."

Jessica was quite happy to take the tests but was far from convinced that she would succumb to the allure of whatever opportunities for sexual adventure she might encounter during her stay. She said as much to Sensi.

"Don't worry; you will be quite safe, nobody here would dream of trying to impose their desires upon you or put you under any kind of pressure. The beauty of making love to another person can only be realised through mutual desire and consent. It would be seen as a terrible violation to try to impose your desires on someone who was unwilling. We also have a custom here that anyone who wears a blue bangle, bracelet or watch strap are discretely saying that they do not wish to be approached and this will always be respected. If you really don't want to open yourself up to the possibility of making love to someone whilst you are here, you can easily pick up a blue bangle in one of the shops. Otherwise you are saying that at the right moment, with the right person, you may say yes which is as it should be between consenting adults. We do not take offence at being approached in Consciência as desire is an instinctive human function that exists whether we wish it to or not. As I said, we believe sex is a joy provided by nature not a sin. Nobody will take offence at being gently declined as one person's desire may well not be replicated."

Jessica was amazed to find herself talking about the nature of sexual desire with Sensi next to this Kapok tree in the middle of a strange village. Even at the

University with her friends she had never been this open about sex and yet here it seemed strangely natural and uncontroversial.

Jessica completed her tests and was joined by Sensi who had been away for a few months and was accustomed to popping into the hospital on her return. Sensi then continued Jessica's short tour. There was a retail area with food, clothing and hardware shops, a community bank and a garage where it appeared that many of the vehicles used by the community were serviced and repaired. Jessica asked whether the community banned the use of private cars.

"Oh no" said Sensi, "it's just that the majority of people find it far more convenient to use a car from the community pool. The community's transport, like the rest of the infrastructure, is funded through each resident's community contribution or through the profits made on community enterprises such as the hydrogen plant and joint agricultural projects. We are not prescriptive here, there are a few private cars owned by residents with a passion for such things. We even have a couple of Harley Davidsons kicking around, one of which is owned by my brother."

Sensi said that there were just over 700 residents in the immediate community but that Consciência was socially and commercially linked to a number of other communities and enterprises in the wider area and even in associated communities across the world. She said that Jessica would have all this explained to her a bit later on during her stay.

Jessica noted that the rainforest came nearly up to the centre of the village except along the main agricultural strip that they had driven along when they had arrived. Sensi explained that it was very important to the community to be close to nature and that many of the tamer animals wandered freely amongst the buildings as they moved from one patch of forest to another. The buildings roughly followed five tracks including the main road that met at the village centre. The forest filled the segments in between. In effect the centre of the village formed a kind of uneven pentagram with the Kapok tree at its centre.

Sensi explained to Jessica that the community was well aware of the global impact of humans on wildlife and there was a consensual ban on taking up any additional land from the pristine forest. This also had the effect of limiting the size of the community of Consciência. The less timid animals of the forest also benefited from some of the additional grains, fruits and nuts that were grown by the residents to supplement their natural diet.

There were no churches in the village which surprised Jessica as she thought that Catholicism in particular was prevalent in this part of South America. She asked Sensi about this.

"We have no rules that forbid anyone from following their religion, but we do not believe that people should try to impose their religious beliefs on others. If sufficient people in the community wanted a church they would be quite free to build it, but there is very little desire for one amongst the current residents. If you follow the second street from the centre on the left hand side of the river, you will discover that the buildings quickly end and there is a path that continues through the forest towards the side of the valley. There are a number of clearings with benches and some covered meditation areas linked to the main path. These are favoured by the community when people want time for reflection or just want to be surrounded by nature and the forest. You are quite free to wander through these areas as the tracks are well marked but please don't wander off into the forest without a guide. It is surprisingly easy to get lost if you are unfamiliar with it."

"If you walk a bit further along the main path it starts to climb up from the valley floor and will take you to some shallow rock pools, fed by a spring that emerges from the valley side. Many residents like to go for a swim in these pools. I wouldn't however recommend visiting the pools if you are bashful. It is the custom to wear clothing in the village out of practicality and because of the sensitivities of some of our visitors, but residents feel no obligation to cover up when swimming or walking in the forest clearings. We don't believe the naked human form is at all offensive. Taking offence at nudity is a very recent addition in the long history of our species and, if you take a moment to reflect upon it, a quite irrational one. Many of us feel it helps to be as nature originally intended us to be when in contemplation. We also find nudity more spiritually liberating when we seek to align ourselves to the natural energies that surround us. I would however thoroughly recommend that you at least wear a pair of sandals as there are all kinds of thorns and insects that you really wouldn't want to step upon!"

Sensi suggested that they meet again at Vanessa's house that evening, a blue bungalow on the same street that led up to the meditation areas and the rock pools they had just discussed. In the meantime Sensi suggested that Jessica took some time to explore the village and absorb some of its atmosphere.

4

Jessica decided to follow the path up towards the swimming pools. After passing the last building she soon came upon a torii or Japanese gateway on the right hand side. Walking through the torii she emerged into a large clearing approximately thirty metres in diameter. The clearing was surrounded by upright stones, similar to the ones she had seen at Avebury, but less than half the size. There were some larger stones equally spaced at four points around the circumference which she estimated to be roughly aligned to North, South, East and West. In the centre was a circular raised platform made from forest timbers with what looked like some kind of stone altar in the middle. Apart from the noise of various birds in the forest and the calling of a distant group of monkeys she found herself peacefully alone.

Jessica walked to the centre of the circle and sat down on the edge of the wooden platform. She shut her eyes and let herself appreciate the gentle breeze waft across her face and the smells of the forest vegetation. As her mind cleared she felt her senses increase, perhaps a residual effect of the events of the previous evening, and she detected the sound of a burbling stream just past the edge of the clearing. She assumed that this stream ran down from the rock pools used by the residents for bathing.

After a while she opened her eyes, stretched her tired limbs that were stiffening from the previous day's exertions, and wandered further up the path. The path meandered through the forest and then went up a slight incline until she came around a bend to meet the stream that she had heard from the middle of the stone circle in the clearing. The path followed the stream, past a small waterfall and emerged next to a pool, about twelve metres by eight metres with a small shingle beach area.

There were three people bathing in the pool, two women, one who must have been about Jessica's age and one who looked to be in her forties. There was quite a resemblance between the two women and Jessica guessed that they might be mother and daughter. There was also a slim athletic looking young man who Jessica guessed must have also been in his early twenties. All of them were swimming in the nude and shared Sensi's beautiful olive skin colour. She noticed their clothing was placed on the small pebbly beach to keep them dry.

Noticing Jessica, the older woman casually waved a greeting and the young man looked across at her and smiled.

Jessica's initial reaction was embarrassment; this was a typically English reaction when exposed to something as startling as nudity. She remembered Sensi's recent words and realised just how stupid this reaction was. Why should people be embarrassed at the sight of nudity? This was the result of a few millennia of processing and conditioning by various controlling societies. For hundreds of thousands of years before such 'civilising' influences humanity had happily existed without any such inhibitions.

Jessica slipped out of clothes, suddenly feeling more self-conscious of all the red blotchy insect bites contrasted by her white skin rather than her nudity. She had a sudden shudder as she entered the water; the spring fed pool was quite chilly despite the heat of the afternoon sun above them. The young man swam over and held out his hand.

"Olá" he said in greeting.

"Hi", replied Jessica, suddenly painfully aware of her lack of Spanish, "I'm Jessica."

"I'm Raul, pleased to meet you" replied the young man in perfect English with only the slightest of accents, something that Jessica suddenly found quite alluring. "Hey are you the Jessica from England that Sensi was bringing to visit us?"

"Yes," replied Jessica, somewhat taken aback that this young man knew about her visit.

"Delighted" he beamed at her, "Sensi is my sister."

The two of them chatted for a while until the chill of the water got to them and then they climbed out and sat on the pebbles to warm in the heat of the sun. Raul offered Jessica his towel as her visit to the pools had been unplanned. After getting dressed they slowly wandered back into Consciência together. Jessica parted from Raul with a friendly wave and decided to go back to her apartment where she suddenly felt incredibly tired. She collapsed into the welcome embrace of her bed and fell fast asleep until the alarm that she had set on her watch beeped her awake.

Jessica dragged a brush through hair that had assumed a wild untamed look that could only be successfully created by falling asleep whilst it was still damp, before setting off to Vanessa's. She came to the blue bungalow that Sensi had shown her earlier that day and, seeing no doorbell, she knocked on the door. "It's open, come on in" came a voice from inside and finding the door unlocked Jessica let herself into the hallway.

Vanessa appeared in a bathrobe from what Jessica assumed was a bedroom followed by a naked Sensi who smiled mischievously at Jessica as she went into another room, shortly followed by the sound of a shower.

"I didn't realise that Sensi was your partner" said Jessica, "she never mentioned this during our trek together."

"Oh, Sensi is not my partner" replied a rather flushed looking Vanessa, "she's a very special friend and lover. We haven't seen each other for three months so there has been a bit of catching up to do!"

Jessica was starting to realise that there were very different cultural norms in Consciência to the ones that she had left behind in England. People here seemed to be completely relaxed about nudity and sex and she was beginning to find this rather refreshing and liberating.

Vanessa invited Jessica into what was a quite a large living room. The first thing she noticed were four strange shaped chairs that looked a bit like upturned oyster shells on legs, each with a big plush cushion placed in the centre. On the wall she saw a number of paintings, the most striking of which was a large picture of two women entwined in a sexual embrace. She noticed that the two women bore a remarkable similarity to Sensi and Vanessa, but what really startled her was that the painting was signed by Alexandra Okereke, and it was an original not a print. Although Jessica was far from being an art expert she had enough interest to know that Alexandra Okereke was fast becoming one of the most sought after artists on the London scene. An original Okereke like this could be worth thirty thousand pounds, maybe even more, yet here it was on a wall in this bungalow in a small village in Peru.

"Vanessa, where on earth did you get this Okereke from" exclaimed Jessica, as she continued to examine the sensual and erotic picture of the two entwined lovers before her.

"Oh that's a present from a very special friend" replied Vanessa. "Can I tempt you to a glass of cold wine or perhaps a cocktail?" The women settled on a bottle of Chilean Sauvignon Blanc and were soon joined by Sensi, her straight black hair still slightly damp from her shower.

"I hear that you met Raul today" said Sensi and to her annoyance Jessica felt herself blushing slightly as she thought of the handsome young man she had met in the pool.

Vanessa looked at Jessica and raised a questioning eyebrow.

Jessica explained to Vanessa where she had been earlier that afternoon and where she had met Raul. She also talked about finding the circle and the altar in the forest clearing. She asked what the circle meant and what the altar was for. Sensi explained that the founders of the community held a great reverence and respect for nature and the circle was created as a place where these feelings could be shared. The majority of those who had subsequently joined the community shared the same conviction that humanity was a part of nature, not apart from it, and revered the natural world.

Sensi explained that some people in Consciência, including herself, believed that there were energies that permeated all natural things. They believed that these energies could be channelled by those who had been trained to tap into them or who were already naturally sensitive to them. There was an initiated group that met together at the stone circle at important points in the cycle of the seasons. At such times they sought to merge their collective consciousness and project this natural energy in the service of the community, the animals, and forest in which the community was embedded.

"That sounds a bit like a witches' coven" remarked Jessica. Sensi smiled back, "you could think of it in that way if it helps you to understand," she suggested "although the roots of the traditional shamanistic tradition that is practiced here are somewhat different in form."

"Roxie and Ellen have explained why you approached them and your journey of self-discovery which they felt could be assisted by visiting Consciência" continued Sensi. "They said you wish to discover the meaning of life." She laughed at this, "well I am not sure we will be able live up to such expectations, you will have to judge that for yourself when you depart. I do think we can at least help you to escape the influences of some of the pervasive illusions that are so prevalent in the world that you have left behind."

"This is why it was thought it might be useful if you were introduced to me" interjected Vanessa. "I have been on my own journey of self-discovery, although my background is somewhat different to yours and I started my journey much later in life. Most of the people who have come to Consciência have gravitated here through dissatisfaction with the contemporary world and a desire to seek an alternative way of living. Some people stay here and become part of the community. Others go back into the societies from which they embarked, driven by a desire to change the dynamics and culture of these societies through actively engaging with them. We hope that we may inspire you enough to wish to join their ranks. The task before those of us who think this way is herculean. Our numbers are comparatively few, although they are growing. Sadly the time remaining, before humanity has done irrevocable damage to our fragile world and its ecosystems, is now very short. For many species it is already too late. They are already extinct, victims of humanity's stupidity, greed and ignorance."

"We think you might find Vanessa's story interesting and entertaining and that it may assist you in defining some of your own goals" said Sensi. "Would you like to hear her story?"

"I would love to" said Jessica with genuine sincerity as she looked at Vanessa. There was an uncommon sense of calmness and inner peace behind the eyes of the captivating woman who sat before her in her bathrobe. This suggested to Jessica that, for Vanessa at least, the battle with some of her inner demons may have been won and she was interested to know how this had been accomplished. She also had to confess that she was very intrigued about a woman who had the sort of friends that would give an original painting by Alexandra Okereke as a present!

Jessica also felt a bit humbled and embarrassed. She had led a rather unremarkable life up until these last few months and felt that she was rather unworthy to be the centre of such attention. "I can't believe how kind you have already been to me" said Jessica, "and I'm not sure I deserve to take up so much of your valuable time. You probably have far more important things to do with it than to waste it on the likes of me."

"There is nothing more important than helping someone who has a real possibility to awaken" said Vanessa, suddenly serious. "The very future of our planet is dependent upon it. Everyone that we help can act as another beacon of light that will attract others through the fog of greed and ignorance that has enveloped our world. Besides," she continued in a much lighter tone, "it's not every day that I get to meet someone who was prepared to throw away their academic career on the basis of a strange proposition from a pair of eccentric women they had only just met. You are either someone who has a great destiny before you or you are completely daft. In the next few days I believe we shall find out which" she said winking at Sensi as she spoke.

"Anyway, that's for tomorrow," said Sensi, "if we can persuade Vanessa to actually put some clothes on we should head towards the great Kapok tree and party a bit."

The three women left Vanessa's bungalow and walked towards the centre of the village where other residents were already congregating. They went to one of a small cluster of cafés and tavernas where they were joined by Raul and a couple of his friends. They had a lovely meal together, plenty of wine, music and dancing until the early hours. Jessica felt herself starting to fall under Raul's spell.

Raul had, like Jessica, recently finished university. He had been studying engineering and chemistry at Massachusetts Institute of Technology or MIT as it was more widely known. He was now helping to improve the efficacy of the hydrogen plant and was also working with an engine team based in South Korea. He was helping to develop new applications for the hydrogen fuel cell technology that was used in the community vehicles. He explained that he had met a young engineer from this company in MIT and had finally persuaded him to allow the community to use obsolete test engines in exchange for the promise to use and market this technology in Peru. He explained that the countries of South America were seen by the South Koreans as a huge future potential market as the economies expanded and their populations grew. It was also core to the ethos of Consciência to promote the use of renewable technology in all its forms.

Jessica would like to have been able to tell Raul that she was attracted to him by his work and his intelligence, but truthfully she was more impressed with his impish cheeky smile and the memory of his firm athletic body gliding towards her across the rock pool earlier that afternoon.

The following morning a slightly worse for wear Jessica knocked on the door of Vanessa's bungalow. She sat down on one of the quirky yet surprisingly comfortable oyster chairs with a steaming mug of coffee and started to listen to Vanessa's story. Within a few minutes she was completely captivated by both the story, and the magnetic presence of the remarkable woman who was sat in front of her.

Part 2 - Vanessa

1

There she was again, the waitress with the smile. It was not just the smile, there was a twinkle in her startlingly blue eyes that showed that this smile was not put on for the benefit of customers alone but seemed to reflect an inner contentment that bubbled to the surface. When was the last time that I smiled like that Vanessa wondered to herself?

Lately she always went into Luigi's on a Friday evening after finishing trading for the week. Tonight it was a spaghetti vongole with a bottle of Amarone, the warmth of the full bodied wine slowly dulling her senses and helping her to forget the stresses of the day.

Vanessa was a very good trader, it had taken years for her to work her way up to become one of the most senior and respected traders at Mallory's Bank. If she had not quite broken the glass ceiling of male privilege that kept so many women from reaching City boardrooms, she was at least putting a few cracks in it. Not that they would ever admit that such a ceiling existed, discrimination was far more subtle than it was twenty years ago when she started in the City after leaving university.

Like many intelligent women, Vanessa had watched less skilled male employees get promoted around her. She instinctively knew that she would have to work twice as hard to prove herself and she set her mind to do so. At what sacrifice? Boyfriends, and even on one occasion a brief relationship with a woman, quickly ended as they became fed up with the long hours, the exhaustion, and the associated tetchiness. Starting a family, huh, no chance! At least she hadn't succumbed to the lure of cocaine like so many of her colleagues.

Vanessa smiled to herself as she looked at the half empty bottle of Amarone on the table. No she had resisted the lure of cocaine but she would hate to think what her alcohol consumption was doing to her liver. Life in the City was often brief with many shining lights on the trading desks burning themselves out in just a few years. At least they had all that money to fall back on, one of her friends had once suggested. The trouble was that City money meant sky high property prices with monumental mortgages, overpriced champagne parties until three in the morning, and tailored suits from the best sources in Savile Row.

She had seen many ex-colleagues suddenly find that all the money had been frittered away. All that they were left with were unpaid bills, a habit they could no longer afford and being completely unprepared for life outside the City. Forget compassion, there was no room for sympathy in the ruthless dog-eat-dog world she had survived and thrived in. She felt a sudden pang of guilt at the pleasure she had felt as she had seen Stephen Wright-Philips escorted from the building last week.

Stephen was about her age and had started in the City within weeks of Vanessa. He had had a classic route to the City, public school education, Cambridge and then straight into a junior trading role through his father's connections. Vanessa had first met him just after she started at Mallory's at one of the unavoidable Friday night team socials in a bar near the Temple. She had spent half the night avoiding his advances which had become ever less subtle with every drink and had been relieved when her friend Sandy had turned up and she had been able to make her excuses.

She had watched Stephen climb the corporate ladder with resignation and some bemusement. He was mediocre at best but he was a member of all the right clubs and was considered influential as his father was now Chairman of one of the biggest investment banks in the Square Mile. Six or seven years before, Stephen had married Charlotte, a presenter from one of the more obscure daytime TV chat shows who was ten years his junior. Charlotte seemed to be a lovely girl, full of life and Vanessa instantly took to her when she met her at one of the Bank's socials. She had recently bumped into her again quite by chance in a coffee shop and had been quite shocked at how drawn she had looked. Another victim of the City she had thought to herself as she sipped her skinny latte. Stephen was married to his work and was consumed by his ambition way before Charlotte came into his life. Charlotte had quickly discovered that the City was the most demanding and unforgiving of mistresses.

Stephen's downfall had come about because he had spent far too much time on the golf course and had been promoted way above his meagre abilities. One of the traders for which he was supposedly responsible had not been off-setting the risk on some of his more speculative trades and this had ultimately cost the bank a cool £20 million. The sum was not big enough to make the papers but it was enough to send Stephen on his way. She had no doubt however that he would soon pop up again somewhere else as it was who you knew, as opposed to what you knew, that seemed the most important factor for success.

Unlike many of her colleagues, Vanessa had not squandered all her earnings in a hedonistic frenzy. She had carefully invested and saved and had rapidly paid off the mortgage on her apartment in Notting Hill. This was a beautiful apartment that took up the top two floors of a renovated terraced house in Landsdowne Crescent. Her flat was not fussy, it was perhaps somewhat understated but her furniture, art and sculptures were highly valuable. Her new kitchen, which she rarely ever seemed to use, had cost her not far short of £30,000 three years ago.

"Is everything ok with your meal madam?" Vanessa suddenly looked up into the eyes of the cheerful waitress. "Yes it's lovely" she said, but why didn't she feel lovely? She had surpassed even her own resolute ambition in her job at Mallory's, earning the respect of colleagues who long ago ceased to care that she was a woman in a male dominated world. She had an enviable apartment, financial security for life, and could still look with some satisfaction at the face looking back at her in the mirror in the morning. She may not consider herself typically beautiful but she still had the elegant charm that had unfortunately attracted Stephen's unwanted attention all those years ago.

There was something about this waitress that was unsettling her and she couldn't work out quite what it was. It was almost like she was feeling jealous of this young woman who flitted between the tables with her quiet confidence and happy disposition. This was disconcerting; if anything it should be the other way around. Vanessa in her expensive designer suit should perhaps be a person to be envied by this waitress who, she imagined, would be struggling just to stay afloat in London on her meagre wages and tips. Not only was there no sign of such envy but on a number of occasions she had felt that she had detected something else in the waitress's eyes; compassion.

She finished her meal and left Luigi's in the taxi that had been called for her. Back in the flat Tabitha started on her regular ritual of rubbing against her legs in anticipation of being fed. Tabitha was the Burmese cat who had shared her apartment for the last eight years and who treated her with the mild distain that only cats have truly perfected. She fed Tabitha, put on Vivaldi's Four Seasons violin concerto to provide a suitable background ambience and settled down to read a few pages of the new novel she had downloaded to her IPad before going to bed.

She turned off the light and tried to get to sleep, never normally a problem after a bottle of Amarone, but not tonight. The look of compassion she had detected in the waitress's eyes had deeply disturbed her and her mind refused to obey her physical desire to succumb to the comforting embrace of her bed. After an hour of tossing and turning she went into the bathroom and turned on the light above the mirror. What had the waitress seen in her face that she hadn't noticed, despite the careful attention she gave it every morning as she carefully applied her makeup? She looked at the eyes staring back at her from the mirror and she had a sudden revelation. The eyes looking back at her looked desperately sad. She recollected her thoughts of earlier that evening as she had tried to remember the last time she had smiled or broken out into laughter through sheer happiness. Here she was, a highly successful, wealthy and attractive woman who seemed to have the world at her feet and yet inside she was suddenly aware of a hollow emptiness and a yearning for something more.

Was it perhaps that it was five months since her last relationship had finished? This was with James, a lawyer she had met at her friend Sandy's dinner party. James was unquestionably quite dishy and she felt no regret that she had quickly succumbed to his advances and they had ended up back at her apartment. They had wild, passionate sex that night, the lovemaking of two hungry bodies that were communicating on their own accord as they succumbed to their animal desires.

They had made love again in the morning, much to the disgust of Tabitha who had to wait an interminable time for her breakfast. Vanessa had spent two years with James in a relationship that gently fizzled out. The initial blaze of passion had slowly burnt down to a barely glowing ember and what was left was insufficient to bridge the growing schism in their relationship. There had been others like David over the years; the thrill of the initial attraction, the joy and physical release, and then the slow realisation after the passion had cooled that they had little else in common between them.

Despite the hard headed professional veneer she liked to show to the outside world, Vanessa had a completely different emotional side to her personality. There had been a few times that the aggressive bullying she had inevitably attracted in her blossoming career from the insecurities of colleagues had penetrated her defences. She can remember Sandy, her closest friend since university days, holding her as she cried uncontrollably to let out all the hurt after one particularly bad day.

The one thing she had learnt was to never, ever let the emotional pain show to those who were trying to harm her. Emotion and empathy were seen as unforgivable character flaws in the investment banking circles where she had chosen to make her career. Oh there was the usual HR blurb about how the bank recognised the stress of the environment and the free counselling that was on offer to employees. This was the official policy of the 'caring' employer.

The unofficial bank policy was far more pervasive. Any indication that a person couldn't cope with the long hours, the blatant sexism and the partying to the early hours then back at the desk by 6.30 a.m. culture, ended all chance of promotion or progression. No matter how good the CV, underlying whispers behind the scenes about the weak character who "couldn't handle the stress" would rapidly drive home the nails into the coffin of an otherwise promising career.

Vanessa was a quick learner and had rapidly become a master at burying her emotions. She had perfected this to such an extent that after all these years she was now virtually immune to the voice deep inside trying to get her attention. She had this startling realisation that earlier in Luigi's, her carefully honed armour had slipped and for the first time in years she felt strangely vulnerable. The source of the sadness in the eyes looking back from the mirror was from the passionate, emotional and unfulfilled Vanessa, the one she had neglected for so long that she had forgotten it had ever existed. Her eyes were telling her that she had paid a heavy emotional price for all the pain, effort and ultimate success in her career and this long neglected aspect of her being was now crying out for attention.

This realisation was not a comforting one. At work the future was subject to analysis by statistical probability and computer algorithms and Vanessa had made great efforts to structure her private life in a similarly rational way. No mortgage, copious provision for private medical care, an enviably large and growing pension pot and a home security system to deter even the most entrepreneurial burglar. These long dormant feelings did not sit comfortably within her rational realm; they came from the mysterious domain of the human unconscious, where emotions, attachments, impulses and instincts resided.

Vanessa shook her head; she was just being stupid and imagining things. She was certainly not going to let an enigmatic smile and an imagined look from a waitress suddenly overturn her carefully constructed life. She went back to bed and this time successfully fell into a deep sleep that was only disturbed by Tabitha padding her through the bedclothes. It might be the weekend but in Tabitha's opinion that was no good reason to delay breakfast.

Despite her attempt to rationalise her emotional misgivings, it was slowly becoming apparent to Vanessa that something had fundamentally changed within her. On Sundays she often liked to walk on Hampstead Heath, a biological antidote to the stark concrete and unforgiving lines of the City landscape. This Sunday everything seemed more vibrant, the colour in the autumnal leaves almost artificial, as if they had been painted by some artist who had been too enthusiastic when mixing the paint on their pallet. The birdsong was louder, she noticed the abundance of waterfowl on the lakes and watched the quirky movement of the squirrels as they played chase through the branches of the trees. Even more disconcerting was the uninvited tear that trickled down her cheek as she sat on a favoured bench and looked out across London spread out before her.

On Monday morning at 7.30 sharp she joined the masses making their way to the multitude of financial institutions that made up the Square Mile of the City of London. She stopped off to pick up a skinny latte from her usual coffee stop as she made her way to her trading desk at Mallorys. Like the other investment banks, Mallorys was always looking out for new opportunities for profit making after the recent collapse in global finance. They were still recovering from the horror stories associated with the 'sub-prime' mortgage scandal and the associated 'collateralized debt obligations' or CDOs. Either the Banking Boards, regulators, or governments didn't remotely understand the risks building in the financial markets, or they had deliberately turned a blind eye whilst they were all raking in so much money. Neither option, too stupid or too greedy was particularly edifying.

These virtually worthless financial instruments had been given AAA ratings by the credit rating agencies and had been traded at huge profits between the various financial institutions. After it all came crashing down it was the governments and, by default, wider society that picked up the tab for this reckless speculation. Most of the proceeds of this speculation were now safely registered by clients and traders in secrecy jurisdictions such as the Cayman Islands or the British Virgin Islands, well out of reach of the taxman and with active complicity of global governments and regulators.

The appetite for creating yet more wealth for the Bank's already extremely wealthy clients, Mallorys had several billionaires amongst its customers, was however unabated and so Mallorys was constantly looking for new opportunities. One that was becoming increasingly attractive was speculating on food. The price in the markets is largely based on supply and demand and the increasingly erratic global climate was playing havoc with some of the basic food commodities that were essential to feed the World's burgeoning population. There had always been some trading in such commodities but this was now occurring on an unprecedented level. Banks and hedge funds now widely speculated on the price of food, forward buying stocks to influence the supply side and then selling at a premium as shortages occurred and the prices rose. It was Vanessa's current job to oversee the management of Mallory's trading positions in the area of food speculation. Vanessa was very good and with her oversight her team had anticipated the market much better than many of her rivals at other competing institutions. This had netted her a personal bonus of over £230,000 at the end of the last financial year.

This Monday Vanessa was however finding it increasingly difficult to get absorbed as the numbers scrolled across the screen in front of her. It all suddenly seemed rather meaningless, extracting yet more money from society to people and institutions that already had far more than they could usefully employ. It was like some kind of crazy, irrational merry-go-round that nobody had the courage to stop and let the passengers get off.

Vanessa reflected upon her own life, the annoying but persistent voice that had awoken inside was asking her what personal benefit she would get by adding yet more money into her already copious financial coffers? Making money had just become a habit, perhaps an addiction and like all habits and addictions, it was hard to give up. If life isn't about making money and influence then what is it for? She had spent so much time and energy getting to the position in which she found herself today that she had never really stopped to consider whether there was any alternative.

After what had seemed like an interminable week she found herself once again standing outside of Luigi's. There are some moments in life that always stand out in the memory. These are times when a person feels truly awake and create the sense that much of life is spent in a semi-awakened state, an alternative sleep mode that is only revealed by such moments. These moments always seem so transitory and all too readily people relapse back into a normal state of consciousness. It is just such a yearning for these moments that makes some people take up extreme sports or even voluntarily risk their lives by joining the armed forces. These extreme moments create a different, if brief; look at the potential of human consciousness. If it were possible to harness such awareness a person could conceivably experience as much in a few weeks as they would otherwise experience in a lifetime.

Standing outside Luigi's was just such a moment for Vanessa. She felt short of breath and her hand trembled as she reached for the door as if she was almost afraid to venture inside. After being greeted by Luigi she was seated at her usual table, deliberately chosen because it furnished her with a view of the busy street outside. Vanessa was an unashamed people watcher and she contentedly observed a cosmopolitan selection of residents and visitors from all over the world bustle past the window as she waited to be served.

"Good evening madam." Vanessa looked once again into the captivating eyes of the waitress who had so unsettled her the previous week. "What can we tempt you with tonight?"

Vanessa ordered a bottle of Barolo and a fillet steak that was so tender that the knife practically cut it by its own weight alone. She watched the people passing by outside the window and wondered what sort of world they were returning to. Were they returning to loved ones, children, a warm and comfortable home or perhaps to a cold lonely flat, arguments, unpaid bills and a fear of a knock on the door? It was a long time since Vanessa had had to face any such fears.

Tonight Luigi's exceptional cuisine and the warm embrace of a fine Barolo wine had failed to work its magic upon her. She paid her bill with the usual generous tip and decided to take a walk in the unseasonably warm evening air rather than ask Luigi to call her a taxi. She wandered down towards the Thames and sat on a bench looking at the lights on the boats that plied their trade upon this historic river as they had done for centuries. For no reason that she could understand the tears started to trickle down her cheeks.

2

"I am sorry to disturb you but is there anything I can do to help?" Vanessa was suddenly startled by the sound of a very familiar voice. She looked up into the concerned face of the young waitress from Luigi's. Vanessa smiled through the tears, "I have no idea what's wrong so I'm not sure you could help, but thank you for your kindness".

"My name's Kaitlin" volunteered the waitress, "I live with a group of friends in an old converted warehouse by the river and was just on my way back when I recognised you."

"Vanessa" said Vanessa in reply.

"I could never forgive myself if I left you alone like this, would you perhaps at least join me for a coffee and a chat?" said Kaitlin. "There is a late night coffee shop just around the corner."

Normally Vanessa was quite reticent and she would have recoiled at the thought of talking to a virtual stranger about her feelings but this was not the normal Vanessa who was sat on this bench in tears. To her own surprise she replied, "yes, I think I'd like that."

As Kaitlin went up to the counter to order the coffee Vanessa reappraised the young woman before her. She had long flowing auburn hair which hung to just below her shoulders which had been pinned up in the restaurant. She was slim, but not skinny and on the tall side. Her taut calves revealed toning that obviously came from someone who was no stranger to exercise. Vanessa would put her age at between twenty and twenty five years old but she had already shown a maturity and confidence that belied her age. She had apple cheeks that were accentuated when she smiled and although she had shown no self-recognition of the fact, Vanessa conceded that she was looking at a beautiful, perhaps even stunningly attractive young woman.

When Kaitlin returned, Vanessa said that more than anything she felt like listening rather than talking and asked Kaitlin whether she would be prepared to talk a bit about herself. Kaitlin was happy to oblige and talked in the free and easy manner of someone seemingly at peace with herself. She explained that she had been working at Luigi's now for three years. The pay and tips were just enough for her to cover her basic living costs and had funded her attendance at UCL where she had studied archaeology. She now spent much of her days working as a volunteer for the Museum of London where she hoped to soon gain a permanent position once she had proved herself in the field.

Kaitlin also revealed that she had a boyfriend called Julian who currently was away in Bangladesh; working for a UK based charity that aspired to reduce the levels of malnutrition in some of the children. Julian was due back in a week's time and they were going to be holding a small party for him on the Saturday when he would be giving a slideshow related to his work. She was really looking forward to his return as he had been away for nearly three months and she missed him a great deal, "except for the piles of rather aromatic clothing he consistently abandons around the bedroom" she laughed.

"Now it's your turn" said Kaitlin, "tell me a bit about you?"

Vanessa explained her lifetime devotion to the world of finance and that she worked in a bank in the City although she did not feel it necessary to explain her work in detail. She talked about living in Notting Hill and love of walking on the Heath on Sundays.

"Sounds like a bit of an idyllic life" said Kaitlin softly, "but it isn't is it?"

"I just feel so desperate" said Vanessa "but I truly don't understand why. It's like something inside has snapped and is rebelling against the life I have so carefully constructed".

"So why don't we shake it all up and see what happens" laughed Kaitlin with that familiar twinkle in her eyes. "Why don't you come along to the warehouse next Saturday, meet the mob and listen to Julian's presentation?"

"Oh no, it would be such an imposition, I really couldn't" said Vanessa.

"Well you really can but I won't bully you into it" said Kaitlin. "We love having interesting people come along and you would be our first investment banker! Who knows, being in a completely different environment might just trigger something inside that may help you to understand why it is you are feeling like this?" She asked Vanessa for one of her business cards and wrote her address and contact details on the back.

Kaitlin gave Vanessa a big hug as they said goodbye. Vanessa was completely taken aback by the evening's events. She didn't really know what to make of this young woman and yet she had somehow felt a strange empathy when she had been in her company. Unlike Vanessa, Kaitlin seemed to be someone who was at peace with herself, and some of her self-confidence had seemed to have rubbed off. Vanessa felt strangely enlivened and the dark feelings of desperation were starting to evaporate, being replaced with a sense of hope or maybe even optimism?

Vanessa passed the next week at Mallory's in virtual autopilot mode. In truth she was so familiar with dynamics of her marketplace now that she could make decisions through a honed intuition that could only be realised through many years of experience. An unexpectedly large typhoon had hit the East of India and the resulting storm surge had caused massive salt water flooding of some of the important rice growing areas. Her team at Mallory's had forward bought 37million tonnes of rice and the market price had risen 30% in just two days of trading.

Vanessa decided to offload about 12 % of their rice options, enough to make a very healthy profit without oversupplying the market and thereby significantly weakening the market price. Rice was now trading at about $610 per tonne and they had bought the options at only $395 so the bank stood to make a healthy $955 million in profit on the deal. Thanks largely to Vanessa's judgement, Mallory's had timed this trading to perfection and had been a first mover. By Friday the market had already weakened to $585 per tonne as other players sought to take profits on the high price.

Normally this kind of successful trading would have left her with a bit of an adrenalin rush but this week she just felt rather detached from it. Her team were boisterous, anticipating the substantial bonuses to come, as she joined them at Flannagans, one of their regular haunts when celebrating a job well done. Tonight Vanessa had no appetite for her team's raucous celebrations, her mind was elsewhere, and she made her excuses early on before heading back to her flat to curl up on her favourite chair with Tabitha.

Vanessa spent most of Saturday afternoon trying to decide whether or not to take up Kaitlin's kind invitation. Part of her saw this as an opportunity for a bit of an adventure, the other part was in dread of feeling old and frumpy and conspicuously out of place. At about 5.00 p.m. she decided that she would put herself into the hand of fate and tossed a coin. Heads she would go, tails she wouldn't. The coin landed on her lacquered oak wood flooring and rolled under the coffee table with Tabitha in hot pursuit. Vanessa lay down, reached under the coffee table and slid the coin towards her across the flooring as she closed her eyes. One, two, three she counted in her head before opening her eyes to see the Queen's head on the coin below. "Cinderella will go to the ball" she laughed to herself.

Choosing what to wear was a real problem. She definitely couldn't wear one of her suits and she felt an evening dress would appear too formal. On the other hand her slouching around the house or walking clothes were completely nondescript and she imagined she might be visiting a rather bohemian group of young people. After much soul searching she found a tie-dye dress at the back of the wardrobe that she had inadvertently kept after her days at the university and a pair of robust sandals. Not perhaps the best choice for the time of year but at least she could pretend she was like Stevie Nicks from Fleetwood Mac, as she had often done when singing to herself in the mirror in her student apartment.

Vanessa smiled as she pulled herself into the dress, it was still quite a good fit after all these years and the addition of a wide belt emphasised the fact that her figure still had the aspect of an hourglass. All those rushed days without time for lunch she smiled wistfully. She had had to dispose of the afghan coat that she had also acquired as a student all those years ago. It had started to develop a rather pungent aroma after many years of abuse and two visits to Glastonbury festival, so she had to settle for a long grey double breasted woollen overcoat to complete the ensemble. She examined the results in a mirror, not exactly a hippy chick but she was still quite satisfied with the result.

She called a cab and by seven o'clock was stood outside a metal staircase that was leading up to a first floor door outside a renovated warehouse on the old dockside. She clambered up the stairs and was just about to pull on the cord by the thick wooden panelled front door when it was opened by a smiling young man in jeans and a Grateful Dead T shirt.

"Hi" said the young man, "I heard you coming up the stairs, they're just great for when we are expecting a raid" he said. Noting Vanessa's sudden alarm he laughed. "I'm sorry, just joking; I have been told my humour is a bit of an acquired taste! How can I help?"

"I've been invited by Kaitlin" said Vanessa, finding herself rather nervous all of a sudden.

"Kaitlin" yelled the young man into the substantial void beyond the doorway. About a half a minute later the familiar smiling face of Kaitlin suddenly appeared behind the young man. "Vanessa, I am so delighted you could make it. For goodness sake let her in Jethro you great oaf!"

Vanessa entered a large room that was the full depth of the building and which ran almost its full length. At the right hand end was a large kitchen area next to which was a big wooden table with room for at least twelve people to sit around it. In the middle was a communal area surrounded by a semicircle of sofas and cushions that faced a large wood burning stove. The smoke from the stove was ventilated through a round metal chimney that went up to the vaulted roof a good 4 metres above the floor. At the opposite end to the kitchen the warehouse was partitioned off but Vanessa could see through a partially opened double door what looked to be a studio area with the paraphernalia of an artist scattered around.

The wall of the warehouse through which she had just passed was pierced by large latticed metal framed windows which could, if desired, be covered over with russet coloured roller blinds. There was a spiral staircase against the opposite wall, positioned just to the right of what she had perceived to be the artist studio. The ceiling had obviously been well insulated during the warehouse's renovation and there were a large number of small lamps sunk into the thickness of the now plastered insulation. There were also eight large uplighters positioned around edge of the room. The overall effect, despite the spaciousness of the room, was surprisingly warm and cosy.

The opposite wall was covered in murals of what looked to be images of nature and creatures and nymphs from Greek mythology. All in all, the impact on someone walking into the warehouse for the first time was quite breath-taking.

Vanessa handed over a bag with a couple of bottles of wine and some chocolate truffles which Kaitlin passed over to Jethro's care. He took these over to a makeshift bar area that had been adapted from one of the extensive work surfaces that virtually surrounded the kitchen and partitioned it from the eating table and the main seating area.

Apart from Kaitlin and Jethro there were seven other people in the room. Slightly to Vanessa's embarrassment Kaitlin picked up a conveniently positioned thin metal rod and tapped a small bronze bell that was obviously also linked to the cord that Kaitlin had seen outside the front door.

Everyone suddenly stopped and turned around inquisitively to look at Vanessa. "Vanessa, may I introduce you to the Rabble, which is the collective noun we have chosen for the disorderly mob that inhabit this warehouse."

There was a quick chorus of "hi Vanessa". Starting from the left Kaitlin identified them as Max, Roxie, Joris, Fixie, Julian, Sinjini and Reggie who waved as he stood over one of the large pots simmering on an impressive dark green Aga in the kitchen area.

"Welcome Vanessa" came a rather deep, husky but unmistakably feminine voice from behind. Vanessa turned and saw a striking tall woman with ebony skin emerge from behind the partition. She was wearing dungarees that were covered in a rainbow of different paint colours and had her dark hair bound up in a brightly coloured band of material. Vanessa guessed she must have been in her late-twenties. "I'm Alexandra" said the woman, rubbing her hand on her dungarees before holding it out in greeting.

Vanessa met a pair of intense dark brown eyes that gave her the rather strange feeling that they were not actually evaluating her physical appearance but rather peering into her essence. The eyes appeared satisfied with what they had found as the face relaxed into a warm smile. "Do forgive my appearance, I am working on a commission which is already two weeks late and my customer is starting to get a bit sniffy with me." Whatever Alexandra's eyes had discovered, something within Vanessa responded to the scrutiny and she felt an instant warmth and affection for the woman standing before her.

Despite the chill in the autumn air outside, the stove and the Aga had combined to make the warehouse pleasantly warm. Vanessa was pleased to hand over her coat to Jethro who was now making up for leaving her standing outside and was playing the convivial host. She was asked if she wanted a drink from the bar. This was well stocked with two hand pumps fixed onto the top of the worktop and a glass fronted door revealed a comprehensive collection of different bottles of wine, beer, and mixers. There were also several different spirits set up in optics behind the bar. There was also a large crystal glass bowl which reputedly contained a copious quantity of 'Fixie's patent punch' which Vanessa decided to sample. The punch was slightly warm, entirely delicious and also revealed within its taste that Fixie was not shy of applying liberal quantities of alcohol of which rum was the predominant influence. Vanessa made a mental note not to get too carried away with Fixie's punch if she was going to last the evening.

Vanessa congratulated Fixie on her creativity. She was a short wisp of a girl in her early twenties with short spiky bleach blond hair with blue highlights. "Fixie is a very unusual name" she enquired.

"Oh it's not my real name, it's just what the Rabble has decided to call me and it seems to have stuck."

"We call her Fixie because if you every want to go out and can't get hold of concert, theatre or any other kind of tickets she will fix it!" said Kaitlin who had appeared at Vanessa's shoulder. "Fixie works at one of the ticket offices down near theatre land in the West End and has contacts everywhere."

Fixie just laughed and skipped over to the kitchen area to help Reggie who was still sweating over an impressive collection of pots and pans that were simmering on the Aga. "She is irrepressible" said Kaitlin, "it's very hard to be miserable with Fixie's around even when the world seems to be throwing everything at you. It was her idea to hold this little homecoming bash for Julian."

"Where do you all sleep?" enquired Vanessa. Kaitlin explained that the ground floor which was reached via the spiral staircase was split into six apartments. Everyone had their own apartment which was individually self-contained apart from Alexandra who had a mezzanine kitchen, bathroom and sleeping area inside her studio. One of the apartments had been empty for three months after Heiner, an Engineer, had moved back to Germany when the research and development department in which he had worked had been relocated.

Kaitlin explained that the warehouse had originally belonged to a kind elderly gentleman who was a Quaker and who had been an enthusiastic supporter of the community that had evolved in the warehouse. The rental had been exceptionally cheap for London and the owner had been very happy to approve a set of house rules proposed by the tenants that allowed them to live in relative harmony. One of these rules was that any new tenant had to be unanimously approved by the others before they could join the Rabble.

Sadly the owner had recently died and the warehouse was now owned by his nephew. The nephew couldn't change the tenancy agreement which was set in trust but there was nothing to stop the nephew selling the warehouse provided that the tenants were given six months' notice. Six weeks ago notice had been served. The tenants had subsequently found out that the nephew intended to sell the site to a property development company owned by a sovereign wealth fund based in the United Arab Emirates.

Kaitlin explained that the Rabble all made a contribution to paying the rent on the warehouse but that this was based on an ability to pay. Even at the discounted rate that had been asked by the previous owner, some of the residents would not have been easily able to afford to live there. By far the biggest slice of the rent was paid for by Roxie. Roxie had inherited a lot of stocks and shares from her late father who died from Lassa Fever whilst working as an oil executive in Nigeria. It was the regular dividends from these investments that largely kept the warehouse going.

Vanessa looked with interest at Roxie. She saw a flamboyant lady whom she estimated was probably about fifty years old but whose whole demeanour and the vivid red streaks of colour in her hair indicated that she still had a youngster's zest for life.

Kaitlin went on to explain that, as an only child and with parents that had long since divorced, Roxie could be considered wealthy as the sole inheritor of her father's estate. This was not however a definition of wealth that she would herself recognise. Roxie was a rare human spirit who measured a person's value by the kindness in their heart and the compassion they showed to others rather than by any material consideration. It was very much Roxie's values that had helped to create the special bond that had developed between the residents and this warmth almost seemed to permeate the fabric of the building itself.

Kaitlin had once asked Roxie why she didn't resent paying more than some of the others. She had laughed aloud and told Kaitlin that the financial investment that helped keep the Warehouse and the Rabble together was paid back a hundredfold in the pleasure and affection she got from their company. "What investment could possibly give me a better return?" If she were to be judged by her own terms Roxie's wealth of spirit far exceeded her material wealth although she would have been the last to recognise or admit this.

Kaitlin explained that Roxie was primarily a writer of novels with the occasional stab at a more serious philosophical work but she had yet to achieve any significant sales for her efforts. This did not seem to remotely bother her as she seemed quite fulfilled by the process of book creation in the way an artist might take delight in creating a picture. It was probably this bond of creativity that had made her especially close to Alexandra.

Alexandra's story was almost the reverse of Roxie's. She had joined the Rabble after being introduced by a friend of Roxie's whom she had met at a woman's refuge. When she had been taken in she was absolutely penniless and made her contribution by painting the incredible murals that now adorned the main area. That was about five years ago but she was now making a name for herself through her painting and her sculptures for which she used different coloured foils over a textured resin base relief to create her own unique style. She painted using more conventional materials and was particularly inspired by the female form and the shapes and patterns of the natural world. Some of Alexandra's art was now fetching good prices from a couple of galleries that had taken her work on. Just the previous week one of her resin and foil works had been sold for five thousand pounds to a dealer from Toronto.

Roxie shared her apartment with Joris who was seventeen years her junior and who worked as a physiotherapist for the local NHS Trust. Although it was quite obvious they adored each other they never admitted to being in a formal relationship. "He's just my friend with benefits" Roxie would chuckle if pushed on the subject and Joris seemed entirely happy with this arrangement. Roxie also had a large and decided overfed ginger tomcat called Marmaduke who was generally loved and who was quite happy to share his affections with any inviting lap that was made available.

Kaitlin explained to Vanessa that Jethro and Max were partners and they both worked as instructors at a local fitness studio and did some additional nightclub door work in the evenings. Vanessa looked with some interest at the obvious muscularity of the pair that was quite evident beneath their close hugging tops and jeans. Jethro in particular obviously made frequent use of the weights in the gym as well as instructing others and his chest and arms were practically bursting out of his t-shirt. If she had been in the market for a toy boy then Jethro might well have been on her shopping list she smiled to herself. Why, she inwardly sighed, was it often the case that many of the most attractive men she came across also turned out to be gay?

She snapped out of her revelry because Kaitlin was explaining about Reggie and Sinjini. They had been together now for about eighteen months. Reggie taught economics at UCL and Sinjini was a dental nurse. To the amusement of most of the Rabble, Reggie seemed to be absolutely hopeless with his own investments. He could often be seen peering nervously at the pages of the Financial Times as yet another company that was a sure fire bet for growth had inexplicably turned into a lame duck. "He could probably benefit from your experience" whispered Kaitlin in Vanessa's ear.

Reggie was however a superb cook and he often volunteered to take over the command of the kitchen when the Rabble decided to have one of their communal get-togethers. Fixie had appointed herself his assistant chef. Although Reggie let out cries of exasperation at her efforts on occasion he obviously enjoyed having her help and basked in the attention she showed as he explained how to prepare different dishes.

At that moment Fixie announced that dinner was served and they gathered around the table to enjoy the feast that Reggie and Fixie had prepared. The majority of the food was vegetarian as some of the residents didn't eat meat or fish. There was a Thai vegetable curry, a beanie hotpot, caramelised onion tart, saffron rice, nan breads, roast beetroot and sweet potato. There was also a substantial lamb Rogan Josh to satisfy the cravings of the meat eaters.

Vanessa found herself sat between Julian, Kaitlin's boyfriend, and Alexandra. Julian had the slightly disconcerting look of someone who had seen rather too much of the world for one so young. He looked rather preoccupied and apart from the occasional exchange with Kaitlin who was sat opposite he largely ate in silence.

Alexandra on the other hand quickly engaged Vanessa in conversation. She had changed into a long robe covered with swirling interwoven red and amber patterns and her hair was curled and pinned up making her look even taller. As she had re-appeared for dinner Vanessa was completely taken aback by the transition. A be-speckled artist in dungarees had left the room. The woman who returned more closely resembled the vision embedded in Vanessa's imagination of the Queen of Sheba.

Alexandra told Vanessa that she had been born in London to Nigerian parents and had been married at a young age to a partner who had been chosen for her. She had left her partner four years before and was forced to seek refuge in a woman's shelter after suffering several years of abuse and ultimately physical violence. The Warehouse had become both her physical and spiritual home and she had found, through the kindness of strangers, the love and support that had always been denied to her by her own family and husband.

Vanessa felt humbled that this magnificent woman was prepared to reveal such personal and painful details to someone she had just met and she said as much to Alexandra. "Both Kaitlin and I have seen a person inside you that you have not yet revealed to yourself" replied Alexandra mysteriously but she refused to elaborate on this statement when pressed.

Alexandra asked Vanessa whether she was interested in art and Vanessa explained that she had quite a collection of art, particularly sculptures. She was asked how she selected them and she explained that this was usually based on the reputation of the artist and the prospects that the works would increase in value. They were not just art but also investments for her long term future she explained.

Alexandra fixed her with that now familiar gaze and after a considerable pause asked "Do you enjoy your art?"

"Well I wouldn't have bought it if I didn't think it wouldn't suit the apartment" she stuttered in reply.

"That hasn't answered my question" said Alexandra. "Do you feel your art, does it change your emotions, does it alter your mood, and does it engage with something deep inside and make you think differently about the world and your relationship with it?"

Vanessa had never been asked such a question before. In her world of finance and commerce, art was largely seen as an investment and the aesthetic qualities didn't really come into play. It was the reputation of the artist and the monetary value placed on the artist's works by others that made different pieces desirable and sought after. She thought about what Alexandra had said and realised that none of her art actually made any real emotional impact upon her. If she came back from a difficult day at the bank it would be Tabitha purring on her lap and the refuge of the imaginary world of her latest novel that would allow her mind to relax and let go of the stresses of the day.

"No" she said quite suddenly "I don't enjoy my art, in fact I don't think I would know how to".

"That's because you have been buying art using the rational aspect of your mind. Art should be chosen through unconscious decisions made by your emotions and instincts" replied Alexandra. "Listen and liberate these instincts and emotions awakening inside you, and trust the messages that they are sending to you. Art chosen by the rational mind has material value alone and maybe a technical appreciation but this is not the purpose of true art. Far greater value can be obtained through art that has the power to alter the harmonies within you. Is a billionaire truly wealthier that a penniless person who has achieved both an inner harmony and a harmony with the natural world around them? Being both at one with themselves and with the immeasurable beauty and magnificence of nature makes a person wealthy beyond compare. Those who see everyone and everything around them as merely exploitable commodities are the true paupers."

Alexandra explained that many of the origins of art had been made by ancient peoples to capture the essence of the natural world around them and the spirits of plants, animals and people. She said that is was the essence of herself and the natural world around her that inspired her work. "If humanity hadn't forgotten that they are part of the natural world and shared in its rhythms, moods and seasons they would never have allowed it to be so catastrophically damaged. Humanity's stupidity and greed has led to it brutalising nature as it has brutalised itself throughout its history. The consequences of disrupting the harmonies of the natural world will be severe and will ultimately change our whole concept of the meaning of civilisation. The current world that applauds and worships greed and self-interest will one day be looked back on as abhorrent and barbaric."

Vanessa had never had a conversation like this before. She looked with fascination at this remarkable woman who was probably fifteen years her junior and yet seemed to have acquired so much more wisdom in her relatively short life. She didn't really understand everything that Alexandra was saying but an inner voice was already growing more assertive. It was telling her that these ideas might well be of importance to her if she was going to come to terms with the inner turmoil that had recently begun to torment her.

"Come on Sinjani, perform one of your dances", Max's voice rose above the general hubbub of conversation from the end of the table.

"No Max, said Sinjani, if I dance after eating all this food I will get a terrible stitch and besides I am sure that the rest of the Rabble and our guest would not be interested."

The table went quiet and Reggie stood up and went over to what looked like some kind of music centre. He put on some Indian dance music and slowly turned up the volume until the melodies filled the room. Max started to clap in rhythm and rapidly everyone else started to join in until the whole table was clapping and calling out "Sin-ja-ni, Sin-ja-ni". Sinjani looked around the table hopelessly looking for an ally but eventually capitulated and moved to the centre of the room as Max and Jethro leapt up to move a couple of the sofas aside to give her room. She looked down and then as she raised her face Vanessa noticed that her expression had completely changed. All of a sudden Sinjani's body burst into a vibrant movement accompanied by a changing dynamic of expressions as the mood of the dance ebbed and flowed. Vanessa was absolutely captivated as Sinjani's whole body conveyed a series of different emotions and passions as the shy looking Indian woman from the end of the table suddenly released this explosion of creative energy.

Finally, in crescendo of sound and music, the dance finished and Sinjani looked daggers at Reggie who held his palms up in submission and turned the music off. The whole room erupted into applause and Fixie rushed over to Sinjani and gave her a huge hug. Vanessa was completely spellbound and felt this sudden inner terror. What if the coin she had so flippantly tossed when she was deciding whether to accept Kaitlin's offer had come up tails? She couldn't remember when she had ever had such a colourful and fascinating evening. What more would the Warehouse and its bohemian residents reveal before the evening was over?

Suddenly the bell by the door clanged loudly and Jethro jumped up to open the door. "It's Sensi" he called out and Alexandra rushed over to the women who walked in and gave her a hug that seemed to go on for at least a minute. When she was finally released Vanessa saw a woman who looked to be about twenty-five years old who she guessed might be from South America from her complexion and her features.

The woman spotted Vanessa, walked across to greet her and gave her a kiss on each cheek in greeting. Much to her surprise the woman said "you must be Vanessa; Alexandra told me that Kaitlin had a new friend called Vanessa whom she was hoping would come over tonight. My name is Sensatez but everyone here calls me Sensi." Sensi's accent again suggested either a Spanish or Portuguese influence to Vanessa's untrained ear, reinforcing the possibility of a South American connection.

"I must say I am extraordinarily flattered that Kaitlin has talked to so many of her friends about me" said Vanessa. Inside however she was far from thrilled to have been the subject of so much evident discussion, it made her feel decidedly uncomfortable and she was suddenly becoming a little wary. There was the conversation with Alexandra about the person inside her that they had seen and now there was this somewhat mysterious woman from South America who was obviously very close to Alexandra. Why were all these strangers showing such an interest in her? Her City instincts started to influence her thinking. Maybe they wanted something from her? Kaitlin must have known that she was wealthy, Luigi's was not cheap and her bespoke business suits were approximately £1,200 a time. She felt her defences going up for the first time since she had arrived at the Warehouse.

She suddenly noticed Sensi smiling at her quizzically, "Vanessa, what must you think about us all talking about you behind your back? I can assure you that there is nothing sinister going on" she said as if she could almost read Vanessa's mind. "I was brought up in Peru and my mother was a curandera or what you would more familiarly call a shaman. Kaitlin had told Alexandra that she had invited a friend over this evening who seemed troubled but could not explain why. Alexandra took the liberty of inviting me this evening as she felt that I had been able to help her in similar circumstances in the past. Alexandra obviously seems to think that I have picked up some of my mother's skills" she laughed and smiled with genuine affection at Alexandra who beamed back at her with her startlingly white teeth.

"I can assure you that I have absolutely no intention to pry into your private life without an explicit invitation to do so" Sensi continued, "but if you do feel that you want to talk later on, I am a pretty good listener."

"Sensi underestimates herself" said Alexandra "she is a true healer of troubled spirits. I would not still be here today if it wasn't for Sensi as I had turned in on myself in a very destructive way. Sensi taught me to understand and love myself again and to realise that we are all part of something far more unique, powerful and precious than we realise."

The conversation was interrupted by Fixie calling out to Julian. "Come on Julian, show us what you have been doing with all this charity money in Bangladesh.

You can't go away for the best part of three months without telling us what you have been up to and you had better have come back with some good tales!"

Julian smiled, it was almost impossible not to with Fixie, but Vanessa thought the smile was also sad and a bit reflective. "OK Fixie, you win, I'll set up my iPad to link in with the screen and show you some slides of what I have been up to. I must warn you all though that some of what I have to share you might find upsetting."

Julian set up the wireless connection to a large LED screen that was on the wall, surrounded by Alexandra's murals and the Rabble jumped onto the ample sofas and cushions with practiced familiarity. Vanessa sat herself down between Kaitlin and Alexandra on one of the sofas.

"I thought I would just do a quick introduction first as some of you are less familiar with what I do in my work. The population of Bangladesh has very high levels of malnutrition, particularly amongst its children which can permanently impair the normal development of the child and lead to lifelong health problems. This is partly because the staple diet of rice lacks all the nutrition that is needed for a balanced diet and many of the population are either unaware of this or cannot afford the variety in their diet for healthy child development. The work of my charity is mostly education about diet but we also distribute essential vitamins and mineral supplements in areas where malnutrition is most prevalent."

Julian started showing some slides of his journey which started with some shots of him having a few days in Thailand with some colleagues. Kaitlin unkindly volunteered that there were obviously no fashion police in Thailand. In a few of the photos Julian was exhibiting a shirt and short combination whose colours and patterns clashed so completely that they were very hard to look at without wincing. He then started showing pictures of some of the villages where he worked and some of the clinics, families and children that he had met.

 "This was something that I didn't expect to see, at least not to this extent" said Julian. He showed pictures of children and families that were obviously suffering from the effects of starvation. "The problem with many of these villagers is that the rice crop had been damaged by the recent typhoon so they didn't have enough for themselves. This shouldn't be a problem as the country had taken measures to build up reserve stocks as this type of severe weather event is relatively common. The problem here lies in the fact that the price of rice has risen over 300 percent in the last three months and the villagers simply can't afford to buy the food that they need."

"What is the reason for such a rapid increase in price?" asked Roxie. "Is it simply the local increase in demand?"

"It's only partly that" said Julian, "the real problem is international market speculation on basic food commodities. Traders in the financial markets can make huge profits by taking options on vast stocks of basic food commodities creating artificial market shortages and then exercising these options when the market price is artificially high." Julian's face was suddenly quite angry, "I simply can't understand how our government legally permits profiteering in basic food commodities when the consequences means malnutrition and death for millions of indigenous people across the world. We live in a world where billionaires cruise the world in their plush super-yachts whilst the most vulnerable are deliberately plunged into poverty and starvation to sustain these obscene lifestyles. Months or even years of hard work on the nutrition projects can be wiped out by just a click of a trader's mouse in New York or London."

There was a sudden hush in the room as the Rabble silently took on board what Julian had been saying. It was no wonder that he had seemed so preoccupied when he had got back from his trip.

Vanessa was absolutely horrified. She had quickly realised that she was one of the traders that had "clicked the mouse" that had resulted in the distressing images that were being shown on the screen in front of her. In fact it was her ingenuity in creating exceptional value from trading in these commodities that had enabled Mallorys to post such exceptional profits from her division. She suddenly realised that the size of her annual bonus could be directly equated to the extent of the misery that was unfolding before her eyes.

To her great distress Vanessa found that she had started to sob uncontrollably as she sat on the sofa and she had no power to stop. Kaitlin instinctively knew Vanessa's response was far more than just a reaction to what Julian was showing. She put her arm around Vanessa's sobbing shoulders but Vanessa violently shook her off. "Don't touch me!" she cried out, "you have no idea who I am and if you did you wouldn't want to be anywhere near me."

Kaitlin pulled back in evident shock at Vanessa's reaction. The rest of the Rabble sat in stunned silence. Suddenly Sensi quietly spoke, "why don't you tell us what this is all about. I know that Kaitlin would not have invited a monster back to the Warehouse, her instincts are far too attuned and in the very the short time I have met you I have shared Kaitlin's instincts."

"But I am a monster" said Vanessa, "don't you realise that I might be personally responsible for killing many people just like those you can see on the screen, maybe even some of these very villagers." She looked at the sunken eyes of yet another severely malnourished child staring vacantly back at her. "I trade in these essential basic food commodities, I get paid huge bonuses for starving and killing people I have never even met. I never ever considered the consequences of my actions but sitting her tonight it is so obvious. Why didn't I realise this was the inevitable result of what I was doing?" Her head just dropped as she sobbed on the sofa. When she had gained more control of herself she quietly added "Kaitlin, now do you see that I didn't deserve your kindness, I don't deserve consideration from anyone here."

"You are not the monster Vanessa" said Sensi, "it is the system you work in that is monstrous and it is obvious that you are also a victim of this system. You exist in a world that is ruled by greed. Greed is unforgiving, it is an insatiable master and it is entirely without compassion. This is what your subconscious has been reacting against and it is this battle within you that Kaitlin spotted when she first met you."

Julian stopped his presentation and looked at Vanessa with bewilderment. He was just about to speak when Kaitlin put her hand on his arm. "Not now Julian, it's not the right time" she said. "Vanessa has to deal with all these conflicting emotions within her first and is in no condition to answer any of your questions. It is also obvious that what you have seen and experienced in Bangladesh has taken both a physical and emotional toll on you. Both you and Vanessa need some respite before you can have that conversation."

Julian looked at Vanessa with her head in her hands on the couch and then into Kaitlin's eyes as she smiled warmly at him. All of a sudden his shoulders dropped and he let out a deep sigh. "You are right as always, I think I will call it a night and get some rest. Goodnight everyone and special thanks to Reggie and Fixie for such a lovely welcome home feast." With that he unplugged his iPad and left the room down the spiral staircase that led to the personal apartments below.

3

"I must go" said Vanessa, "I am so sorry and that I have ruined your evening. Thank you for your wonderful hospitality and your kindness, I promise I won't bother any of you again." With that she made to get to her feet but found that her legs suddenly lacked the strength to support her and she sat back down onto the sofa.

"I refuse to allow you to go anywhere until you have given yourself a chance to digest what has taken place here tonight and you are not under any circumstances be left alone," said Alexandra. "I insist that you at least stay tonight as my guest and see how you feel in the morning."

"I couldn't possibly impose" said Vanessa, "you have all been so kind to me, even though I was a stranger to all but Kaitlin before tonight. Now that you know what I have done and what sort of person I truly am, how could you possibly want me to stay?"

"We already know what kind of person you really are" said Sensi, "even though it is obvious that you don't know this yourself, and above all you need love and support. When you have had some time to think and rest you can then decide what you want to do. I believe your life will be very different in the future as you find a different path that is in harmony with your true self. In your heart you already know this, you can no longer deny your true nature by trying to rationalise your emotions. Emotions can't be rationalised, they must be accepted as they are and this requires a very different type of understanding. It's time you opened up your heart and trusted it to guide you. Most people think that wisdom equates to the amount of knowledge that a person has accrued but nothing could be further from the truth. Look how much knowledge you had of the financial markets but have you acted wisely with all this knowledge? Wisdom is created when there is a harmony and a balance between rational intelligence and emotional intelligence. You have been deeply out of harmony with yourself and if you are out of harmony within, you cannot possibly be in harmony with the world around you."

Without waiting for Vanessa to answer Alexandra and Sensi each put an arm around her and gently guided her towards Alexandra's studio at the end of the room. They helped Vanessa up some stairs to a mezzanine area above the studio which was laid out below. The mezzanine was partitioned off from the rest of the studio behind a stud wall covered with different fabrics and drapes. Inside was a kitchen area with just enough room for some worktops and appliances and an oak table with four chairs. Beyond the kitchen was the bedchamber with an en-suite bathroom. The bedchamber was lit with dimmed coloured lights of different hues. The walls were covered with some more of Alexandra's naturalistic murals, some drapes to add to its sense of cosiness and a number of hung pictures which at a glance seemed largely to be of nude women.

There was a super king-size bed in the middle of the back wall of the bedchamber, a large built in wardrobe along one of the side walls, a dressing table and what looked like a large padded, massage table. Despite the chill of the night it was lovely and warm in Alexandra's bedchamber and Sensi added to the sensual stimulation by lighting up some incense sticks. Alexandra put on some gentle background music and turned around to face Vanessa.

"You need to completely relax for a while Vanessa, you are understandably very distressed after what you have just been through. Now is not the time to attempt to make sense of it all whist your emotions are in turmoil, you need to allow your mind to still and your emotions to calm. The best way to achieve this is through a complete relaxation of your physical body." She glanced at the massage table and then to Sensi who smiled and nodded. "Sensi would like to give you a massage with some essential oils if you will permit her to do so?"

Vanessa had no more will to resist; she was led to the bathroom area, told to undress completely, and given a beautiful white silk robe, covered with a pattern of lotus flowers. When she returned she found that both Sensi and Alexandra had also changed into similar robes. Alexandra lay on the bed, propped against the headboard with pillows whilst Sensi gestured for Vanessa to come over to the massage table. She stood in front of Vanessa and slowly pulled on the cord that held the robe together. She gently but insistently slid her hands over Vanessa's shoulders, gently removing the robe and Vanessa found herself being guided naked to the massage table. There was a small opening near the top of the table where she was told to place her face leaving her lying on her front feeling somewhat nervous and exposed.

"Just relax and listen to the music" said Sensi as she sat astride Vanessa and started to massage her neck. As Sensi's fingers worked their magic Vanessa quickly forgot her nervousness. She became aware of the warmth of Sensi's thighs around her lower back. She found that her body was responding to Sensi's caresses, the warmth, the music and the incense and she was starting to become aroused. A delicious feeling started in her groin and slowly spread, her arousal increasing as Sensi's expert hands worked their way down her body. Soon Vanessa lost all sense of time as she succumbed to this enveloping cocoon of sensations.

Sensi asked Vanessa to turn over and once again straddled her on the bench. Her fingers once again started their work, beginning on her forehead and around the eyebrows before moving down to the side of her face and neck. Vanessa opened her eyes and saw that Sensi's robe had fallen open and she could see firm rounded breasts glistening with perspiration as Sensi worked on Vanessa's body. As Sensi's hands moved down towards her own breasts, Vanessa could feel her nipples harden in anticipation and she let out an involuntary gasp revealing her arousal. "Switch off your mind and listen to your body" whispered Sensi. "Give yourself permission to succumb to your desire."

Vanessa gave herself over completely to the gentle assault on all her senses that was taking place and her arousal grew in intensity. Sensi's hands worked their way down her body until they were circulating and caressing her breasts. As if by accident her hand gently brushed the top of one of Vanessa's engorged nipples eliciting yet another involuntary moan of arousal. "Do I have your permission to release the tension within you?" said Sensi in a sensual voice that seemed to communicate not just with Vanessa's ears but also to directly caress the growing desire deep within her. "Please" whispered back Vanessa, a pleading urgency in her voice.

She closed her eyes as Sensi's hands reached the moist mound between her legs. Something touched her most sensitive spot and her hips arched off the couch as her body started to respond to the stimulation. Vanessa raised her head and saw that Sensi's head was now between her thighs which had instinctively parted as her arousal had increased. Sensi's tongue teased and tormented her, one moment delving deep between her now parted and engorged lips, the next moment switching its attention to her clitoris. The intensity of Vanessa's arousal escalated rapidly as Sensi's tongue became ever more insistent. Suddenly she completely lost control, an almost primeval cry escaped from her as she erupted into what was undoubtedly the most intense orgasm of her life, her thighs involuntarily clamping Sensi's head in her moment of ecstasy.

As the intensity of her orgasm dissipated Vanessa sat up on the bench and gently steered Sensi to lie on her back in her place. She turned around until her vulva was above Sensi's face and beneath her she saw that Sensi's mound of Venus was completely without a trace of hair. Sensi's labia were also swollen and had already parted slightly, like a ripe fruit opening up to reveal the delights within. The glistening between these lips revealed to Vanessa that Sensi was already in a high state of arousal.

Vanessa slowly parted Sensi's engorged labia and detected sweetness, almost like honeyed nectar, as her tongue met the moistness within. Her tongue traced a path upwards until the tip touched the sensitive tip of Sensi's clitoris nestled within its hood. She was rewarded with a gasp from Sensi who then returned to pleasuring Vanessa with increased urgency. Expert fingers entered Vanessa and found a very special place at the top front of her vagina that swelled in response to the attention it was receiving. This would soon deliver Vanessa another powerful but entirely different orgasm to her first. Both women were now completely lost to the language of their bodies. Their urgency continued to increase and their bodies fell into a beautiful harmony of movement that finally grew into another explosive climax that simultaneously engulfed their whole beings.

Vanessa was now physically drained but she retained a delicious, tingling, warm sensation, the sensual aftermath of their combined passion. After a few moments she raised herself off Sensi and turned around. She sat looking into the beautiful dark eyes of this extraordinary woman who a few hours ago had been a complete stranger to her, but with whom she had now shared the deepest of intimacies. Sensi leaned forwards and their lips tentatively brushed. Vanessa responded, putting her arms around Sensi her lips parted and both women shared the kind of deep passionate kiss that can only truly belong to lovers.

Reluctantly the lovers parted from their embrace and Vanessa walked over to sit on the edge of the bed where Alexandra was sat smiling at her. In Alexandra's hands was a sketch pad in which she had captured the two women whilst they were lost in their lovemaking. Vanessa now took in more of the detail of the pictures around the bedchamber noticing that many followed similar themes. She smiled as she noticed that Sensi featured in several of the scenes that had been captured by Alexandra's expert hand. She felt encompassed in this womb of femininity and warmth and, at a gestured invitation from Alexandra, she climbed onto the huge bed, snuggled beneath the duvet, and fell into a deep and dreamless sleep.

4

Vanessa woke to find herself spooning the naked body of Alexandra who lay alongside her in the bed. The lingering smell of female musk upon Vanessa's body reminded her of the extraordinary experiences of the night before. She raised herself up in the bed, the movement stirring Alexandra who leisurely stretched out her arms with a contented sigh and raised herself up in the bed. Alexandra kissed Vanessa on the cheek and then sprung out of the bed, a pair of firm rounded ebony buttocks moving towards the hook where she had hung her robe the night before.

"Coffee?" she called out to Vanessa enquiringly.

"Oh yes please" replied Vanessa with genuine enthusiasm. She was told to help herself to the bathroom and she luxuriated in Alexandra's power shower, the jets tingling her skin as they blasted away the residues of the previous night's passion. She returned to the bedchamber to find Alexandra sat up in the bed with a steaming mug of coffee in her hand. She patted the bed next to her and Vanessa joined her, gratefully picking up her own mug from the bedside table.

Before talking to Alexandra, Vanessa picked up her iPhone from the bedside table and called up Bridget to ask her if she would feed Tabitha. Bridget was her kindly neighbour who had rescued her many times before after unplanned late nights in the office. Her conscience now allayed, she turned to Alexandra with a quizzical look in her eye. "I am still trying to come to terms with what happened last night" she said, "where is Sensi this morning?"

"Sensi left about 7.30, she has a plane to catch and will probably not be back for two or three months" answered Alexandra.

"I have a lot questions and rather mixed feelings after last night, it's a shame that she had to leave so early" said Vanessa. "Did you both plan to seduce me last night?" she enquired with a quizzically raised eyebrow.

"Oh no, nothing of the sort was planned and anyway Sensi wasn't seducing you as such, she was starting the healing process" replied Alexandra. "The human mind is a very complex thing and its various parts often end up in conflict with each other. Sensi intuitively felt that you were on the verge of a damaging breakdown as the rational part of your mind, the part that has supressed your instincts and emotions for so long, started to recoil at the images in Julian's presentation. This just accelerated a change that was already happening within you, a positive change that comes with increasing awareness, but Sensi was also worried that this was spiralling out of control."

"Many spiritual teachers through the ages have stated that a person has to die before they can be reborn. This teaching was not meant to be taken literally. What the teachers knew is that from a young age we are programmed by our society with cultural beliefs and norms and these influence all our thinking. In order to take on new ideas and gain a different understanding, a person first has to let go of all the myths and illusions that constrain our ability to think freely and objectively. Your internal conflict is part of a process of awakening but this is a dangerous time. It can leave a person in despair as old certainties disappear and new ideas and understanding have not developed to replace them. It is not uncommon for people who have started the process of awakening, without love and support, to become very depressed and even suicidal."

"The most basic elements of the human mind, the ones that are already present in the human unconscious when we are born, are our instincts. Our sexual energies and passions emerge from these during puberty. Although the effects of cultural conditioning may have an impact upon the nature of our fantasies, true sexual energy and the associated physiological responses remain largely unaffected. Sexual release can therefore be the best place to start when trying to calm a human mind that is conflicted as a result of the process of awakening."

"It is also the authenticity of our true sexuality that makes it such a threat to those who wish to programme and control us for their own ends. Many organised religions in particular, reinforced by the social norms of society, try to repress sexuality, calling it sinful and shameful. The part of the human mind that Freud would call the ego then tries to repress sexual energy and as a result this can have very damaging consequences. Women in particular can be brutally forced to deny their sexuality. They are often horribly oppressed by men through the patriarchal cultures and religions that have been invented as mechanisms of control. I am living proof of the lengths that some cultures will go to deny women their sexuality."

Vanessa was quite taken aback. She wasn't sure where this conversation was leading and she was being exposed to many new ideas that she had never even considered before. She saw the flash in Alexandra's eyes when she was talking about how the structures of society were designed to repress female sexuality and this also struck a chord with her. She remembered all the sexism, harassment and gender discrimination she had had to put up with in the City during her career.

"There is no reproductive reason for the female orgasm and the pleasure associated with it but everything that has evolved in nature has purpose and meaning. The female orgasm is intrinsically linked to both physical and psychological wellbeing" continued Alexandra. "By stimulating your sexuality and releasing this energy Sensi hoped that she could start your healing process. She hoped that the sexual release that you experienced would start the process of rebuilding an inner harmony. You are an incredibly sensual woman Vanessa. Watching Sensi slowly release the pent up energy of your sexual passion was just beautiful and wonderful to watch." Alexandra gave Vanessa a huge grin of delight at the memory.

"It was wonderful to experience too" replied Vanessa grinning back, a familiar tingle in her clitoris reminding her of the joy of the previous last night's encounter. She had been quite amazed at the power of her reaction to Sensi and she felt a longing to further explore her newly awakened sexuality. "I do feel very different this morning Alexandra. I have no idea what my future holds but I am certain that there is no possibility of going back to the life I have led. Sensi really is a remarkable woman. What does she do?"

Alexandra chuckled at this. "I think you above all people should understand what she does. Reflect on how different you feel this morning compared with how you felt before Sensi first embraced you. You experienced what she does, that's why you are feeling alive this morning rather than sat at home alone in your apartment feeling depressed and in emotional conflict with yourself."

"I can also hear that you haven't lost all your programming yet" continued Alexandra teasingly, "you are definitely still a work in progress. I suspect that by asking 'what does she do?' you were enquiring about the nature of her occupation. Why is it that we often use that which is probably the least important part of a person's true self as the thing we define them by? We put so much importance in material status and income but how important is this really to us? I am not naive, everyone has to find enough to sustain themself in life but being preoccupied with material things rather than inner wellbeing is very damaging for a person's real potential. The answer to your question is that Sensi is a bringer of light to a world shrouded in the darkness of greed and ignorance."

"I don't understand what you mean" replied Vanessa. "I have never heard of a bringer of light before."

"Sure you have," said Alexandra. "By light I mean the light of wisdom and this can manifest itself in the most unexpected places. Buddha, Jesus and the writers of the Bhagavad Gita are often called bringers of light, although sadly the teachings associated with them are frequently misunderstood or deliberately distorted and abused. The teachings associated with Jesus in particular are horribly muddled up with a misogynistic, narcissistic, psychopathic mythical God. This is the God that the rulers of men created in the image of their own overblown egos as a justification for their own tyranny and to legitimise their control over the rest of the population. They also like to use their God as an excuse to deliberately supress the rights and aspirations of women."

"Children can also be the bringers of light before they have been fully educated and conditioned by society. An innocent child, not yet corrupted and indoctrinated by the lure of selfish materialism, may question why is it that some people have far more than they need while others don't have enough? A true understanding of the reasons for the great inequality that has developed in our world brings much in the way of enlightenment. You in particular have begun to reflect on the wisdom of feeding the appetites of the enormously greedy for yet more wealth at the expense of the poor and starving of the world. Even in our country the queues at the food-banks grow in correlation with the growing wealth of the billionaires."

"The unconditional love of a mother holding her new-born baby brings great joy and light to the world. If we could all hold such a love for the babies we don't know, for all the babies around the world whose futures are cut short by greed, self-interest and ignorance would our hearts not surely break? There is much enlightenment to be had if we but stopped to reflect on this and our world could be a very different, harmonious and joyous place."

"All those who know how to truly love, and by this I mean a giving unselfish love, not a possessive self-interested love, bring light through their actions. Sensi is a bringer of light, but Sensi also loves in the context of a great intellect and intelligence. Such a combination of both rational and emotional intelligence is what I mean by wisdom. It is sadly all too rare to find in the heads of our poor muddled species. Those who lack compassion and empathy for the wellbeing of others lack the ability to accrue wisdom and their actions reflect their weakness."

"So are you saying that Sensi's purpose in the world is to spread wisdom?" said Vanessa. "It's funny, nearly all my life I have valued status, money and wealth and have sought the admiration of my peers. Nobody has ever really suggested that I should value compassion and wisdom before."

"We live in a society that values material wealth and celebrity and have been deliberately conditioned through mass indoctrination and a complicit media to accept this as normal" said Alexandra. "Don't be too hard on yourself Vanessa. If we lived in societies that truly valued wisdom and educated their children wisely it would be a very different world. Sadly humanity has very little time left to understand this. Mother Nature is very ruthless with those that disturb her balance and harmony and the consequences of human stupidity will be very severe."

"You were right of course about what I really meant when I asked what Sensi did" reflected Vanessa. "Can I ask a different question, can you tell me how you met Sensi and ask where she comes from?"

"That's two questions cheeky one" laughed Alexandra. "How we met is the easier one to answer. I'm afraid I can't tell you very much about where Sensi comes from so I will tell you what I do know about this first. Sensi has told me that she was born and brought up in Peru. She lives in a community called Consciência which seems to be made up of a group of people from all over the world who seem to share both a common perspective on life, and a similar ideology. I don't know enough about this community to tell you much more about it. What I can say is that if Sensi feels she belongs there, it must be a truly remarkable place. Sensi seems to act as some kind of wandering ambassador for this community, seeking out other kindred spirits, but I don't really understand enough to tell you more. I can tell you that I love her very much and she has positively changed my life more than any other person I have ever met."

"Are you and Sensi also lovers?" asked Vanessa.

"Not in the sexual sense that you had the joy to experience with her last night. I love her very much and we often hug, cuddle and lie together, embracing the sensuality and warmth that this brings. I also love her for her mind, her emotions, her compassion, and the way that she has this strange intuition. She seems to intuitively know when other people need kindness and support. She identified your hurt and inner turmoil immediately and knew how to respond. This is why I found it so amusing when you asked whether we planned to seduce you."

"It is obvious that you love her very much. Don't you get jealous when she gives her love and affection to others?" said Vanessa.

"Part of me will always be jealous;" replied Alexandra, "this comes from the possessive and insecure part of all minds that constantly seek affirmation of their worth from others and demand love and attention. We can't shut this off completely, even after years of meditation, but through understanding we can choose not to succumb to such demands. This part of the mind is fuelled by an inner fear and insecurity that we are all born with. Freud would say that it emirates from something he called the human Id, and it is the source of much of human activity. The Id is the realm of instincts, emotions and sexual passion we discussed earlier."

"So you consciously try not to be possessive of her affections when these feelings arise?" said Vanessa.

"It would be absurd for me to succumb to fantasies about possessing a person like Sensi when the main reason I love her so much is her free spirit. How could I ever justify trying to deny others the joy that Sensi brings to me when I value it so much myself? It would be like picking a rare and beautiful orchid and bringing it back home, knowing that by the very act of possession you will inevitably destroy the essence and beauty that attracted you to it in the first place." Alexandra smiled at Vanessa, "watching Sensi liberate your pent up sexuality yesterday evening was truly beautiful."

Vanessa was now even more intrigued about the mysterious and sensual woman that had made love to her. She asked Alexandra to explain how they had met.

"We met at a woman's refuge in Kennington" replied Alexandra. "I had just escaped from a very abusive relationship and was probably at the lowest ebb of my life. I felt so utterly worthless that I didn't really care anymore whether I lived or died. It wasn't that I even felt angry, hurt or desperate any more. Those feelings had come and gone and I was left with a feeling of complete emptiness."

"Please let me know if any of my questions upset you, it's the last thing I want to do," said Vanessa. "Do you mind if I ask how you came to be at the women's refuge?"

"I was at the refuge because my husband had beaten me yet again and this time he had hurt me so badly that I ended up in hospital with two broken ribs and an eye that was so bruised that it had completely closed. I can't even remember how many times he had hit me during the five years we were together but I can remember that the first time was our wedding night."

Vanessa was horrified; she could not understand how anyone could bring themselves to harm the beautiful, caring woman who sat next to her on the bed. She just couldn't imagine what could have initiated such anger and violence. She asked Alexandra what had provoked such a response.

"It was because I screamed at him in agony at the pain he was causing me and refused all of the further attempts he made to penetrate me" replied Alexandra, a hint of anger now evident in her voice. "Do you remember that I said to you earlier that I was living proof of how far some cultures will go to in order to deprive women of their sexuality?"

"I do," said Vanessa "but I didn't really understand what you meant."

"Let me show you" and with that Alexandra moved around in front of Vanessa on the bed. She leant backwards and pulled the cord on her robe which slowly parted, initially revealing to Vanessa's eyes a pronounced cleavage that became a pair of firm uplifted breasts with large areolae and nipples. Her eyes travelled downward as the robe slowly parted until she suddenly let out a gasp of dismay. Where Alexandra's vagina and labia should have been was completely smooth with a jagged scar running down the middle to a small opening at the bottom. It was like nothing she had ever seen before.

"Oh Alexandra, what has happened to you" she cried. Out of impulse she leant forward and put her arms around Alexandra in a futile gesture of protection as if she could in some way take away the tears of hurt that now showed in Alexandra's eyes. The two women just held each other for a while until Alexandra gently pulled away, a slight smile now showing although her eyes glistened as she attempted to hold back her tears. "In my culture it is simply called cutting" she said "but you may have heard of it as female genital mutilation or FGM."

"Why would anyone do such a thing?" said Vanessa. She couldn't comprehend that such a beautiful woman had been so horribly mutilated and she shuddered inwardly as she started to imagine the hurt and pain that Alexandra must have experienced.

Alexandra explained that when she was about eleven she had been taken around to her auntie's house by her mother one weekend. She had been surprised to see that there were three other women there that she did not know. Before she could even grasp what was happening her dress was taken off and she was forcibly held down on this bed by four of the women whilst a fifth reached down between her legs. She was suddenly screaming in agony, she had never felt pain like it before and after what seems like an eternity she believe she must have passed out. She awoke to a terrible throbbing pain between her legs, the area between them covered in a rough dressing stained with her blood.

Her mother had told her that she was now 'clean' and that she was a proper woman who would attract a good husband. In a bizarre way she later realised that her mother and aunt had actually believed that they were doing the best for her future. Despite this, Alexandra had never forgiven them for what they had put her through and the consequences that it had had upon her life. After some considerable time, when the bleeding had stopped and the dressing had been removed, Alexandra summoned up the courage to see what had been done to her. She picked up the mirror she used when dressing her hair and placed it in front of her, facing towards the area between her legs where her vagina and labia should have been. To her horror she had seen that the women had cut off her lips and the precious bud at the top of her vagina and had crudely stitched her vagina up until there was just a small opening left at the bottom so she could pass urine.

This was just one way that women were oppressed in her culture which believed that women were little more than the possessions of their husbands. By denying a woman any chance to celebrate her sexuality, it was hoped that she would remain faithful to her husband and not be led astray by any unfulfilled sexual longings. Naturally, as a direct result of this horrific practice, many of these husbands spent much of their spare time having sexual relations with uncut women, the same women that they were happy to pour scorn upon when selecting a bride. This was what ultimately happened with Alexandra's husband. Alexandra was so traumatised by what had happened to her and the intense pain when he tried to force himself through the small opening in her vagina that their marriage was never consummated. Her husband physically and emotionally took out his rage and frustration upon Alexandra in-between his affairs with 'uncut' women and his steadily increasing consumption of alcohol.

Alexandra had had no say in the selection of her husband and there had been little that could be remotely described as courting. The marriage was arranged by her parents with another family and, apart from a couple of brief supervised visits, the wedding night was the first time they had truly been alone together. She told Vanessa that the fact that she had been cut was ironically seen by her husband's family as a major selling point. It didn't prove to be so attractive to her eager husband on the wedding night though she told Vanessa tearfully.

"Surely such terrible hurting of a child is illegal? Couldn't you have had the people who did this terrible thing to you arrested?" asked Vanessa.

Alexandra explained that this would mean getting her mother and aunt prosecuted, destroying her family and being ostracised and made an outcast by her community. The mutilation of girls in this dreadful way had been illegal for over twenty-five years and yet there had never been a conviction in the UK despite the knowledge that this was happening to thousands of young girls every year. Part of this was because the victims were so unwilling to come forward because of community pressure and part of this was because the doctors, nurses, teachers and police saw this as a 'culturally sensitive' issue and were reluctant to effectively intervene.

Alexandra asked Vanessa to imagine the outcry if pretty blond white girls were routinely mutilated in such a way, or someone was going around cutting the penises off young boys. It would be on the front page of every newspaper. When it came to the torture and mutilation of defenceless young girls from minority ethnic groups nobody seemed willing to talk about it. Alexandra did acknowledge that this media silence was finally starting to change. A number of brave women were actively campaigning to protect the next generation from going through this horror, but there was a long way to go before society would even start to put an end to this awful violation of young girls.

This was the woman that Sensi had met at the refuge, a woman so physically and psychologically abused over the five years of her marriage that she had now reached the point where she felt utterly worthless. Even her own family had turned against her as they blamed Alexandra, rather than her abusive husband, for the unhappiness in the marriage. Sensi was visiting Gabriela, a cousin who had moved to London from the Consciência community to run the refuge, when she had been introduced to Alexandra. Something in Sensi had made Alexandra completely open up to her in a way that she had never opened up to anyone else before. "I'm afraid I just cried on her shoulder for about an hour" she confessed but Sensi had not seemed at all perturbed about this. Her passing words after this initial visit were that she saw a very special and beautiful person both physically and spiritually and that if Alexandra would permit her to visit again she would help her to rediscover herself.

Two weeks later Sensi had come back to the refuge and had persuaded Alexandra to come and meet her friend Roxie at a place called the Warehouse. Roxie had immediately charmed Alexandra but even more importantly, there was something about the Warehouse that made her feel strangely secure and safe. Roxie encouraged Alexandra to move in and join 'the Rabble' but at first she was very reluctant. For one thing she was penniless. In the eyes of the authorities, physical and psychological abuse and a terror of strangers were no excuse for not spending hours at a Job Centre.

Without any support from the state, Alexandra had only survived the last few weeks through the great kindness of Gabriela and her staff. The great tragedy of this was that the refuge was likely to close next year as the grant it received from the council was going to be cut. Alexandra could not imagine what would have become of her without the care the refuge had provided; in all likelihood she may well have died on the street.

She also felt that she was such a worthless person she did not deserve the kindness of strangers and she did not want to feel further indebted. In a perverse way the abuse she had endured had almost become comforting for her. She could equate the way her husband despised her to the way she had come to despise herself. She found the kindness of Roxie and Sensi almost frightening. She felt that if she even dared to hope that she had a future it might weaken her defences and she would end up getting hurt all over again. The numbness and emptiness she had developed were her protection against the unbearable emotional pain of constant rejection. She dared not contemplate ever allowing herself to be indebted to another person again, let alone to be unconditionally loved by one.

Despite all these misgivings there was something about Sensi and Roxie that she could not help believing in. She could not detect the remotest sense of guile or subterfuge from either of them. Roxie had explained to her that everyone at the Warehouse contributed in their own way and that Alexandra would also eventually find a way of contributing but there was no hurry. First she had to heal.

They had pressed Alexandra as to what made her feel positive and she had explained that she used to escape from the hurt of the world through her art. Sadly she didn't have much she could show them as most of the art she had created had been destroyed by her husband during his frequent rages. Roxie's eyes lit up in delight at hearing this. "Isn't that wonderful Sensi, we have an artist in the Warehouse." Roxie and Sensi literally dragged Alexandra by the hands to the studio area partitioned off from the main body of the Warehouse. "I believe there was another artist in this studio before we moved in and we have had no idea what to do with it. Would you like to tidy up the mess and see what you can make of it?"

"That was four years ago" said Alexandra "and now I couldn't imagine living anywhere else. Through all the love and support I have had from everyone I have met at the Warehouse I am now proud to be the woman I am. I paint about the natural world and about the essence and spirituality of women and our powerful connection with the forces of nature. I think this has been my way of compensating for the fact that my own sexuality was so violated. I feel that my art is a release for my repressed feelings in another form. Perversely it may be that I could only create my art with an intensity of feeling that could only have come through having been hurt so badly."

"One regret I do have is that I have never been able to bring myself to successfully paint or sculpt male images. I have tried to do so on a few occasions, but I can never seem to mask the suppressed anger that wells up when I remember the violence and humiliation that I was subjected to. This is particularly sad as I now share the Warehouse with some truly beautiful male souls whom I have grown to love dearly, and who have shown me nothing but kindness. Somehow all my attempts to express men through art have turned out crude and ugly. I think this may perhaps be a sad legacy of the abuse that I will never truly escape from."

Vanessa was absolutely stunned by the beautiful woman sat next to her who had just shared so many intimate details of her life with a virtual stranger. She also knew that the passion and ideas that Alexandra had shared with her were awakening a whole new set of feelings within her. She simply had to find out more about wisdom and the power of love and compassion and what these could mean to her. Above all she felt that she must maintain contact with Alexandra at all costs, she had never met another woman like her. Come to think of it she had never before met women like Sensi, Roxie or Kaitlin for that matter. It seemed that the Warehouse had acted like some kind of spiritual magnet that had drawn these remarkable people together and Vanessa also felt herself being strangely drawn and captivated by the community there.

"You do realise that through our mutual love of Sensi we are now becoming spiritual sisters?" It was almost as if Alexandra was actually reading Vanessa's mind. "Whatever you decide to do with the rest of your life I hope you will still want to keep in contact with me."

Vanessa once again warmly embraced Alexandra, "even though we only met yesterday evening I don't think I could bear the thought of not seeing you again and you not being a part of my life."

"I am delighted" said Alexandra "but now I think you should probably get dressed because I think you should have a chat with Julian about last night. He will have very mixed feelings about your presence and if you want to come and visit me again you will have to find some way of making peace with him. He was very upset with what he saw in Bangladesh and he may now understandably associate you directly with some of the misery he saw there."

"He is right to" replied Vanessa. After the euphoria of her time with Sensi and listening with increasing captivation to Alexandra as they sat on her bed, the reality of her current situation started to dawn upon her. Tomorrow was Monday morning and she would be expected to turn up at the office and start trading food commodities again. The thought of doing this now made her feel physically sick. There was no way she could go back to her old job but contractually she had a three month notice period to serve before she could leave. She also had to now look Julian in the eye and explain and justify a life that she could not even explain or justify to herself.

5

Vanessa got dressed into the somewhat crumpled clothes she had been wearing the evening before and, after a lingering kiss with Alexandra, she opened the door in the partition and re-entered the main living area of the Warehouse.

The only other person in the room was Roxie, who had a strangely knowing smile on her face when she saw Vanessa. "I see the girls have worked a bit of their magic on you" said Roxie, "you look so much better than you did last night. Do you fancy a bit of breakfast, I'm just scrambling some eggs or perhaps you fancy something else?"

Vanessa realised that she was absolutely famished and she readily accepted Roxie's invitation to join her. They sat at the table that had been miraculously cleared from the previous night and Vanessa felt a pang of guilt that she had had no thoughts about helping to tidy up. She voiced her guilty conscience to Roxie who assured her not to worry. She told Vanessa that Jethro and Max had sorted it all out before they went off to the gym, "they can be such sweet boys at times" she had chirped.

They made idle chit chat over breakfast and Vanessa eagerly accepted the offer of her second mug of coffee of the morning. It was Vanessa who broached the subject of Julian with Roxie. She explained how embarrassed she was about the previous evening and the revelations of how she may well have contributed to the suffering of the people Julian was trying to help. She asked Roxie if she thought Julian would be prepared to sit down with her so she could make some attempt to explain, both to Julian and herself how she had been so oblivious to the consequences of her actions.

"Why don't I give them a call" said Roxie "and see if they are up and about yet. Don't be too disappointed if they are still in bed; don't forget that they haven't seen each other in three months." Roxie's face now wore a very similar expression as the one that greeted Vanessa when she emerged from Alexandra's studio. To her great annoyance Vanessa found herself blushing.

Roxie had a brief exchange on the phone and informed Vanessa that Kaitlin and Julian would be up in a few minutes. Vanessa had some trepidation as she heard footsteps coming up the spiral staircase; she was not even sure how Kaitlin would greet her after the previous night's events. She needn't have worried as Kaitlin's face broke into her familiar smile as she saw Vanessa and she skipped across the room and gave Vanessa a huge hug and a kiss on the cheek. Vanessa saw that Kaitlin's beautiful auburn locks were decidedly tussled this morning and she felt the heat in her cheeks again as she remembered her own lovemaking with Sensi.

Julian emerged a few seconds later looking rather tired but relaxed. He also smiled at Vanessa but his eyes were more serious as if he too felt awkward about the tension that had arisen between them. They sat on the sofas and Roxie went to make some coffee for Kaitlin and Julian. After a few awkward seconds both Vanessa and Julian started to try and speak at the exact same moment which led to an embarrassed laugh. Vanessa gestured for Julian to speak first.

"I just wanted you to know that I am not personally angry with you Vanessa" he started. He went on to explain that it was the system that caused so much inequality and hardship that was the source of his anger. He said that he understood that Vanessa was just part of the system and was just making her own way in life staying within the letter of the laws that have been laid down by society. "These rules are killing people and destroying the planet" he told her with a flash of anger in his eyes. "There are no longer any constraints on the greedy and those who celebrate self-interest and wealth above all other values. I often feel a sense of despair. All the work that thousands of charity workers do to mitigate the harsh effects of a world that celebrates greed, can be overturned in a few seconds by some callous decision in the City of London or Wall Street."

"It must be very hard to personalise your actions" said Roxie as she returned from the kitchen area to join them. "If you were eating and there was a starving child sat next to you on the table looking at your food I would defy anyone but the most hardened and cynical not to share their meal. What if the child was out of sight but in the next room and you heard the child crying, aware that you were eating whilst they had nothing? Again you would find it difficult to ignore the suffering. If the child was next door, you could start to depersonalise the child. Surely there is someone else that could feed this child? If the child was in

Birmingham, yes you knew that there was poverty and that many families were going to food banks but maybe they brought it upon themselves? Surely the council should be doing something? Bangladesh? Not my responsibility! This is how people can become billionaires, own multiple houses, drive around in a Bentley and travel to their luxury mansion abroad on-board their private jet. They could alleviate the suffering of millions by redistributing their wealth instead of hoarding it, but they have de-personalised this suffering to the extent that they no longer feel any sense of responsibility. What they like to convince themselves is that there is no cost to others through their deliberate systematic extraction of resources from society. The truth is that many people suffer as a direct result of such an addiction to material things. Vanessa, you are just one small cog in a huge machine that was built to serve the interests of the few at the expense of billions of others."

"You must forgive Roxie" said Kaitlin although her look of deep love and affection towards Roxie showed that she didn't feel in her heart that there was anything to forgive. "I think I told you that Roxie was a writer of novels but I probably didn't tell you that she has also written several philosophical works about the nature of society."

"You are quite right to chastise me my dear" said Roxie, "Vanessa has not had a chance to speak a word yet and I am already blurting out my opinionated views at her. Please forgive me Vanessa; we want to hear your thoughts and feelings."

"Please don't apologise" replied Vanessa, "what you have told me has really helped me to try to explain to myself how I remained so blind to what was going on around me. It is now obvious to me that the hunger for wealth at any costs must have an opportunity cost from those from whom this wealth has been redistributed. For decades now the growth of wealth in most developed societies has only been really benefiting the few. I am more than aware that average salaries for the majority have been largely stagnant whilst the wealth of the few in a position to exploit the system has grown exponentially. Just as you have said I have always thought it was someone else's problem to make the world a better place, not mine. I have never taken any personal responsibility for my actions except to the extent that I could financially benefit by being very good at what I do."

"At the risk of sounding all philosophical again" Roxie, glanced teasingly at Kaitlin as she spoke "this is the true secret of how we could make the world a very different place. If everyone genuinely cared about the impact of their actions on others we would live in completely different, and much happier and fulfilling societies."

Vanessa looked Julian firmly in the eyes. "I cannot ask you to forgive me for what you know that I have done in my past as I cannot forgive myself. There is no real justification for deliberately choosing to look the other way and pretending to be ignorant of the consequences of what you are doing. I realise now that I have been lying to myself for years and I am starting to believe that this is the reason I have become so out of harmony with myself recently. I am just so grateful that I met such a lovely person as Kaitlin." She smiled warmly at Kaitlin who responded by moving over to Vanessa and giving her another kiss before reseating herself again next to Julian. Kaitlin put her arm around Julian as Vanessa continued, her voice now revealing the turbulent emotions rising up inside her.

"What I pledge to all of you is that I shall find some way in trying to use my skills to help the people who are suffering as a result of this stupid system we have created. I will no longer be part of the problem; I wish to become part of a solution, whatever that may look like. I would ask you all a personal favour," Vanessa's eyes suddenly glistened with tears again "will you help me find the right path because at the moment I feel very afraid for the first time since I was a small child. I also feel terribly alone." She lost the battle to keep control of herself and the tears started to slowly roll down her cheeks.

"Well you have no excuse in feeling alone" the words coming from a familiar husky voice from behind. "I for one am starting to fall in love with you and looking at the faces around you I have a feeling I am not alone." Roxie, Kaitlin and Alexandra gave Vanessa a group hug whilst Julian smiled with the embarrassment that many men often have when trying to adequately cope with emotional situations.

When the women eventually parted Julian ventured a question, "what are you going to tell them at the bank?" he asked. "Surely they will expect you to continue in your work through a notice period but I just don't see how you could continue to do that feeling as you do now. I hate the thought of you going back into that office tomorrow."

"I really don't know what I will do" Vanessa replied "this seems all so sudden but in reflection I think I have known for quite a while that I need to escape from that environment."

"Come on Roxie" said Alexandra "switch on that head of yours, there must be some way of rescuing Vanessa here?"

They all looked at Roxie whose brow furrowed with concentration as she applied herself to the problem. After some time she spoke to Vanessa, "have you ever known other colleagues who have been immediately released by the bank and in what circumstances?"

"Yes" Vanessa replied "this is usually when the management have convinced themselves that the employee may be going to work for a rival and they then see that any access to information becomes an immediate commercial threat. It is not unusual in these circumstances for the employee's computer access to be immediately suspended and sometimes they even get security to escort such an employee from the premises."

"So the solution to our little problem is that we need to convince them that you are a commercial liability" said Roxie. "It's a sad truth that the only thing that really motivates the greed obsessed is an imminent financial threat. My radical plan is that you go in on Monday morning and tell them the truth. You tell them that you have become increasingly disturbed about the impact that trading on basic food commodities is having on the poor of the world and you are handing in your notice as a consequence. You can also say that you are not able to conduct certain trades if you strongly suspect that they will cause significant hardship but that you are willing to take on any other role that they may like you to undertake. Nothing will unsettle your managers more than to know that they have an employee with an objective human conscience in the trading room. You have become an instant liability my dear."

6

Roxie proved to be absolutely right in her conviction. As soon as Vanessa had got back to her apartment she drafted a resignation letter giving three months' notice which explained the reasons she could no longer continue to work at Mallorys, just as Roxie had suggested. She emailed this to her manager, Lionel. She knew Lionel would have the email alert of his iPhone active even on a Sunday afternoon. She reflected that she had always done the same thing with her phone, even when she was supposedly away from it all on holidays. After a couple of hours she received a confirmation from Lionel that he had received and read her letter. Lionel asked her to turn up a little later than usual at 10.00 a.m. on Monday morning so that he would have a chance to consider the implications of her sudden resignation.

When Vanessa arrived at Mallorys she found that the barrier wouldn't open as she tried to swipe her way through with her pass to gain access to the trading floors. She approached the security desk to discover that a message had been left from Lionel asking to be called the moment Vanessa arrived at the bank. Security also asked Vanessa to hand over her pass.

Lionel, met her in the public foyer and explained that the bank was grateful that Vanessa was prepared to work her notice period but that in the circumstances they felt that she should be put on immediate garden leave. He also asked her to hand over her company laptop. She handed this over to him without comment. There wasn't anything of interest on its hard drive anyway, as all the company information was held on remote servers to which she now no longer had access. Lionel said that all Vanessa's personal belongings were already being boxed up and that they would be sent by carrier to her apartment that afternoon. He offered his thanks for all her loyal support to the bank and in the next moment was he back through the barrier and out of her life forever. In the matter of a mere ten minutes her investment banking career was over and she found herself standing outside Mallorys with her old life closed behind her and a new life just beginning.

Although the events of the morning had effectively realised the plan that had been proposed by Roxie, Vanessa felt in a state of mild shock. She went to her usual coffee bar and ordered a large skinny latte and found that her hand was shaking as she picked up the cardboard cup from the end of the counter. Her long dedicated service to Mallory's was apparently worth a mere ten minutes of her manager's time. Like an entry on an accounting sheet she has merely been moved from the asset to the liability column and order had been re-established. One small consolation that she could take away was that Jeremy, her understudy in the team, lacked the intuition that had so often kept her one step ahead of her rivals at other banks. She suspected that Mallory's figures would quickly reflect this. The painful recollection of Julian's presentation on the misery caused by such trade gave Vanessa a small measure of satisfaction with this knowledge.

She made her way back to her flat and a far from happy Tabitha who made a short demonstration of turning her back on Vanessa and ignoring her before eventually succumbing to the warmth of her lap. At about 2.30pm there was a chime which signified the entrance bell had been rung. Vanessa let the courier into the building using the remote access control in her flat and directed him to take the lift to the second floor where she met him on the landing. He carried a single double walled cardboard box into her front room and left her staring at the only remaining physical evidence of her career at Mallory's.

Vanessa decided to call her oldest friend Sandy and arranged to meet her at a wine bar near London Bridge station at 6.00 p.m. She had not told Sandy on the phone what had happened and she waited until the first glass of Pinot Grigio had been consumed before telling Sandy that she had left Mallorys that morning. Sandy was completely taken aback, "I thought Mallorys was your life" she exclaimed. "If you were so fed up with Mallorys why didn't you at least secure a promotion to another job in banking before handing in your notice? I can think of half a dozen firms that would have been delighted to poach you with your performance record. You have worked so hard to get where you are, why have you suddenly just decided to throw it all away? I'm afraid I don't understand you at all Vanessa."

Vanessa tried to explain that she had suddenly realised that most of her activity had produced no real benefit to society and worse than that, it actually caused harm. Sandy just couldn't seem to grasp what Vanessa was concerned about. She just told Vanessa that it was not her problem to set the rules. As long as she was working within the trading guidelines and what she was doing was not actually illegal it was someone else's problem to sort out the resulting mess. "It's just not your responsibility" she said impatiently as Vanessa tried for the fourth time to explain to her friend why she just had to walk away from Mallory's.

That was the trouble with the UK today, reflected Vanessa, nobody was taking responsibility but the rich just kept getting wealthier and the poor and vulnerable were becoming increasingly destitute. Even in London there were now food banks being created by some of the charities and church groups to feed people who could no longer afford to heat their homes and feed their families. Margaret Thatcher had famously stated that there was no such thing as society and the way things were developing she might well end up being proved correct.

Most of her ex-colleagues and the banks and corporations they worked for took great pride in taking every opportunity to avoid paying tax. They saw making any contribution to wider society as a game for mugs. If people were starving it was their own fault for not doing better at school or finding a good enough job. This was just the collateral waste of the capitalist system and those who were driven to destitution were not human beings, they were simply statistics.

Vanessa shivered, just a few days ago she probably had the same mind-set and she could see that Sandy simply couldn't relate to what she was now saying. The scary thing is that many of her former friends and colleagues were not actually evil people. They were just so desensitised through long exposure to a collective culture that celebrated greed and self-interest above all else, that they no longer even considered there to be any alternative.

After the extraordinary events at the Warehouse, Vanessa now realised that such a cynical and exploitative perspective on the nature of the world left her feeling emotionally cold and empty. She hungered for the warmth of the company of Alexandra, Sensi, Roxie and the Rabble as she listened to her friend Sandy bemoan the latest increase in her gym membership fee. She now knew without any doubt that she had left this old world behind but what was her new world to be? She felt that all the anchors and certainties of her old life had been cast away and she now voyaged forth into an unknown. She would need some help and she could see that, through no fault of Sandy's, it could no longer come from her old friend.

After a couple of hours of small talk with Sandy, Vanessa made an excuse that the she was tired after the dramatic events of the day and the two women parted with a kiss to each cheek and a promise to 'catch up again soon.' The truth was that Sandy reminded her too much of her old self, and she was uncomfortable with the conflicts that were still going on within her.

Rather than go back to the flat she decided to return to the same bench where Kaitlin had found her and where the extraordinary chain of events that had so dramatically changed her life had started. She sat again looking at the river and observed one of the lighted up party boats carrying noisy revellers down towards Tower Bridge. Although it had been ten days since she last sat on this bench it now seemed half a lifetime ago. Here she was without a job and without any plans for the future and yet for the first time in months she felt strangely at peace with herself. She pulled a chunky circle scarf more tightly around her neck, tucked it into the top of her long woollen coat to block out the chill of the London air, and just let her mind wander as she took in the view of the river.

"Hello stranger" said a familiar voice and she turned in delight to see the familiar face of Kaitlin with her beaming smile. Vanessa leapt of the bench and gave Kaitlin such a long affectionate hug it was almost as if she had just met her long lost sister.

"Kaitlin, how wonderful" said Vanessa, "I didn't know you worked Monday's."

"I don't but I had a text from Sensi saying that she sensed that I might find you here and we have all been a bit concerned about you. How did it go at the bank today?"

"How on earth would Sensi know that I would be here?" exclaimed Vanessa, "even I didn't know until about an hour ago."

Kaitlin smiled back at Vanessa, "I stopped trying to work out how Sensi seems to know such things a long time ago. She seems to have some kind of mysterious sixth sense. She often seems to just turn up or will suddenly intervene just when we need her the most. Now stop dodging the issue and tell me what happened at the bank this morning."

"On one condition," said Vanessa, "let's go to the coffee shop you took me to last time and I'll tell you there."

"It's a deal."

They purchased their coffees and sat at a table by a window so that they could also indulge in their mutual pleasure in watching people passing by. Vanessa then explained to Kaitlin how Roxie's plan had worked to perfection. "They definitely see me as a liability now and I am sure that word will have been rapidly passed around the City that I have has lost my marbles! I have almost certainly burnt my bridges, at least until people's memories start to fade, but what is the way forward? I have never really done anything apart from finance before."

"What do you mean by the way forward and doing things?" asked Kaitlin.

"What am I going to do for a living? What kind of career could I develop instead? It's a frightening thought but I might be absolutely useless at anything but manipulating numbers on computers and speculating. I have a dreadful feeling that I may be virtually unemployable."

"Do you need to be employed?" asked Kaitlin.

The question took Vanessa aback. She had never thought about not being employed in the traditional sense of the word. She remembered Alexandra teasing her about her cultural programming when she asked what Sensi did. In the UK's Anglo-Saxon work ethic society being 'unemployed' was almost like admitting to being a social misfit. It made people uncomfortable and judgmental. How dare you get off the hamster wheel and stop financially contributing to society? She had already started to comprehend from the recent events at the Warehouse that making a contribution, as defined in traditional economic terms, often harmed the world much more that it benefited it.

Kaitlin continued, "If you already have accumulated enough money to meet your life's needs, and only you can make that judgment, why spend your life trying to acquire any more? I'm not saying that your life shouldn't have a purpose. I can't begin to imagine what it must feel like to believe that there is no purpose to life, but why should that purpose be about creating any more money?"

Vanessa thought about what Kaitlin was saying to her and it frightened her a bit. For most people in countries like the UK, as far as she could work it out, the purpose of life fell into three main categories.

The first and predominant purpose in life was to earn as much as you can and buy material things with your money so that society could equate you to being successful. It was most important for the human ego and a feeling of wellbeing to be considered successful in terms of the established cultural norms. The trouble was that she had tried this and ended up sobbing in the arms of a young waitress on a riverside bench. The thought made her smile as she looked into Kaitlin's eyes. Kaitlin was quite right; chasing ever larger pots of gold at the end of financial rainbows was not going to bring her any additional happiness.

A second purpose in life was to have children. Many people devoted their lives to the wellbeing of their children and their own wishes often became surrogate to the desires and aspiration of their children. Vanessa had never had the right relationship to consider having children and if she was honest with herself she had never felt remotely broody. She had lost count of the number of times that people had asked her if she had any children and she found that she almost had to justify why she didn't have any.

It was another cultural norm that women were supposed to want children and also adore other peoples' babies and children. Vanessa fell into neither camp. It was one of the positives of working at Mallorys. Many of the women who worked there had sacrificed any chance of motherhood for career progression. Oh the various financial institutions would all say that they had parent friendly policies and that motherhood and career were entirely compatible. Behind the scenes they would be working out how they could side-line any woman who was inconsiderate enough to get pregnant whilst staying within the letter, if not the intent, of the anti-discrimination legislation. Fellow employees would give hearty congratulations when a colleague became pregnant, whilst secretly scheming about what opportunities this would present to leap-frog her in the corporate pecking order.

A third purpose in life that people often clung on to was a devotion to a particular religion. In many parts of the world religion completely influenced every aspect of society, usually to the complete detriment of women's rights and their autonomy. Devotion of this type was however becoming increasingly rare in some developed western societies such as in the Scandinavian countries where society was becoming increasingly secular and atheistic. Even in the UK with the Queen as the head of the Church of England and bishops sitting in the House of Lords, religious affiliation was often more about a social statement than any reflection of a true belief. In the USA however it was still virtually impossible to get into any public office without claiming to be a believer.

Vanessa could never relate to this male God that had been pumped down all the children's throats at school assembly. Somehow a raging genocidal God that demanded worship or condemned you to burn for an eternity in the fires of hell seemed less than appealing, especially when this usually went hand in hand for women to be explicitly subservient to a male partner. After all it was supposedly an evil woman called Eve who gave Adam the apple and the authorities of the prevailing Abrahamic religions had taken great pleasure in punishing women for it ever since. The thing she found even more incredulous was that this was supposed to be a loving God, particularly according to the Christians. A bit like a divine Al Capone who could have been considered a loving mafia Godfather she mused, the kind of Godfather that gave you offers that you couldn't refuse. If you were not extorted, mugged or shot it was obviously a demonstration of compassion!

So if life wasn't about making money, having children or devoting yourself to God then what was left? Sure there was hedonistic pleasure, which she certainly had no objection to in principle, but all this really provided was a distraction rather than an objective purpose. Hedonistic pleasures seldom left any lasting contentment once the experience had passed. They became a bit like materialism, you were just left looking for the next high to distract your mind from the fact that life could otherwise be deemed to be eminently pointless.

Maybe this was why many increasingly alienated young people succumbed to the temptation of drugs? For the briefest moment they no longer had to worry about the future of their lives as their thoughts were temporarily suspended or distorted. At the other end of the spectrum you had a disproportionate number of celebrities turning to drugs having found out that material riches, fame and fortune were brief superficial highs which left desperate lows in their wake when the cameras and applause were gone. There were many examples of so called celebrities who had ended up in a downward cycle of despair, some ultimately taking their own lives to escape the emotional pain.

Vanessa tried her best to summarise these thoughts and doubts and explain them to Kaitlin who listened thoughtfully to her and admitted that she did not have the answer to Vanessa's dilemma. Kaitlin was a young woman in love, with a passion for her developing career in archaeology, and a strong desire to bring up a family at some point in the future with the right partner. Whether that partner was Julian she was not yet sure but her heart leapt every time she saw him and he was a very kind, if somewhat intense young man. Kaitlin had plenty of purpose, direction and joy in her life at present.

"I think you need to talk to Roxie," said Kaitlin, "she is the philosopher amongst the Rabble and I am sure that she will be able to give you some useful advice for the next step on your life's journey."

"Do you think she would mind?" said Vanessa, "I would hate to impose on her kindness yet again."

"I think she would be delighted," replied Kaitlin, "can I give her your mobile number?"

Fortunately Vanessa had her own personal mobile that she had kept for family and friends. Her business mobile had also been confiscated by Mallorys that morning although Vanessa had the foresight to copy the address book to her personal computer in case she ever had any future need of her long list of contacts. She gave Kaitlin the new number for Roxie and asked that she pass it on to Alexandra as well.

With that the two women left the café and parted with another big hug. Although she had only known her briefly, Vanessa realised that she was beginning to really love this remarkable, kind and beautiful young woman.

7

The next day Vanessa was determined to focus on the practicalities of her current situation. There was no great panic to do this but Vanessa felt that it was a useful distraction for a mind that was still whirling with the events of the last few days. If there was one thing Vanessa was good at, it was being a pragmatic problem solver. This had served her well on the many occasions at Mallorys when the markets had one of their frequent unpredicted wobbles and less experienced and resolute traders wobbled in sympathetic panic. Market wobbles did not just present risks; they also revealed new opportunities to be exploited for those who could keep a calm head. Vanessa was determined that this unplanned and unexpected wobble in her life would also reveal new and positive opportunities, but these needed to be of a spiritual rather than a financial nature.

Financially Vanessa was very well placed; Kaitlin was quite right when she made the observation that she did not need to accumulate any more money to be safe and secure unless she deliberately chose to embark on a hedonistic frenzy. She assessed her accrued assets.

Short term liquid assets including cash in the bank and readily convertible stocks and bonds amounted to approximately £1.75 million. She had an additional £850K in longer term assets that were not readily accessible in the short term as there was a significant penalty to be paid if they redeemed before their maturity dates. Her art and sculpture collection amounted to about £150K and her flat was now probably worth £1.3-1.5 million, values were changing daily in London so it was hard to be sure. She was also due about £90K in bonuses from Mallorys to be paid at the end of the fiscal year. This gave her total assets of a bit over £4 million. These investments would give her a growth and dividend return of at least £100K a year without having to dip into the actual asset values.

Vanessa also had an ample pension pot that would provide a fairly substantial annuity in fifteen years when it matured. All in all Vanessa was a financially secure woman of considerable means and she had no immediate need to seek paid employment. Vanessa was by no means exceptional; her assets were very meagre compared to many others who worked in the City or whose assets were being managed through the City's various financial institutions. There was a small but highly influential minority whose wealth could be measured in the hundreds of millions of pounds or even billions. She wondered if they ever stopped to think that their continued wealth creation was essentially pointless in any objective sense. This obsession with money was all pervasive and seemed to override any objective reasoning as to whether it served any useful purpose.

Suddenly Vanessa's mobile pinged, signifying that she had received a message. It was from Roxie who had invited her to breakfast at 9.30 the next morning at the Warehouse. The text finished with a strong hint that refusal was not to be considered an option. Vanessa found her mood changed immediately when she thought about visiting Roxie at the Warehouse in the morning. These lovely people who had refused to judge her and who had made unconditional overtures of friendship had started to capture her heart and she felt a developing longing to be in their company again. She reflected on her previous evening with Sandy and how she had tried and failed to get her old friend to understand what she had been going through.

The next morning Vanessa could hear the small bell ring inside the Warehouse as she pulled the cord outside the door. After a short pause the door was opened by Joris, who Kaitlin had described as Roxie's friend with benefits and who was looking somewhat the worse for wear.

"Oh hi Vanessa" he said with an accent that revealed his Spanish nationality, "do come in. Sorry I am a bit jaded this morning but Roxie insisted that we went to one of her friends 'special parties' last night. We didn't get back in until after two o'clock in the morning. I have asked Roxie not to drag me out to one of these parties when I have a shift the following day but she is deaf to my pleas."

"Oh shut up Joris" came Roxie's familiar voice from the kitchen area, "you know you love it. Now stop complaining and sort yourself out or you will be late for work."

Joris just raised his eyes to the heavens without further comment and disappeared down the spiral staircase towards the living quarters.

In contrast to Joris, Roxie seemed to be full of life and energy as she hummed to herself in the kitchen preparing breakfast. Her face seemed to have an almost incandescent glow about it as she went about her task.

"Vanessa, it's lovely to see you again" she chirped, "thank you for accepting my little offer of breakfast, it's so good of you to come over. Is scrambled eggs with smoked trout ok?"

"That would be delicious" replied Vanessa. "It really is kind of you to invite me."

"Not at all my dear, I am lacking inspiration for my latest literary effort and your company is making me feel less guilty about my constant prevarication."

"I must say you are looking wonderfully energised this morning, what was so special about this party last night that seems to have taken such a toll on Joris?"

"Joris like so many youngsters today seems to lack stamina," Roxie replied with a sigh, "I shall either have to put him on a training regime or trade him in for a younger model. As for the nature of the party, I shall just keep you guessing for now," she said with a conspiratorial wink. "Who knows, maybe one day I might entice you to come along to one so you can discover for yourself."

Vanessa was becoming increasingly intrigued but sensed that she would get no more out of Roxie for now and that it would be inappropriate to pry too deeply.

The two women sat together at the end of the dining table and ate their breakfast of smoked trout and eggs accompanied with fresh coffee and pomegranate juice. Roxie poured them both a second mug of coffee from an impressively large bright orange stoneware cafetiere and they took themselves off to one of the comfy sofas. Roxie asked Vanessa to explain again what had happened at the bank although she had been given a bit of an idea from Kaitlin.

"I'm not surprised" said Roxie after Vanessa had explained how her whole dismissal process had lasted about ten minutes, "someone with a resolute conscience is an anathema to many corporations. Most people can be bullied, bribed or cajoled to leave their conscience behind when they come to work; those that can't are a genuine threat to the unscrupulous. Most large corporations are now run to meet the interests of a few greedy people in the boardroom. Any link to shareholders is increasingly tenuous in the modern digital age where ownership of a share can be a transaction that lasts a few seconds. People in the societies that spawn their profits are considered exploitable assets and there is virtually no sense of responsibility for any of the carnage caused. You have successfully become an instant liability my dear."

Vanessa then told Roxie about her conversation with Kaitlin and her thoughts about wealth, children or religion being a source of direction and purpose direction in life. Now she had given up chasing wealth and had no interest in children or religion she felt rather adrift and purposeless. "Kaitlin felt that you might be able to provide a different perspective" she explained to Roxie.

Roxie smiled, "Kaitlin frequently flatters me" she said. "Before I say anything I would like to make an important caveat, which is that nobody knows the truth. All you will get from anyone is an opinion which may be more or less informed, depending on how much the person knows about the subject and how honest they are with both themselves and the person listening. I am happy to share my opinions, but ultimately you need to decide using your own knowledge and experience whether you think they have any merit."

 "I think that it would be fruitless and inappropriate on my part to begin trying to suggest any particular path that could provide you with the sense of direction that you are seeking" continued Roxie. "I would suggest that it would be more useful to begin by illuminating some of the more obvious illusions that obscure where such a sense of direction might be found. Are you happy to proceed on this basis?"

Vanesa readily accepted these conditions and listened attentively to what Roxie had to say.

Roxie explained to Vanessa that her current condition had been caused because some of her own illusions about her life in investment banking had already been painfully exposed. Roxie went on to explain that many people, perhaps a majority, didn't really need a purpose in life, they just had to be sufficiently distracted not to be overtly bothered by such questions. These people would happily devote their lives to watching sport on the television, becoming absorbed in the latest soap operas or counting the days to the next pay-packet and the subsequent retail therapy. Most politicians and corporations survived in their current form based on the assumption that the majority of the population was happy to be exploited or manipulated provided that they were sufficiently distracted.

Another tool used to control any inconvenient aspirations of the majority was fear. Those who exploited society deliberately placed concerns into the minds of the population that, should they even attempt to change the established order of things, the consequences would be damaging and harmful to them. At times of war the threat is obvious and populations will make enormous sacrifices for the perceived common good. At other times the threats are more nuanced. Should the population show any indication that they are sufficiently restless to be disturbed from their distractions, they are deliberately fed propaganda and fear by those pulling the levers of power to keep them in line. A population that loses its fear is the greatest threat to those who exploit society because this could lead to revolutionary change.

"What do you think happened in the financial collapse that started in 2007?" Roxie asked Vanessa.

Vanessa explained about sub-prime mortgages and complex derivatives that nobody really understood and how the banks had borrowed vast sums of money against these assets that were ultimately worthless. This had led to many banks being intrinsically bankrupt with their liabilities far larger than their assets. Governments had to borrow the money required to rescue the banking system leaving the accrued billions of pounds of debt in the hands of the population. Vanessa also confessed that her understanding was from someone who was embedded in the financial system. She was interested to know Roxie's perspective observing the system from outside. "What's your opinion about what really happened Roxie?"

"I don't want to try to teach you to suck eggs Vanessa with all your knowledge" protested Roxie.

"We already know how much my so called knowledge lacked wisdom" said Vanessa in response. "Please Roxie, I really do want to know what you think."

"Well if you are really sure my dear I shall try to do my best. You have already explained the gist of what went on but I believe the truth is actually far simpler. Most people believe that money in society is generated by central banks accountable to governments. In reality, as I am sure you know, it is created by commercial banks when they issue debt. When someone borrows money it creates a liability which is digitally balanced by an asset in the banks database. This is based on the expected payment of this liability with interest. A bank is considered solvent when the expected realisation value of these assets exceeds the liabilities of the debtors. Once these assets in the banks database have been created, this 'money' can be traded and exploited. The interest and charges attributed to all this trading can then be systematically extracted. The only thing required to create this money is the creation of a realistic asset, or more importantly, something that it is possible to get people to believe is a realistic asset."

"I'm not sure I fully understand what you mean by getting someone to believe it is a realistic asset?" said Vanessa.

"Let me try to explain another way" said Roxie. "Let's pretend that I am a budding amateur painter who has just produced my latest effort. As an unknown painter with no reputation my effort is worth maybe £5.00 to any prospective buyer that may take pity on me. In effect I have created an asset that is worth £5. I decide to put my painting into an auction where by chance it is spotted by an unscrupulous art dealer. The art dealer believes that my work could be confused with the work of a famous painter; let's say for instance a Jackson Pollock. This is a bit unlikely I have to admit, if you have ever seen any of my pitiful efforts. The dealer, or rather an obscure company based in the Cayman Islands which is owned by the dealer now buys my painting for £5.00. The dealer then works in conjunction with a renowned art critic who categorically professes to the world that their painting is the genuine article, a previously undiscovered Pollock. This makes my painting worth a potential £500,000 to the dealer when his company sells the painting at auction."

"We have now created a potential £499,995 of additional wealth that didn't exist before. This is pretty impressive as you have to remember, should the art world discover the painting is a Roxie not a Pollock, the true worth of the asset is still only £5 not £½ million pounds!"

"Now that the painting has been verified as a Pollock it is possible for someone to borrow money against the expected value of this asset to purchase it. This borrowing is created in the database of their bank and viola, nearly £½ million of real money has been created where none existed before. Now humour me and let's suggest that this money was borrowed from the bank by a museum in order to secure this 'Pollock' for the public interest. After the auctioneer's commission the art dealer's company in the Cayman Islands now has nearly £½ million of real money. As the Cayman Islands is a tax haven there is no tax payable by the dealer, and the public purse has accrued an additional £½ million pounds of debt, plus an additional liability for the interest owed to the museum's bank. Horror upon horror it is now discovered by the museum that the newly purchased Pollock is actually a virtually worthless Roxie! The museum no longer has a tangible asset to cover the liability accrued, but the museum still has to pay off the debt to its bankers unless of course it goes into liquidation, in which case the bank has to write the loan off as a bad debt."

"Now all we need to do to explain what has been going on in the financial markets is change the characters. The Roxie painting was the millions of sub-prime mortgages taken out on vastly overpriced property that the mortgage holders couldn't possibly repay. These were basically worthless unsecured debts. At this point nobody would be seriously taken in, let alone invest in them."

"The art dealer was the traders in the investment banks that invented a cunning financial device called a CDO (Collateralized debt obligation) which most people didn't understand but which the traders insisted were sound financial instruments. In our scenario the sub-prime mortgages were the Roxie but the rebranding of this debt into CDOs made them into potential financial Jackson Pollocks."

"The role of our art expert was taken up by the various credit rating agencies that, for a suitable fee, said that these CDOs were indeed sound financial instruments and who gave them top AAA ratings. The Roxie, the sub-prime mortgages, had now been verified as Pollocks, secure AAA rated investment opportunities by the so called experts."

"I think I understand what you mean" interjected Vanessa. "By validating the worth of the CDOs the ratings agencies effectively created supposedly low risk valuable financial assets where before the same assets as high risk sub-prime mortgages were considered virtually worthless. They created a Pollock out of a Roxie."

"Exactly my dear," continued Roxie with approval "but unlike the mere £ ½ million of new money created in my little tale, this ploy created hundreds of billions of pounds of new money. The investment bankers traded these CDOs at great profit many times over and extract vast amounts of this new money through fees, charges and bonuses which were then placed in nice secure tax efficient financial instruments. The banks created vast amounts of debt on their balance sheets, secured against the value of these AAA rated assets which worked absolutely brilliantly as long as the majority of investors failed to understand their true nature. When it was eventually discovered that these CDOs were actually worthless, it left the banks with vast sums of unsecured debt which were then transferred to the public through the aforementioned bank bailouts. Meanwhile these traders, colluding politicians and their ultra-rich customers are now sitting on mountains of cunningly extracted wealth whilst the societies from which they systematically extracted it are now left holding unimaginable amounts of debt. In order to pay off these vast debts, the public have been subjected to 'austerity measures' by the self-same politicians who actively colluded in creating this debt in the first place. This has caused absolute misery to millions of the poorest and most vulnerable in our global societies."

"This is absolutely dreadful" said Vanessa, "it's just like the trading I was conducting in basic food commodities. Just another scam to transfer money from those who can least afford it to those who already have vast wealth and don't need it. What an insane world we live in."

"So very true my dear girl. The major difference from my little metaphor is that the museum might have been able to sue the art expert to try to get the money back. In our real life situation apparently it is all perfectly legal. It would appear that the millions of people left with this debt can do absolutely nothing about it and those that have extracted these vast sums continue to fund and lobby political parties and politicians to make sure they never will be able to."

"As you observed Vanessa, the financial crisis was caused by deliberate mechanisms that transferred the ownership of vast amounts of financial assets, funded by society, to a relatively small number of very wealthy people. These people have now safely extracted these assets away in different, more financially secure forms, to murky tax havens in the Cayman Islands, Bermuda, British Virgin Islands and the like."

"Do you think this was all deliberate or do you think that the financial institutions and politicians really did believe these CDOs were as low risk and valuable as they were made out to be?" asked Vanessa.

"I am personally convinced that this was no accident my dear" continued Roxie. "Those involved must have known that sub-prime mortgage based CDOs were worthless, just like they knew before the 2003 stock market crash that the majority of dot.com companies were worthless. The only other explanation is that they were incredibly stupid and incompetent in which case it is quite a coincidence that these incredibly incompetent people seem to have ended up with all the money. It is estimated that there is somewhere between $20 and $30 trillion of assets now sat in tax havens that have been systematically and deliberately extracted from global societies leaving billions of people in debt. The traders in the investment banks are undoubtable looking for the next dot.com boom or sub-prime mortgage scam as a mechanism for extracting yet more wealth from society. In the meantime, here in London, they are currently treading water by trading the profits accrued from yet another carefully instigated debt fuelled property bubble."

"The reason that these people have completely got away with this is that their active accomplices in politics and the media create a stream of propaganda arguing that this is the nature of capitalism and if anyone tries to temper or control these excesses, society will collapse. Anyone who challenges unconstrained greed and capitalism must be a communist in these people's eyes. The wider population is becoming very agitated by the torments deliberately placed upon them by the ultra-greedy of our world. Sadly at the moment they are more frightened of the consequences of doing anything about it than they are exorcised by the distress caused to them."

"So what you are saying is that one of the illusions that we have to get rid of is that capitalism serves the interests of the majority of people" said Vanessa.

"Certainly capitalism that isn't heavily constrained by society to mitigate its worst excesses is extremely damaging and erodes and destroys societies and their democratic systems. The small number of people in today's global society who now control most of the world's wealth feel no loyalty to the billions of people that they continue to exploit to get this wealth."

"How does this help me in my quest for new meaning and purpose in my life" asked Vanessa.

"The important lesson here is that you will never find a true purpose through the pursuit of greed" replied Roxie. "Greed feeds the worst aspects of the human psyche and is ultimately always destructive. This is because the pursuit of greed also requires the suspension of empathy and compassion for anyone else. There is always an opportunity cost with greed, paid for at the expense of somebody else, but ultimately the biggest cost is the damage done to the person who is seduced by it. What do we call a person who lacks compassion and empathy Vanessa?"

"An investment banker" laughed Vanessa as she mocked herself.

"Funnily enough banking is one industry that is recognised to hold a disproportionately high number of these people."

"Go on Roxie, I give up" said Vanessa.

"They are called psychopaths or sociopaths if you prefer" replied Roxie. "The characteristics of a sociopath are of someone who is full of their own self-importance. They lack empathy and compassion for others and can't identify with the hurt that they cause to other people. They are prone to pathological lying and manipulation and are often parasitic, preying on others for their own benefit. Above all they never accept responsibility for their actions or the harm that they have caused and feel no guilt or remorse. Sociopaths can cause terrible damage."

"I have never thought of it in those terms before" reflected Vanessa. "Are you are saying that the pursuit of greed for greed's sake is comparable to the action of a psychopath or sociopath?"

"How could it be otherwise?" said Roxie. "The opportunity costs of someone hoarding vast amounts of wealth are absolutely immense. We are moving towards a world where approximately one hundred people own as much wealth as the poorest half of the world's population. Only a psychopath could calmly observe billions of people suffer terrible hardship, early death and deprivation and feel absolutely no guilt or obligation towards those people. Relatively few psychopaths actually turn into pathological killers in a direct sense but in a way these are the ones we should be less afraid of. A serial killer may kill tens of people before they are caught and locked away. The actions of those who systematically plot to extract the wealth from the world's societies kill millions through lack of healthcare, malnutrition and a host of other associated social evils."

"It is the same with the natural world. These people and the corporations they control are often directly responsible for destroying the ecology of our fragile planet. They cause incalculable harm, often to the point of extinction to the fellow species with which we share our Earth, just in order to feed the demands of their insatiable appetites."

"It is hard to argue that human societies are so often driven by the pursuit of greed and ambition" said Vanessa "you only have to look in the newspapers to observe who is celebrated to realise this. What I think you are implying that we are actually living in pathological societies?"

"My dear girl you are a wonder" exclaimed Roxie, "you have absolutely grasped the crux of my argument. I think this is the origin of much of the anguish and misery you have recently been through. The financial world that you were working within was major factor in creating and sustaining a truly pathological society. You are not a sociopath Vanessa. It is not surprising that you were struggling to continue when you were embedded in such a toxic environment? On reflection, is it any wonder that your spirit rebelled so strongly?"

"I don't understand how I could have been a part of this for so long without recognising the harm that was being caused" exclaimed Vanessa. "I don't think I am stupid but I genuinely didn't recognise what was happening as a result of my own actions, until the harsh reality of Julian's presentation broke through."

"There is a difference between emotional intelligence and rational intelligence Vanessa and you were deliberately supressing your emotional intelligence as a survival tactic. Don't forget that there is a huge propaganda campaign linked to protecting these vested interests. It is no coincidence that the majority of our media is owned by billionaire plutocrats. As we have already discussed one of the key characteristics of the sociopath is that they are extremely manipulative and the easiest way to manipulate humans through their emotions is to own and use the established media as a vehicle for disseminating your propaganda."

"Despite the obvious fact that all these trillions of pounds and dollars have so obviously been transferred into the pockets of the few at the expense of the many, the media will call the culprits 'wealth creators' rather than the blindingly obvious fact that they are wealth extractors. They talk about the trickle down of benefits from the rich to the rest of society rather than the flood up effect that channels wealth from the poorest to the richest. In the USA and the UK average wages have been flat or indeed falling in real terms for decades whilst top executives award themselves yearly double digit increases."

"Don't forget another key characteristic of our sociopath is this sense of self-aggrandisement. These people genuinely believe they are worth being paid hundreds of times as much as the actual workers who really create the wealth. Don't forget these are the self-same people who virtually bankrupted the global financial markets through their extraordinary incompetence. They blackmail and threaten politicians and societies, saying that they will remove their assets and effectively cripple whole countries if any attempt is made to rein in their excesses. Fear is by far the most effective mechanism used by our global sociopaths to manipulate the minds and control the actions of the masses."

"The worst part of all is that through the development of our pathological societies we have become a pathological species. We are like a virus that is destroying the host that sustains all life; we are destroying the natural ecosystems that sustain all life on Earth including our own. It may indeed already be too late to reverse this process but in the best case scenario we may have no more than twenty years before the damage caused to the Earth's ecosystems is irreparable."

"Oh Roxie" lamented Vanessa, "I have grown really fond of you but I am starting to wish that I had never started this conversation. You have left me feeling nothing but despair. Is there really so little hope? The only rational action in response to the scenario you have painted is to put a gun to my head to be spared the pain of witnessing the inevitable misery to come."

"Well if you do that you will never get to have such extraordinary sex with Sensi again and I can't think of a better reason for sticking around!" replied Roxie.

"Roxie!"

"I am really jealous you know" continued Roxie undeterred, "I have never really had any bisexual inclinations and I am sure I have been seriously missing out on a lot of fun as a result."

Once again Vanessa felt herself blushing as she remembered that wonderful sensuous evening with the beautiful Sensi. She felt that familiar tingling sensation already stirring at the thought and she shifted her weight on the chair and looked at Roxie who was looking at her with a knowing smile.

"I am sure that you haven't just started playing with your hair at the thought of me have you" teased Roxie.

Vanessa was completely ambushed as she realised that she had started to unconsciously play with her hair as she had started to reminisce of her time with Sensi.

"Ok" said Vanessa raising the palms of her hands towards Roxie in submission "you have convinced me that there are good reasons to continue with my life but is the joy of sex really the only positive argument you can provide?"

"Well it's a pretty good starting point" laughed Roxie. "Let's have another coffee before we continue. Would you like to continue?" Roxie suddenly remarked with genuine anxiety. "I have become a bit of philosopher in my advancing age and sometimes forget that others around me may not share such enthusiasm. As you have already witnessed, Kaitlin often has to reel me in when I get carried away."

"Please don't stop now" said Vanessa with genuine sincerity, "you may not have left me in a very comfortable place but I am genuinely fascinated by what we have discussed so far. I want to hear more, regardless of the emotional consequences."

"Well you will be pleased to know that I am actually going to offer a glimmer of hope to you next. I suggested to you that the first step to finding a new purpose in life was to peel away the illusions that surround you. When you draw them out of the shadows they seem so obvious but the behaviour of people is completely dominated by such illusions. The vast majority of people remain blissfully unaware of the mechanisms and dynamics that so cruelly manipulate them. Identifying the illusions that mask the world around them is the first step to genuine freedom a person can take. First however I think we both require another fix of caffeine!"

Vanessa felt a brush across her cheek from Marmaduke's tail as he leisurely strolled along the back of the sofa. He returned to nuzzle to her cheek and then slowly clambered down onto the seat to take possession of Vanessa's lap. This was not altogether pain free and Vanessa winced at Marmaduke's feeble attempts to retract any of his painfully sharp claws during this settling process.

"Oh my, you are honoured" remarked Roxie as she returned with yet another steaming mug of coffee, "not everyone is considered so worthy of his lordship's attention."

"I hope you have returned as the bearer of hope as well as coffee as promised" challenged Vanessa.

"Indeed I do, and we are both part of that hope."

"In what sense" asked Vanessa?

"Why my dear, because we are both women of course!"

"So you are saying that merely by being women we create hope? Sorry Roxie I'm afraid that you have lost me again."

"It's not that simple but let me explain further. Women are far less likely to be sociopaths than men; certain studies that I have seen suggest that for every female sociopath there are seven males. I think I need to explain this a bit more. Dr Robert D.Hare the Canadian psychologist devised a checklist based on the anti-social tendencies and characteristics of psychopaths. The maximum score for the test is forty. In the USA anyone scoring over thirty is considered to be a psychopath. Interestingly in the UK this figure is only twenty-five. The scary conclusion that can be drawn is that American society is so pathological by nature that showing serious levels of psychopathic or sociopathic tendencies is considered to be normal, perhaps even desirable behaviour. You only have to look at the extraordinary inequality in American society and the cynical and callous disregard for the needs of the poor and the vulnerable to understand the truth of this. Sadly our own society is moving in a similar direction and is also becoming increasingly pathological so we have little room for smugness or complacency."

"So what you are implying is that women are intrinsically less pathological than men?" said Vanessa.

"Exactly."

"What is the difference between a psychopath and a sociopath" asked Vanessa.

"These terms are often freely interchanged and the difference is rather nuanced. Some schools of thought believe that the vast majority of psychopaths are genetically programmed to turn out as they do and that there is virtually nothing that could be done to fundamentally treat them. Others believe that early environmental influences and experiences may also have shaped the psyche of these individuals and may be more inclined to use the term sociopath. If you happen to be a victim it's a bit of a moot point!"

"Ok, let's say that I can go along with you on this," said Vanessa "although I have met some women in my time who would be definitely score near the top of Dr Hare's scale. How does this knowledge bring hope?"

"Firstly you have made a very good point. Just because there is a higher tendency in men to develop sociopathic characteristics, the majority of men would score low on the scale and are as appalled by greed, ignorance, lying and cruelty as most women. Also, as you have pointed out, there are some women who are complete sociopaths, as bad as any of their male equivalents. Sadly we also find a disproportionally high percentage of these women holding the levers of power and influence alongside their male counterparts. We must therefore be careful not to make too sweeping a judgement about any one individual based purely on their gender. I do however believe it is quite reasonable to take note of the difference in the propensity to develop psychotic tendencies between the genders."

"With the exception of a few ancient societies, men have always dominated and controlled the levers of power, usually through control, coercion and the threat of physical violence to supress the rights and aspirations of women. Do you know that it is estimated that there are over one billion women in the world who are living with the physical and psychological scars of violence and abuse? This equates to roughly one in three of all the women on the planet. In the UK it is less than a hundred years since women were even given the opportunity to vote. For the first time in millennia, in democratic developed countries, women are actually starting to get hold of some of the levers of power. Sadly in many other parts of the world, often using religious ideology as an excuse, the physical oppression and control of women by men is actually getting more extreme not less."

"I have seen some signs of career progression for women in banking circles," replied Vanessa, "but the number of women getting to the top is still pitifully low. There is a strong underlying patriarchal culture that actively discourages compassion, caring and sensitivity, the very human qualities that you are saying offer a source of potential hope."

"You have grabbed the problem in a nutshell. The underlying pathology of our greed based culture creates an extremely hostile environment for people whose personalities don't share these pathological characteristics. The purpose of most large banks and corporations is defined as 'maximising shareholder value' although we know in reality this usually equates to maximising the money flowing into the pockets of boardroom directors. There is no social obligation, no requirement for sustainability, no obligation to the needs, concerns and families of employees except when this could impact upon profits."

"Virtually all the constraints that have been placed on corporations have had to come from state intervention in the face of frenzied lobbying and opposition. The capitalist slave owners insisted that the British Empire would be virtually brought to its knees when William Wilberforce wanted to abolish slavery. There were similar protests when the Government in the Victorian era slowly introduced legislation to stop the worst exploitation of child labour. For decades now this tide of social progress has been stemmed and even reversed through intense corporate lobbying and the collusion of politicians. We have now built a globalised corporate society without obligation or any social conscience. If you put the culture and behaviour of many corporations to the sociopath test they would score very highly indeed. Is it any wonder that many women struggle to thrive in such emotionally and spiritually hostile environments?"

"I'm still struggling on the hope front here Roxie!"

"The hope comes from the statistical fact that in democratic countries women could change the rules of the game if they really wanted to, and had the courage and to do so. There is no reason at all that the individualistic, greed based, pathological model of government and corporations can't be rejected and a very different set of social priorities adopted. The established culture would scream and threaten and coerce and bully and do everything in their power to stop any such progress. At least they can no longer overtly use direct physical violence and intimidation of women to do this. If women want a viable and sustainable world for their children and their children's children then they have to take urgent action to create this sustainable future. As we have discussed, the window of opportunity to do this is now very short. In a world dominated by greed and short term self-interest the prevailing social dynamics are nearly all pointing the wrong way."

"Are there any glimmers of light at the end of the tunnel or is it just a ruddy great locomotive heading our way" said Vanessa.

"Indeed there are" replied Roxie. "Have you ever heard of a book called the Spirit Level written by Richard Wilkinson and Kate Pickett?"

"Sorry, no."

"What the authors discovered is that the wellbeing and happiness of societies, above a certain base level of income, was dependent upon relative equality not the amount people actually earnt. The more unequal a society had become, the more social issues and problems were incurred such as violent crime, number of offenders locked up in prisons, poor health, shorter life expectancy, obesity etc. It is my belief that you can correlate inequality in a society with the degree of greed based pathological characteristics. Not surprisingly the USA and the UK were right up at the unequal end of the table and inequality continues to grow exponentially because there are few social constraints in our society to prevent this. At the other end of the scale are societies that are far more equal and where wealth and opportunity are better shared amongst the population. These are the Scandinavian countries such as Norway, Finland, Sweden and Denmark."

"How do women fit into this picture?" asked Vanessa.

"Well in the Scandinavian countries roughly forty to fifty percent of the politicians are women. In the UK it is a paltry 22.6 percent, heavily biased towards the left wing and the marginally less pathological parties, and in the USA it is a miserly seventeen percent. The underlying culture in Scandinavian countries is based far more on collective responsibility and mutual obligation than the highly individualistic cultures you find in the USA and UK and other similar countries."

"Is there is a chicken and egg situation here?" observed Vanessa. "Are there more women in politics in these countries because they have more equal and caring societies and women can thrive, or do they have better societies because there are more women in their political establishments?"

"I think a shift in culture has to be established before a significant number of women would be able to tolerate the political establishment" reflected Roxie.

"Another useful example of just how different the respective cultures of these societies are is to look at their prison populations. Let's take a figure of how many people are locked up in prison per 100,000 of the population? In Norway and Sweden when I last looked at the figures it was sixty-six and eighty-two respectively. In the UK it was about 145 and growing. In the greed and self-interest capital of the world where inequality is worshiped as 'the American way' it is a whopping 700 plus or ten times what you would typically find in a Scandinavian country. There can be no greater indictment of just how pathological the USA has become as a country. There is a close correlation between the increase in inequality in the USA and the increase in the number of people that are being excluded from society and locked away."

"So the glimmer of hope you offer is that the women of the world, the ones that are not still directly repressed and intimidated through physical violence, could exercise their democratic mandate and could therefore choose to change the nature of our society?" said Vanessa.

"It is merely a glimmer I'm afraid, don't forget that the established patriarchal culture and the plutocrat owned media will use every tool in their possession to prevent this. The most effective tool usually used against women is the fear that the prospects for their own children could be worse if things changed. The opposite is actually true as the current momentum of a greed dominated global society is leading us to a point that, for the vast majority of women, the future prospects for their children are simply appalling. The levers of power in our current world are in the hands of remarkably few people who are pathologically addicted to their individual wealth and the power it can buy. These people have no intention of changing this dynamic any time soon, even if it costs humanity the very ecology of the Earth upon which all life is dependent."

"Wow," reflected Vanessa, "this has been some conversation Roxie, my head is reeling. You have completely succeeded in eliminating any remaining vestiges of remorse I may have had about deciding to leave behind my life in the City! I need to think about all you have told me, do you have any advice about how I move on from here?"

"You mean apart from dramatically improving your sex life" laughed Roxie.

"Yes, although I might just come back to you on that!"

"Discover what it really means to be a human being and in particular what it really means to be a woman. We are far more powerful than you can even begin to imagine. It is no accident that men have been trying to constrain and control us for so long, they fear being emasculated should we collectively understand and unleash the potential within our true natures. Love, compassion and caring for others are far more powerful than greed, ignorance and self-interest when used collectively and constructively. They also fear the true power and nature of our sexuality; look at how religion and oppressive cultures have tried to control it for so long? Look at what they did to poor Alexandra to deny her the right to truly experience her sexual nature? Anyway let's face it; it was the allure of Helen of Troy that launched a thousand ships, not Achilles's bum!" laughed Roxie. "My word of advice is to go and have a chat with Alexandra, she can reveal more to you on these subjects than I can and she may well help to reveal the next step on your personal journey. Now I demand a hug!"

At that moment Kaitlin came bursting through the front door and the two women immediately knew that something was very wrong.

Part 3 - The Warehouse

1

A very flushed looking Kaitlin came straight over to the sofa and slumped down next to Vanessa. She was shaking slightly but it looked like this was more through anger than fright.

"What on earth's the matter dear" said Roxie with genuine concern in her voice, "I've never seen you like this."

"That's because I haven't experienced two of Justin Stempson's hired thugs intimidating and threatening me before," replied Kaitlin.

"Who is Justin Stempson?" said Vanessa with alarm.

"Do you remember at the party that I said that the Warehouse used to be owned by a lovely Quaker gentleman who sadly died recently and it was now owned by his nephew?" said Kaitlin. "Well Justin Stempson is the nephew and he is none too happy that we have shown no sign of departing the Warehouse. We still have over three months left on our existing contract which he would cancel in a minute if he got the chance. I suspect his investors are starting to get a bit nervous so he has decided to up the ante a bit to 'persuade' us to start vacating the building."

"Tell us exactly what happened" said Roxie.

"I was just passing over the footbridge by the canal at the end of the road when this thickset guy in his thirties appeared and stood at the end blocking my exit. As you know it is quite narrow so there was no way of getting past. I heard a voice behind me say 'hello sweetie, nice day for a walk' and I looked over my shoulder to see another younger guy in a blue hooded sweatshirt blocking my exit the other way."

"I was really alarmed as I had no idea what these men wanted and there was nobody else around. 'It's a bit dangerous for a pretty young girl like you to be walking alone in these parts' said the first man. 'Who knows what could happen, particularly after dark. Sadly there are some very unpleasant people about, don't you agree mate' he called to his accomplice. 'Very unpleasant, I blame the police, nobody's safe these days' came the reply. 'If I was you I would consider moving' continued the older man, 'neighbourhood's gone all to pot since those druggies and hippies moved into the Warehouse. Attracts a bad crowd that sort of place, not the sort of area that a lovely young thing like you should be hanging out in.' At this point he slowly moved to one side leaving a small gap for me to pass. I had to physically squeeze past him which he obviously enjoyed, and I heard his chum chuckling behind me. As I got past him I literally ran and I heard them both laughing. One of them called out 'Mr Stempson sends his compliments.' At least the distance of the voice let me know that they weren't pursuing me. I am so angry but I have to admit to being a bit scared about what might happen next time."

"There will not be a next time" said Roxie with sudden steel in her voice.

"Are you going to call the police?" Vanessa asked Roxie.

"There is no point, Stempson will deny everything and we have got no real evidence. There is no CCTV down at that end of the wharf."

"So what are you going to do then Roxie?"

"Stempson has made a very big mistake which he will very rapidly regret. We all reluctantly accept that we will have to move although it's hard to see where. Time is getting very short and London is becoming horrendously expensive to rent in. What we will never accept is someone threatening one of our family. I am calling a 'Rabble Rouser' tonight to sort this all out."

"What on Earth is a Rabble Rouser?" asked Vanessa.

"When anyone in the Rabble needs help or when the security of the Warehouse is threatened we call a special meeting to collect our thoughts and develop a plan of action" replied Kaitlin. "We were planning to call one anyway about the impending end of the contract but I think Roxie feels that it can't wait after this incident."

"Right" said Roxie, "Kaitlin, you call Julian and also get hold of Jethro and Max. Tell them that they have to make excuses at the nightclub but we need them looking after our door tonight. I'll contact the rest and make sure that they rendezvous as a group first before coming back this evening. I don't want anyone coming back alone tonight if it can be avoided. I don't think Stempson would be stupid enough to instigate any real violence yet but I'm not prepared to take any chances. I'll also get Sinjini to pick up some CCTV for the outside of the property on the way home. Before she switched into dentistry Sinjini completed an electronics apprenticeship" she explained to a bemused looking Vanessa. "She is a wiz with that sort of thing. Vanessa, unless you have very urgent business elsewhere I want you to stay. You will have been observed coming here and I don't want to run the risk of you being followed. Besides, it's a great chance to catch up with Alexandra; she will love to see you again. Any questions?"

"I can stay if you really think it's a good idea" said Vanessa. "I'll get my long suffering neighbour Bridget to sort out Tabitha again."

"I'll get on to Julian and the boys" said Kaitlin. "I'll have to phone Luigi as he will be expecting me tonight. I hope he can manage at such short notice."

"That's sorted then, let's gets started. Vanessa, go and check on Alexandra and explain what has happened. You will probably find her covered in paint as usual as she is working on a new commission for the gallery. Can you ask her whether she could arrange to get the sisters together? We could really do with a different dynamic at the Warehouse and time is short. I know that this makes no sense to you Vanessa, but Alexandra will understand what needs to be done."

Vanessa went to the door in the partition that separated Alexandra's studio from the main living area and pressed a button on the frame next to the door and she heard a buzzer going off inside. She felt a little nervous but also quite excited about seeing Alexandra again after the circumstances of their last meeting. After a few moments the door opened and Vanessa saw the familiar sight of Alexandra in her paint splattered dungarees.

"Vanessa, what a delight" she exclaimed and immediately embraced Vanessa in a huge hug. As the two women parted Alexandra planted a long kiss on

Vanessa's lips. Vanessa noticed a mischievous glint in Alexandra's eyes when she finally pulled away.

"Coffee?" she asked.

"Oh no thank you, Roxie has been plying me with coffee for the last two hours and I can already feel the effects of all that caffeine. I'm afraid it's not just a courtesy visit, although it really is lovely to see you again. Something has happened and Roxie is organising a Rabble Rouser for tonight."

Alexandra raised her eyebrows at this and invited Vanessa into the studio where they plumped themselves opposite each other on a couple of large colourful beanbags. Vanessa explained what had happened to Kaitlin on her way home and she could see Alexandra's face harden at the news. She realised that she was talking to a woman who had suffered a lot of abuse at the hands of a man and could imagine what conflicting emotions Kaitlin's experience might stir up in Alexandra.

"Then she said something that I don't understand so I hope I have got this right," Vanessa continued. "She asked if you could get the sisters together because there was an urgent need for a new dynamic in the Warehouse situation. Does this make any sense to you?"

"It makes perfect sense" replied Alexandra, "I shall see if I can get the sisters here on Friday evening. It's a full moon on Friday which is a perfect time to instigate a process of transition."

"Can I be really nosey," said Vanessa "who are the sisters?"

Alexandra looked into Vanessa's eyes very intently for what must have been a full two minutes before her face relaxed and the familiar smile returned. "If you really want to know about the sisters there is a price to pay. I have started to paint that sketch I made of you and Sensi together. I am fine capturing Sensi as I have done so many times before, but I have been struggling to do justice to your form and especially your essence. If you are prepared to model for me for a while, I shall explain about the sisters and what Roxie is asking from us. Is it a deal?"

Vanessa barely hesitated and in a few moments she was laid out naked on a silk sheet draped over an antique looking chaise longue. Alexandra settled in front of her with some charcoal to sketch with and an easel and she started to explain about the sisters whilst Vanessa listened with a growing sense of wonder.

"Have you ever heard of Wicca?" she asked Vanessa.

"Isn't that something to do with witches or devil worship?"

"It is to do with witches and absolutely nothing to do with worshiping the devil. The Devil you understand is a perverse construct of Christianity. They use the concept of the Devil to divert blame from their mythical Abrahamic God for all the harm, cruelty and misery that people inflict on each other. The physical form of the Devil used by Christians would be familiar to the Greeks and Romans who worshiped Gods of nature like Dionysus, Pan and Faunus. It is also a familiar image to those who follow Wicca as it represents the male aspect of the forces of nature that pervade all living things. It helps those who practice Wicca to visualise such forces. Much that is called magic that is associated with Wicca is created through channelling the natural forces that surround us all through a process of visualisation."

"So are you telling me that the sisters are a witches' coven?" exclaimed Vanessa in amazement.

"Got it in one. Most covens consist of male and female members and use the dynamic between the male and female aspects of nature in their work. The sisters are an all-female coven; many of us have suffered abuse and violence at the hands of men and find it easier to practice our Craft without the presence of men. We are led by a high priestess and we work primarily with the mother goddess aspect of the Earth and the natural world. We also draw upon the male aspect of our own natures that resides deep within the psyche of every woman."

"Unlike the patriarchal Abrahamic religions and other religions created by men, Wicca understands and celebrates the power of the female aspect of the natural world. Wicca as a religion could be said to be a fairly modern phenomenon as much of its structure comes from the work of Gerald Gardner in the 1940's and

50's. Many of the traditions and practices of Wicca are however very ancient, preceding Christianity by thousands of years. You are probably aware that nearly all the important Christian festivals come from previous pagan and Dionysian festivals based on the movements of the sun, moon and planets and their impact on nature."

"So is Roxie actually asking you to put some kind of hex or spell on Justin Stempson?" asked Vanessa.

"No, Roxie wouldn't dream of asking us to do something like that and we wouldn't have anything to do with such an idea if she did. Our practice involves focusing on creating a desired positive dynamic; we will have nothing to do with anything that is deliberately intended to cause harm. There are very few witches that would be associated with such practices. Creating negative and harmful energies frequently rebounds upon those who would desire to control them. Giving a more simplistic viewpoint that anyone can relate to, would you rather conjure up feelings of love within yourself or hate? Hate damages not only those who are targeted with it but also gnaws away at the psyche of the person in which it arises. Many Wiccans believe that any dynamic that is deliberately created through practicing the Craft rebounds threefold on the person that created it. It would be rather unwise to lay yourself open to the possibility of your intention to do harm rebounding back with three times the impact. It is far better to send out positive energy such as healing, love and compassion. What Roxie is asking us to do is to create a positive visualisation for the future of the Warehouse and for those who reside within it."

"So would this involve casting a spell on the Warehouse or something of this kind?" said Vanessa "I'm sorry if I sound a bit surprised but I don't believe in magic and I am a bit taken aback to find that you do."

"Do you believe in energy?"

"Yes of course."

"Everything in creation can be considered to be energy stored in different forms" said Alexandra. "You and I are stored energy, our brains pulsate with electrical energy and energy permeates everything in our natural world. In natural magic we believe that together we can create a harmonisation between ourselves and the energies in the natural world around us. Through concentrated thought and visualisation we believe it is sometimes possible to directly influence the world around us because we are all intrinsically a part of that world. You could consider it to be something like the theory of the butterfly effect. This suggests that through the complex interconnectedness of all things, an event as small as a butterfly flapping its wings in one part of the world could influence the formation of a hurricane somewhere else."

"So you are saying that Wicca is a religion that tries to change the world through a process of influencing the natural energy that surrounds us?"

"It's far more than that Vanessa. The primary purpose of Wicca is to help each of us to discover our true natures. Once we understand our true nature we can understand the nature of the world around us and can both influence nature as we are influenced by it. The conscious part of our minds is just a very small part of our psyche. There is a whole world of instincts and emotions that influence everything we think or do that we do not properly understand. Have you every stood in a forest and felt some kind of spiritual awakening inside?"

"I know I often go to nature when I am trying to escape the stupidity or frustrations of work and the people around me" replied Vanessa, reflecting on her recent walk on Hampstead Heath.

"Why?"

"I don't know, just feel somehow different, it seems to put things into a proper perspective. I love the feeling of detachment when I am standing on a high hill or walking on the seashore, it seems to put the trivialities of daily life into a different perspective."

"Something inside you is relating to the energies in the natural world and it's helping to create a better sense of harmony within you," said Alexandra. "Wiccans believe that there is a spark of the divine in all of us and that through ritual, contemplation and meditation we have the potential to become one with the nature of the divine that permeates everything in the universe. Most of us are very far removed from understanding our true nature. Wicca is therefore primarily a religion of self-inquiry and self-knowledge that can also be used to positively influence in the world around us."

"Do you believe in Gods" asked Vanessa.

"That's a good question" replied Alexandra. "Ultimately the divine is one; it is the true nature of the universe that surrounds us and the natural world. There are different aspects of the divine; in particular we worship the Great Goddess and the Horned God which represent the female and male aspects of the divine in the natural world and of our own natures. The process of visualisation of the Goddess and the Horned God is also a process of visualisation of the male and female aspects within every one of us. This has similarities to Hinduism; Brahman is the unchanging reality of the universe and also represents the true nature of the self, a state which can only be realised by the fully enlightened. The many different Hindu Gods and Goddesses represent different aspects and manifestations of Brahman. For goodness sake stop fidgeting will you! How am I supposed to capture your likeness when you are wriggling all over the place?"

"Sorry! How's that?"

"Better."

"How does Wicca relate to religions such as Christianity and Islam?" asked Vanessa.

"Apart from the fact that the organisations and officials of these religions have remorselessly persecuted and repressed witches throughout the ages it doesn't" replied Alexandra. "The Abrahamic God is a myth created in man's image and is a manifestation of the worst aspects of man. I deliberately use the masculine here. This God is used as an excuse for people to unleash the most appalling atrocities on each other and upon the natural world around us. It represents the worst possible role model. The overtly patriarchal and misogynistic aspects of the Abrahamic religions have also been used to repress and persecute women for millennia."

"That's a hugely controversial perspective" said Vanessa.

"Why?"

"Well isn't this God supposed to be the God of love and mercy?"

"Well in the sense of the love of a truly despotic ruler that sanctions mass genocide of men, women and children without mercy. Some sad individuals have tried to work out how many people God killed in the bible and it apparently amounts to about two and a half million souls plus the virtually complete obliteration of his faulty human design in Noah's flood. The Abrahamic God represents the least developed, crudest, cruellest aspects of human nature. His followers would have us believe that such a primitive despotic creature somehow managed to create our magnificent universe and everything in it. This is even less probable than holding a belief that Einstein's theory of relativity was really written by a hamster! If you were to systematically tick off a psychopath checklist you would find that the Abrahamic God ticks virtually every box."

"It's interesting that you used the word psychopath" said Vanessa "because Roxie said that our greed based societies are intrinsically pathological. Are you saying that everyone that follows the Abrahamic God is pathological too? If this is the case, what hope is there for our crazy world?"

"You're fidgeting again! Only someone with psychopathic or sociopathic tendencies could truly model their behaviour on the behaviour of God as depicted in the Old Testament, the pages of the Koran and similar texts. He exhibits narcissism, demands constant worship, is genocidal, creates the most horrific tortures on a whim, is constantly angry and completely devoid of empathy. This God also takes no responsibility for any of his actions and frequent failures, but blames it all on humans. Above all he has an incredible sense of self-aggrandisement. Fortunately the vast majority of the followers of this God don't relate to most of these characteristics except when they are truly wound up on mass by their religious leaders, but the fundamentalists; now they are truly scary. To be a woman in the hands of fundamentalist followers of the Abrahamic God is a truly horrific prospect. This is the daily reality of millions of women in the world who suffer the most appalling violence and abuse."

"But don't Christians also believe in love, mercy, kindness and forgiveness" argued Vanessa. Weren't these the most important aspects of Jesus's teachings?"

"Ah. Now you have hit the crux of the matter. You have a religion based on the teachings of a loving compassionate son of a raging psychopathic God. This is the problem that Christianity has always had; it doesn't know whether to be caring, kind and compassionate, or torture you and burn you to death at the stake. Fortunately many followers are in the son's loving camp and can be very special humans but a surprising number, sadly almost certainly a majority, use the father's characteristics as their role model."

"The logical conclusion is that the teachings attributed to Jesus and the teachings related to the Abrahamic God come from two completely different traditions. Roxie has done quite a study on this. She is convinced that the teachings attributed to Jesus came from an Eastern tradition, probably influenced by Hinduism and Buddhism. Roxie argues that Jesus's teachings were linked to the Abrahamic God, some considerable time after his reported death, by the Jewish Pharisee Paul. Roxie actually argues that Jesus, if indeed he existed at all as the evidence is extremely scarce, was probably put to death for blasphemy because he refused to believe in the Abrahamic vision of God. Virtually all the resurrection tales and references to 'miracles' come from texts either linked to Paul's sphere of influence, such as the Gospel of Mark or post Paul Christian writers. There are other equally contemporary texts such as the Gospel of Thomas that present a completely different aspect to the teachings attributed to Jesus. If you want to know more about this stuff I suggest you read Roxie's book although it's a bit esoteric for most readers."

"If what you say is true, then billions of people have been following a lie!" exclaimed Vanessa.

"Can't you get argumentative without moving your head? You really are a most troublesome model!" replied Alexandra in frustration. "Naturally they have been following lies or if you would prefer myths, fables and various allegorical stories. All these different religions, even within their own strands, contradict themselves to a greater or lesser extent anyway. It is therefore a statistical certainty that the vast majority of followers are misled in one way or another."

"Any person who genuinely tries to follow a path of self-awareness and development evolves on a path that is the complete opposite of the Abrahamic God with all his anger and petulance. How could the universe have been made by an all-powerful psychopathic entity that doesn't even exhibit a vestigial level of spiritual development? This God is a tool invented and used by powerful people through the ages as a vehicle to help them to control and oppress human populations and women in particular."

"Couldn't some of the same arguments be said about Wicca?" challenged Vanessa.

"Wiccans accept that it would be only those with complete knowledge who could genuinely understand the truth of reality. By following a path of self-enquiry and by trying to relate and understand the nature of the natural world we hope to get nearer to the truth. Every practitioner is encouraged to keep their own journal which we would call 'a book of shadows' to record what works for them. The truth exists; it is the true nature of our universe. It is only by trying to strip off the layers of illusion that we can even hope to approach aspects of the truth. We are destined never to fully understand it."

"I can tell you talk a lot about this to Roxie, she is always talking about stripping away layers of illusion" remarked Vanessa.

"Roxie and I have regularly 'burnt the midnight oil' debating such topics. To continue on the subject of Wicca, in a way our path of enquiry into our true nature is a bit like a scientist who seeks the truth in the observed material universe. Unfortunately, without emotional and spiritual wisdom scientific knowledge is often used to create great harm to the Earth. Science without spiritual wisdom is leading humanity headlong towards self-destruction. The difference is that we seek the spiritual truth of our nature by observation, practice and experimentation using our emotions and instincts to guide us as well as our logic. We seek to care for and live sustainably and in harmony with the natural world of which we are all a part. Sadly too many people see the Earth merely as an exploitable asset that can be utilised to furnish short term monetary gains. This comes at a devastating cost to human generations yet to come and the diminishing number of other species that share our fragile world."

"I am sure that Roxie has told you that she believes that women have a higher propensity for emotional and spiritual wisdom and I agree with her on this. In both the unconstrained capitalist world of avarice and greed and the world of the angry patriarchal religions these qualities are systematically controlled and repressed. It is only if women can find the strength to liberate themselves from these controls and celebrate their true nature that there is any hope for a sustainable future for the Earth. As Roxie and I have often discussed, the time to intervene before catastrophic and irreparable damage has been done to the Earth's ecosystems is very short. You will however be delighted to know that I have finished sketching you so you can wriggle about as much as you like now!"

Vanessa got up and stretched before settling herself down again in front of Alexandra. It now seemed the most natural thing to be sat naked in front of this remarkable woman and she felt no immediate desire to break the flow of the conversation by getting dressed. "You talk almost as if you believe the natural world is a living intelligent thing" she said.

"Are you so sure it isn't? We know the universe is capable of being sentient because we are sentient and we are part of the universe. I think many scientists see life as an accidental product of amino-acids forming and producing complex protein chains that eventually evolved to create more complex life forms. I believe that we may be part of a much larger natural dynamic and that life on Earth, rather than being an improbable accident, may actually be the inevitable result of the properties of that dynamic."

"I don't believe that the universe is sentient in the way of the petty petulant Abrahamic God that is based on a particularly flawed despotic human model. That doesn't mean that it doesn't have an overall purpose and destiny that is way beyond our current understanding. We are a very tiny part of the vast universe. Imagine trying to understand the nature, desires and aspirations of a Vanessa from the perspective of a single brain cell or even an atom of carbon within such a cell. Logically I recognise that the universe is a thing of almost unimaginable beauty, complexity and magnificence. Spiritually I also feel an intrinsic part of the universe and that perhaps my life has a purpose within it that is beyond my understanding. Perhaps it is to strive to preserve our beautiful and fragile Earth from the terrible devastation that other humans would wreak upon it. Physically however my stomach is now telling me it's nearly half past two and that lunch is long overdue!"

After sharing a light lunch of crisp breads, humus and salad Alexandra invited a rather tired Vanessa to an afternoon nap and the two women fell blissfully asleep, curled up together in Alexandra's sumptuous bed.

2

"Come on you two, shift your bums or you will miss out on this humongous Chinese takeaway that the boys have brought back with them" Fixie's familiar voice from the studio below broke into Vanessa's dream.

The two women exchanged a kiss, clambered out of Alexandra's bed, got dressed and went into the main living area of the Warehouse. The whole of the rest of the Rabble were stood around the familiar large wooden table next to the kitchen area raiding an enormous Chinese takeaway. "Hi Vanessa, do tuck in, veggie stuff at the window end, prawn and squid in the middle and a selection for the carnivores amongst us at the wall end" said Max.

Vanessa, with the slight feelings of guilt often experienced by meat eaters in front of conscientious vegetarians, raided the sweet and sour chicken and crispy fried beef with relish. After the takeaway had suffered considerable attrition from the combined attentions of the Rabble, Roxie called the meeting to order and they all moved to the circle of sofas in the middle of the room.

Roxie explained what had happened to Kaitlin earlier to everyone and Jethro who was sat next to her put a protective arm around her shoulder. Roxie also reported that Fixie's Z4 BMW Roaster, for which she had a parking space at the end of the wharf, had also been seriously damaged. The screen and headlights had been smashed and there was a big dent in the middle of the bonnet. This Justin Stempson is not mucking about thought Vanessa.

"It's obvious that Stempson's developers are starting to get twitchy" said Roxie. "Hiring this muscle will have cost him and I think we all know just how much he hates parting with his money, unless of course he is spending it on himself. We have a number of issues to sort out my dears, let's put them into two categories. The first and most imminent category is the sudden threat of violence and intimidation. He really is a very silly boy but unfortunately we can't just ignore this. The second category of issues relates to the fact that we are running out of time before we have to vacate the Warehouse. Much as I loathe him for it, Stempson does have the right to take vacant possession at the end of February. I just don't see how we could possibly afford to make him a reasonable offer, let alone one that he would actually accept from us."

"You're right Roxie, I can't see us ever being able to make an offer remotely close enough to one he would even consider. Money is everything to a man like Stempson" said Reggie. "Even as it stands the building must be worth two or three million pounds but if the site was redeveloped it could be worth upwards of fifteen million pounds. Taking the cost of redevelopment aside Stempson is likely to be made an offer for three to four million for the plot. We can never hope to compete with any offer that the wealth fund behind the development company is likely to make."

"It just makes me so despondent" said Max. "London is fast becoming an investment bubble for rich overseas investors that are running out of ideas of where else to plant their money. All this money is coming in, but the only people it benefits are the rich bankers and investors. Ordinary people like us are being driven out of this city. Sorry Vanessa, no offence meant, you being a banker and all."

"None taken" said Vanessa, "anyway I am now an ex-banker and everything you have been saying is perfectly true. The trouble is that many of the politicians and the crowd at City Hall are amongst the same group of people that are directly benefiting from all this speculation. It is absolutely no coincidence that for years the politicians of all parties have done nothing to curb the dreadful shortage in housing. Market value is all about supply and demand and by deliberately restricting the supply they have ensured that the haves in society have seen their investments continue to grow. They are completely indifferent to the fact that this causes untold misery to everyone else. They are also too afraid now to do anything about it because the debt raised against over inflated housing values is the only thing keeping the economy going. The real economy has been declining for years now."

"Call to order my dears" said Roxie, "I want to deal with the most pressing issues first which are those relating to that stupid boy Stempson's pathetic attempts to intimidate us all."

Not that pathetic, thought Vanessa who was becoming increasingly alarmed after hearing what had happened to Fixie's car. She had seen the car parked earlier, a nearly new Valencia orange coloured Z4 although she hadn't dreamed that it had belonged to Fixie. She was struggling to think how Fixie could possibly afford to have such an expensive car with the wages she earned working at a West End ticket office. She had to admit that it did rather suit her though; Vanessa thought that there was even a chance that one day the car might match the ever changing colour of Fixie's hair.

"Sorry Roxie, what's the plan?" asked Max.

"We have to pool our resources to put a stop to his shenanigans. Firstly we need to know who the hired muscle are and persuade them that it is their best interests to find a new employer. Who can handle this?"

"Already in hand" said Jethro. "I put the word out amongst the different teams that operate the doors in the pubs and clubs. There are only half a dozen major teams and I am sure that someone will have heard something. We have also let it be widely known that anyone who threatens someone living in the Warehouse is directly inviting mischief with Max and me."

"That's wonderful boys, thank you. Next we need some CCTV rigged up so that we can monitor the wharf and access areas and record any suspicious activity in the unlikely event that we need to get the police involved. Sinjani, can you handle that?"

"After your phone call I went to Maplins in Eldon Street and bought everything I need" replied Sinjini. It's all in that box over there by the wall. I have arranged with the practice to come in at lunchtime tomorrow so I can sort it out in the morning. I need to put a 10mm hole through the wall over there by the door. Do you think you could put that through for me Max if I lend you Reggie's drill?"

"Consider it done" said Max.

"I have also bought some software that enables us to put up to four images at any one time on the screen, although I think I can probably get sufficient coverage with just 3 cameras. I can always buy more if you think it's necessary."

"That's fantastic dear" said Roxie, "let me have the invoice and I will reimburse you from the central kitty."

"I think that's all we can realistically do for the moment to protect ourselves from any escalating stupidity from Justin Stempson. Now we can turn our minds to the issue of the fact that most of us will shortly be without a home" said Roxie.

"Excuse me, can I ask a question?" said Vanessa. "I know I don't live here and do tell me to butt out if you think it's none of my business but in the short time I have known this Rabble I have become very fond of you all."

"It's very mutual my dear. Now fire away with this question of yours" replied Roxie.

"What are you going to do about Fixie's car? It's just not fair that he can get away with it and her insurance premium will go through the roof after the cost of repairing all that damage."

"I'm afraid there is little that we can do to protect Justin from the consequences of his actions," replied Roxie. "We could perhaps plead that he doesn't actually come to any physical harm" she said glancing at Fixie. "I am sure you have heard of the law of Karma Vanessa, in which it is stated that the consequences of your actions come full circle? Well I'm afraid there is very little we can do to prevent Justin finding out that the law of Karma can move very quickly in these parts."

"I don't understand" said a confused Vanessa.

"The thing is it's not actually my car" said Fixie. "My dad gave it to me to use as a 21st birthday present but technically he owns and insures it. I'm afraid he will not be too pleased about the re-sculpting of the bodywork undertaken by Stempson's goons."

"But what can your father possibly do about it?"

"My father is a bit of an unconventional businessman who has unfortunately spent rather too much of his life at Her Majesty's pleasure" said Fixie.

"To be blunt Fixie, although I know you love him dearly, even you have to admit that if you peek under the thin veneer of business legitimacy your father is basically a gangster" said Jethro.

"Harsh but true" sighed Fixie. She turned to Vanessa, "have you ever heard of the Frankie McNeal gang?"

"Weren't they the outfit that were suspected of doing that bullion heist on the M20 motorway near Dover? I remember that someone was arrested but I don't remember anyone ever being charged or convicted for that job" said Vanessa.

"The very same" said Fixie "although I have made it a point never to talk to my dad about what he may get up to or I would just spend my entire time arguing with him. In the street where my father grew up in many of the children ended up becoming either being crooks or cops. I am cross enough that he spent such a large part of my childhood behind bars. He has assured me that his new enterprises are all entirely legitimate but I have heard this many times before. He may well still be a gangster but he has always been very kind to me and my mum and I can't help still loving him despite what he gets up to."

"So you see Vanessa that the incident involving Fixie's car is likely to resolve itself without the need for any action from the rest of us" said Roxie. "Now for the situation that we have only three months left before we will have to vacate the Warehouse. Has anybody come up with any ideas about how we can preserve our Rabble or about how we might remain in the Warehouse?"

Roxie looked around the room but nobody had anything new to offer. They discussed again just how much money they would need to pay even the site value. It was well beyond their means, even if Justin Stempson would have been prepared to let them buy it which was doubtful. It was agreed that they would give it another four weeks and if nothing had changed then they would have to split up and try to find alternative accommodation.

Roxie said that she and Alexandra would help to coordinate the property search. Sadly the chances were that most of them would have to relocate to the outskirts of London or beyond if they were to be able to afford the rent on even the most basic accommodation. Finally she told the Rabble that the sisters were coming together on Friday evening at seven o'clock for two to three hours and would everyone give them space to exercise their craft without disturbance. With that she declared the Rabble Rouser closed and they each went away with their allotted tasks and much to think about.

3

Vanessa was feeling quite depressed about the whole situation. For the first time in probably twenty years she had finally found a community of people with whom she felt she really belonged. Sure she had shared a common interest with her colleagues in the City whilst at work with them but that had never really transferred outside the working environment. Somehow the social life associated with work and her colleagues had always felt a bit forced and superficial, especially with the hindsight of recent events at the Warehouse. She couldn't believe that she was almost certainly going to lose this oasis of knowledge and friendship almost as soon as she had found it. She expressed her views to Alexandra.

"Don't you dare give up on us yet" said Alexandra, "we still have time and I still have a hope that something positive may arise after Friday's meeting of the sisters. You are welcome to come and observe the coven if you wish to do so but you would not be able to participate and would have to keep quiet so as not to break our concentration. You could observe from the small window you see up there that allows me to get extra ventilation into my bedroom. If this is to be allowed I must ask you to commit to not sharing anything of what you see or hear with anyone outside the group, even with the Rabble. I shall also have to clear this with Cyrene, our high priestess first and she may well decline."

"I would really love to see what goes on and I promise to keep secret what I hear and observe, thank you" replied Vanessa. "How do you become a sister in the coven? Can anyone join in?"

"Anyone wishing to join would have to be accepted by the whole group. It is very important that all the members in a coven can get along and that they can explicitly trust one another. If you introduce the wrong personality into the group it can destroy the balance and this affects the potential to create effective natural magic. The collective will of the group acts as a magnifier to the individual will, dramatically increasing the potential and the level of energy that can be produced. This can only happen if the group is in harmony. Joining a coven is not like joining a local church. Before you can actively take part you have to go through a process of initiation. This requires a lot of self-work and determination if you are to attain the necessary ability to concentrate and visualise to a level required to make magic. You would work with the initiate who advocated your proposed admission to the coven and they would help guide you through this process. There is however no guarantee that you will be successful. The chance of success also depends upon your own propensity for being able to channel nature's energies."

"The purpose of the coven is twofold. Firstly it is a chance for all the members to evolve in their own right and awaken the latent capabilities and potential of their human psyche. In normal life we only use a fraction of the potential of our human mind. Secondly it is to produce magic, to impact upon the external world of which we are all a part and change the dynamic within that world with a sense of purpose. Only an initiate has the capability of working within the coven to enable magic to take place. There are three levels of initiation depending upon the level of personal development attained. The high priestess of our coven, Cyrene, is a level three initiate. I have attained level two and Kaitlin is a level one."

"Kaitlin!" exclaimed Vanessa in surprise. "I had no idea that she was involved with Wicca."

"Why would you" laughed Alexandra "do you expect us to all walk around in pointy hats or ride around on broomsticks! If you hadn't been invited you to Friday's Rabble Rouser I wouldn't have mentioned it to you at all and you would have been none the wiser."

The two women went back to Alexandra's apartment and talked about Alexandra's new work and the increasing interest she was receiving from the gallery that marketed her work. She had been approached through the gallery by an art magazine that focused on upcoming talent. They wanted to do a feature article on her for their February edition which was a great compliment and had the potential to bring her work to a far wider audience.

4

The sound of a masonry drill screeching in protest as it was being driven through a steel reinforced concrete lintel very effectively awoke Alexandra and Vanessa from their slumbers. She looked at her watch, it was only 7.30. Max and Sinjani were wasting no time in getting the CCTV set up. Vanessa peeked through the small window that Alexandra had pointed out to her the previous evening that opened up into the main living area. She could see Max up a stepladder trying to force the drill bit through the lintel above the window next to the main door of the Warehouse. There was a sudden jerk in his arms as the end of the drill lost its resistance as it broke through to the outside.

By the time Vanessa had showered, got dressed and entered the living area Sinjani had already got the first camera working. This was discretely placed outside above the main entrance and was linked using Bluetooth technology into the LCD TV on the back wall. Sinjani was now experimenting by zooming the camera in and out using software she had downloaded onto a laptop. She smiled at Vanessa and wished her a good morning before going back to her task in hand. Reggie was in the kitchen fixing up some croissants and some pain-au-chocolat and there was a wonderful aroma of coffee. He invited Vanessa to join him and at that moment Roxie appeared in one of her more colourful dressing gowns.

"Max dear, you know how much I need my beauty sleep. If I get any more wrinkles I will blame you" she chided with mock reproach. Max responded by giving her a big peck on the cheek. "Nonsense Roxie, your beauty is ageless. You will still be pristine and beautiful when the rest of us are all wizened and decrepit" he replied.

"You daft boy" she responded but Vanessa could see that Roxie appreciated the flattery.

Vanessa was just deciding if she could get away with a second Pain-au-chocolat without completely ruining her waistline when the doorbell rang violently. They all glanced at the monitor to see the unwelcome sight of Justin Stempson and his two hired thugs standing outside.

"Max, do you think you might find Jethro and slip out the fire exit at the back. I think Stempson's hired help might benefit from a little chat don't you?"

Max gave a rather evil smile and nipped off down the spiral staircase to find Jethro.

Roxie waited a couple of minutes to give the boys enough time before going to the door which had just been rung for the third time. Vanessa went with her to offer what little support she could.

"Why Mr Stempson, how kind of you to grace us with your presence. What can we do for you?"

"You can clear off out of my property you stupid bitch" shouted Stempson "and take the rest of these fucking weirdo's with you. Who the fuck are you?" he said glaring at Vanessa.

"We shall be happy to oblige on the 28th February, in the meantime we would very much appreciate it if you left us in peace as your uncle would have wished" replied Roxie calmly.

"Don't bring that old fool into it. If it wasn't for his stupid contract I would have had you kicked out of here 6 months ago. I have no intention of poncing about for another 3 months waiting for you to piss off, it's costing me money and the developers are getting fidgety. My friends here have come along to help you pack."

"Hello Gary" Jethro had suddenly appeared next to the older of the two hired thugs whilst Max stood behind the younger one who was still wearing his blue hoody. He now obviously felt confident enough to have the hood down. "You must have come upon hard times to be working for a loser like Justin Stempson."

"Hello Jethro" said the thug rather nervously. "What are you doing in these parts?"

"Why I live here Gary! I'm surprised Mr Stempson didn't see fit to tell you. How extraordinarily remiss of him."

"Fuck"

"Language Gary please, I'm sure my friends don't want to hear your expletives. Now are you considering a new career move or do you and your friend fancy stepping a quick tango with me and Max?"

"I'm not afraid of him" said the younger thug facing off at Max who seemed to be more interested in examining his fingernail than in the person evident set to square up to him.

"Well you bloody well should be you tosser" said Gary "that's Max Schroeder."

She might have just imagined it but Vanessa was sure that the younger thug turned distinctly pale with this new information. Kaitlin suddenly appeared at her shoulder seemingly amused at what was taking place outside.

"Come on, we're off" said Gary.

Max stepped calmly in front of them effectively blocking their exit still examining his fingernail.

He looked up and fixed Gary in the eye. "Aren't you forgetting something?"

"What's that?" said Gary nervously.

"Shouldn't you apologise to the ladies for your rude manners and for causing them alarm and distress?"

Gary's face turned red but he turned to the three women standing at the doorway and said "I would like to apologise for any distress we may have caused you. There seems to have been a bit of a misunderstanding." He glared at Justin Stempson leaving the distinct impression that this was by no means the end of the matter.

Max raised one eyebrow at the younger thug who looked down at his feet and then muttered "sorry."

"Oh I'm so glad that we are all friends again" said Jethro "although I suspect Max is a little disappointed at missing out at an unexpected opportunity for a bit of practice. Anyway, I'm sure you boys are busy so don't let us hold you up any longer, thanks for popping in to say hi."

With one last smouldering glance over his shoulder at Justin Stempson, Gary and his partner made a rapid exit from the Warehouse.

"Well boys, I'm glad you had the opportunity to have a nice chat with your friends" said Roxie. Now Mr Stempson you were saying something about packing?"

She was speaking to Justin Stempson's back as he was running away down the steps of the entrance gantry and heading towards a brand new 7 series BMW parked on the wharf.

"Oh dear the stupid boy seems to have spent more of his inheritance on a new car" observed Roxie. "Without the sale of the Warehouse he must be virtually broke. His uncle spent most of his money on charitable causes in his last few years. There can't have been much more than fifty or sixty thousand left in liquid assets and he seems to have been spending his inheritance like water. No wonder he is getting itchy feet about getting us out of here."

"I don't suppose you noticed but that BMW was the twelve cylinder version and you don't get much change from 100 thousand for one of those" observed Jethro. "Even with his inheritance he must have borrowed a lot of money and with his background and credit rating he certainly wouldn't have got it from a reputable bank. I bet his repayments are eye watering and I'm sure that the lender is not going to be the forgiving type if he slips up."

As they went back inside Vanessa turned to Max. "Why were they so nervous about you Max? I can't help but notice you are obviously very fit but I thought that they would be more frightened of Jethro because of the size of him." Vanessa caught herself thinking about how she would have liked to have discussed his fitness in more intimate detail except for the inconvenient fact that he had a partner, and a gay one at that. There was something about the atmosphere at the Warehouse that was playing havoc with her hormones.

"Jethro would have easily coped on his own without my help" said Max, "I doubt whether Gary would have been stupid enough to try it on with Jethro even with his new apprentice with him."

"Apart from working in the gym and the door work, Max also dabbles in a bit of mixed martial arts or MMA cage fighting" said Jethro. "I'm seriously worried that one day someone is going to permanently damage his face and ruin his ravishing good looks. I keep asking him to quit but he just won't listen!"

"Jethro is rather understating Max's talents" said Kaitlin. "He is the current East London champion and hasn't been defeated in over a dozen boughts. I went to one of his earlier fights but I was too upset about watching him get hurt so I haven't been again." Max put his arm around Kaitlin and gave her a good natured squeeze. "Jethro, how do you know Gary?" she asked.

"He used to work on the doors but recently lost his license after being caught selling tabs to the punters on the side. I have heard that he has recently hired himself out as low grade muscle but I didn't think times were so bad that he would end up working for a jerk like Stempson. If I had known it was Gary I would have saved Sinjani the trouble of putting in the CCTV. I would be amazed if he shows up again and word will soon spread. Stempson will not be able to find anyone else willing to work for him for the money he can pay. He certainly can't afford real professionals with his debts."

5

Vanessa left the Warehouse after a quick round of hugs and goodbyes and headed back to her flat. She spent half an hour watching Tabitha's bottom as she showed her evident distain about being deserted yet again before making peace with the aid of half a tin of Sheba laced with a couple of sardines. If only all troubles in life were so easy to negotiate she thought.

On Friday afternoon she went on a large shopping spree for ingredients for a feast at the direction of Reggie. Vanessa was very conscious of the hospitality that had been shown to her by the Rabble and when she heard that a feast was planned to thank the sisters after they had finished their work she had insisted on providing the food. She took a taxi to the warehouse for 6 o'clock and the kind driver helped her to carry all the shopping to the door.

She found Jethro and Max moving all the sofas back towards the walls in the main living area. After they had cleared a large space in the middle they rolled up the large Turkish style rug that covered the area to reveal a large circle about 6 metres in diameter marked out on the wooden floorboard surrounded by unfamiliar symbols. There were four points which were soon marked out by Alexandra with large single candle stands, each with a different coloured candle. These were equidistant around the circumference of the circle and were slightly offset to the natural angle of the walls. She guessed that perhaps they represented the points of the compass. There was a large pentagram in the middle of the circle touching the edge at five points with the tip pointing at the green candle which Vanessa estimated to be facing to the north.

"Thank you boys" said Alexandra who was supervising their efforts. She was wearing a thin white silk robe with a large downward pointing pentagram on the front and Vanessa could see from the way that the material clung to the contours of her body that she was naked underneath.

To her surprise Vanessa saw Alexandra pick up a besom, a traditional twig broom and watched her as she carefully swept the area within the circle. So witches do have brooms after all she thought. The picture would be truly complete if Alexandra suddenly started to fly around the room on it. When she had finished she came over to greet Vanessa.

"I prepared this yesterday" she said "although it will have to be properly consecrated by Cyrene before we commence. This is the first time that the coven has met at the Warehouse. Cyrene felt that the effect would be greater if we concentrated our energies within the actual fabric of the building itself. Cyrene is just getting ready in my bedroom, come and meet her."

Vanessa followed Alexandra into the studio and waited for Cyrene to join them from the bedroom above. The first thing she noted was an extraordinarily shapely leg appearing at the top of the staircase leading down from the mezzanine floor. A vision of voluptuous womanhood followed in a similar silk robe to Alexandra's except that the large pentagram was pointing upwards, the tip of the point resting between a swell caused by a pair of large breasts that moved freely under the material as she walked. The woman was a dark brunette; her almost black hair was long and straight and ended just above the tantalising curve of her bottom. Vanessa guessed she would probably be in her mid-forties.

Vanessa was just about to speak when Cyrene raised her hand to silence her. She walked over to Vanessa and a pair of serious green eyes met hers in a gaze that seemed strangely similar to the one that Alexandra had fixed upon her the first time they met. Once again she felt that she was having part of her soul assessed as she was calmly evaluated for what must have been a full minute.

"You are right Alexandra, there truly is a lot of power locked up in this woman but it has been deeply buried for a long time. Hello Vanessa, I'm Cyrene and I've been looking forward to meeting you." She slowly kissed Vanessa on each cheek and there was now a mischievous twinkle in Cyrene's gaze that made Vanessa blush and initiated a familiar stirring.

"I'm going to ask you to give me your word that you will endeavour not to share anything that you see or hear this evening with anyone outside the coven. I can only ask you to try, it is extremely difficult for anyone to truly hold a secret, such resolve usually requires a continuity and focus of will that can only be crystallised as a result of considerable work. All I ask of you is that your intentions are genuine. Do you so promise?"

"I promise" said Vanessa with commitment.

"Good, I am happy. Perhaps one day we might persuade you to become an initiate to the Craft but I sense that at the moment your mind is too focused on what you would call the rational world, rather than our world of instinct, emotion and intuition. I think you have further to go on your own internal journey before you may become open to such ideas. I do hope you do because I believe your latent capability could be powerful and would serve you well once if you learned how to harness it. Now I must go out and greet the rest of the sisters and consecrate the circle. I think it is going to be quite an evening, I haven't worked out the source but there is a tremendous wellspring of energy emanating from this place."

Over the next thirty minutes the rest of the sisters turned up and used Alexandra's studio as a changing room. Kaitlin joined them and Vanessa noticed that like some of the others she had an upside down triangle on her robe. She caught Kaitlin's eye and asked her what this signified. She told Vanessa that it was the sign of a first-degree initiate; it was the sign of water and of the womb. The first initiation signified a form of rebirth. Of the thirteen sisters that made up the coven Vanessa noticed that there were nine first degree initiates, three of the second degree and Cyrene the high priestess of the third degree.

They were now all gathered in Alexandra's studio then, at a sign from Cyrene, they all entered the main living area of the Warehouse. This was now only lit by large candles placed around the circle that Alexandra had previously prepared. Vanessa took up her position in the darkness of Alexandra's bedroom next to the little window so that she could observe what was going on.

To her surprise she saw Cyrene walk clockwise around the outside of the circle to where a free standing wooden coat stand had been placed. At this point she disrobed, hung her up her gown and entered the circle entirely naked. At the centre of the circle was a wooden altar on which there was a burning candle, an incense holder, a small clear vase like vessel containing water and a bowl of a white substance that she subsequently discovered was salt. Alexandra later explained that these represented the 4 elements of fire, air, water and earth. There were also a number of other items including what looked to be some kind of wand, a sword, a besom and a large black handled dagger which Alexandra later explained was called an athame.

Cyrene took vessel containing the water and sprinkled a little of the salt into it. She then chanted what sounded like some kind of exorcising spell as she drew the athame from the altar pointing it at the vessel. At this point all the other sisters walked clockwise each disrobing at the same point as Cyrene had until they were all stood naked equidistant around the circle. Vanessa couldn't help but notice Kaitlin's beauty as she unselfconsciously disrobed and took her place at the edge of the circle.

Cyrene took the vessel and slowly sprinkled the salted water around the circle with a consecrating chant that was taken up by the other sisters who walked clockwise outside the circle at the same pace as Cyrene. Cyrene then picked up the athame and once again walked the circle chanting as she went with the tip of the blade pointed at the circle. She then laid the sword and the besom across the circle forming a cross and anointed each of the sisters as they leapt over this cross with more consecrated water. Once all the sisters were inside the circle the sword and besom were removed leaving the sisters secure within the now consecrated circle.

The twelve sisters now started to dance within the circle in a clockwise direction around Cyrene singing a chant of consecration and purification in the names of the goddess Aradia and the god Cernunnos. Alexandra then took each of the elements in turn off the altar and took it to its appropriate quarter signified by the four candles and Cyrene cast a pentagram in the air using the athame invoking the elementals responsible for each element to assist the sisters in their work and to grant their protection to the circle.

Once the consecration ceremony had been completed the sisters, now joined by Cyrene once again, danced around the circle singing some kind of chant whose intensity increased as they danced until with a simultaneous cry they stopped still in complete silence. There now followed a period of contemplation or meditation after which Cyrene again moved to the middle of the circle and knelt behind the altar facing to the north. Each of the sisters sat with their back to the circle facing Cyrene in contemplation. All of the sisters seemed to be in a sort of trance as if they had collectively formed some sort of group consciousness which was now being channelled through Cyrene as a focal point.

Cyrene then went through a ritual which Alexandra later explained was a process of opening up the seven energy centres which ran up from the base of the spine to the crown of the head which were commonly known in Eastern esoteric traditions as the chakras. This was to let the natural energy that permeates the universe to flow through the sisters and be channelled through their collective will for the purpose of creating natural magic.

Cyrene then spoke, "we call on Aradia and Cernunnos, the divine Goddess and God that are both apart and yet within us all to bring harmony to this place. I call upon my sisters joined here together to visualise joy, laughter, love and compassion emanating from this dwelling for years to come and to cast out the forces of disharmony and chaos. Create a shield of love as a protection from those driven by greed anger and avarice that would seek to cause them harm. Bring guidance to those that dwell within, deliver the divine light that banishes ignorance and hate and drive back the threatening shadows that seek to surround and eclipse this place."

The sisters bowed their heads in concentration as they each opened up their consciousness. They reached out to their sisters to form a powerful unified collective will that would be used to channel the forces of nature in the service and protection of the Warehouse and the Rabble. Cyrene repeated her call three times, each with a greater intensity and Vanessa felt the hairs on her skin stand up in response as if there a force of static electricity was beginning to surround her.

Cyrene began a slow chant from the altar and as she did so Vanessa felt the intensity of feeling increase until her whole skin was tingling. Cyrene's chanting started to change in tone until the words stopped and instead familiar sounds of a more sexual nature started to emanate from her. She leant back over her heels until she was lying on her back and her skin started to glisten in the light of the candles. Slowly her pelvic area started to gently thrust upwards into the air as though she was responding to the movements of some invisible lover. Several of the sisters also started to moan with desire and Vanessa felt a familiar tingling starting to emanate from her own love bud as her body instinctively responded to the sexually charged atmosphere.

Vanessa slowly undid the button at the top of her jeans and pulled down the zip to enable a finger to slip into the slippery wet warmth between her lips. She let out a moan of desire as she started to move her finger, caressing her bud underneath its little hood; the movements increasing in frequency in time with Cyrene's thrusting hips in the circle below. Several of the sisters were now joined together within the circle in various sexual embraces writhing and moaning with increasing arousal. Eventually Cyrene let out a cry of ecstasy as she was overcome with an intense orgasm that was shared by many of the sisters and by Vanessa who had brought herself to a simultaneous climax as she watched the sisters below.

After a considerable pause, where the only sound was the deep breathing of the breathless sisters, Cyrene burst out in joyous laughter. "Well my sisters. I have never experienced a reaction quite like that before; there really is the most incredible atmosphere in this place." The sisters started to compose themselves and knelt back in their allotted place inside the circle. One of the sisters was sobbing uncontrollably and Vanesa saw to her consternation that it was Alexandra. Cyrene stood up and walked over to her. She gently moved Alexandra to the side and still within the safety of the circle sat behind her enveloping her with her arms.

"What is troubling you my sister" she said softly, "you are surrounded by those who would love and protect you and yet the tears run from your eyes. How can we help?"

"You already have" replied Alexandra, "I am not sure whether these are tears of joy or sorrow? I have experienced sensations that I have never felt before and I am now feeling the grief of loss, knowing that I may never get the chance to feel such pleasure and such joy again. Maybe it would have been better to have never known such feelings than to have known and then lost them?"

"Tell me what you felt my sister"

"I felt a sensation in a part of my sex that no longer exists. I felt sensations where my clitoris and lips would have been before they were hacked off and cruelly sown together. For a brief few moments I felt whole again. It's as if my etheric body had replaced the parts of my physical body that had been removed and for the first time I felt what it must be like for a woman to experience the true power and joy of her sexuality. I also now know just what I have been missing all my life because of what was done to me and it hurts, it really hurts Cyrene." With that she lost control and started sobbing again as Cyrene gently rocked her in her arms.

The sisters gathered around Alexandra and Cyrene in a protective huddle until eventually the wave of distress had passed and she felt able to take her place in the circle again. Cyrene then took control once more and took the sisters through a process of closing their chakras and deconsecrating the circle.

The sisters gathered their robes from the stand near the edge of the circle and returned to Alexandra's apartment where they showered and cleansed each other and got dressed back into their normal clothing.

6

Alexandra and Cyrene joined Vanessa in Alexandra's bedchamber. Vanessa threw her arms around her friend in understanding of the conflicting emotions that the recent experience in the circle had raised within her. She just couldn't begin to imagine what it must be like to know that the people who were supposed to have loved her had so cruelly acted to deny her one of the most beautiful experiences of life and womanhood. She looked into Cyrene's eyes and saw that they were glistening with love and compassion for her sister.

"I am sure you meant well" said Vanessa to Cyrene "but couldn't you have anticipated how your sexual magic might have impacted upon Alexandra?"

"Well that's the mystery" replied Cyrene. "Witches do at times practice ecstatic magic as sexual energy, properly focused, can be extremely powerful but we would only do this with a lot of preparation. Such power when unleashed without the necessary precautions in place also has the possibility of creating danger and bringing disharmony to the coven. The release of sexual energy that you observed and, looking at your flushed cheeks and neckline also experienced, did not originate from those of us within the circle. Through our craft we unexpectedly created a conduit for a very powerful external energy source that it would appear originated from within this location."

"We seem to have opened a gateway that has let this energy flow through but please do not be afraid. I could detect no harm or malicious intent in the force that entered the circle and in any event our preparations would have prevented this from happening. We take no precautions to prevent sexual energy and love entering the circle as these will merely increase the potency of our magical practice and that is what flowed into the circle today. I am completely mystified as to where this has come from. In over twenty years in the Craft I have never experienced anything with such a powerful intensity before, the closest I have ever come to this has been when I have deliberately summoned it through ecstatic ritual."

"When you all disrobed I thought that this might have been because there was a deliberate sexual element to your Craft" said Vanessa.

"This is a mistake that many people make about the Craft, they seem to think it is just an excuse for some kind of sexual orgy but this is completely missing the point. Natural magic requires the opening up of our own energies and connecting with the natural energies of nature that flow around us. Any barrier between our natural state and the external world of nature lessens the effectiveness of our work. This is why many covens practice their work in the nude or skyclad as we would describe our natural state. I am not saying that we don't sometimes deliberately use sexual energy but this is nothing to do with being skyclad. As I have previously said we normally make special preparations and take extra precautions when practicing ecstatic ritual. Some members of the craft are also less comfortable about ecstatic magic and would not normally be prepared to take part in such work."

"It is the difficulty that physical barriers present to our work, barriers that separate us from the natural world when we are trying to make a connection, that makes tonight's events all the more surprising. I warned Alexandra and Roxie when we were asked to assist that practicing our craft in a steel framed brick clad warehouse could severely reduce the impact of any effect we could initiate. Ideally we would choose to practice in wooded glades and forests where the energy of the trees complements the energies of the sisters. This is not just known to witchcraft it is understood in many wisdom traditions. Advanced practitioners of any of the martial arts that utilise chi or natural energy, know through experience that their ability to channel chi in their art is enhanced in a natural environment such as woodland. Trees are wonderful stores of natural energy; even people with very little sensitivity can pick up some sense of this energy when walking in the forests. This is of course an ideal, it is rare to find such seclusion these days and often it is too cold and wet to make this a practical proposition."

At that moment Kaitlin appeared, now dressed in jeans and T shirt looking worried about Alexandra. "Don't fret so" said Alexandra smiling at the concern evident in Kaitlin's face "I'm fine now; it was just such a surprise to have such an intense experience. Did you feel it too Kaitlin?"

Kaitlin blushed and nodded. She was actually quite shy when it came to discussing the subject of sex and her own feelings but she still couldn't help smiling at her memory of the evening's events. She was still feeling quite sexually charged and she thought that Julian had better not have any silly ideas about going to sleep when they retired for the night.

Alexandra picked up her phone and gave Roxie a quick call to tell her that the sisters had finished their work and that it was safe for everyone to come back into the main living area again. By the time Alexandra and Cyrene had showered and wandered down to join the others the rug had already been replaced over the circle and the sofas moved back.

Vanessa noticed that it was not just herself and the sisters that had been affected that night. Everyone was looking rather flushed and there were the little smiles and glances between partners that gave evidence of recent lovemaking. Roxie had made no attempt to disguise the fact as her hair was a still a tangled mop and poor Joris, by his demeanour, looked like he had been struggling to satisfy her demands.

Vanessa helped Fixie and Reggie in their kitchen fiefdom as they prepared a feast of Indian food for all the guests using many of the ingredients that they had asked her to buy for them. Every now and then Sinjani would also wander over and offer words of advice to Reggie about how much spice to add to the dishes and they would have a good natured argument. The smell of delicious spices filled the air as the Rabble and the sisters laughed and chatted to each other. Looking around Vanessa felt it hard to imagine that in just a few weeks all this would be over and in all likelihood the bulldozers would be moving in to reduce the Warehouse to a pile of rubble.

Vanessa reflected on the events of the last few weeks. Less than a month ago she was a senior trader in Mallory's, her main priority being how to exploit the markets to squeeze out extra value for wealthy clients. The developing inner turmoil and the kindness of strangers had opened up a whole new world of possibilities and she realised that she had become very attached to this eccentric yet wonderful community. Just as these feelings were developing and growing towards the Rabble and the Warehouse it looked like they would both simply vanish leaving her once more adrift and she had a sudden feeling of vulnerability.

She caught up with Roxie and explained how she was feeling.

"You do know that the Buddhists say that attachment is the source of all suffering and they do have a point" said Roxie. "If we equate our security and feelings of wellbeing with material objects and other people we immediately leave ourselves vulnerable should anything befall these objects of our attachment."

"Everything in the universe is in a constant state of flux. If we seek true security and peace of mind the source lies within us not in the world outside. This is very difficult to find because our own human psyche is also in a constant state of flux and even the attachments we make to what we perceive to be ourselves are as fragile and illusory. The personality that we have developed in our minds that we equate to be ourselves sits in the outer layer of our consciousness. To know our true nature we have to peel back these surface layers and seek that which lies deeply hidden within"

"Having been all philosophical about what you have been saying will not make a jot of difference to how we will both feel if we can't find a way out of our current difficulties. I feel that you are already a part of our little community and that our futures are now somehow entwined. I for one am beginning to fall for you Vanessa and I know I am not alone in this. I hope that the sisters have somehow worked their magic and that something will happen as a result that will change the direction of future events. We must place our faith and hope in their work because, in the world of instinct and intuition, faith is vital element if what is desired is to have any chance of become a reality. We each have to visualise a better future if it is to come to pass."

The two women kissed each other gently on the lips. This was not a kiss of passion but a kiss of loving affection between two women who were now emotionally bonded. Attachment may ultimately be the cause of all suffering reflected Vanessa, but attachment also creates love and it is such feelings of warmth and love that makes life truly worth living.

Suddenly the brass bell that doubled as a doorbell was being rung by the irrepressible Fixie. "Can I have your attention; Cyrene would like to say something on behalf of the sisters."

"Firstly we would all like to thank you for your interest in our work and for inviting us to join you here tonight. We know that most of you will not understand what we have been attempting and probably think we sisters are as mad as an army of frogs. You do all know Alexandra and Kaitlin and your love of them and your faith and acceptance in their judgement complements us all."

"It has been an incredible evening and I can sense that each and every one of you has been in some way affected by the energies that were released here this evening. The work of magic is not experienced through rational evaluation. It can't be picked up and examined; rather it is felt in the instincts and emotions, the psychic realm of intuition."

Cyrene then laughed as she continued, "it is also the realm of sexual energy which I think many of you also discovered this evening."

There were knowing smiles and looks between the Rabble and Kaitlin gave Julian a look that made him blush, just as she had blushed earlier when confronted by Cyrene. Julian felt a familiar stirring down below and he made a discreet adjustment in the position of his growing manhood within his jeans to ease his discomfort.

"I can't tell you what will happen as a result of the work that we have undertaken this evening, magic seldom manifests itself directly. If we have been successful the results will probably result in unexpected coincidences or meetings, what we often describe as synchronicity. Those who have been working in the craft a long time get accustomed to this and see it as a perfectly natural consequence but for those of you outside the Craft you may experience some surprising events."

"I have talked about the importance in the Craft of intuition and tonight my intuition is telling me that the solution to the challenges placed before you may lie in Kaitlin's hands." Kaitlin's eyebrows both rose with sudden interest. "I believe that the future of the Warehouse is intrinsically linked to the source of the powerful energy that we released tonight. Please give our sister Kaitlin your love and support in the days ahead as she seeks to unravel this mystery."

Roxie then stood up and gave Cyrene a warm hug. "On behalf of the Rabble we would like to thank you for your kindness and support in coming here tonight and for your work to try to help us continue to thrive as a community into the future. I think each of us has been in some way touched by your Craft tonight. Regardless of the eventual fate of the Warehouse I feel that we now have eleven new sisters as part of an extended family which is not constrained by the walls of this building. I know after speaking with Cyrene that you will take no payment for the work you carry out on behalf of others but we at least hope that you enjoyed Reggie and Fixie's wonderful feast."

Everyone burst into spontaneous applause as Reggie and Fixie bowed with false modesty.

Kaitlin went up to Cyrene before she departed. "Where do I start to look?" she asked.

"Don't worry, it will come to you. The solution must somehow lie in the history of this place and perhaps your work within the Museum of London maybe of some advantage. What could have happened here that could have left such an extraordinary residual energy? There must be clues somewhere that can lead you to its source. I don't know how but I am convinced the solution to your problem is also tied up with this knowledge. Why don't you try to persuade Alexandra to help you, she has greatly developed her intuitive skills since joining the Craft and these may assist you in your search. Good luck!"

With that Cyrene departed and the other sisters soon followed. Most of the Rabble who were in a loving partnership also seemed to disappear very quickly downstairs, as the atmosphere in the Warehouse still seemed to retain some of its earlier potency.

Vanessa started to help Jethro and Max clear up in the kitchen but she could see them exchanging knowing glances and she soon shooed them off, finishing the task of clearing up herself. Although she was not a member of the Rabble, at least not yet, it seemed perfectly natural. After she had finished she decided to pop in on Alexandra again before leaving just to make sure that she was feeling ok. She did not underestimate the experience that Alexandra had gone through and she didn't believe her in her assertion that she had got over it.

She went into the studio to find Alexandra splattered with paint in front of a picture of a grotesquely deformed female vulva on the canvas before her. Vanessa quietly sat on a beanbag and watched as Alexandra continued working on the canvas until eventually she threw down her brushes and sat at the floor staring at the picture. Vanessa went over to her and gently sat behind her cradling Alexandra in her arms.

"I just had to externalise what they have done to me after tonight" said Alexandra quietly. "Ever since I was mutilated I have taken the view that it was just something that I had to accept and that I should move forward and get on with my life. The problem is you never really move forward when so much of what makes you a woman has been deliberately taken away from you. If the consequences were not so dramatic the practice of female genital mutilation would not be so widely practiced by the misogynistic cultures where it prevails. The malevolent purpose behind this dreadful custom is to reduce a woman to a possession whose sole reason for being is to fulfil the desires and breeding requirements of whichever man she belongs to. For the first time this evening I fully understand what has been taken away from me and I want it back."

"How can you get back what has been taken away from you in such a way?" asked Vanessa.

"There are some surgeons who specialise in surgery that tries to correct at least part of the harm that has been done. Most people think that a clitoris is just a small bud nestled at the top of a woman's vagina but it is actually the tip of a long organ that may be as large as the penis of some men. When the mutilation takes place the tip is removed with many of the nerve endings and this is then covered in scar tissue. For some women, if the organ is extended so that the tip is where the original clitoris would have been and the scar tissue removed, some of the sensation can return. There is no guarantee and it will never be the same as it was before, but I feel I must at least try. I refuse to submit to what has been done!" She shouted the last few words in defiance at the grotesque painting in front of her and Vanessa could begin to see the return of the wonderful formidable woman she had first encountered.

"Corrective surgery for victims of FGM that hopes to restore some sensation has been taking place in France, Spain and the USA for some time" Alexandra continued. "There is now a French trained surgeon called Nathalie Deneuve operating on victims in London. I have been thinking about contacting her clinic for some time but after tonight I have decided I am definitely going to give it a try. For the first time in my life I actually have a considerable income coming in from my agent at the gallery and I can afford the surgery." She turned around to face Vanessa, "would you come with me when I have my consultation and hopefully, if they think I am suitable, for the surgery?"

Vanessa clasped Alexandra's hands and held them to her chest, "it would be a privilege, and of course I will come with you."

"Could I ask you for something else? This is very difficult for me to ask and I will not be at all offended if you say no."

"What can I do to help?" replied Vanessa.

"When the surgery has healed, would you be prepared to make love to me? I have grown close to you Vanessa; I trust you and I couldn't contemplate anyone else touching me down there. I know it is a lot to ask and I really will understand if you don't share my feelings."

This time Vanessa said nothing but she leant forward and gave Alexandra a long sensuous kiss on the lips as a reply. The two women climbed up to Alexandra's bedroom, took off their clothes and curled up into each other's arms.

7

The next morning Alexandra and Vanessa caught up with Roxie making breakfast in the main kitchen.

"Vanessa wants to move in with me" said Alexandra.

"Well my dears I wish I could feign some kind of surprised reaction but I have really been expecting this ever since that first evening with Sensi" replied Roxie. "We have all seen the way you have looked at each and for the tenuous excuses that Vanessa has come up with for spending the night cuddled up with you in your bed. The only real surprise is how long it has taken you both to get around to it. The other problem is of course that you may not have a home to offer Vanessa for much longer."

"I want to be here to help in any way I can" said Vanessa. "I shall keep the apartment and if the worst comes to the worst I can at least offer a temporary home to Alexandra and a couple of others from the Warehouse until we can find something better."

"You are a darling" said Roxie. "I shall have to ask the others first as this is a rule we created when our little community first formed. Everyone has to accept a new person joining the Rabble and if anyone feels strongly enough to object we have to take their concerns seriously. We are a ragtag mixed bunch but we also have a precious harmony and if anyone feels that this harmony may be damaged by a new arrival they have a right to be heard."

"I fully understand" said Vanessa thoughtfully. "I would also have to bring Tabitha with me and everyone would have to agree to that too."

"The only person who might object to Tabitha is Marmaduke and he is so laid back he probably won't deign to register that Tabitha even exists" laughed Roxie.

"When will you be able to let us know the rest of the Rabble's decision?" asked Alexandra.

"I shall talk to them all today and let you know this evening. Would you give me some time and space to sort things out my dear" said Roxie looking towards Vanessa. "Do you think you might be able to pop back about 7ish?"

"Of course, thank you so much" said Vanessa. She gave Roxie a big kiss on the cheek and went to collect her handbag before heading back to her flat to start sorting things out. This was very much a spur of the moment decision and she had to think through the practicalities and implications of what she had decided to do.

After Vanessa had left the Warehouse, Alexandra asked Roxie if she felt that anyone would object to Vanessa joining them.

"The only person who might is Julian if he has any lingering issues with the work Vanessa used to carry out at Mallory's bank" replied Roxie. "Not that he is here very often anyway but we do need to consider his feelings. My view is that most of us have already accepted Vanessa as one of our own. She seems to belong here. I strongly suspect that Kaitlin's first invitation to Vanessa was as a result of the enhanced intuition that she has developed through practicing the Craft with you and the sisters. If she is part of the strange synchronicity associated with your work, she may yet be an important player in the fate of the Warehouse and the future of our dear little family."

Vanessa returned to the Warehouse at just after 7.00 in the evening with a sense of trepidation. She could not quite decide whether this was because she might be rejected or because of the implications for her future if she was going to be accepted.

Alexandra, Reggie, Sinjani, Roxie, Julian and Kaitlin were waiting for her. As it was a Saturday night the boys were busy doing door work and Fixie was out partying with some of her friends.

They seemed a bit subdued and she noticed that Kaitlin couldn't look at her and was looking down at her feet. Her heart sunk, it looked like she was not going to be accepted after all.

Suddenly Kaitlin leapt up in the air with a yell, "Yeah Vanessa! Welcome to the Rabble" and they all gathered around Vanessa in a group hug. After they had parted Reggie pulled out a Jeroboam of Champagne that had been strategically hidden behind the kitchen worktop.

"We thought this would remind you of the days in the City that you have left behind" he laughed as he popped the cork on the huge bottle.

Vanessa found it a bit hard to take in, for the first time for as long as she could remember she felt that she was being accepted for who she was as a person, rather than for her proficiency in producing wealth or as a future networking prospect. A few tears of happiness trickled down her cheeks as her heart soared and the emotions became a bit too much to hold in. This time it was Alexandra who comforted Vanessa and the two women kissed deeply as the others whooped and cheered in delight.

They all sat around the table as Reggie and Sinjani brought out a tapas comprising about a dozen small dishes which they all tucked into with relish. Vanessa deliberately sat down next to Julian.

"Thank you" said Vanessa, "it means a lot to me that you are prepared to accept me after my time at Mallory's"

Julian gave her a genuinely warm smile "there is more joy in heaven over one lost sinner who repents" he replied.

"That's pretty rich coming from one of the world's most confirmed atheists" remarked Kaitlin.

"What will you do now Vanessa?" asked Julian.

"I really don't know in the long term but my immediate plans are to support Alexandra and to do anything I can to help keep this community together. After that I shall try to make sense of my life and what, if any, purpose it may have. I have learnt so much from all of you and in particular from Roxie, Alexandra and the sisters that all my previous concepts of what my life was supposed to be about now seem rather trivial and pointless. I feel a bit like a boat on the ocean that is being tossed about by the waves, blown by the winds and drawn by the tides to unknown destinations. I feel both helpless and excited at the same time. At least I don't feel alone in my quest as I am surrounded by a wonderful crew."

With that she stood up and proposed a toast, "the Rabble!" They all lifted their glasses in response, "the Rabble" they cried and drained their glasses.

"Come on Reggie, stop hogging that bottle" chided Sinjani and Reggie happily walked around the table topping everyone up."

"I see I'm just in time" said Fixie as she breezed in through the front door. She joined them around the table and started to eagerly raid the remains of the tapas.

After she had been passed a glass of champagne she declared that she had come bearing gossip.

"I have heard on the grapevine that Justin Stempson has had a rather unpleasant surprise" she confided mysteriously.

"What's happened dear?" said Roxie. "Come on, don't keep us in suspense."

Fixie took a deliberately long slow sip of her drink, relishing the universal attention now focused upon her.

"By some unknown means his beautiful BMW has been somewhat restyled. Rumour has it that he parked it outside his house as usual and when he woke in the morning he found a large metal cube of compressed metal where the car had been. Apparently it took him quite a while to realise that this apparent attempt at modern sculpture was indeed all that remained of his most prized possession. It was left with an anonymous note saying that he was very lucky that he was not also inside the vehicle when it was crushed."

"It was your dad's crew wasn't it?" said Kaitlin.

"Probably" said Fixie. "He was really mad when he heard what had happened to my car although I will never get him to admit that he had anything to do with it. He wouldn't have to; he just needed to let the right ears know how he felt about Justin Stempson and his posh BMW. Poor Justin!"

"Poor Justin indeed" said Roxie. "If it's Fixie's dad you can be sure that the police will never be able to pin it on him. That's if Justin is stupid enough to actually go to the police with the virtual certainty of even worse retribution if he does. Equally there is no way that the insurance company is going to pay out on such a claim as it is absolutely obvious that this is no accident and it's certainly not fire or theft! He is now left with a large debt borrowed against a car that no longer exists and you can be sure that whoever lent him the money will have heard about it. His only hope now is that the Warehouse sale goes through without a hitch before he runs out of money to pay for the instalments on his debts."

"Well everything suggests it will" said Kaitlin "but Cyrene was pretty sure that there was something about the Warehouse that might yet bring us some hope and she has placed this task firmly in my hands. Its Sunday tomorrow and, apart from the public galleries, the museum will be virtually empty and I will get unimpeded access to the computers and the archives. Alexandra, Vanessa, are you able to come along with me tomorrow and see what we can turn up between us?"

Alexandra glanced at Vanessa who nodded enthusiastically, "We'd be delighted to" she replied.

The following morning, the three women were sat in the office in the museum which Kaitlin shared with three other volunteers in the archaeology department.

"Right" said Vanessa, "brainstorming time, tell me everything you can remember about the Warehouse and I'll jot it down on this flipchart."

"Those management instincts are still present I see" laughed Alexandra affectionately.

After about 15 minutes they took stock of what Vanessa had captured on the chart. The current building was rebuilt after the blitz in 1948. The previous building had also been a warehouse for importing wine and could be dated back to the great fire of 1666.

The Warehouse address was simply Friggs Wharf. This was previously recorded as Friggs Place on an old map of London that Kaitlin had found which showed what the area was like before the Wharf front was reconstructed in 1783.

Kaitlin had found the plans of the Warehouse which were fortunately held in the National Archive to which the Museum had an automatic web link. It looked as if the 1948 building had literally been built on the foundations of the old building which was constructed in 1669, three years after the great fire. Interestingly, in the planning notes it recorded that the old building had originally been three storeys high instead of the two in the new building. It was recorded that the lower story had become obsolete as the increased height of the new Wharf that was constructed in 1783 made access to the lower level impractical.

None of these facts seemed particularly helpful but undaunted they decided to look through all the online archives to see if they could find any further information about either Friggs Wharf or Friggs Place that might be of any interest.

"Hey, did you know that our Warehouse is supposed to be haunted?" remarked Vanessa who was using one of the spare terminals in the room. This is the fourth entry I have found of locals reporting sounds of strange laughter and foreign sounding voices. Here's a report from a newspaper from 1852, 'night-watchman Eric Samuels was sacked after he refused to enter the Warehouse on Friggs Wharf because of hearing what he described as demonic laughter.' Now I wonder what that was all about? Let's put in ghost, phantom, apparition and Friggs and see what it comes up with?"

They found 13 different entries from papers and articles going back to 1703. This recorded that a local vicar had gone mad after reportedly seeing the ghosts of a group of Roman Soldiers moving into the warehouse at Friggs Place. The other strange aspect about the soldiers was that only their bodies above the waist were visible and it looked as if they walked straight through the wall where there was no doorway to give them access.

"So our Warehouse is supposed to be haunted but I don't see how that helps us at all with our problem" said Alexandra. "I can't see the developers being deterred from their plan in case the building might be haunted. It will take a lot more than that to deter Stempson, particularly now his money worries are even more acute."

"We must be missing something" said Kaitlin. "Cyrene was sure that there was something about the history of the place that was important but there is nothing here to help us. We have been at this now for four hours so I suggest we call it a day and I will see if I can find out anything else on Tuesday when I am in next."

Reluctantly they agreed and somewhat disheartened they made their way back to the warehouse.

8

Three days later on the Wednesday everyone got a text from Roxie, "Kaitlin has called a Rabble Rouser for tonight; she has found something that might be important. Please try to make it if you can."

That evening they were all gathered together in the Warehouse waiting to see what Kaitlin had discovered. Vanessa noticed with concern that Max's face was severely bruised and that Jethro was glowering at him.

"Max, what on earth has happened to you!" she exclaimed. "I hope it's not Stempson's thugs up to their tricks again."

"Don't give him any sympathy" said Jethro crossly. "He has been fighting a bought with the North London MMA champion. Look at the state of him!"

"Should see the other guy" said Max. "Anyway I won didn't I?"

"On a split decision" retorted Jethro, "next time you may not be so fortunate."

Fixie rang the bell to call the Rabble to order. They all turned to look at Kaitlin who was standing excitedly in front of a Roman Map of London that was up on the large flat screen television.

Kaitlin explained that she had gone into the Museum on Tuesday to find a note in her email from her boss Dr Diane Evans. The email asked her to have a quick look at the document that she had placed in an envelope on her desk to see if it revealed anything interesting. In the envelope was a translation of a short extract from the work of the Roman historian Gaius Marcellinus who was known to have written about the Roman occupation of Britain between 137 and 155 CE. Dr Evans remarked that the text referred to the wonders to be found at the Temple of Venus in Londinium. The slight problem was that the Museum had no other record of a Temple of Venus in Roman London. There was a Temple of Mithras near Temple Court Victoria but the map indicated there was no record that a Temple of Venus had ever existed.

"How do you explain that?" asked Fixie.

"Well the trouble is that the Roman occupation of Britain was very poorly documented by the historians of the time so we have very partial knowledge" answered Kaitlin. "I have no idea where Dr Evans got hold of this extract from Marcellinus as he was rather obscure even in Roman times. It is quite possible that a temple existed that we have not previously heard about. Another possibility is that it burned down and was never rebuilt in a fire that destroyed much of Roman London about halfway through the 2nd century CE. Later historians may not have even been aware of the existence of an earlier temple."

"This is all very interesting Kaitlin, but how does this help us?" asked Reggie."

"It might just be possible that the Warehouse is built on the site of the missing temple" Kaitlin explained. "If that is the case, any development could be delayed for years whilst the archaeologists decided whether there was anything important that needed preserving. If the find was significant they would probably not permit any development to take place at all that could further jeopardise the site. In either scenario the developers would soon lose interest and look for riper, less problematic pickings."

There was a murmur of interest from the Rabble.

"This is all pure conjecture Kaitlin. What makes you think that the site might be here? As far as I can remember the most antiquated find we have made was Reggie's old chewed sock down the back of the sofa, courtesy of Marmaduke" asked Sinjani sceptically.

"The clue may be in the name of the Warehouse. Many modern names are corruptions of previous Saxon or Viking place names. Friggs could just be such a corruption of Frige."

"Who or what is Frige?" asked Sinjani.

"Frige was the Saxon Goddess of love" replied Kaitlin. "If there was a previous Roman name associated with Venus, the Roman Goddess of love, it's just possible that the Saxons renamed it after their own Goddess to incur her blessings. If it was just the name I would be less excited but we all felt the powerful reaction when the Sisters exercised their craft on Friday. If we add that to the evidence in the archives about all the strange goings on and hauntings, it's just possible that there is something to it. I know it all sounds a bit tenuous but surely we should try to find out a bit more?"

"How can we do that?" asked Jethro.

"We need to see if there is any access to the earlier foundations of the building" replied Kaitlin. The building this replaced was considerably lower and had three storeys. Have any of us ever contemplated raising the manhole cover in the corridor downstairs near the bottom of the spiral staircase to see what's underneath?"

"Let's do it" said Max leaping to his feet.

It was agreed that Max, Jethro and Kaitlin would go down together, partly because there were only three hard hats in the building and nobody knew what they might find when they went down. They set up a couple of powerful lights that Jethro and Max had stored away from days odd jobbing on building sites and, with the aid of a crowbar, they eventually managed to prise open the old manhole cover in a cloud of dust. There was a void about four metres deep below them and the lights revealed a floor that was covered in what looked like several centuries of dust.

The party lowered down a ladder and the three of them descended to the floor of the basement. The lights revealed a large chamber that seemed to run the whole length of the Warehouse with sturdy brick arches holding up the weight above them. Kaitlin examined the brickwork closely. Apart from a bit of patching up in a few places near the roof all the bricks and the associated lime mortar looked consistent with the original warehouse that would have been built after the Great Fire in 1669. It looked as if the top two storeys that had been rebuilt after the blitz had simply been constructed on top of the original lower storey of the 1669 building. It was quite a testament to the skill of the builders of nearly 350 years before that this part of the building had endured virtually intact.

Brushing away the dust on an area of the flooring revealed rather uninteresting terracotta coloured clay floor tiles, certainly nothing to indicate anything from Roman times. Disappointed they were about to go back up when Kaitlin suddenly raised her hand. In four places towards each corner of the chamber the bottom metre of the wall was broken by some old stonework that butted several centimetres into the chamber. The stonework was completely different to the bricks that made up the bulk of the walls and it looked like the face of it had been simply chiselled away.

Kaitlin examined the stonework closely and looked at the few centimetres at the side that had not been distressed by the chiselling. Excitedly she turned around to Jethro and Max. "I can't be 100 percent sure she said, but this stonework looks like it could have been Roman. They favoured using Kentish Ragstone for major construction projects which they could transport up the river and this is what it looks like these remnants are constructed from. If these were truly the foundations of a large Roman building this would be entirely consistent with building practices at the time. It is a very hard limestone and is extremely strong and resilient."

"Why would they have just left four small parts of the original Roman building?" asked Max. "It doesn't make sense. Why wouldn't they have used all the old building or demolished it all. Why just leave these four remnants?"

"It makes perfect sense" explained Kaitlin, "the original building, if it was a temple, may well have been circular. What the builders after the Great Fire have done is cut directly through the circular foundations leaving the stonework exposed where the circle was cut. It would have made no sense to remove the limestone as it provides considerable extra strength at no cost. Just look at the old walls, they were nearly two metres thick and the distance between them is at least thirty metres, this must have been quite a building."

"Can you prove its Roman?" asked Jethro.

"It would be hard to do so just from these walls alone" replied Kaitlin. What we really need to find is some artefacts and any that remained would be buried under this flooring. We would have to take the flooring up to see what's underneath."

"No time like the present" said Max lifting up the crowbar.

"Stop!" shouted Kaitlin. "If we are going to do this it needs to be done very carefully so that we don't run the risk of damaging anything that may lie beneath the floor tiles."

"Would the museum do it?" asked Jethro.

"We haven't enough evidence yet" said Kaitlin. "What I propose is that I ask Steve, one of the volunteers who works with me at the museum, to help me for a couple of days to see what we can uncover. If we find anything that's convincingly Roman we can then approach Dr Evans to make the find official. We will need some proper lights put up in here and it would be a great help is if we can remove all this old dust from the flooring."

That weekend the whole of the Rabble dedicated themselves to clearing the terracotta floor of the basement. Sinjani set up some strip lights along the centre of the arches and even managed to get hold of an extractor fan to clear the dust as they systematically swept and shovelled up the dust of over three centuries. Jethro borrowed an old pickup from a friend and parked it discreetly round the side by one of the fire exits in case Justin Stempson happened by. By Sunday evening the work was done and ready for Kaitlin and Steve to set to work.

They decided to clear an area near to where the centre of the old stone building would have been. This was a bit difficult to judge as the old stonework was closer together on one side than on the other. By measuring the difference in distance against the width of the warehouse Kaitlin estimated that the original diameter would have been about thirty three metres so they chose an area exactly in-between the stonework, close to the brick wall but far enough away from it to avoid any 17th century foundations.

They carefully removed about four square metres of tiling with considerable difficulty as they were laid on top of a layer of lime mortar. Underneath about four centimetres of mortar was a layer of gravel. Kaitlin and Steve gently removed the gravel making sure that there was nothing that could have been of interest. Underneath the gravel they hit a layer of soot and charcoal which they assumed may have been from the Great Fire of 1666. Underneath this layer was old debris from what may have been a wooden medieval building on the same spot.

After sifting through about fifteen centimetres of this debris which contained bits of tiling and pottery but nothing remotely Roman, they came across another layer of soot and charcoal. This was quite an exciting find as it was just possible that this could have been from the conflagration of approximately 150 CE. Very carefully they sifted through the soot and the material underneath. They had now been working patiently together on the site for nearly three days.

"Hold up" what's this exclaimed Steve. He carefully brushed away some of the finer debris to reveal a metallic object. "Kaitlin, I think it's a silver denarius!"

"Let me look" said Kaitlin excitedly. "You're right but which Emperor is on the coin?" They turned on Kaitlin's laptop and looked up Roman coinage to see if they could identify a possible date. "It's Pius, I'm sure it is, exclaimed Kaitlin. Look at the head; it's identical to this denarius recently sold at auction. Antoninus Pius was Emperor from 138 to 161 CE so that could be consistent to the date of the reported fire which we know was definitely after Hadrian's visit to Londinium. They certainly must have left in a hurry to have dropped this coin and for nobody to have picked it up."

"It's a great start" said Steve "but all it proves is that we have hit a layer of Roman debris which is not that remarkable as we know the Warehouse stands within the walls of the old Roman City."

They carefully brushed away the dirt under where the coin had been found and immediately revealed a hard surface. The hard surface was smooth and appeared to be a dark blue in colour. A bit more careful brushwork and they were staring in wonder at what were unmistakably Roman mosaics. The original Roman flooring was still intact underneath the Warehouse after nearly two millennia.

Two days later they had convinced a very cynical Dr Diane Evans to cut short a conference in York and meet them at the Warehouse site.

"This had better be good or I will have you both spending the next few months dissecting medieval dung" she said challengingly. Kaitlin and Steve escorted their supervisor down the ladder leaving an excited but somewhat apprehensive Roxie, Alexandra and Vanessa awaiting the verdict in the main room above.

Diane Evans first examined the remnants of the stone walls and it was immediately obvious to Steve and Kaitlin that they had captured her imagination. She then went over to the area of floor that had been uncovered and carefully examined the mosaics revealed. With a raised eyebrow she contemplated her wayward staff. She was not sure whether to be delighted with their skill and imagination in discovering such an extraordinary site or cross that they had started an excavation without asking her permission first. She decided on the former and burst into a wide grin.

"It's amazing, simply amazing" she exclaimed. "I can't believe that we have no record of a building of this magnitude. Initial observation would suggest that this is one of the most important Roman finds we have ever discovered in London, well done you two, really well done."

They all congregated in the main living area and discussed what would happen next over some very welcome coffee.

Roxie explained Justin Stempson's plans to Dr Evans and that the Warehouse was imminently going to be demolished and redeveloped into a high value housing scheme.

"Oh no it isn't!" said Diane Evans. "Nothing is to happen to this site until it has been properly excavated by the Museum of London. I will be making sure that there is an immediate protection order placed on this Warehouse and I will be asking Kaitlin and Steve to carefully recover the exposed mosaics and replace the flooring until we are ready to proceed."

"Will you not be able to start immediately?" asked Vanessa.

"Unfortunately we would not be able to start on a project of this magnitude for at least three years" replied Dr Evans. "All our main archaeologists are tied up supporting the excavations linked to Cross-Rail and there is no way that I would authorise anyone else to start on an excavation of this significance. I'm afraid this structure will have to remain exactly as it is until then."

"As an aside Diane, can I just ask you how you came across that extract from the works of Gaius Marcellinus? He really is a rather obscure historian" said Kaitlin.

"Oh, that really was rather strange" replied Dr Evans. "I was working late at the museum on Friday night preparing some material for the conference in York. I had to go down to the archives to photocopy some material on the construction of Viking long-ships and nearly tripped over the Marcellinus which had somehow managed to fall out of one of the flies onto the floor. I gave it a quick glance as I thought that perhaps one of my staff had pulled it out and hadn't replaced it properly. It's also a complete nightmare if something is misfiled. I am always so busy and never get the time to really catch up with you all and find out what you are working on. Anyway, I knew that you had a personal interest in Roman Londinium and it's not every day that we get a reference to a lost temple so I decided to pop it in your tray. It never remotely crossed my mind that you would be living above it. What a remarkable coincidence that turned out to be."

Alexandra and Kaitlin exchanged a knowing smile; they were not quite as surprised as Dr Evans over such a strange coincidence.

That night in the Warehouse the partying went on into the early hours. They had stopped Justin Stempson from demolishing the Warehouse and this was a justifiable cause for celebration. They had just won the opening skirmish but in their hearts they knew that the battle for the future of their little community was far from won.

9

The following evening there was a loud ringing of the bell announcing a visitor. Fixie opened the door to a very drunk Justin Stempson who tottered into the room.

"You bastards, do you know what you have done" he shouted at Fixie and Sinjani who had joined her from the kitchen area.

"Sinjani, call Roxie and the boys" said an unimpressed Fixie. As Sinjani went to buzz the others, Vanessa and Alexandra emerged from the studio to see what all the noise was about.

Roxie appeared from the staircase and saw Stempson slumped on one of the sofas obviously very much the worse for wear.

"Why Justin dear, how nice of you to pop in to see us again" said Roxie in a voice that suggested a favoured niece had just arrived. "What can we do for you this evening?"

"They're going to kill me you stupid bitch" exclaimed Stempson.

"We really wouldn't go that far" said Max who had just entered the room with Jethro close behind him.

"N n no not you" stuttered Stempson, suddenly feeling very exposed, "the bloody Albanians."

"Why would they do that dear" replied Roxie not rising to the insulting way she was being addressed.

"I owe the Albanians 150 thousand plus thirty grand interest and its due by the end of the month. I was going to clear the debt with the deposit that was promised by the developers who have now pulled out because of this stupid Roman bollocks."

"Tsk, tsk, please mind your language in front of the ladies Mr Stempson" cautioned Max.

"You don't know these people, if I don't pay them in ten days' time I will be as good as dead and I don't expect it will be a quick. These people take pleasure in causing pain. You got me into this mess; you've got to get me out of it" pleaded Stempson.

"How can we possibly do that dear" said Roxie.

"You want the Warehouse, you can have it. I don't care if I never set eyes on the fucking place again" he suddenly looked nervously at Max who was waggling a finger at him mouthing 'language'.

"Are we to take it that you are making an offer to sell the Warehouse to us?" interjected Alexandra.

"Two million and it's yours, but I need it now!"

"And if we don't come up with the money?" asked Jethro.

"Then I give the Warehouse to the Albanians and you can argue with them!" slurred Stempson, the effect of the alcohol clearly starting to tell.

"Come back tomorrow morning dear, when you have had a chance to sober up a bit and we will let you know our answer" said Roxie.

"I want your answer now" screamed Stempson in a stream of spittle.

"You're leaving" said Jethro who grabbed Stempson under one armpit and virtually lifted him out of the door slamming it behind him.

"Well that's a turn up for the book" said Roxie. "It's actually a really good offer; this place must be worth at least three million on the open market even with the protection order in place. The trouble is there is no way we can raise that sort of money."

"How much could you raise?" asked Vanessa.

"We have about 100 thousand pounds invested in the group kitty that we could draw on if we were all agreed and I have about 600 thousand in liquid assets of my own" said Roxie.

"Roxie no!" exclaimed Alexandra, "you can't spend any more of your money on this place."

"She's right" said Fixie, "we couldn't ask you to do that after all you have already done for the Rabble."

"I would be more than happy to" smiled Roxie, "but it's academic anyway as it is nowhere near enough."

The others calculated how much they had in their own savings and it amounted to another eighty-five thousand between them. They had £785,000 if they spent everything.

"It's hopeless" said Fixie, "we might as well accept it that Stempson will give this place to the Albanians."

"Can't we just make him an offer with what we've got, he's pretty desperate" observed Max.

"You are quite right, it's much more than the £150,000 he owes the Albanians but two million is still a very fair offer" said Roxie. "Just because he is desperate doesn't mean that we should deliberately extort him for our own ends. He is a very stupid and ignorant person but are we the sort of people who would exploit this? What kind of community would result if we allowed ourselves to adopt those kinds of values at its inception? No I'm sorry but integrity is worth more than bricks and mortar, I'm afraid it's hopeless."

"We've got more than enough."

Everyone looked around at Vanessa.

"What do you mean dear" said Roxie.

"I have more than enough to cover the balance" said Vanessa "accept Stempson's offer in the morning."

They all stood looking at Vanessa in disbelief.

"We can't possibly ask you to do this" said Fixie.

"You can't ask me to defend my own home?" replied Vanessa. "You all accepted me into your hearts and asked nothing in return. I have known more love from the people in this place over the last couple of weeks than I have known in all of my adult life. Unconditional love from former strangers who have shown me nothing but kindness and who have asked for nothing in return. Do you remember the woman you found on the bench that cold night by the river Kaitlin? That woman doesn't exist anymore. Are you really expecting me to allow all this to collapse for the sake of money that I don't need? What could I buy with that money that is worth more than all the love that was so freely given by the people here? I don't have any family other than the one that I have found here and I don't intend to lose it any time soon!" The last sentence was stated with the power of a woman who had recently been making split second decisions on billion dollar trades and was used to getting her way.

"Vanessa is right" said Roxie. "I think we should accept her offer, love really is the most precious thing anyone can obtain in life and she has truly found love amongst us."

In the next week the lawyers had drawn up the documents and the Warehouse belonged to newly formed 'Rabble cooperative.' There was also a very plush apartment for sale in Notting Hill. Marmaduke had treated a newly arrived Tabitha with the complete indifference that Roxie had predicted, despite a considerable amount of puffing up and hissing on Tabitha's part. In the studio at the end of the Warehouse two very close friends were adjusting to the fact that they now shared their intimate space with another person. They both recognised that for such independent women this was going to bring its own challenges but at this time they were both just living in the moment and tomorrow would have to take care of itself.

10

"You must be Vanessa" said a man who quickly introduced himself as Richard Maverley, the proprietor of the New Dimensions Gallery in Berners Street. "It's such a pleasure to meet you at last; Alexandra has told me so much about you. Since you moved in three months ago her art has been simply inspired."

Vanessa looked at a tall handsome black man of African lineage in his early thirties wearing a very smart blue three piece pinstriped suit that strangely reminded her of her time working in the City. Tonight was a very special evening for Alexandra; it was the first time that any gallery had arranged an exhibition that was specifically dedicated to her work.

"The pleasure is all mine" said Vanessa and this was not just out of politeness. Not only was this man scrumptiously sexy but he had been the first person to recognise Alexandra's true potential and he had patiently mentored her into becoming an artist of considerable renown. There was a lot of spare money sloshing about in London looking for a home and some of this was now finding its way to the New Dimensions gallery, attracted by Alexandra Okereke's growing reputation.

"Vanessa!" Alexandra ran over and hooked arms with her friend. "May I have the pleasure in escorting madam through my exhibition" she said with a good impression of someone with a plum in their mouth.

"You may" replied Vanessa falling into her part as she was escorted into the screened off part of the gallery that was dedicated to Alexandra's work. There were twenty-eight paintings and eight sculptures in the exhibition with prices ranging from £8,000 to £35,000. One painting was not for sale, this was a large painting of two women consumed in an act of passionate lovemaking, one of which showed more than a passing resemblance to Vanessa. She could already see that over half of the exhibits had already been sold and the exhibition had only been open for just over an hour. "Wow" she exclaimed, "what happened to that virtually unknown artist in painted dungarees that I met just four months ago?"

"She's still here" answered Alexandra. "If I am honest with you I find all of this a bit distasteful. I suspect that nearly all the buyers couldn't give a damn about my work; they just see it as a future investment, a way of making even more money that they don't need. Still, most of it's going to a good cause so Richard has taught me to smile like a lady and show the appropriate gratitude and servility as the great, the good and the just plain greedy sign their cheques."

What the visitors to the exhibition didn't know was that the majority of the money from the sale of Alexandra's work, after the agreed commission had been taken by the gallery, was directly supporting the refuges for women subject to violence and abuse. Alexandra's recent success had enabled her to more than replace the funding that had been cynically cut from the refuge by the local authorities and they were now even planning the start-up of a second refuge. Alexandra was never going to forget the lifeline that the refuge had provided for her when she was hurt, alone and afraid with nowhere else to go.

Vanessa had asked Alexandra why she hadn't named the trust after herself as was often the case with rich patrons. "I am trying to help protect vulnerable women not create a monument for the glory and satisfaction of my ego" she had replied testily. "Anyway, many of the people who now buy my work would probably think that we would accept much less for them if they thought the money was going towards the refuges. Most of them don't value society at all, they don't feel a part of it, but they do hold greed in high regard. It's more productive in the long run if they think that I am hoarding this wealth for my own ends and that I share their values."

Vanessa had noted with some reflection the glance that Alexandra had given to Richard when she had spoken about him; there was a lot of affection in those beautiful brown eyes. Perhaps this was not surprising after all he had done to support her but somewhere deep in Vanessa's heart was a little stab of jealousy that she noted with some surprise. She was the first person to acknowledge that love should not, and could not be possessive between free spirited souls if it was to survive. Such a love was damaging and controlling and would eventually destroy everything that was beautiful in a relationship.

The trouble was that love didn't obey the dictates of the conscious mind. Emotions have their own way of exerting their independence and of reminding a person that they follow a completely different set of rules. Love could be the most beautiful, ecstatic power in the world and also cause a person pain beyond endurance.

One week earlier the two friends had experimented with lovemaking for the first time. Once the future of the Warehouse had been secured, Alexandra had booked herself in for the corrective surgery that she so desperately hoped would restore the potential for sexual pleasure. This was the pleasure that every woman deserved as a birth right. Gently the two women had caressed each other and Vanessa had tentatively touched the rounded bud that had been restored in a newly formed fold of flesh at the top of Alexandra's now opened and healed vaginal opening. Alexandra's lips could sadly never be properly replaced so her vagina still looked rather strange and unfamiliar to Vanessa.

To their mutual delight Alexandra could feel some sensation where there had been none before and had reached a level of arousal that had caused her sex to moisten in preparation for an anticipated act of lovemaking. Disappointingly this was as far as it went and both women had realised that there was just something missing. The incredible chemistry that had spontaneously occurred when Vanessa and Sensi had first made love was just not there.

They promised to try again and did so three days later. Again the experience was pleasurable but it still failed to deliver the women the satisfaction that they were seeking. Vanessa decided to speak to Roxie about it. Roxie's reputation for sexual knowledge and her own sexual appetite were quite legendary, both within the Warehouse and within certain circles beyond its walls. Roxie, Vanessa had subsequently discovered, was an unapologetic swinger. She relished the scene and actively sought out new and stimulating sexual encounters, dragging poor Joris along in her wake!

"My dear girl, the problem that you are having is that you are confusing your emotional love of Alexandra and her mutual love of you with mutual sexual attraction" said Roxie. "These are two completely different things and the failure to recognise this causes no end of pain and confusion to the vast majority of our poor species who simply do not understand this. There is a world of difference between being in love with someone and being in lust with someone. Do you understand what I am saying here?"

"Sorry Roxie, not really" replied Vanessa apologetically.

"Well dear, let's start by taking lust out of the equation. Let's start with Tabitha."

"Tabitha! How does Tabitha fit into this?"

"What would happen if something happened to Tabitha, say she was run over or someone was deliberately cruel to her? You would feel a deep aching pain just below your sternum and you would be very upset, most likely brought to tears. Am I correct?"

"Yes of course."

"Why of course? Logically the cat is of no practical use to you; it brings in no profit and can't offer you any security. At best it sometimes deigns to show you a little affection. In fact, in coldly logical terms it is an economic parasite that just uses you to survive and you would be financially better off if you just got rid of the pesky thing. Yet you have made an emotional attachment to this creature and as such would be devastated if it came to any harm. This is the power of emotional attachment, I expect you would go to extraordinary lengths to protect Tabitha and be prepared to spend a fortune on vets' bills to make her well again."

"You know I would and you would be just the same with Marmaduke" replied Vanessa.

"Moving on, if you like someone and they have a similar affinity to you, returning your affection you may well start to develop an emotional attachment to them and this can happen surprisingly quickly. If this emotional attachment becomes strong enough and crosses a certain threshold it could be called love. Where this threshold lies has never been properly defined which makes love such a confusing and also a much abused word because everyone has their own definition. My best attempt at this is that love is present when you are prepared to make sacrifices that may cause hardship and disadvantage to yourself without thought of personal gain, in order to help and protect the other person. In the case of both Alexandra and yourself it is obvious to anyone that is close to you that you crossed that threshold many months ago so it's safe to say that you are both in love with each other."

"Part of your personal journey of self-discovery will be to understand that, by the criteria I have described, it is even possible to come to love people you have never met and even develop genuine feeling of love for the Earth on which we live so precariously. This is however a conversation for another day. So do you now understand where love comes from and the powerful hold it can have upon you? You will also note that we have not mentioned sex at all yet have we?"

"Yes I'm with you now" replied Vanessa.

"Ok my dear so now let's talk about lust which, as you know, is one of my very favourite subjects" continued Roxie. "Lust comes from a completely different part of the human psyche, it comes from the instinctive part of the brain; the animalistic mammalian part that is embedded in what Carl Jung would call our collective human unconscious. We have virtually no control over who we may fall in lust with; all we can do is to choose to ignore the powerful instinctive signals that are being produced. Every day we will meet people with whom we fall in lust with, this may even be with people who we don't even like!"

"Whether we choose it or not our bodies and our unconscious reactions to our lust will clearly communicate this reality to the other person. Just watch how a person's pupils dilate and how they will unconsciously play with their hair or become slightly flushed. We have virtually no control over any of this except in the taking of a decision not to act upon it. I find all this one of the most delicious aspects of being a human, don't you my dear?"

"I've never really thought about it in this way before. I've always kind of assumed that love and lust were two sides of the same coin" said Vanessa.

"Well my dear you really couldn't be more wrong, they are entirely different coins. Now don't misunderstand me, if you are in love and in lust with the same person the sparks will really fly because two powerful aspects of your psyche will be stimulated at the same time. If we were to be strictly accurate the emotional bonding aspect of such an experience is the lovemaking and the sexual bit is the lustmaking. See how the very language we use acts to confound us?"

"Our society is really screwed up because the difference between love and lust is simply not understood by the vast majority of people. If I come over to you and give you a big warm hug and a kiss, as we often do, I am expressing affection and emotional closeness, lust just doesn't come into the equation. I have never been sexually attracted to other women, much to my eternal regret when I consider all the fun I may have missed out on as a result."

"Oh Roxie, you are just impossible" laughed Vanessa.

"Don't knock it my dear bisexual friend! To continue, we live in a society where we cannot show any affection to each other or to the children who should be collectively loved and protected. This is because we have decided that love and affection is virtually the same thing as sexual attraction and therefore it is a dangerous thing that must be avoided. We now live in a society that collectively is almost an emotional desert and this has had terrible consequences for the state of the world that we now live in."

"Going back to yourself and Alexandra, it may sadly be the case that you are both in love but not really in lust with each other. Alexandra has had her sexuality repressed for so long now she has to rediscover what these new feelings and impulses mean and she is probably very confused. She may just need a little time and patience before she knows how she truly feels. What really hurts is when you are in love and lust with someone but they are not in lust with you. This can cause a lot of difficulty because lust is a powerful force and it can turn in on a person if it has no outlet."

"Many people also fall in lust with each other only to later discover that they have never actually been in love at all. Many relationships and even marriages start simply because there is a very powerful mutual lust. Unfortunately lust has a tendency to wane once it has been fully satiated and if there is no enduring love in a relationship to hold it together such a relationship is likely to fail. It is also surprisingly common for people to forge relationships based purely on a perfectly rational intellectual decision on the prospects for mutual security and material benefits. Such a practical relationship may require little emotion and no lust at all but I am now straying from my main point so I will also leave that discussion for another day."

"Owing to the unavoidable fact, as previously stated, that in the vast majority of cases mutual lust wanes over time, I would personally recommend anyone embedded in a loving long term relationship should give swinging a go" continued Roxie mischievously. "The reason that people get so upset and angry about affairs is the associated breach of trust which is very much linked to the emotional bonds they have made. A breach of trust is seen as a breach of love and also may create strong feelings of insecurity in the partner who may fear that lust will draw their partner away."

"Our minds are having sexual affairs all the time whether we like it or not and we have no control over this no matter how much we try to repress it. It is a great shame to see so many loving relationships end because one or other partner has finally given in to the demands of lust. It's far better to explore the excitement of sharing new lusts together and as an added bonus it often brings new zing to a previously lacklustre love life!"

"Oh Roxie, I fear the world is not truly ready for such wisdom" said Vanessa.

"True my dear girl, so very true. Has our little chat helped at all?"

Vanessa replied by initiating one of their big hugs and kisses.

It was in the context of this conversation that Vanessa noted Alexandra's body language whenever Richard was near to her and it was slowly dawning on Vanessa that Alexandra was showing every sign of being in lust with him. Part of her was overjoyed at seeing her friend's sexuality blossoming after all that had been done to her, but another part was wrestling with the implications about what this might mean to their relationship.

"Alexandra!" Richard called out from across the gallery. The two friends, still arm in arm walked over to Richard and a lady who was conspicuously covered in the sort of sophisticated bling that would make any insurance assessor break out in a cold sweat. They were standing in front of the painting of the two women locked in sexual embrace that was not for sale.

"Lady Fullerton is absolutely captivated by this painting and wishes you to reconsider your decision not to sell it. I have explained that you are unlikely to change your mind but she insisted on talking to you herself" said Richard.

"It's absolutely captivating" purred Lady Fullerton, "I have never seen a painting that so powerfully conveyed such passion and yet at the same time such beautiful feminine intimacy. Name your price, I simply must have it."

Alexandra forced the smile that Richard had painstakingly trained her to produce with prospective customers, "I'm afraid Richard's absolutely correct Lady Fullerton; this painting is not for sale. Anyway it's out of my hands as I no longer own this painting."

Both Richard and Vanessa were taken aback by this. Alexandra was a force of nature when she had made up her mind about something. She had told both of them that she would never sell that painting and yet here she was standing in front of them directly contradicting herself.

"Well who is the new owner" exclaimed Lady Fullerton, "perhaps I could persuade them to part with it if the price is right? Do tell me."

"Yes do tell us" said Richard quizzically with a raised eyebrow.

"Why the picture belongs to Vanessa here of course" smiled Alexandra putting her arm across Vanessa's shoulder, "it could never truly belong to anyone else."

Vanessa looked at Alexandra with tears glistening in her eyes. This was the moment captured in paint that had completely changed her life. Alexandra was right; it would never mean so much to anyone else.

"How much would you take for the picture?" enquired Lady Fullerton, "name your price, you will find I have very deep pockets if I really want something."

Vanessa could not supress the laugh that burst out from between her lips, much to Lady Fullerton's surprise and obvious distaste.

Vanessa composed herself and then politely replied "Well Lady Fullerton, I am sorry to have to tell you that I will never sell this painting. I will however offer you something which I believe is of far more value to you; some advice. Beyond a certain quantity, and I'm sure you would consider it to be a surprisingly low quantity, money is utterly worthless, indeed it is positively harmful. Understanding the truth of this would be an opportunity for you to discover riches beyond your wildest imagination. I'm afraid I have to tell you that you have nothing of any real value to offer me for this painting." With that she calmly walked away to look at some of the other paintings leaving behind a completely bemused Lady Fullerton and a gallery proprietor who was grinning from ear to ear.

11

"Beautiful" the comment came from a familiar sounding deep feminine voice from behind Vanessa. Vanessa was contemplating a picture of a curvaceous naked woman with extraordinarily wide hips, standing under a waterfall like some fertility goddess, her arms held above her head with an expression of blissful happiness on her face. She turned to see Cyrene, the High Priestess from the sisters looking directly at her.

"Hello Cyrene, I didn't know you were coming tonight. It is a wonderfully sensuous picture isn't it? The beauty of nature expressed in the waterfall washing over the essential beauty of womanhood" replied Vanessa.

"I wasn't talking about the picture" said Cyrene, "but I was appreciating the beauty of womanhood."

Vanessa blushed slightly at the compliment but was also pleasantly flattered at the sudden attention from this mystical lady who closely matched Vanessa's vision of what a Celtic priestess from pagan times might have looked like. She still remembered that long leg appearing at the top of Alexandra's staircase followed by the voluptuous figure, the swell of the breasts under the silk robe and the long straight dark brown hair. She remembered how the same green eyes that now unashamedly appraised Vanessa had first weighed up her character and her fitness to be drawn into the mysteries of the sisterhood. She also found herself with familiar feelings of arousal that had been her frequent companion since she had started living at the Warehouse.

"The woman and the waterfall in the picture are part of the same divine whole, we are all a part of greater nature" continued Cyrene. "Water and earth are the two female elements, air and fire being the male elements. Without the air and the sun, the latent possibility of nature cannot be realised. Without earth and water all that is left is gas and fire that scorches and destroys everything in its path. Power has to be harnessed and brought into the service of nature if it is to be turned from a destructive to a creative force."

"It is the Goddess, the great Earth mother that delivers life but men fear being tamed by the power of the Goddess and rage against her. It is this rage exercised through violence and oppression that is channelled towards women the world over. A third of all our sisters across the world are subject to abuse and physical violence yet, although they seek to deny her, the Goddess also lies within the breast of every man. If they continue to forcefully deny her nature and wisdom our male dominated global societies will follow the path to self-destruction and take most of the Earth's other precious life with them."

"That's quite a statement to make over one picture" remarked Vanessa.

"It's quite a world we live in" replied Cyrene. "By the way, I wanted to thank you and the rest of the Rabble for allowing the sisters to use the basement at the Warehouse, at least until the excavation starts. There really is the most extraordinary energy down there, quite unlike anywhere else we have known. Now that we better understand the origins and nature of the energy that we accidentally tapped into the first time, we take suitable measures to control and channel it more effectively."

"It's genuinely our pleasure" said Vanessa, "the Sisters didn't have to help us when you gathered to help defend the Warehouse. You did it through kindness and it has just given us an opportunity to pass some of that kindness back. What are you focusing on now when you gather for your work?"

"If we have a sister who needs help for herself or healing for a friend or relative who is in distress it will be a priority for our work" said Cyrene. "Our primary overarching work is to try to focus on healing the Earth and protecting nature from the terrible harm caused by human ignorance. We know we may have very little effect against the commercial vested interests and human greed that rages against the harmony of the natural world, but we feel an obligation to try. As you discovered at the Warehouse, we often don't know what effect our work may have or what dynamic it may create. Sometimes a seemingly insignificant change, perhaps the projection of love and calmness when there is anger and disharmony in the community around us, may ultimately have a dramatic impact in the long term. Even a slight influence upon a developing change of events can ultimately lead to a completely different outcome."

"You mean an influence like the mysterious way that an obscure file found its way into the hands of Dr Diane Evans, at exactly the same time that the Sisters were meeting in the Warehouse" observed Vanessa with a knowing wink. "That small, seemingly unrelated incident, ultimately led to the Warehouse community being saved."

"Yes we hope for something like that to happen although we can never truly predict the outcome of our work. Just about anything that happens can also be put down to coincidence which helps to keep the cynics happy. This is very useful as it helps stop people prying too deeply into our work. Wicca works far better in the shadows than in the glare of unwelcome publicity. I think Alexandra may have already told you that we call such coincidences synchronicity. For dedicated practitioners of Wicca these strange coincidences become increasingly frequent as they develop their abilities. That is why it is so important to practice the Craft in a state of inner harmony and with positive intent. Now it's my turn to enquire what you are focusing on Vanessa. What are you planning to do with your life now that you have joined the community at the Warehouse?"

"I can't answer that, I don't think I have ever felt so unfocused," replied Vanessa. "It's almost as if I am adrift on a large sea with no idea which direction the shore lies or what I might find when I get there."

"The distant shore lies within you but the barriers put up by your conscious mind are preventing you from journeying there" said Cyrene. "To reach your destination you will need to start to trust the instincts and emotions that reside in your unconscious but your human ego presents a formidable obstacle and there is no easy way to accomplish this. You will almost certainly need a guide to help you."

"Could you perhaps be this guide?"

"You have a long way to go on your journey before I can reach you. You are a very logical and rational person Vanessa and you have spent a lot of time in a business world where love, compassion and trust are most often treated with derision and as evidence of human weakness. It is this warped and twisted philosophy that is corrupting and destroying everything of value in the world. It creates an almost impenetrable barrier to attaining the most valuable thing any human can possess."

"What is it that is the most valuable thing in the world?" asked Vanessa.

"Self-realisation" replied Cyrene.

"This is the destination of the inner journey you have talked about?"

"Yes"

"How will I find my guide?" asked Vanessa.

"I have a feeling that your guide will find you when you are ready for the next step on your journey. What are you doing about eating tonight?"

Vanessa was taken off guard by the sudden change in direction of their conversation.

"I hadn't really thought about it" she replied, "I was going to see what Alexandra was planning to do."

"I think Alexandra is going to busy for quite a while yet" observed Cyrene.

Vanessa looked over to see Alexandra laughing with a group of people and she also observed that Richard had placed a protective arm around her shoulder. At that moment Alexandra rolled her head unconsciously but completely naturally against Richard's arm demonstrating that she was completely comfortable with the intimacy and familiarity of the gesture. Once again Vanessa felt a small pang of jealousy at the affection that Alexandra was showing to this charismatic man. There was no doubt in her mind that Alexandra was succumbing to Richard's attention and the way that he looked at her with such evident pride and affection showed that the feeling was entirely mutual.

Vanessa went over to Alexandra when there was a break in the conversation.

"I hope you don't mind but Cyrene and I were thinking of sloping off to get something to eat" she said.

Alexandra looked at her friend with a sudden feeling of guilt. She had for a moment forgotten that Vanessa was there. She had been completely captivated by the attention that her work was receiving and, she suddenly realised, the attention she was receiving from Richard.

Vanessa kissed Alexandra gently, the look in her eyes communicating the conflict of emotions that had been going on within her, the kiss sending the message that she understood what was happening between Alexandra and Richard and it was going to be ok. Alexandra looked back at Vanessa with an expression of love and gratitude. Both women accepted without the need for further words that there was an inevitable dynamic underway that would permanently change the direction and nature of their relationship.

"Be warned," whispered Alexandra in parting, "I think Cyrene is trying to seduce you."

"Oh I do hope so" whispered Vanessa back, parting with a conspiratorial wink.

Later that evening Alexandra found herself back at Richard's maisonette in Fulham. They had eaten an intimate meal at a small gem of a Greek restaurant that Richard discovered near the gallery. Neither of them wanted the meal to end but they realised that they could no longer avoid the increasingly less subtle signs conveyed by the host that it was time for them to move on.

"Would you like to come back for a coffee" asked Richard tentatively.

"I would love to" replied Alexandra, not wanting the evening to end but equally feeling a sense of trepidation.

They had taken a taxi back to Richard's and they had gone into Richard's kitchen so that he could prime his Italian coffee machine. As he turned away from the machine Alexandra was directly in front of him and without further comment she put her arms around him and kissed him passionately on the lips. Richard responded, revealing all the pent up desire and affection that had been building within him over the months he had spent with this extraordinary and beautiful lady.

They went into his bedroom and Richard gently put his hands behind her neck and untied the bow that held up the flamboyant halter neck evening dress that she had been wearing at the gallery. Her firm rounded breasts had not needed any additional support. They dropped slightly under the demands of gravity as they were released from the dress's embrace then gently bounced and parted beneath his gaze, the nipples already hard with her arousal.

Alexandra undressed Richard, revealing to her for the first time his toned muscular body. His maleness was already protesting against the strain of his Calvin Klein boxer's. Alexandra let out a small gasp as she released it from its captivity and it lay throbbing in the palm of her hand.

"Richard, I'm frightened" she said, "I don't know how I'm going to respond, this is the first time in my life I've ever really wanted to be intimate with a man. I'm also afraid that you will be repulsed when you see what has been done to me." Richard was aware of Alexandra's past and her operation and had been sympathetic when an important commission had to be delayed owing to her physical and emotional recovery from the procedure. Alexandra realised it was quite another thing to openly reveal her most intimate parts to the scrutiny of Richard's gaze.

Instinctively she covered herself protectively with her hand as he gently slipped her knickers down her legs. Richard had been trying, and miserably failing in his attempts, not to overtly notice Alexandra's beautiful long slender legs since the very first time they had met.

Richard laid Alexandra back on the bed and gently but insistently removed her hand to look at her. His eyes glistened in hurt and anger as he saw what had been done to her and a great affection welled up inside him. Nobody was ever going to hurt this beautiful woman again, not while he was alive to prevent it.

He lay beside her and they kissed and embraced, both exploring the new delights of the body next to them. Nature took over the dynamic that was increasing between them and Alexandra rolled Richard on his back and she straddled him, gently slipping his engorged manhood between lips that were already wet in anticipation.

She gasped with an initial stab of pain and shock as his fullness penetrated her. She paused and looked down at Richard who smiled in encouragement. This was so different from the attempted forced penetration that had happened when her drunken husband had tried to violate her all those years ago. The pain subsided as she relaxed and slowly she started to rock backwards and forward upon him, savouring the sensations that were beginning to well up inside. The pace of her movements increased as she abandoned herself to the insistence of her own body and Richard's body responded instinctively to her increasing passion. The sensation continued to build until; with a cry of release Alexandra had her first ever climax. Moments later Richard also erupted deep within her.

Alexandra collapsed into Richard's arms and lay there relishing his warm protective embrace. So this is what she had been missing for all these years. She looked at Richard's face and the love that was shining for her from his eyes and knew that her life would never be the same again. She started to gently cry, her head resting on Richard's powerful chest. She was not crying for herself, she was crying for the millions of women in the world who had been deliberately hurt and mutilated to ensure that they would never be able to experience such joy.

Three miles away on another bed Vanessa gripped the headboard above her head and groaned in ecstasy as Cyrene's tongue dipped once again into her most intimate crevice.

12

Vanessa and Alexandra met up at the Warehouse late the following morning. They sat facing each other on Alexandra's bed having been armed with fresh mugs of coffee by an irrepressible Roxie. Roxie was simply bursting to know what had gone on the previous night. She couldn't help notice that the two women had arrived back separately and that they were still wearing the same evening clothes that they had departed in the night before. Fortunately she was sensitive enough to the situation to know that this was not the right moment to have her questions answered.

Alexandra told Vanessa about the previous evening and how special Richard had made her feel and Vanessa told Alexandra that she had allowed Cyrene to successfully seduce her which made them both laugh.

"I'm going to move into Heiner's old apartment downstairs" said Vanessa. She raised her hand as Alexandra started to protest. "You are showing severe symptoms of being in love and there will be no room for a third party to be hanging around while you and Richard discover how you really feel about each other. It's wonderful Alexandra, celebrate the passion, relish it. I love you but I think we have both come to realise that the love that has developed between us is more like the love of sisters than that of lovers. I am not even going to try to compete with Richard to be the centre of your world."

Alexandra admitted that she felt the truth in what Vanessa had said and over the next couple of days she helped her friend move into the spare apartment. Tabitha had already technically moved out some weeks before as she had decided to adopt Marmaduke rather than hiss at him and they were often found curled up together at Roxie's. Vanessa still spent quite a bit of time with Alexandra in her studio as Alexandra was determined to maintain her independence from Richard, at least for the immediate future.

Vanessa had watched with a sense of joy the evolution of Alexandra's painting of the horned God Cernunnos. This was the first male figure Alexandra had painted without wanting to tear it up in frustration. She wondered wistfully, as she looked at the developed musculature and suggestion of restrained power within the pagan figure, just how much Richard had been an inspiration. She had yet to see him out of his business suits. Alexandra had taken a different fork in the path of life that was inevitably drawing her away from Vanessa. Vanessa knew she too had to set out on her own path but she had no idea where this might take her. She had no sense of direction, let alone destination.

This suddenly changed when Sensi turned up at the Warehouse completely unannounced. She had been in Germany visiting a community down near the Black Forest and had stopped over in London to visit her cousin at the woman's refuge and catch up with her friends at the Warehouse. As soon as Vanessa and Sensi caught sight of each other the embers of their previous passion burst into a ferocious fire and it was several hours before they re-joined the Rabble to chat and celebrate Sensi's visit. Both Sensi and Vanessa realised that their relationship was probably based more on mutual respect and lust rather than emotion but they relished it nonetheless.

The following morning, having temporarily satiated her sexual passion, a more subdued Vanessa told Sensi how she was feeling. She felt loved and contented at the Warehouse but she still didn't feel that she had a sense of purpose and this was making her restless. The energy and fierce intelligence that Vanessa had employed to make her so successful in the City were still present and needed to be harnessed and re-directed.

"That's one of the main reasons I stopped over in London" said Sensi. "I wanted to invite you to come to visit us in Consciência. I think moving to a completely different environment may help you to find yourself and I also have another reason for asking you over."

"What's that?" asked a genuinely intrigued Vanessa.

"Our community is now part of a small but growing global network of people who want to build a different world and this increasingly requires joint financing and international cooperation" replied Sensi. We are also heavily investing in other local communities in Peru who like what we do. These communities are also keen to develop alternative models but they need our assistance in order to develop. We are struggling to find the experience and expertise to effectively manage our investments. We want to ensure that we invest ethically but equally we have to invest sustainably to meet our vision for a long term future. I thought with all your experience that you might be prepared to help. Will you come?"

"I don't know why you thought of me" exclaimed Vanessa, "I can't look back on any of my investment banking decisions and consider that they were ethical. On reflection most of the activity I saw and participated in was harmful rather than beneficial. Rather than being an asset to the world, the City acts like a huge leech that sucks the lifeblood out of societies for the benefit of a tiny global minority. I was just another player helping to pick over the bones."

"Exactly" exclaimed Sensi triumphantly "and Roxie is in full agreement with me."

"Have you two been conspiring again" admonished Vanessa.

"Of course!"

"I still don't understand."

"Roxie told me of this quaint English expression that you may have heard of. She said that you could be our poacher turned gamekeeper. Do you understand now?"

Vanessa reflected on what they were saying. It was true that she knew her way about the investment market as well as anyone and it was an attractive thought to be able to use her skills in a new way.

"Anyway it would be an adventure for you, and you will also get to see a lot more of me" said Sensi with a deliberately naughty expression.

"What the heck, why not!" said Vanessa in capitulation. She looked again at this remarkable young woman with the olive skin and the long black hair who was sat before her. They had the familiarity of lovers who had shared every sort of intimacy and yet she realised that she knew virtually nothing about Sensi. She did know that despite her relative youth, Sensi had a depth of wisdom that Vanessa could not even begin to comprehend.

Three months later Vanessa was walking through the arrivals gate at Lima airport. She quickly noticed a strangely familiar looking and rather handsome young man holding up a sign with her name on it. He waved at her, a big friendly smile of greeting on his face.

"Hi I'm Raul" beamed the young man. "I'm Sensi's brother and I have come to take you to Consciência. I have strict instructions from my big sister to show you as much as I can of the beauty of our wonderful country on the way. I am your dedicated guide and you are to consider me your humble servant." Vanessa was being whisked away to begin a whole new adventure in Peru.

She had no comprehension at the time that eighteen months later she would have a resident's Visa and be talking to a young English woman called Jessica about the importance of finding meaning and purpose in her life.

Part 4 – Consciência

1

"Wow," said Jessica "that was an amazing story but there is still so much I wish to know. What is it about Consciência that has made you stay and how have you used your skills to help them? What are the long term goals and values that you talked about?"

"Such is the nature of young people. No matter how much information you give to them they always seem to end up with yet more questions" chuckled Vanessa. "Before we talk anymore about such things I think that you need to know how Consciência came into existence and the ethos behind it. I also think that you have heard more than enough of my voice but luckily I have found a volunteer who seemed remarkably enthusiastic to tell you a bit more about our community. You will find this kind person at the taverna by the Kapok tree where we ate the other evening at 7 oclock."

"How will I recognise them?" asked Jessica.

"I'm sure that won't be a problem" smiled Vanessa, "it's a small village."

That evening Jessica wandered over towards the taverna and saw a familiar figure waving at her. She felt her heart leap at the sight of Raul once again.

"Tonight we eat, drink and make merry" said Raul "and tomorrow morning I shall take you for a walk and explain how Consciência came into being."

The following morning Jessica was sitting on a rug with Raul on a vantage point on top of an outcrop of rocks that overlooked the community.

"The story of Consciência begins nearly thirty years ago with the crash of a small light aircraft further up the valley, near the ruins where you camped with Sensi on your way here" said Raul.

Jessica wondered just how much Sensi had told Raul about what had taken place at the ruins but decided against interrupting him.

"There were two men in the plane. The pilot was killed outright and the passenger was badly injured and severely concussed. They were found by a young woman who lived mostly alone on what you would call a smallholding near the top of the valley. This woman was a shaman and healer, qualities that she had inherited from her own mother, what we would call a curandera. The name given to her by her mother was Iluminada but she liked to be called Lumi. She would also one day become Sensi's and my mother. You may have already noticed that Sensi has also inherited the same intuition and aptitude for natural magic as her mother. For some reason it only seems to run on the female side of the family. As far as I can tell, I seem to have no particular sensitivity at all although I share their love and passion for nature."

"Why was she living on her own?" asked Jessica.

"The Catholic Priest in the nearest town had condemned the practices of my mother as the 'work of the devil' and many of the community felt obliged to publically shun her. Rather than put up with this ignorance and bigotry she decided to move away and find peace with the world of nature near the ruins of her ancestors. Secretly many of the villagers would still come to my mother for advice and guidance and she would always find time to listen to their problems and assist them in any way she could. The Christian fanatics never truly succeeded in destroying our pagan ancestry although thousands were tortured and put to death in their efforts to do so. At least this intolerance and ignorance is now largely channelled by the use of words and no longer by the hot irons and flames of the inquisition. Many of my own ancestors were not so fortunate."

"Sensi said that they used to practice human sacrifice here. That doesn't sound any better than the worst the Christians got up to" challenged Jessica.

"Both Christianity and the religion practiced by the ancient society that left the ruins were patriarchal religions" replied Raul. "Religion was largely about the strict control and manipulation of the population. The God worshipped by the old civilisation was an angry vengeful God just like the Christian Abrahamic God. Both demanded unconditional worship or terrible retribution would be meted out and both were specifically intended to create fear in the population. Both religions also had a class of religious leaders who were supposed to interpret and intercede with God on behalf of a supposedly ignorant population. In both religions the religious class worked hand in glove with secular leaders who liked to assume God's mantel in practice, if not in name, for their own political ends. My mother's craft comes from a completely different tradition; it is a religion that seeks to be at one with the natural world, its followers seek to live in harmony with the great Earth mother who nurtures all life. It is a religion of respect and love for all living things including each other."

"I thought the Christian God was also supposed to be a God of love?" said Jessica.

"Have you ever read the Bible, and in particular the Old Testament?" teased Raul.

"Not as such" admitted a slightly chastened Jessica.

"I thought not. Read it first and then come back and tell me all about your God of love. In the meantime shall I continue with the story?"

"Please, I'm sorry to have interrupted" said Jessica.

"Don't apologise, the questions were good" said Raul with sincerity.

Raul went on to explain how his mother was determined to try to save the life of the man from the plane. The man was far too ill to be moved far and there was no road in the valley in those days, only a poorly defined path. She managed to pull him clear of the wreckage, years of surviving alone on her smallholding and off the fruits of the jungle around her had made his mother much stronger than her small frame would suggest. With the help of some branches, some creepers and some large palm leaves she constructed a crude travois frame and managed to drag him back to her home. She reset a dislocated shoulder and wrist and splinted his forearm where the bone had been broken. The man was barely lucid when he started to recover from the concussion and he had also contracted a fever. On several occasions he had to be physically held down to prevent him harming himself when crying out in his sleep. Lumi also created herbal medicines that aided the healing of bruised organs that had been so violently shaken in the crash.

When he had sufficiently recovered the man struggled to explain that his name was Owen Rogerson and that he was an industrialist from Boston in the United States. Lumi had virtually no English; her first language was a Panoan dialect although she was also fluent in Spanish. Owen Rogerson's Spanish was fairly rudimentary but somehow, with patience, they eventually managed to understand each other. He explained that he had been looking at the possibility of opening up a manufacturing facility in Peru or Ecuador as he could get much cheaper labour in South America and he could therefore undercut his competition and make more profit. He had chartered a plane and pilot to fly him from Quito to Lima when the plane had split an oil line and crashed into the valley where Lumi had found him.

During his fever Owen had experienced a terrible recurring dream. He was wandering through a magnificent large building with beautiful Greek style pillars and marbled flooring, the white light reflected by the flawless stonework almost dazzling his eyes. At the centre of the building was a large reception hall with a huge dome high above. As he continued to walk through the halls and galleries he suddenly started to notice a few cracks and blemishes appear. At first he thought he must have just missed them but the cracks started to get more frequent and wider and the staining got worse until he found himself walking through a gigantic filthy ruin. As he returned to the centre of the building he looked up at the dome which started to crumble before his eyes and as the masonry plummeted down upon him he would awake crying out, trembling through a combination of his fear and his fever.

One night he was immersed in his dream when a beautiful young woman approached him as he returned towards his inevitable destiny with the crumbling dome.

"Why have you chosen to walk through these ruins?" she asked him.

"When I entered this building, it was magnificent" he replied "I did not choose to wander through these ruins but I can't find my way out again."

"Didn't you know that all things made by the hand of man inevitably decay? Even the things that man holds most precious rapidly lose their lustre.

Attachment to such things causes terrible suffering" she replied. "Come to me." The girl spread her arms in an offering to embrace him.

As he walked towards the girl the ruins and the girl faded and he found himself wandering naked and alone through a beautiful meadow surrounded by waving grasses and wild flowers. He had never felt so at peace before. He heard the girl's whispering voice repeating in the gentle breeze "rejoice now you are whole again" and as he slowly regained his senses his fever had broken.

"How do you know so much about this man and his dreams?" asked Jessica.

"He told me about it."

"You have met him? Is he still here?" she asked.

"Yes I have met him but do you really want me to ruin the story for you by telling you how?"

"No don't! Please continue" said Jessica eagerly.

Raul went on to explain that in the weeks that it took for him to heal he fell increasingly under the spell of the gentle young woman who looked after him. He noticed that she had a great affinity for the wild animals who showed no fear around her and some of which would let her feed them from her hand. Sometimes he would find her sat by a fire in a trance like state, occasionally speaking Panoan words that he didn't understand. He was somehow sure that she was aware of his presence but this did not seem to disturb her in the least. On two occasions he was sure that he heard the growl of a Jaguar just outside the dwelling and Lumi's voice gently greeting the animal but when he went to look, all he could see was a large shape disappearing into the shadows of the trees.

"He doesn't trust strangers and in particularly he doesn't trust men" said Lumi. "I think he is very wise."

"I wouldn't do anything to harm him" said Owen.

"People like you are destroying his world" said Lumi without hostility. "You care only for money and power and take no responsibility for destroying the priceless creations of the Earth Mother. You will lead our world to ruin and she will not forgive you for your ignorance. The Jaguar is wise to stay away from you."

"If you feel that way about me, why have you spent so much time helping me to get better?" asked Owen.

"I have chosen the path of the healer and it is not for me to judge your future actions. You must take responsibility for your own life. Perhaps one day you may come to see the world differently if you choose to reflect upon your recent experience. Now come and sit by the fire and try this stew I have prepared for you, it will make you feel stronger."

After eight weeks Owen felt strong enough to travel with Lumi back to the nearest town where there was a telephone. He noticed how some of the people crossed the street when they saw Lumi coming and he found himself increasingly angry at such ignorance. Lumi was probably the kindest and most beautiful person he had known. He looked at her again and probably for the first time realised just how physically beautiful she really was.

"Don't judge them too harshly" said Lumi gently, "people fear what they do not understand. The priests tell them that if they turn back to the old ways their souls will be damned for an eternity. Is it any wonder that some of them choose to look the other way? The priests are starting to lose their influence over some of the people. An increasing number are turning back to nature to seek answers and despite all the hostility and threats and I have many more visitors than I used to. Now I must leave as you need my help no longer."

"I know I can never repay you for your kindness" said Owen "but please accept this small token of appreciation." He pulled out the equivalent of 600 US dollars' worth of Peruvian sols from his wallet and offered these to her.

"I see I have healed your body but not your spirit" said Lumi calmly. "If you want to repay me I ask you to reflect on why the Jaguar runs into the shadows when you are near." With that she turned away from him and walked back up the path without a backward glance.

Owen returned to his company in the US to find that his position on the Board had already been replaced as they had assumed him to be dead. With some embarrassment from the rest of the Board they returned him to his Vice President of Operations role and within a few months he had almost forgotten about the crash and his time in the jungle. One night he was working very late in the office looking at some disappointing production figures. The company's competitors in Japan were producing rival products at virtually half the price. He knew that if he didn't improve the productivity in the manufacturing of this product range, the company would have to issue a profits warning and this would impact badly on the share price.

His eyes blurred as he tried to take in the figures and he unwittingly fell asleep, slumped over his desk. For the first time since his fever broke after the accident he had the recurring nightmare of walking through the ruins but this time he saw Lumi instead of the girl as he returned to his fate in the domed hall. "Why have you chosen to be walking again in these ruins?" she asked him. "I can't find my way out" he replied in desperation. "I have shown you the way" replied Lumi "yet still you choose to walk in these ruins?"

Owen awoke with a start. He finally understood what the nightmare was trying to tell him. Nothing that he was doing was going to last. His company and thousands like it were consuming the Earth's resources at an alarming rate. Their products, like the products of their competitors, were deliberately designed to become obsolete and to be replaced by new offerings to wet the insatiable appetites of consumers. Was this what he really wanted for his life? Did he really want to look back on his life knowing that his primary achievement was that he had maintained the company share price? Did he really want to work sixty hours a week just to pour yet more profits into the hands of wealthy capitalists, capitalists just like him who didn't even need the money anyway? Could he really continue to close his eyes whilst the precious Earth was irreplaceably damaged for such a feeble reason? In fifty years' time would there be any wilderness left for the few remaining Jaguars to run to and hide? He thought of his time with Lumi and realised that he had never felt more awake than he had been in that small dwelling nestled at the edge of the Peruvian rainforest.

Owen was not a naïve idealist however. He knew that the people of the world couldn't and wouldn't go back to the days of living off the land and that the tide of technological advance could not be stemmed. Was it even right to attempt to do so? There must be a way for humanity and nature to live symbiotically in harmony with each other? Intuitively he felt that if there was an answer, he would find it back in that valley in Peru in the foothills of the Andes. He also realised for the first time that he had truly fallen in love with Lumi, the bewitching curandera who had nurtured him back to health and who now called out to him even in his dreams.

"That is how my father came to settle in the valley and how the community of Consciência began" said Raul.

"Owen Rogerson was your father!" exclaimed Jessica.

"He is my father, he is very much alive and has told me how much he is looking forward to meeting you" said Raul, "but before you meet Owen I must take you to meet Lumi. Lumi is the spiritual custodian of our community and she is interested to meet the girl that so captured the imagination of our friends in England that they have shipped her 6,000 miles to visit us."

Jessica was rather alarmed at the prospect of meeting Lumi. She still had no real understanding why Roxie and Ellen had placed so much faith in her and what was really expected from her. She felt like a bit of a fraud. She was genuinely worried that Lumi would see through her façade of false confidence and would be disappointed with what she saw underneath.

"When Lumi is not called to sit on Consciência's Community Council, or tend to someone who needs her help, she is still to be found in the smallholding where she nursed my father at the top of the valley" continued Raul. "She values her solitude and likes to spend time immersed in collecting her plants and being close to the animals and natural spirits of the forest. Owen has to spend much of his time in the main village when he is not away on business but please don't misunderstand this. Owen is only ever truly content when he is at Lumi's side and he will sometimes shut himself away with her for days on end to escape from the outside world. Come; let me take you to meet my mother."

2

Jessica and Raul strolled back into the village and picked up one of the electric buggies. Raul wanted to encourage Jessica to get used to using the vehicles so she happily took the wheel. They travelled back up the same road that she had originally travelled down when she had first arrived at Consciência with Sensi. Just past the last of the farms Raul directed Jessica to pull into a small parking space at the side of the road. They had left the metalled surface half a kilometre behind and the road had now become little more than a dirt track. Next to the parking space was a small path that disappeared between the trees. They followed this path for about three kilometres until they came to a small clearing where there was a modest mud brick house and a large garden planted out with vegetables and herbs with an orchard behind. There was also an array of solar panels which seemed rather out of place in such a remote rural location.

Raul called out in Spanish and was answered by a woman's voice in the distance from within the forest. A few minutes later a woman entered the clearing carrying a weaved reed basket full of different plants and fruits. Her similarity to Sensi was startling and it was immediately apparent where Sensi had inherited her beauty from. Although her complexion revealed a lifetime of living outside in the elements and she must have been well into her fifties, she was still a very striking woman. She was wearing what looked like loose fitting light brown dungarees and she immediately broke into a smile and waved on seeing Raul and Jessica. As she approached her expression changed, she frowned and started to waggle her finger at Raul whilst lambasting him in Spanish. Raul just smiled happily as he was verbally chastised by this feisty woman.

When the woman, who Jessica fully realised by now must be Lumi, had finally stopped chastising Raul he turned to Jessica. He said "Jessica, this is my mother Lumi. She was just reminding me how worthless I was, how I so seldom come out here to see her, and how I would try the love and patience of any mother."

"Jessica, how lovely to meet you" said Lumi in perfect English with just the slightest tinge of a North American accent which Jessica suspected might be through Owen's tutoring influence. She went up to Jessica, kissed her on each cheek, linked arms and whisked her into her home. They entered a room which looked to all purposes like a spacious kitchen. There were a large number of clay and ceramic containers as well as many modern equivalents, a huge wooden table and a wood burning stove for cooking. To Jessica's amazement there was also an iPad on the table.

Lumi smiled as she saw Jessica's expression. "I suspect that my two lovely children have given you the impression that I was some kind of eccentric animal skin wearing magic woman cut off from all civilisation. If I didn't have this link to the antenna in the village and Skype I wouldn't hear from them for months on end" this was accompanied by another sharp look at Raul who raised his eyes in mock exasperation as his verbal chastisement continued.

"If you didn't want us to go out into the world you shouldn't have packed us both off to university" he said rather unconvincingly in response. Despite this exchange it was obvious to Jessica that Raul absolutely adored his mother and she sensed that the feeling was entirely mutual.

"Come over here Jessica and sit down. I have a drink that I make from honey that you might enjoy." She poured the drink into three beakers and joined Jessica and Raul at the table. Jessica sipped the drink and found it delightful; it tasted rather liked honeyed blueberries.

Jessica found Lumi looking at her with the same strange intensity that she had experienced when she had first met Sensi. Despite her initial fears of meeting Lumi she felt no sense of intimidation under Lumi's gaze, instead she suddenly had the strangest feeling of déjà vu. It almost felt as if she had met this woman before although she knew that this couldn't possibly have happened in this lifetime.

"Sensi has told me that you are looking for a new sense of purpose and direction in your life and she feels that I may be able to help you" said Lumi. "Do you have any idea on what the purpose of your life might be?"

"Roxie and Ellen told me that the secret of life is love but they said I had to discover what this meant" replied Jessica. "Sensi also told me on our journey to Consciência that the secret of life could only be revealed through an internal journey but that this was virtually impossible to take directly as it had to be experienced rather than understood. She said that I would have to take many indirect paths to eventually reach my destination."

"Sensi is wise beyond her years" said Lumi. "It is possible that I may be able to help you. I sense that your latent essence and intuition is very strong, even stronger than Vanessa's which is quite remarkable."

"Have you also helped Vanessa?" asked Jessica.

"Vanessa spent three months with me when she first arrived at Consciência" replied Lumi "and I helped her to develop her relationship and empathy with the natural world. Sensi had seen in Vanessa a person who already had a comprehensive understanding of the nature and dynamics of the material human world. Despite now being so disillusioned by what she had seen and experienced, she still had yet to develop an understanding of her own essential nature. Vanessa had a very strong spiritual essence that had been ruthlessly suppressed by her own consciousness. This was a defence mechanism built within her psyche to enable her to survive and successfully compete in such a hostile environment. Apart from my own daughter, and I sense perhaps you Jessica, Vanessa has the greatest potential for using and channelling natural energies of anyone I have met. I think that might explain why Vanessa and Sensi's lovemaking had been so powerful during their first night together, a coming together of essences. It is a great delight that she has chosen to stay amongst us and help us to grow and develop the vision we have for Consciência. I think Sensi is even more delighted than I am, though I can't possibly imagine why" she said with a wink.

"I can't believe that Sensi discussed her lovemaking with you!" exclaimed Jessica in disbelief. She would never contemplate discussing such things with her own mother.

"This is quite natural between us and I didn't need her to tell me on Skype what had happened. I sensed what had happened; we have a special kind of connection." Lumi suddenly turned to Raul who was listening in rapt attention with a big grin on his face, "go and make yourself useful, one of the solar arrays is on the blink again."

Jessica's eyes lingered on Raul as he went outside and when she looked back Lumi had a knowing look on her face that made Jessica blush in embarrassment. This truly was a woman from which it seemed to be impossible to hide secrets. Jessica perceived that Lumi instinctively knew more about her true nature and desires than she did herself.

"Don't be alarmed" said Lumi reassuringly as if she had read Jessica's mind, "desire originates in the human unconscious and will reveal itself to those who are experienced in observing such impulses. I can assure you that Raul betrays the same feelings and is as equally unaware that he is revealing this to me as you have been. I leave it entirely up to you what you decide to do with this knowledge. What is seldom understood is that all thoughts pass through and are influenced by the unconscious part of the human mind before they manifest themselves in conscious thought. This means that every sight, smell, sound or sensation is emotionally conditioned before our conscious mind is even aware of it."

"The consciousness, what many of your learned psychologists might call the ego, is just a small veneer on the surface of a mind that is far more powerful than you can even begin to imagine. The modern world has virtually lost this understanding and most people actually believe that human action results largely from some kind of rational reasoning process. Nothing could be further from the truth. Those who manipulate the mass of humanity for their own ends know this only too well and almost always use emotional signals rather than rational reasoning to influence the masses."

"Fear is one of the most popular emotions they like to create, particularly when this is associated with harm to someone or something that is loved. For example a politician may say that an education proposal from the political opposition will 'permanently harm your child's future.' They know that your powerful emotional reaction to the word harm, in association with the protective instincts you have for your child, will be far more persuasive than any rational evaluation of the policy. Even if you attempt to rationally evaluate the policy, your thoughts will already be emotionally conditioned by an association with harm, regardless of any objective reality that the policy might actually be beneficial. Such people know that by influencing the emotions they will change the actions of people almost as effectively as a remote control with a model plane. Collective human action is almost entirely initiated by the deliberate manipulation of unconscious emotional impulses. This has resulted in devastating consequences for both humanity and other forms of life on Earth."

"You make humanity sound like robots or automatons that are controlled by unconscious thought processes which they can't control and don't understand" said Jessica. "You also make the politicians and capitalists that hold the levers of power in our societies sound like manipulative puppet masters."

"If you observe collective human behaviour you will see that there is a lot of evidence to support what I have asserted, but it doesn't have to be that way" replied Lumi. "The first step to developing an independent will is to actually understand what is happening. Using your puppet analogy, you first have to develop the ability to observe the strings and the pull they have upon you before you can cut them and escape the control of the puppet masters. Even if you can't stop your conscious thoughts being preconditioned by your emotions, you can begin to observe this process taking place."

"So are you saying that if we know that all our thoughts are coloured by our emotions and instincts before they develop, we can begin to regain control of our ourselves by observing their impact?" said Jessica.

"Or deliberately choose not to do so. Not all such impulses are negative. The internal journey that Sensi talked about is the journey that both aspects of your human nature, the conscious and the unconscious, must make in order to come together as a united whole. It is this bringing together of both aspects of the human mind, the conscious and the unconscious, that is the source of wisdom and enlightenment. The unconscious is where love, compassion and acceptance are to be found as well as the sources of fear, greed, anger and intolerance. It requires a well-developed consciousness to understand the source of these impulses and mitigate those that would cause harm whilst allowing yourself to celebrate and nurture those impulses and qualities that bring joy."

"You will also frequently hear it said that some people have 'monumental egos'. It would be far more accurate to say that the ego or reasoning capability of such a person is actually very weak. They lack the understanding to interpret their own emotional and instinctive responses to the world around them and make wise balanced judgements. Instead they believe that their impulses are created in their conscious mind and they blindly follow an agenda completely oblivious to the knowledge that their conscious mind is merely a puppet and the strings are pulled by powerful unconscious impulses. If these impulses are love, empathy, caring and compassion, this can be a very beautiful thing to observe even if the actions arising from these feelings are not effectively directed. If these impulses are ambition, greed, fear, anger and envy the actions they provoke can be immensely destructive."

Jessica thought about Raul and how delighted she had been when she saw that it was Raul waiting to meet her at the Kapok tree that morning. "So my conscious thoughts at the sight of Raul and the impression he has made on me have already been strongly influenced by unconscious desire before I was even aware of this myself?" said Jessica.

"Knowing this, would you want to stop such desires?" asked Lumi.

Jessica smiled; she had rather enjoyed experiencing her growing desire for Raul. "Probably not" she said, "but knowing this I shall be careful not to get too infatuated with him until I have had a chance to observe his character a bit better!"

Lumi smiled at how rapidly Jessica was developing an understanding of what she had said. Her daughter had been right about this girl, she was special. "It may not have been just at the sight of Raul that your emotions were influencing your thoughts; it may also be the sound of his voice or maybe his smell. You will find that even his touch or the taste of him when you kiss will influence your mind when your body has learnt to recognise it" said Lumi. "The impulses of all the senses pass through this emotional and instinctive conditioning before reaching your consciousness. There is also another level of understanding, if you like a sixth sense, that of essence and intuition for those who have developed such capabilities. Most women have a much higher natural aptitude for intuition and emotional sensitivity than the majority of men. This is a very useful ability to develop to help protect yourself from harm. Have you ever met someone who is very charming on the outside but who intuitively makes you feel very uncomfortable?"

Jessica thought of some of the people she had met at university. There was one man in particular who was quite popular, the secretary of the student union. He was attractive and superficially very charming but something about him had made the hairs on her neck rise every time he was near her.

"Yes" Jessica answered, "I have met people like that before."

"Work on developing this skill Jessica, it is particularly important if you ever come across a person that would be classified in your civilisation as a psychopath or sociopath. There are far more of these people about than you would imagine. They are highly manipulative and have virtually no control of some of their darker unconscious impulses and see no reason to constrain their behaviour. Now tell me more about your quest and why you have journeyed to Consciência?"

Jessica explained the circumstances as to how she had arrived at Consciência, the impact the loss of her sister's life had had upon her and her subsequent search for a sense of meaning and purpose for her own life. She also talked about how awake she had felt after her night in the ruins with Sensi but how this had faded, just as Sensi had predicted.

"Your unconscious may have important information that it is trying to pass to you that you cannot reach through reasoning alone" said Lumi. "It is almost certain that this is where the source of your restlessness has come from, just like it was the source of Vanessa's frustration and subsequent anxiety with her life and career. I do have the power to open up your consciousness to be receptive to these impulses but there are also dangers with this process. The process I propose may assist you on your path towards self-knowledge or it may exacerbate darker tendencies that could have the opposite effect upon you. It's possible that the experience could even initiate what you would understand as a neurosis. I think this is very unlikely as your intuition is already powerful but the risk still remains and in a worst case scenario it could be irreversible."

Jessica paused for a few moments as she evaluated what Lumi had told her. "I have come too far along this path to turn back now" she answered with conviction looking firmly into Lumi's eyes. "I am willing to accept the risk."

"Your unconscious mind may not reveal what it is trying to communicate in an obvious way" said Lumi. "Communicating with the emotions and instincts is not like popping into a library and reading a book. This is a very complex process and the knowledge revealed is often manifest in the form of a type of dream full of visual metaphors that may take some time to interpret. Now, are you ready to start?"

"I am."

3

Jessica and Lumi walked into the forest until they came to a small clearing which had a traditionally weaved rug laid out in the centre. Lumi pulled out what looked like an elongated rock crystal on a cord from her bag and a small incense burner with a tile on which to stand it. She laid down the crystal and put the burner on its tile in the middle of the rug. She pulled out a small pouch, placed some incense in the burner and lit it.

"Please take your clothes off Jessica. We are opening up the part of your mind that has been shaped by the lives and experiences of countless generations before. It has even been shaped by the lives of the animals from which we have evolved, passing back through millions of years of evolution. It is the part you that you are born with, the instinctive part of the mind that is common to us all, what the psychologist Jung would have called your collective unconscious. It helps to remove the trappings of convention and society and be as nature intended when undertaking such a journey into your inner self."

Without question Jessica did as Lumi requested. Lumi also removed her clothing and the two women sat cross legged opposite each other on the rug. "The process we are going to undertake is a form of hypnosis during which I shall encourage your ego to relax its grip on your mind. This will help enable your unconscious to reveal what the barrier of your ego has been suppressing from your consciousness. Are you still happy to proceed?"

"I am."

"Please lie down on your back on the rug and relax. Listen to the sounds of the forest, the wind in the leaves and the calls of the animals and birds." Lumi knelt down on the rug behind Jessica with a knee either side of her head. She held the long clear crystal on a cord above Jessica's eyes on which she asked her to fix her gaze and she began to spin it in the U shaped space between her breasts. Lumi then started to chant as Sensi had done the night in the ruins.

Jessica let Lumi's chanting and the background noise of the forest seep into her mind as she watched the crystal spin, slowly the scene faded and her eyes closed as she gently slipped into an altered state of consciousness.

The noise of the animals had changed. There was alarm and fear in their calls and Jessica stood up to see what was going on. She stumbled slightly as she did so. There was something different about the ground, it felt as if it was slightly moving beneath her feet. It was not like she would imagine an earthquake to be, the movement was too slight and regular for that. There was no sign at all of Lumi and the air was colder. She also realised that she was clothed in some kind of thick woollen garments which were completely unfamiliar to her to protect her from the chill of the cold wind.

A small herd of deer rushed past her in terror, seemingly completely oblivious to her presence. There was an acrid smell of smoke in the forest and in the distance she heard noises that sounded like trees being cut down with axes and chainsaws. There was a large tree in front of her and she decided to climb it to see if she could detect the source of the commotion. She climbed higher and higher until eventually she climbed out above the forest canopy and she was completely startled by the panorama laid out before her.

Jessica suddenly understood why the ground was moving. The forest was growing on top of the deck of the most enormous ship she had ever seen and the pitching movement was caused by the movement of the waves as the ship ploughed forward. The ship must have been twenty kilometres long and at least two kilometres wide. It was obvious from the remains of the stumps that once the forest had covered virtually the whole deck of the ship but now it was just a few acres of woodland near the bow. There was a group of men chopping down the trees and other men with rifles were shooting any animals who tried to escape from the forest. The carcasses of the animals were thrown with the wood onto flatbed train cars that were periodically dragged by a small steam engine along metal rails towards a towering ship's bridge at the stern.

Above the bridge there was thick black acrid smoke billowing out of four enormous chimneys and she could now detect the throbbing sound of the massive engines that were driving the ship forward through the waves. She turned towards the bow and she noticed that there was a huge iceberg in the distance that the ship was relentlessly heading towards. She heard the screaming of a monkey as the tree in which it sheltered was cut down beneath it, it's infant in its arms. Two shots rang out and the carcasses of the mother and infant were thrown casually onto the next car on top of some logs.

In absolute horror Jessica climbed down the tree and ran through the forest towards the men. As she burst out through the trees she screamed, "Stop! What are you doing?"

"You shouldn't be here Miss" said a burly man with a red hard hat that seemed to distinguish him as some kind of foreman. "You could get shot running out of the trees like that. You should be with the other passengers on the deck below."

"Why are you destroying the forest?" she asked in distress as yet another carcass, this time of a young deer was thrown onto the growing pile.

"To fuel the ship of course" said the man looking at his colleague as if it was the dumbest question he had ever been asked.

"Well you have to stop, you can't do this to the animals, they're absolutely terrified" she shouted in exasperation.

"What's that to me?" said the man with complete indifference. "I have a shift quota to get through and you are holding up my work. If you don't like it I suggest you speak to the captain."

"Where will I find him?" asked Jessica.

"Why on the bridge of course, where else?" he replied. "You can take the next train back if you don't fancy walking."

Jessica sat on the flatbed looking at the bloodied bodies of the animals and the chopped up remnants of forest trees as it rumbled up towards the bridge. The sound of the engines got louder and louder as she approached and she heard the deep rumble of the huge screws turning beneath the waterline.

A large group of filthy workers were emptying the carts, throwing the wood and the carcasses of the animals onto a conveyor belt that disappeared deep into the bowels of the ship. She could feel the heat of enormous fires that heated the boilers radiating out of the hold.

At the base of the bridge was a large metal hatch that was open and she passed through into the gloomy corridor behind. She went down a metal staircase and found herself on a walkway above what looked to be a huge metal storage hold that was filled with murmuring people. They all seemed to be looking down towards their feet as they slowly shuffled about. She could see that this hold was one of many that disappeared far into the gloomy darkness that lay beyond.

She went back up the staircase and bumped into a man in a white uniform who looked like some kind of officer.

"I must speak to the Captain" she said to the officer.

"Captain's busy with the ship" he replied.

"Please, it's terribly important" she pleaded.

With a deep sigh the officer gestured with his head for her to follow and she followed him along several corridors and up staircases until she entered the bridge where the Captain stood staring out through a window across the vast deck in front of him. He leant forward towards some kind of microphone and shouted, "give me more steam, we are barely doing thirty two knots and so help me I'll cut your pay if you let the ship slip below thirty."

"Captain, this girl wants a word with you, says it's urgent" said the officer who just turned and left her alone looking at the large powerful back of the Captain.

"What do you want?" snapped the Captain without bothering to turn around. "Can't you see I'm busy?"

"I want you to stop destroying the forest and the animals" she said.

The Captain now turned around in annoyance to face this intruder that had the audacity to disturb him. "That's absurd, the ship will run out of fuel and stop" he snorted at her.

"How far is it until we reach our destination?" she asked.

"There is no destination," said the Captain, "the purpose is to keep the ship moving forward, not arrive at a destination, that's what we all get paid for."

"Why keep going if there is no destination" she said in confusion.

"We must keep going, it's called making progress" he said. "What's the point of it all if we stop?"

"You must stop" she said, "you're heading for an iceberg."

"There are no icebergs" he said in contemptuous reply. "Talk of icebergs is just a silly myth to scare weak minded people and stop the ship and I won't listen to such stupidity. Now get off my bridge, I have a ship to run."

Jessica ran back down the corridors and staircases to reach the hold where thousands of people were still shuffling around. She stood on the gantry above the hold and, trying to make herself heard above the throbbing drone of the ships engines, she screamed "we must get the Captain to stop the ship, there will soon be no forest or animals left and we will hit the iceberg. You will all drown." A few people looked up at her incuriously and then resumed their shuffling and murmuring.

She ran back up towards the deck and met a woman with a small boy. "You must take your child off the ship or you will both be drowned" she said grabbing the woman's shoulders.

"Don't be silly" she giggled, "why would I do that?"

"There's an iceberg ahead" and the Captain refuses to stop the ship.

"If there was any danger the officers would tell us" she replied. "One day my boy will be an officer and he will be very wealthy" she said with pride.

"Where are the lifeboats?" cried Jessica, "I haven't seen any lifeboats."

"We don't need lifeboats, as I said to you, we are all perfectly safe" said the woman. "Come on Jose." With that she squeezed past Jessica on the gangway and headed towards a metal ladder to climb down into the hold and re-join the others.

Jessica ran back onto the deck. A large monkey on one of the flatbed cars, although badly hurt, was still alive and was screaming in terror as one of the men tried to force it down the hatchway towards the furnaces. Jessica covered her ears; she couldn't stand listening to its cries any more. Ahead of the ship she saw the huge bulk of the iceberg looming above the bow of the now doomed vessel. It was not white but filthy, crusted with dirt and soot, dark and menacing. She turned around in desperation and suddenly saw a dazzling bright light coming from a hatchway that she had not noticed before. She ran through the hatchway and into the light as the screams of the terrified monkey faded behind her.

4

Jessica's eyes opened, her head resting on Lumi's lap. Lumi's hand was gently stroking her forehead and in the distance she could hear a troop of monkeys chattering and whooping as they passed through the canopy of the forest far above. She felt the warmth of the sun on her body and the smell of the vegetation that surrounded her. How beautiful this world was, how precious and yet how fragile. Lumi was looking affectionately down at her but Jessica also noted some concern in Lumi's eyes as to how she would emerge from her experience.

Jessica sat up, she turned around to face Lumi and wrapped her arms around her, seeking the warmth and comfort of her embrace. When she parted there were tears in her eyes but these were not just with the sadness that the memories of her experience had left with her but something else was stirring. There was a fire in her breast, a renewed sense of energy and a determination that she had never felt before. She knew that she could never be the same woman ever again. She did not yet fully understand what her dream had revealed to her but she felt it was an allegory for what was happening in the actual world. She knew with conviction that she must now dedicate her life to challenging the direction that humanity was taking. Somehow she had to stop the ship and protect the forest and the animals from the pointless slaughter and exploitation. She looked again into Lumi's eyes and understood immediately that she was not alone.

Lumi asked her about her experience and Jessica found that she could recollect everything vividly and with complete clarity, including the unbearably painful emotions she endured as she had helplessly watched the animals being brutally hurt and slaughtered. How could someone inflict such appalling suffering and misery with calm indifference? Everything in her was repelled by what she had witnessed and yet she knew that this was not just a dream. Across the world there were countless examples of such people inflicting terrible harm and misery on each other, the animals, and the natural world on which all life depended.

She asked Lumi if she would help her to interpret the dream.

"I have my views on what the dream has revealed but I think that first you should talk further with Owen, Sensi and Vanessa. Listen to what they have to say in the context of what you have experienced here today and much will be revealed to you. What I will say is that we are all the children of nature, nurtured in the womb of the great Goddess through the creative processes of the universe. Collectively we are also the custodians of our beautiful yet fragile world. This is without doubt the most important responsibility that we have and yet this is the responsibility about which we are the most negligent. Humanity is racing along a path that will ultimately destroy everything of beauty and value unless we can light a beacon of wisdom to illuminate the true path. Without such illumination the prospects for all life on Earth are bleak."

"Where can we find such illumination?" asked Jessica.

"The light of wisdom has shone for centuries and yet humanity lacks the eyes to see. Jesus is reputed to have said, 'the Father's kingdom is spread out upon the earth, and people don't see it.' I would argue that it is the mother's kingdom, as it is the womb of the Goddess that is the birthplace of all life, but the point is still well made."

"I had no idea that you believed in Jesus and God" said Jessica.

"I have said no such thing. What I have said is that there is wisdom revealed by some of the sayings attributed to a person called Jesus. As for the Abrahamic God, it is nothing but a reflection of the egos of the men that created it. Those who suspend reason to worship such an entity are merely substituting the worship of their own ego for that of a more powerful projected one. Remember when we discussed how the ego is governed by unconscious impulses?"

"Yes, you said that a weak poorly developed ego is dominated by impulses from the human unconscious yet lacks the awareness to realise this" replied Jessica.

"Clever girl! Do you also remember the different aspects of such impulses?"

"Yes, you said that some were the sources of love, empathy and compassion and others anger, greed, hatred and fear" replied Jessica.

"Sadly the impulses manifest in man's monumental projected ego or 'God' as described in the religious texts such as the Koran and the Old Testament almost universally fall into the latter category. How is it possible to act wisely and worship such an entity?" said Lumi. "We are born into this beautiful world, an island paradise in the vastness of space. Yet countless people who worship this angry God are trying to turn our Earthly paradise into a vision of hell, all for a vague promise of finding another paradise after death. It is hard to even begin to comprehend such madness."

"Raul told me to read the Old Testament before I talked about God's love and now I am beginning to understand why" said Jessica reflectively.

"What I didn't say was that men are far more susceptible to the forceful destructive unconscious impulses than women" said Lumi. "Women, by their very nature and through their capacity for giving birth, are inclined towards protecting life and are more influenced by their intuition and emotions that nurture these feelings. It is no accident that the Abrahamic faiths are remorselessly patriarchal and that women are seen as an influence that should be feared, dominated and controlled. The Abrahamic God provides an excellent allegory of a rampaging male ego, demanding to be worshiped and punishing and destroying all that stands in its way. As a result, all across the world women are hurt, raped, abused, repressed and controlled and the result is greed, avarice cruelty and ruthless exploitation. It brings me great sadness to witness billions of women coerced into following Abrahamic God faiths through intimidation, cultural imperative or simply misguided belief. Such women, often unwittingly, are actively colluding in their own control and oppression."

"So are you telling me that it is because of the inherent nature of men that the Earth is in such peril?" said Jessica.

"Both men and women have a responsibility. Within a few generations we have depleted the Earth of much of its scarce minerals, hydrocarbon deposits and water aquifers. These precious resources took hundreds of millions of years to create and yet in just a few decades we have permanently deprived future generations from their precious inheritance. We have poisoned the Earth's atmosphere, caused the extinction of thousands of species, and polluted the rivers and the oceans. All of this has been done to satisfy humanity's insatiable addiction to greed."

"That we live on the edge of the precipice of global catastrophe is principally the result of the actions of ignorant men with weak egos and women who lack the strength and confidence to assert a different set of values. Such men are like empty shells whose purpose in life is either serving the cravings of their own ego or latching onto a more powerful ego and mindlessly serving it as some kind of dominating substitute for the limitations of their own. These are tragic figures. Hidden within the unconscious of every man is the female perspective, what is sometimes described as the anima. It is this that is the source of balance and wholeness that can give real joy, love and meaning to life. Men whose egos are strong enough not to be threatened by such impulses and who open up to the influence of their anima can also use their energy and strength to love, nurture and protect. It is in such men that wisdom may be found."

"What about women? You have said that part of the problem is that women lack the strength and confidence to stand up against the harm being done to the world and thus share the responsibility for what is happening" said Jessica.

"For much of humanity's existence, physical force and intimidation has been a dominating factor, whether between individuals or between states and societies. In such circumstances it is hardly fair to blame women for not standing firm against the dominance of male orientated societies. There is now a beacon of hope, at least in the parts of the world that are no longer dominated by patriarchal religious doctrines and intimidation through the threat or use of physical abuse."

"Women in some societies, through ongoing hard fought battles for equal rights, have finally gained a real opportunity to assert themselves. They could change the direction that humanity has taken tomorrow if they chose to follow their inherent emotions, their instincts to love, nurture and protect, and collectively decide to act. This is all very recent. Nearly all existing cultures, and the associated structures of society where power and influence is exercised, are still dominated by active or latent masculine influences. Unless women rise up and decide to challenge the predominant culture that constrains their true nature, there is very little hope. Many men possessed of wisdom would actively support them, for how can true value be found in a world devoid of compassion and love?"

"Roxie told me that the meaning of life was love and I think I am now starting to understand what she meant" said Jessica.

"Sensi can help you to understand what Roxie meant about love" said Lumi.

"I will ask her for her guidance when I see her" said Jessica.

Lumi continued her explanation of the different aspects of human nature. "Just as the anima, the female perspective lies embedded in the unconscious psyche of every man, the animus or male aspect lies embedded in every woman. Just as every man who wishes to gain wisdom must open up to his anima, so every woman who seeks wisdom must also open up to the influences of her animus. It is by balancing the conscious and the unconscious aspects of the human psyche in both men and women that wisdom is to be found. This is where a person can truly find their independent self, no longer a slave to either their unconscious emotional impulses or the cravings of the conscious ego. This true self, the wise self, can only be created through reconciling and harmonising these competing aspects of our natures."

"The Jessica that emerged from the hypnosis induced dream just a few moments ago has changed from the one that lay down before. There is a new energy and conviction in you now that was not present before. Through your experience you may have started to open up to your own animus, your internal male aspect, and this makes you a formidable positive force for change in the world. Just remember that this newfound energy and conviction needs to be harnessed and used to serve your female nature not to subvert it. There are many examples of women who have tried to succeed in a hostile patriarchal world and have completely succumbed to the demands of their inner male perspective. They have ended up subverting the love, empathy and compassion in their nature with dispassionate greed and ambition. There is no hope or wisdom to be found by following such a path."

"I think I understand" said Jessica. "What you are saying is that it is the balancing of the male and female perspectives of our natures that takes us on the path towards wisdom. This can only be realised in a person when their ego is sufficiently strong to understand this as a desirable development not a threat to its own self-serving agenda. Every enlightened person will need to work together, both women and men, if we are going to stand up to the selfish and ignorant who predominantly hold the levers of power. This offers a path of hope, a chance to change the direction humanity is taking before it is too late" said Jessica with excitement.

"The dynamics between the male and female aspects, yin and yang, permeate everything and are the source of creative energy in the world of nature" replied Lumi. "In our human world our evolution has long been out of balance, it has been dominated by the male aspect. This imbalance manifested itself in your dream in the form of the Captain and the mysterious unknown influences that manipulated and controlled him. As you have understood, the only hope is to restore a natural balance is through the power of wisdom and that is an enormous challenge, maybe an impossible one. You recognised this in your dream when you cried out to the shuffling crowd in the ship's hold to no avail. You couldn't break through their inherent ignorance and apathy."

"I refuse to accept that it is impossible" said a defiant Jessica. "I shall find others who think as we do and we shall join together to cry out louder and longer. I am sure that this is the path that I must now follow, the path that I was seeking when I came to Consciêcia. We can't just allow ourselves to destroy such a rare and precious gem as our Earth simply because we are just too stupid or lack the will to act." Jessica thought again of the ignorance of the Captain of the ship in her dream, destroying the last of the trees and animals so that the ship could make progress towards an inevitable destiny with calamity. The parallels with the situation that the Earth now faced were becoming all too clear to her.

Lumi and Jessica got dressed and, with their arms entwined, they walked back to Lumi's dwelling where they found Raul testing the transformer linked to the solar array with a meter.

"It's all working fine now" he said. "You really should let me cut down that fig tree that is near the panels. As usual it was the discarded figs from the monkeys that had almost covered the panels making them virtually useless."

234

"We can easily clean the panels but that colony of red howler monkeys cannot replace that food tree in their habitat" said Lumi. If we cut down the tree we will drive them away and into conflict and competition for food with another troop. As a result of such a thoughtless action many could die. If you make me choose between the electricity and the monkeys you know what my answer will be!"

Raul put up his hands in submission and turned to Jessica with some concern. He didn't really understand the nature of his mother's abilities but he knew that it was not something to be taken lightly. There was something different about Jessica since the two women had walked into the forest together. There seemed to be a new bond between them and there was a confidence in Jessica's demeanour and the way that she walked that she hadn't shown before.

Jessica walked up to Raul, linked her hands behind his head and gave him a big kiss on the lips. "Come on, you're taking me for a swim" she said. She kissed Lumi goodbye and waltzed off back down the path towards the village.

Raul scratched his head with a stupid grin on his face and looked at his mother with bemusement. "You are going to have a job keeping up with that one" laughed Lumi. So much for Jessica's pledge to suss out her son properly before falling for his charms she thought to herself. Such was the way of lust between people and for these two she thought that perhaps love might follow. One thing she had learnt despite all her years and wisdom, never ever try to give advice to young people on affairs of the heart. She remembered how she had felt all those years ago as she had walked nonchalantly away from Owen after taking him down to the nearest town so that he could return to his previous life. Her voice had been calm, her advice had been sound, but her heart had cried out in protest at every step as she turned her back on him and walked away. She remembered the first time they had made love together when he had returned to her; she had never felt such a passion with any other man. She picked up her mobile phone and sent a text; Owen was going to get very little sleep tonight!

5

Jessica persuaded Raul to take her to the pools again where they had first met and they swam, laughed and finally lay together on a towel on the small shingle beach deliciously soaking up the heat of the afternoon sun after the chill of the water. Jessica told Raul what had happened with his mother and the dream and her determination to do everything she could to help preserve what was left of the Earth from the avarice of people. She put her head on his chest and he gently played with her hair as she talked.

Jessica asked Raul if he had any idea what he planned to do with his life. He explained that the work on the hydrogen plant and the fuel cell research kept him pretty occupied since university but he felt that he probably needed a new adventure although he had no idea what that might be. What he didn't choose to reveal was his growing attraction to Jessica and an admiration for her passion and resolve. A part of him was already hoping that she might play a significant part in his future.

"Of course my real future lies with the band" said Raul, "it can only be a matter of time before the world discovers our genius!"

"You never told me you were in a band" said Jessica lifting herself up onto her elbows.

"I didn't want you falling in love with me just because I'm a rock star" he said with mock haughtiness.

Jessica pushed him off the towel onto the shingle and ran screaming into the pool with Raul hot on her heels, she tried to swim away but he was far too quick for her and he grabbed a kicking heel and pulled her back under the water. She turned to face him spluttering and laughing and they found themselves waist deep in the pool, their lips almost touching. They looked into each other's eyes and this time it was Raul who kissed her. Her lips responded and they had a slow lingering kiss, followed by another and another. With the tingling energy of two young people, whose bodies already knew that they would soon be lovers even if their minds were still catching up, they walked hand in hand out of the pool and made their way slowly back to the village.

That evening Raul's band was playing in the village hall and Jessica had to admit that they were pretty good. The hall was packed and Jessica saw Vanessa and Sensi in the crowd. Raul's band played a mix of rock covers, mostly in English but also some songs that Raul had written himself. Towards the end Raul picked up a classical guitar and the band played a slow song in Spanish that hushed the audience and she detected a note of sadness.

When the song had finished she asked Sensi what her brother had been singing about.

"The song is called the last butterfly" she replied. "It is about a man in a concrete world of the future, where nature has been destroyed by human greed, remembering as a boy seeing his last butterfly. He remembers the light glistening off its wings like the sparkle of a thousand diamonds and he laments that his children will never see such beauty again." Seeking to change the mood that had suddenly overcome Jessica, Sensi provocatively asked, "so have you fallen in love with my brother yet?"

"Sensi!" rebuked Vanessa "don't be so unfair to the poor girl; they have only just met each other."

"I am remembering when we first met" replied Sensi mischievously.

Jessica was looking at Raul on the stage where the band was now playing a Mötley Crüe number dedicated to 'girls, girls, girls' and every few seconds he would catch her eye as he gyrated with the microphone stand.

"Now that's what I call a chat up line" laughed Sensi. "That brother of mine can be so corny at times but you gotta love him for it."

Raul walked Jessica back to her apartment after the show and they kissed at the doorstep.

"Tomorrow we can meet Owen if you'd like to?" said Raul. "He is spending some time with Vanessa looking at an investment proposal. It's for an organic vineyard in Chile that requires some venture capital to expand. The vineyard is being partly staffed by ex-offenders as a way of introducing them to the wine growing industry so that they can start up new lives after prison. It sounds just like the sort of project that we should be supporting but Owen needs to convince Vanessa first. She is very pragmatic about such things and doesn't let her heart rule her head if she thinks a project isn't viable. They said that we could meet them at the café about 10.30 when they break for coffee. What do you think?"

"I simply must meet the man who managed to capture Lumi's heart" replied Jessica eagerly, "he must be quite something."

"Well I have to admit to being a little biased" said Raul. "I'll pick you up here after I have popped into the plant to check the overnight production figures."

They parted with another lingering kiss and Jessica told herself not to look back as she went to close the door behind her. She didn't want Raul to think she was too keen. She caught Raul looking back over his shoulder at her with his cheeky smile as she completely failed to heed her own advice.

The next morning Jessica and Raul overheard Vanessa saying "I know it's a wonderful cause but these proposals are simply not viable" to a sandy haired man as they entered the café. To Jessica the man looked to be in his mid-sixties but she thought the years had sat lightly upon his shoulders. He was powerfully built but there was a kindness and gentleness in his expression that she instantly liked. "They will either need to find a way to take another 10% out of the costs or increase production volumes by at least 30% just to recover the overheads" continued Vanessa. "With this proposal we will not only be setting up the capital cost of the new plant but still subsidising every single bottle they produce. I'm sorry Owen but this project proposal as it stands is simply not tenable."

"Owen trying to pull a fast one again" said Raul looking at his father affectionately.

"Getting Vanessa to release the purse strings is like getting blood from a stone" sighed Owen to Jessica but it was obvious that he held Vanessa in high regard.

"Don't listen to him Jessica, I am far too soft a touch" said Vanessa. "He will get his money if the twelve Stoics eventually pass the proposal but is has to come through me first. We will send someone down there to help them look at their processes and I am sure that with a bit more work we will get there."

"The twelve Stoics?" questioned Jessica.

"The Stoics are what we call our community and social enterprise board," said Owen, "we entrust them to maintain our vision and we think it's a better title than director as it emphasises what we feel to be important in the role. It's a delight to meet you Jessica, despite the dodgy company you choose to keep."

Raul responded by sticking his tongue out at his father.

A young woman greeted them at the table and they ordered coffees and some locally produced flapjacks.

When the coffees had arrived Jessica turned to Owen and asked him to explain how the community of Consciência came into being and the underlying philosophy behind it.

"I had absolutely no plan when I came back to see Lumi except to be with the beautiful and mysterious woman with whom I had fallen in love. I just knew I had to get away from the corporate world and all the greed and backstabbing that went with it. I guess I was just looking for a refuge and love but there was no way that Lumi was going to let me get away with that for long."

Owen explained that Lumi had told him that she used her skills to heal people and animals and that he needed to use his skills to heal the world that he had thought he had left behind him. Lumi had explained that everything that he held precious about where she lived would eventually be destroyed. He knew she was right unless a very different vision for conducting finance and business could be created. He also knew that the entrenched interests between the corporations and the politicians that colluded with them would mean that change had to come from the grass roots, not from those who held the levers of power in the contemporary world.

Owen had accumulated about $5 million in assets during his career and he used these to set up a development fund for a concept that was beginning to form in his mind about creating a different kind of community. He used a considerable amount of the money to run a string of adverts in international management magazines and financial publications seeking people who were also looking for an alternative perspective on life and who might want to join him.

After three years there were about thirty people living in a jumble of lashed together dwellings and Owen had felt that there was enough experience and skills in the group to formalise the community and its objectives. One of the first things they had to decide was where to build the new community and they sought Lumi's advice on where she felt would be the most auspicious location. Lumi advised them against building near the old ruins at the head of the valley. She explained that the tortures and sacrifices made over the centuries had left a legacy of energy that could be destructive if not properly understood and channelled.

Further down the valley there was a basin where three streams joined the main river that had sculpted the valley out of the hillside. This created five lines of water with the main stream making two of them as it passed through this conjunction of the waterways. Lumi suggested that they build the community centre near this confluence in the form of a pentagram that represented the four elements of earth, air ,fire, water and essence or the essential nature of the human spirit. This would create harmony and balance within the future community and help promote the spiritual growth and understanding in the world which was one of its founding principles. It was also Lumi that suggested that they call the community Consciência which roughly translated meant conscience or awareness, both of which were important elements to keep at the forefront of their thinking as the community developed.

They formed a community trust to coordinate the community's accounts. The initial pool of community funding was created from the donations of those who had joined the community. Part of these funds was used to purchase the valley for the community from the relevant authorities. The purpose of Consciência was not to escape from the world but to engage actively with it promoting a different set of values. The early arrivals were not 'new age' hippies looking to create a commune, although Owen confessed to being somewhat sympathetic to such values. Amongst those invited to join were engineers, financiers, lawyers, builders and teachers. As the community grew they also made efforts to attract local people from the area. The farmers, mechanics and craftsmen who joined them helped them to develop and maintain the growing community and support the infrastructure needed for the community to thrive.

Fairly early on in the development of Consciência they ran into problems with some of the founding members who felt that they should have a bigger say in what was going on as they had donated the most to the trust fund. It quickly became apparent that old world problems of greed and manipulation were starting to permeate the community and a majority of the founders who were passionate about their mission felt that this had to be prevented at all costs. Social values and skills, rather than wealth, were the primary requirements for joining the community in its early days. Despite this there were some very wealthy people, like Owen himself, who had been spiritually despondent about the values of the world in which they lived despite all their wealth, and who had decided to join them.

Lumi warned Owen and the majority of the founding group that greed would destroy their community just as effectively as it was destroying everything of real value in the outside world. If the community was to survive they had to eliminate greed from within their midst and the only way to do this was to starve it of sustenance. A meeting was held and it was proposed that there should be a limit to the wealth that anyone joining the community could retain. It was certainly not their intention to create some kind of communist egalitarian model but there had to be a cap placed on how much wealth was acceptable for those choosing to live within the community.

"How did you decide on what this figure should be?" asked Jessica.

"That is a very good question" said Owen. "We had no intention of removing personal choice or creating some kind of monastic pledge of poverty coupled with the wearing of hair shirts to purify our souls. We believe that life should be fun and there is joy to be had in hedonistic pleasures provided that they do not cause substantial harm to other living beings." Owen turned to Vanessa, "I believe your Wicca sisters back at the Warehouse had an appropriate saying for this."

"An it harm none, do as thou will" replied Vanessa "which means if your actions do not harm anyone else then you should feel liberated to do what gives you fulfilment in life."

"Who is to judge if harm is being done" asked Jessica.

Owen looked at Jessica with growing respect. "That is absolutely the core question that we have to constantly ask ourselves. When we stop asking this question the community is certain to fail. Everything we do in life has consequences as everything is interconnected. The Buddhists believe it is impossible to fully understand the implications of our actions but that we are at least responsible for carrying out our actions with positive intentions not to cause harm. This is one of the reasons why we created the twelve Stoics in the community."

"I thought you said the twelve Stoics were the equivalent of your board of directors, part of your business enterprise" said Jessica.

"We don't separate the community and business here" replied Vanessa on Owen's behalf. "Consciência is what we choose to call a social union. It's a bit like being in a trade union but trade unions primarily just look out for their own workers interests. We believe it is important to look out for the interests of the whole community but even more importantly, that the community is looking out for the interests of the world around them and the sustainable future of the Earth. The future of the community depends on the business activities and investments that are intrinsically linked to what we do here."

"How do you decide who the Stoics should be?" asked Jessica.

"Four of them are elected every year for a period of three years" replied Owen. "They are democratically elected by everyone who lives in Consciência. Once someone has completed their term they cannot be re-elected for another three years. This prevents dominant personalities being able to gain too much control."

"Personalities like Owen's" said Raul cheekily.

"I shall ignore the interruption" said Owen with a withering look at Raul. "Everyone is eligible to stand but there are two guiding principles. Firstly at each election two women and two men are elected as we believe it is essential that there is an equal balance of the sexes maintained within the Stoic Council. I know Lumi has discussed the differences between the female and male aspects of nature and that the interaction between the two creates both creative energy and balance. In addition to the Stoics is the position of the Guardian. The Guardian safeguards our vision and values and will intercede if she feels that any of the decisions being made by the council of Stoics violate any of the founding principles. Ultimately the Guardian has the authority to veto any decision although it has never come to this as her wise council has always proved to have been persuasive."

"She?" asked Jessica.

"We decided very early on that the Guardian had to be a woman. You have seen the terrible damage that is inevitable when people follow the demands of their own ego rather than the needs of others. Poorly developed male egos are far more prone to the destructive elements of our human unconscious than female egos, although there have been explicit examples in history where this hasn't been the case."

"Consciência cannot be complacent about this danger in a world dominated by patriarchal societies. In contrast, our community values the qualities of love, empathy, caring and compassion. We have therefore deliberately created a community where matriarchal values are a dominant influence. We seek to help others not control or manipulate them for selfish ends. These properties come more naturally to women and Lumi has educated me to understand that greater nature is the fertile womb from which all life emerges and depends. Nature is the realm of the great Goddess, the female aspect of creation. A female Guardian helps to ensure that the values upon which Consciência has been founded cannot be overlooked when important decisions are made about the future of the community. For both these reasons the Guardian will always be a spiritually enlightened woman who nurtures the essential guiding spirit of the community and the qualities we aspire to uphold. The Guardian can only be changed by a vote of at least nine of the Stoics or by deciding to resign."

"Who is your current Guardian?" asked Jessica.

"Why Lumi of course" said Vanessa. "Who else is better placed to look out for our spiritual wellbeing than the person who inspired Consciência's creation."

"You didn't answer Jessica's question about how much wealth is enough?" said Raul.

"Thanks Raul" said Owen. "We decided that $350,000 US of assets was enough for anyone to enjoy the fruits of life and this was a realistic and achievable figure that could be obtained through hard work and enterprise. This has been amended over the years by the Stoic Council to take account of inflation and now sits at $435,000 US. Beyond this it would have to be questioned why anyone should be so attracted to gaining more. There are so many more important things in life than just amassing wealth for the sake of it and if someone lacks the wisdom to realise this they have no place in Consciência. We also think that the opportunity cost of more wealth is too high and violates our principle of not causing harm."

"I don't understand what you mean by opportunity cost" said Jessica.

"Vanessa is better placed to explain this to you" said Owen.

"This is usually used as a financial term" said Vanessa. "When you are making an investment you should look at other options as to how the money could otherwise be invested that might provide a better return. Some companies use the average rate of return on their current investments as a baseline figure, or a cost of capital, to assess the viability of a proposed new project or investment. Ideally the new project should increase the average rate of return and therefore make the company more profitable. The rate of return on the finances required for the new project that could be obtained by alternatively investing it at the average rate of return is known as the opportunity cost of the proposed new project. This is how the world generally sees opportunity cost through the lens of wealth acquisition. We naturally see it very differently. Accumulating personal wealth beyond the amounts that we have discussed is far less valuable than channelling this resource towards the wellbeing and happiness of people or the welfare of the animals with which we share this beautiful planet. Do you understand what I have explained?"

"Not really" said Jessica.

"I'm not really surprised" interceded Raul, "you have lost me too Vanessa."

"Ok let's come up with a few examples of how we might look at opportunity cost in Consciência" continued Vanessa. "Recently a special diamond was sold at auction for $83 million. This diamond has no useful purpose at all except to inflate the vanity and ego of its new owner. As you will be well aware from your discussions and experiences with Lumi, inflating the ego is not a benefit but a terrible affliction for any human. In an objective sense this person has spent $83 million to cause further psychological harm to themself. At the same time that this diamond was purchased a violent typhoon struck the Philippines, one of the most violent on record. This typhoon killed thousands of people and left many more homeless and exposed to starvation and disease. $83 million of emergency aid spent on food medicine and shelter would have saved many lives and prevented the hardship of thousands more. Do you now see the opportunity cost of the $83 million?"

"Now you have put it that way, it's impossible not to" replied Jessica, "but I have never really thought about it in such stark terms. It seems so obvious and it makes me feel a bit stupid. There must be millions of obvious examples where resources are being misdirected at great cost to others who need them more."

"Don't be too harsh on yourself Jessica" said Vanessa. "There are remarkably few people who do recognise such absurdities. In the majority of people the ego deliberately supresses such inconvenient thoughts as it does not want to be constrained by conscience from following its appetites. In Consciência we would see such an opportunity cost as utterly unacceptable. Let me come up with a couple more examples, one on a smaller scale and one on a massive scale. I recently saw an interview with a very wealthy man who was boasting that the watch on his wrist was worth a bagful of Rolexes. Now a watch is for telling the time and you can pick up a very good one for $100 that will more than adequately meet any of your timekeeping requirements. The rest is vanity. How many scholarships for students from poor backgrounds would this watch have bought? Such an investment in students would also be recycled back into the community for the benefit of all as they take their learning back out into the world. What is the opportunity cost of that silly watch?"

"Here is a much larger and far more damaging example" Vanessa continued. "In Indonesia there are huge companies that are burning vast tracks of native rainforest to produce palm oil. They are destroying the irreplaceable habitat and wildlife and polluting the air of many other countries in the region through the resultant forest fires. Much of the profits from these plantations are hived off to secret accounts in tax havens so even the population of Indonesia do not substantially profit from any tangible social benefit to enhance their lives. All this is done to feed the crazy egos of a few wealthy people. The opportunity cost of this action when combined with hundreds of corporations like them across the planet will be the ultimate demise of most of life on Earth and the very future of humanity itself. We have now reached the absurd situation where less than 100 people on the planet own more wealth than the poorest 3.5 billion or half the world's population."

"Now Jessica, do you see why we constrain personal wealth accumulation in Consciência? Greed is a cancer that destroys everything and we dare not expose ourselves to the possibility of it taking a grip again in the community. Six of the original founders of Consciência left the community after we made the decision to limit personal wealth which reflected that they were not really committed to our values. Future generations, who will be living with the appalling legacy of the current generation's obsession with greed, will see the obsessive wealth accumulators of today as some of the very worst tyrants in human history."

"Don't these people always insist that their wealth is creating industry and jobs for the greater good?" questioned Jessica.

"This is the trickle-down theory that is a busted flush" said Owen. "The more inequality has grown the poorer the majority of people have become. Flow up rather than trickle-down is the far more accurate description. It's perfectly possible to make wise decisions on behalf of large organisations without personally profiting to excess from it. Vanessa and I do this in our own way in the management of Consciência's Social Enterprise Fund. True personal reward comes from seeing how we have used these resources to improve the wellbeing of others and also help create a sustainable future for our precious Earth."

"When you come up with better prepared proposals than this one that is" teased Vanessa waving the file they were discussing earlier under Owen's nose.

"Point taken" said Owen smiling at Vanessa. "Maximizing shareholder value' is the mantra that drives the activities of most corporations today. This justifies the pursuit of wealth regardless of the cost to the rest of society provided that the law, largely influenced by these self-same organisations, is not actually broken. Many of today's corporations don't even manage to look out for shareholder value any more as executives unashamedly run corporations to maximise their own personal rewards instead."

"There have been far better historical models for creating and running businesses. The Quakers for instance set an excellent example and created many companies whose founding purpose was for the greater good of society and their workforce. These Quaker companies were in their day some of the most successful that have been created. Did you know that one of the biggest banks in the UK was originally a Quaker bank whose founding principles were honesty, integrity and plain dealing? It now mired in seemingly endless controversies about miss-selling scandals and fines for fraudulent rate rigging."

"Any excess profits we make through our Social Enterprise Fund go into supporting the germination of new social enterprises. These might be social investments in communities that are sympathetic to our values or investment to protect wildlife and the rapidly vanishing habitats it depends upon. As an example, last year we managed to finance ten university scholarships for bright students from local schools. We also managed to finance a new maternity and aftercare centre covering a catchment area of 500 square kilometres. This offers free healthcare to mothers and children who need it where before there was none. What is more rewarding? Having hundreds of thousands or even millions of pounds in pay and bonuses that you don't conceivably need or knowing that your efforts have helped save the life of babies and mothers that may otherwise have died?"

"Vanessa, did you have to give up any of your assets in order to join the community here at Consciência?" asked Jessica.

"I would rather say that my previous material assets live on in the future wellbeing of others rather than being given up" replied Vanessa. "In this regard I see them as far more profitably invested than they were before. In answer to your question, I had to be prepared to divest myself of several million pounds as a condition of joining the community here in Consciência" replied Vanessa. "It wasn't a difficult decision to make, much of it is now helping my friend Alexandra to provide shelter and counselling for abused women in London, and the rest went into the Consciência Social Enterprise Fund that I now help to manage. My happiness and the quality of my life have also both improved beyond recognition from the time when my priority in life was fixated with chasing personal wealth."

"Doesn't giving up so much money make you feel vulnerable?" asked Jessica, "you may now have to rely on other people to support you whereas before you were independent."

"That is the terrible logic of a greed based society" answered Vanessa. "Nobody is actually secure on their own; we all depend on each other in one way or another but the more individualistic society becomes, the less people equate their happiness and security with the society they live in. Greed is actually the best indicator of someone plagued by self-doubt and insecurity. Placing your faith on material wealth is a false security. All too easily such material empires can come crashing down. True security comes when people are looking out for the needs of one another not through financial isolation. When I had all my wealth there was only really me looking out for my wellbeing and interests and it was only the chance kindness of strangers that helped to show me a different path. In Consciência there are hundreds of people who would come to my assistance if I needed it and this doesn't count all the friends we have made across the world. I have never felt happier or more secure in my life than I do now."

"What people don't realise is that an obsession for accumulating wealth is an addiction, as bad, if not worse than a drug addiction" said Owen. "It can completely dominate someone's life to the exclusion of all other considerations. This is why wise teachings associated with the Buddha, Jesus and the writers of the Bhagavad Gita warn so strongly against accumulating wealth. It is not possible to take a personal journey to find your true self if your conscious moments are dominated by greed and an addiction to money. I know this from bitter experience, I shudder to think what my life would have been like if a random accident hadn't brought me to Lumi and even then I very nearly wasted the opportunity."

"Alfredo, who you met at the reception desk at the Village Centre, was one of the early founders of Consciência and refuses to this day to keep any significant financial assets at all" continued Owen. "When he came to us originally he brought $137 million with him which he handed over in its entirety immediately after we set out the rules for the retention of personal assets. He was probably more aware of the dangers of not bringing in this ruling than anyone else in the community at the time."

Owen went on to tell Jessica Alfredo's story. Alfredo had made a fortune through property speculation in the USA. The whole focus of his life had been dominated by a crazy, irrational, yet all-consuming desire to create ever more wealth. He had no time for people who were vulnerable, disabled, unemployed or unable to afford proper healthcare. These people were just a statistic to him, a drain on society. If they were poor it must have been because they hadn't tried hard enough to succeed, he reasoned. They deserved their fate. Anyway they were the problem of the state he convinced himself, even though he used every trick in the accountant's book to make sure the state got as little from him in taxation as possible to support them.

One evening he was visiting a tenement block that he had just acquired at auction. He wanted to see whether there were any squatters in the building that he would have to get evicted before he sent the bulldozers in. When he got there the building appeared to be deserted. He also noticed with some considerable satisfaction that the new padlock his company had placed on the gate in the wire mesh fencing that closed the building off was still in place. He picked up a Maglite torch that he had brought with him and undid the padlock to have a closer look. There was a corrugated iron sheet that was supposed to be sealing the doorway but on closer inspection with his torch he noticed a shadow down one side that shouldn't have been there. The sheet had been forcefully bent back leaving a gap big enough to squeeze through. Someone had obviously found another way onto the site, bypassing the padlocked gate.

Alfredo squeezed past the corrugated iron and heard the sound of voices and music coming from the first floor. Now any sensible person at this stage would have let caution be the better part of valour and have come back in the morning with a security escort to evaluate the situation, but not Alfredo. He was suddenly furious with these people who were likely to cause a severe delay the development of the land and cost him thousands in court fees. Any vestiges of common sense deserted him, overridden by his sudden anger. He couldn't stand squatters, he believed they were the worst type of human scum. In his fury he virtually ran up the stairs towards where the sound was coming from and hammered with his fist on the plywood board that the squatters had rigged up as a makeshift internal door. The door opened to reveal a slim dark haired girl in an afghan coat appraising him calmly. Suddenly a huge guy in a motorcycle jacket appeared behind her virtually blocking out the light from the room with his powerful frame. Alfredo's sense of self-preservation finally kicked in with a rush of adrenalin. His instincts had no debate about whether fight or flight was going to be the best option; he was definitely going to make excuses followed by a rapid exit. The girl asked him what he wanted but when he tried to speak he couldn't. Alfredo suddenly felt a great pressure on his chest and a terrible shortness of breath, his legs collapsed underneath him and he rapidly blacked out on the landing.

The next thing Alfredo remembered was waking up in a hospital bed. The doctors told him that he had had a heart attack and that his heart had stopped. Fortunately a medical student at the scene had kept him alive long enough for the paramedics to get to him. He called his site manager and told him that on no account was anyone to do anything with tenement until further notice. A few weeks later he returned to the block and found the couple of squatters who had so enraged him on his first visit. This was how he got to know Greg, a trainee doctor and motorbike enthusiast and Marion, a nurse who, along with seven others were using the building as temporary low cost accommodation whilst they completed their medical training. Greg had instantly realised what was happening and kept him alive through CPR until the paramedics had arrived with a defibrillator.

Owing to speculation from people like Alfredo, many students like Greg and Marion simply couldn't afford to live legally near the medical school. Some of the fabulously expensive buildings in this desirable part of the city were actually virtually empty; their owners just sitting on them as an investment. As available property became scarcer through the action of the speculators, the price of housing rocketed. Whilst empty buildings sat accumulating money for emotionally empty owners, thousands of people lived in increasingly abject poverty, their earnings virtually wiped out by spiralling mortgage costs or rents from unscrupulous landlords.

Alfredo had realised that these two people, whom he had so despised for being in his way, had not only saved his life but were also training to save other people's lives. He looked at his own life, his empty selfishness and lack of any empathy or compassion for anyone else and he despised what he saw. He set up an investment trust fund that paid for the redevelopment of the tenement into a community health centre and continued to support its ongoing running costs. The Harley Centre, named after Greg's bike passion and with a dig at the consultants in expensive suits from Harley Street in London, was now administered by Greg and Marion. They had subsequently married, and were now two of Alfredo's dearest friends. He found out about the alternative society that Consciência was trying to create via one of Owen's ads and he brought his remaining wealth which was not committed to the long term upkeep of the Harley Centre, with him. Once the vote on limiting personal wealth had been taken at Consciência, a motion that Alfredo wholeheartedly supported, he immediately handed it all over to the Social Enterprise Fund.

"I talked to Alfredo about his total aversion to personal wealth," said Vanessa "I felt it was rather an extreme position to take. He told me that his greed had been an all-consuming addiction and just like a heroin user or an alcoholic; he dare not expose himself to another fix. He hated the sort of person that it had turned him into, in his own words 'a loathsome parasite feeding on the misery and misfortune of others.' He had pledged to never again open himself up to the risk of greed seeping back into his consciousness."

"Alfredo says that he had never felt so contented with his life since the day he gave it all away. Security in his life now depends on the happiness and security of the community. He devotes his energies in supporting Consciência and those who live or visit here, living off the modest salary that his job provides. I have actually made provision for Alfredo in the accounts, and he does have a personal legacy should he ever need it although he has no idea it exists. Whilst

Consciência thrives we would never let Alfredo or any other member of our community be in need of help without offering love and support, but sadly we can't guarantee the long term existence of Consciência."

"Why is that?" asked a startled Jessica.

"If humanity continues on its current path of rapid population growth and unconstrained exploitation it will soon be beyond the ability of the Earth's rapidly depleting resources to sustain it. Humanity will soon reap the climatic rewards of its ignorant meddling with the balance of the natural world and there will be terrible famine, poverty and inevitably war" said Vanessa. "We will not be able to live as an island in such circumstances; desperate hungry men with guns will soon find our little haven and tear it apart. We, along with many other people of conscience, are trying to influence humanity to change direction. We wish to steer it away from continued population explosion and the shameless exploitation and destruction of precious natural environments but it is far from probable that we can do this in time. The two choices facing humanity are either a rapid and radical change of values and direction or a catastrophic and an inevitably violent collapse."

"Is there no hope at all?" said Jessica in growing despair. What Vanessa and Owen had said brought back similar emotions to the one she had felt in her dream and she shuddered as she remembered.

"Of course there is hope Jessica" said Vanessa. "Your presence here today brings hope. When we got that call about you from Ellen and Roxie it was another ray of light in the darkness. Above all there is still such capacity for love in the world and where there is still love there is still hope."

"Lumi said I should talk to Sensi about the meaning of love" said Jessica.

"And so you should" said Vanessa, "now if you young lovebirds have heard enough I think you should leave me with Owen to thrash out what we need to do with this proposal."

6

Jessica and Raul left Vanessa and Owen in the café and unselfconsciously joined hands as they walked together. "Everyone seems to think we are falling in love" said Raul rather awkwardly.

Jessica pulled Raul round until they were facing each other.

"What do you think Raul?" she said "do you think we are falling in love?"

"No" replied Raul, "I think I have already fallen in love with you."

"Lumi would say that you have just fallen in lust" teased Jessica.

"I fell in lust the first time I saw you in the pool" replied Raul "but since I have got to know you better I know that my feelings for you are not just sexual attraction. You captivate me; I am finding it virtually impossible to concentrate on anything else I am supposed to be doing."

"Lumi would still call it infatuation" said Jessica.

She noticed the sudden hurt in his eyes at her teasing. He went to turn away from her but she pulled him back and kissed him deeply and passionately. "It's a very lovely infatuation" she said as they eventually pulled apart. She knew without a doubt that she wanted to make love to this handsome, sensitive, talented and captivating man. She didn't care if it was lust, infatuation or love. In the short time she had met Raul he made her feel more alive than any other man she had ever met. Maybe it was the atmosphere of this strange community on the other side of the world, maybe it was partly as a result of her experience with Lumi? Whatever it was she knew that she was going to completely succumb to her desire if the opportunity presented itself.

"I want to talk to your sister about love" she said to Raul as they sat on a bench by the great Kapok tree, "and I don't want you to be earwigging in on our conversation either" she added as she saw him break into a mischievous grin.

"I'll see if I can get hold of her" he said. "Where can I find you?"

"I want to check up on my emails and write down the detail of my experience with Lumi before it fades" said Jessica.

"I'll call you in a bit and let you know what Sensi says"

They parted with another kiss and Jessica virtually skipped back to her apartment. Despite everything that Owen, Vanessa and Lumi had talked about, despite her dream, or trance, or whatever it was that happened in the forest, she had never felt so optimistic about the future.

A bit later she got a call from Raul telling her that Sensi had invited her to a picnic lunch at the stone circle the following day. He asked her what she was planning to do that evening and whether she wanted to go out but she declined. She suddenly felt overwhelmingly tired and after making herself a sandwich and a glass of milk, she fell into a deep but rather troubled sleep. Recollections from her daydream and other seemingly disconnected visions and thoughts whirled around in her subconscious as her psyche tried to make some kind of sense of it all.

The following morning Raul picked her up after breakfast and he showed her around the facility where he worked and talked about their future plans for improving the efficiency of their hydrogen production and the associated fuel cell technology. Despite his claims of being completely captivated by Jessica, once Raul started to explain his work she could see how much it meant to him. She didn't understand all of what he was explaining but she loved seeing his passion and enthusiasm. Raul was absolutely convinced that energy needs of the world in the future were going to be largely met through the use of hydrogen.

"We haven't even scratched the surface of the potential for hydrogen associated technologies" he said. "Instead of working out how to extract more carbon based fuels from the Earth to pollute the atmosphere and contaminate the ground and the waterways, we should be focussing on how to use this wonderful source of clean energy. If our work here at Consciência achieves nothing more than help prove the viability of such technologies it will all have been worth it. Sadly there are huge sums of money being made by people who extract and sell carbon based fuels and many of the politicians are in their pockets. It will be a tough battle to make inroads against such odds but the alternative if the world carries on as it is will be cataclysmic."

Jessica left Raul at the plant and used one of the electric buggies to make her way back to the village centre. She parked up the buggy and walked up the path towards the stone circle enjoying the sounds of the animals and birds emanating from the canopies of the trees. There had been a heavy shower whilst she had been with Raul and this enhanced the smell of the lush vegetation. As she passed under the torii she saw Sensi sat on the stone altar at the centre of the circle. She looked up and waved at Jessica as if she had somehow sensed her presence. As Jessica entered the circle she saw a deer spring into the safety of forest and there were squirrels playfully chasing each other around the stones.

"I hope you are being gentle with Raul" said Sensi after they had kissed each other's cheeks in greeting. "Despite the rock musician image he likes to portray, he is quite sensitive underneath. I remember he was heartbroken when his first serious girlfriend split up with him after university."

Jessica thought of her teasing and the hurt look that she had received from Raul as a consequence and felt mildly guilty.

"Have you two made love yet?" asked Sensi much to Jessica's amazement.

"Sensi!"

"Well everyone else can see that you can barely keep your hands off each other so it seems a reasonable question."

"Not that I'm used to sharing details of my love live, especially with boyfriends' sisters but the answer is no" replied Jessica.

"Aha, you used the term boyfriend! So you do admit that you fancy him?"

"Yes"

"So the issue is that neither of you have the confidence to take the first step."

"There is no issue and anyway Sensi I did not come here to discuss my love life!"

"That's a shame."

"But I do want to talk about love or what is meant by the word love. Roxie told me that love was the answer that I was seeking but that I didn't understand what was meant by the word. Lumi suggested that I should talk to you about it."

"Well you could say that there are two types of love" said Sensi. "There is conscious love and there is unconscious love. The love that you are developing for Raul comes into the second category, unconscious love. My friend Roxie would say that you are mostly in lust with Raul but as you have got to know him you are developing a deeper attachment and this is moving into the realm of love. Love is often first detected if you are faced with the object of your attachment facing harm or of being lost. It is surprising how quickly a person can make such an attachment; it is almost instantaneous if the object of the love resonates with similar imagery embedded in the unconscious. Such attachments are most often triggered by imagery except when a person has lost their sight. In such cases the other senses develop to trigger the internal imagery that is part of what Jung would call humanity's collective unconscious."

"You said the object of the attachment triggers unconscious love. Don't you mean person?" asked Jessica.

"No not at all. The object could just as easily be a favoured pet or even an unknown animal whose image had triggered a response. If I showed you a picture of a baby marmoset I can almost guarantee that you will love that marmoset before the conscious part of your mind has even properly registered the image. This is a lovely aspect of humans, they have an extraordinary capacity to love and an instinct to nurture and protect. If I told you that the marmoset had been orphaned because its mother had been shot by a poacher and frightened and alone it would almost certainly die, you would become quite distressed at the thought. This whole process may just have taken a few seconds. The object could even be a favourite view, plant or tree. The site of a beautiful rainforest being cut down and burned certainly causes me emotional hurt when I see it."

"So you are saying that I haven't consciously chosen to love Raul but that this attachment has been made in my unconscious because he resonates with imagery that I have embedded there?" said Jessica.

"Yes but for goodness sake don't go analysing all your feelings in such a way or you will take all the joy away" said Sensi. "Feelings of love and affection are what make life so wonderful and the fact that you don't consciously choose these feelings makes them all the more powerful and exciting. When you are close to Raul you should relish the sensations that he creates in you. Yes you will be hurt if the relationship ends or your love is not returned but such hurt proves that you were truly alive. I believe the saying is that it is better to have loved and lost than to have never loved at all. I fully agree with this saying. We don't have to be completely naïve when we give into such pleasures, we can do so in the knowledge of the emotional dangers they present and acknowledging such risk still take the plunge."

"What about conscious love, what do you mean by that?" asked Jessica.

"The first step is to understand and acknowledge the process of unconscious love. If we understand this process we can consciously use it to channel energy and focus on the things we choose to care about. This is a process of deliberately creating the imagery knowing that it will trigger an emotional response and an associated passion to act. There are pitfalls in this path, as you deliberately open up your emotions to these images you will also open up the pain that goes with them when the focus of your attachment is under threat. This is why so many people shut off the hurt and suffering around them. They know it is there but they deliberately suppress these feelings to avoid the hurt or the associated guilt of not acting."

"Can you give me an example?" asked Jessica.

"Well let's take the marmoset shall we? If I told you that through the actions of poachers and illicit farming, hundreds of marmosets were being killed each week this would have virtually no impact upon you. It is not imagery; it is a statistic and as such stimulates virtually no emotional resonance in your unconscious. You could however decide that you will deliberately expose yourself to associated imagery. Look up the website of the few people who care enough about marmosets that they provide shelter. Deliberately look at the animals, the harm and hurt they have suffered. Get to know the names that have been given to some of the orphaned marmosets in the shelter. The unconscious emotional reactions that this will stimulate will create compassion, a strong desire to nurture and protect and even righteous anger. These emotions will all be triggered in exactly the same way as the earlier example of the baby marmoset but this time you will have initiated this by refusing to accept these creatures as statistics but as vulnerable animals they are instead. This is after all the real situation and the appropriate response for any caring person."

"In the dream I experienced when I was with Lumi it was the screaming of the monkey at the end that I can never forget" said Jessica.

"This was a similar process although the original instigator of this process was not a conscious decision but originated in the unconscious realms of your mind. In your dream your suppressed feelings were actually reaching out to your consciousness to make you aware of the turmoil that was going on within you. It forced your consciousness to face up to the emotional cost of the terrible damage we are doing to our natural world by creating a specific visualisation in your consciousness. This visualisation then triggered your powerful emotional response."

"It seems all very complicated" said Jessica.

"Did anyone ever tell you that it was simple?" chided Sensi.

"Just the opposite" admitted Jessica.

"Let me give you another example" said Sensi, one that is very personal to me. "In London I have a very special friend whom I love very much. When she was young she suffered a terrible mutilation, her vaginal lips and clitoris were cut off with a razorblade and her vagina sewn up. It is horrific to think what she had to go through and it has impacted upon the rest of her life. I can tell you that it is estimated that 24,000 girls every year are at risk of going through this same terrible ordeal in your so called civilised country. It has been illegal for nearly thirty years and yet to date, nobody has ever been convicted. How do you feel about that?"

"Well it's terrible" said Jessica.

"That is a rational response, not an emotional one" said Sensi. "You haven't effectively visualised what I have been telling you. You have listened to the words, you have heard the statistics but you don't really care yet. If Raul came into this clearing you would probably forget what I have said in an instant. The authorities in your country also don't really care. Stopping such an appalling practice is in the culturally sensitive, rather difficult box and they would really like to look the other way. In fact for nearly thirty years they have been effectively doing so."

"Genuinely caring is an emotional response and the emotions are triggered by visual imagery. Now let's say I was to introduce you to a little girl in the village. I then took you with this little girl to a room and asked you to watch while three adults held her down whilst a fourth cut her with a rusty blade and I made you listen to her screams and see the blood soaking in to the towel underneath. Then you would care, in fact I suspect you would have tried to physically protect the girl from the adults responsible even if it put you at personal risk. You would probably never fully recover from seeing such an appalling thing and it's highly likely that you would campaign fervently to get it stopped. If a video of such a thing was played on your national news programme without hiding any of the horrors, the authorities would be forced to act overnight at the public outrage. They would however never allow it, making the excuse that it would be too distressing to watch and thereby avoiding having to deal with such a situation. Well I'm sorry but people need to be distressed if there is any hope of stopping the many horrors going on in our world."

"Are you saying that our politicians understand this process?" said Jessica.

"A powerful emotional response from those they seek to control is the greatest fear that politicians and those who manipulate them have. They go to extraordinary lengths to objectify the victims of their actions. The poor, disabled and vulnerable become statistics and are described as lazy or shirkers so that the rest of the society don't identify with them. They hate personal stories that show the real victims of their policies, the hungry child, the person crippled with pain because they can't get healthcare. This is why it is so important to own and manipulate the media."

"The first thing any tyrant does when they are taking power is to take control of the media and manipulate the emotions of the majority. Their favourite emotion to trigger is fear because frightened people lose all sense of rationality when the survival instincts kick in. This is what the Nazi's did in Germany. The Jewish people were objectified; they were no longer real men, women and children with hopes, loves, fears and desires for their future life like everyone else. The Jewish people became the scapegoat for economic failure, a segregated statistic and also a source of fear because of the threat of associated persecution to those who stood up against the outrages going on."

"I still don't fully understand what this has to do with love" said Jessica.

"By opening our eyes and deliberately choosing to see what is going on we can trigger the natural and most beautiful of human emotions. These are the emotions linked to love, compassion and empathy. These emotions cut through the illusions; illusions deliberately placed before us by those who want to manipulate and control us, and reveal to us what is really going on."

"Don't you mean see what is going on" said Jessica.

"No, no, no! You haven't understood, you must feel it with your emotions if you are to understand the reality of what is happening in the world. The visualisation is just a part of the process that you deliberately use to trigger such feelings. This is the path that leads to wisdom. It is about having the intellectual intelligence to see the manipulations that are put up to disguise what is happening and the emotional intelligence to overcome the selfishness of the ego which has its own agenda. This is about choosing the path of conscious love. When you hear a statistic about cruelty, or poverty or injustice, visualise what it really means and trust and act upon the emotions that result."

"I think I am beginning to understand you now" said Jessica. "Love is an aspect of our true nature and we can use this to care passionately about the world around us if we can trigger it through a process of internal visualisation. Knowing this we can learn to consciously love by deliberately seeking to visualise what is happening when we hear stories wrapped up in statistics that would normally never trigger an emotional response. We would never allow ourselves to cause so much damage to our beautiful Earth and nature that sustains all life if we truly chose to visualise the consequences. Perhaps we could save our world if enough people became intelligent enough to choose to love it."

"Don't forget that the Earth is the womb of life, the realm of the Goddess" said Sensi. "Our universe is full of suns with their raging fires and gases which could be considered as male aspects of the universe. It is only when very special conditions exist; water and the nutrients of the earth, the female aspects of our universe's nature, that the destructive character of these forces can be harnessed and become creative. Once harnessed these are the forces that can stimulate the creation of life itself. This is a rare and precious phenomenon in the vastness of the universe. In our human world the male aspect of our species has long dominated, constraining the creative power of love to nurture and care for our beautiful Earth. Raging unchecked egos worship greed and power, preventing the conditions for love and compassion to flourish. We need to seek the Goddess that exists in the psyche of every person and listen to her voice if there is to be any hope for our world. The Goddess is a very powerful visualisation and this visualisation is a potent source of natural magic if you can learn to harness it."

"I think I understand what Roxie was telling me now" said Jessica. "The meaning of my life is to open up to my true nature, to visualise what is happening in the world around me and to consciously choose to care and to love."

"There is another powerful benefit for our individual development through consciously choosing to love" said Sensi. "The human ego desires to be the central focus of our existence. If we choose conscious love, our focal point sits way beyond the selfish demands of our own ego. By focusing beyond the petty demands of the ego our human psyche can bypass the barriers that the ego had deliberately created to supress the aspects our nature associated with love. This has the desirable aspect of gradually weakening the control that the ego has over our unconscious emotions. It helps to enable the ego to mature beyond its own petty cravings. As I am sure that Lumi explained to you, wisdom is when the conscious and unconscious aspects of our psyche come into balance. This is a powerful benefit of an external focus brought about through the power of conscious love; it helps us on the path to self-realisation. Wisdom teachers have being trying to tell humanity this for thousands of years and yet we have proved to be very poor students."

"An external focus for love can initiate self-sacrifice, where the needs of the self are put aside to serve a greater purpose, in extreme circumstances even being prepared to sacrifice life itself. This concept of self-sacrifice will be immediately understood by many parents should their own children be threatened by harm. This powerful desire to protect your own children is unconscious love; it is programmed into the very essence of the majority of people. If such parents also consciously chose to create love by deliberately visualising the needs of all the Earth's children and loving them with the same intensity as their own, humanity would soon stop its orgy of destruction. Ultimately the futures of all the children of the Earth are entwined. Nobody will be immune from the consequences of our collective actions. Those people who care too little and are too apathetic to act are not protecting their own children. They are condemning them and their grandchildren and all future generations to the malign consequences of their ignorance and selfishness."

"Thank you so much Sensi" said Jessica. "No wonder Roxie laughed at me when I asked her for the meaning of life and she told me it was love. She knew that the Jessica that was stood before her at the time would never have understood what the answer meant. I will never be able to repay the love Ellen and Roxie have shown to me by sending me to Consciência."

"The best way to repay such love is to pass it on to others" replied Sensi. "This is the only payment they would desire. I believe the only obligation they put on you was to publish your story on your return so others could learn from your experiences should they chose to do so. Now after all this analysis on the nature of love, please don't forget what I said earlier," cautioned Sensi. "Unconscious love is also powerful and wonderful and should be celebrated and enjoyed. Analysing such love would be like jumping on a roller coaster and spending the entire ride trying to find the brake, where is the fun in that? Life should not be all about reason and control, it should also be about impulse and desire and laughter and, yes the associated hurt and the crying too. On this subject, when are you going to seduce my brother? You are likely to be old and grey before he summons up the courage to ask."

"Sensi, you really are impossible!" exclaimed Jessica but she was laughing as she did so.

"So what are you planning to do now after our discussion about love? Do you start to see a direction to follow to take you forward in your life?" asked Sensi.

"I think that was vividly revealed to me in the revelation I experienced with Lumi" replied Jessica. "The purpose for my life is to consciously look beyond my own immediate desires. Through conscious visualisation I shall choose to love this wonderful Earth and all of the creatures that depend upon it. The destiny for humanity should be as the protective custodians of this precious natural world but instead we just see it as a source of exploitation to feed the meaningless cravings of our petty selfish egos. We humans are capable of the most incredible love and kindness but all too often we demonstrate the most appalling cruelty, greed and selfishness instead."

"Using the power of love I intend to devote my life to being a responsible custodian of our Earth and I intend to start this work as soon as I return to the UK. Vanessa has told me that I can stay in her room in the Warehouse in London for a while if I would like to. In my revelation with Lumi, the only way to protect the forest and the animals was to get the captain to stop the ship, a ship that was consuming them to fuel a journey towards its own inevitable destruction. The captains of our global ship steer a similar path in places like the City of London and Wall Street, destroying the very fabric of our planet and the natural world as they ply their trade. These are the high temples of human greed and this is where the battle for human consciousness and a very different set of values must be won or else all will be lost."

"I now understand that the shuffling masses in the hold of the ship represented the ignorant and largely apathetic majority of the people of Earth. Just like the calming messages from the ship's crew, they are deliberately numbed, mollified by the misinformation pumped out by a media largely controlled by self-serving plutocrats. Most of the Earth's population are unknowingly shuffling inextricably towards their own demise. It may ultimately prove to be a futile effort to wake these people from their slumbers but I will find others who have awoken and together we will make a very loud clamour indeed!"

"I will also succumb to the perils and joys of unconscious love and cry myself to sleep at the hurt should it all go wrong. I shall take the greatest joy that I have been blessed enough to be born on this beautiful gem of a planet, a small speck of life in the vastness of the universe, like a tiny oasis in the desert. I shall discover how to visualise the true nature of the Goddess that is manifest in all forms of life and learn to live in harmony with her and benefit from her wisdom."

Sensi didn't say anything, instead she just held Jessica in her arms in a lingering loving embrace. The two young women finished their picnic and Sensi then took Jessica on a walk into the forest to share some of its delights with her. She showed her how to find certain fruits and medicinal herbs, where it was likely that she could spot the deer and how to identify the sounds of the different troops of monkeys. She also told Jessica that Lumi had offered to let her stay with her for a month so that should could learn more about listening to her inner unconscious and interpret what it was saying to her. Lumi also offered to share some of her experience in harnessing the energies that permeated the natural world and how to consciously channel these for positive purposes such as healing. Jessica told Sensi that she would be delighted to accept Lumi's offer also knowing that this would give her at least another month with Raul.

7

Jessica returned to her apartment to check on her emails and messages. She had a text message and she flushed with excitement as she read it. The message simply said that Raul loved her and if she loved him too she should meet him in the stone circle just before 8 o'clock this evening. She decided to lie on the bed and get some rest but thoughts of Raul and their rendezvous initially prevented her from sleeping. The weather was also getting hotter and more humid and the breeze had dropped. Although the apartment was very well insulated she still felt prickles of sweat forming on her skin. Eventually she succumbed and slept until the early evening.

Jessica had a shower and put on a loose fitting halter neck turquoise dress which was transparent enough to reveal the contours of her body underneath without being overtly explicit. She added a single blue topaz stone mounted on a chain that now rested tantalisingly between the swell of her breasts. The outfit was completed by a pair of silver sequined slip on sandals that she had picked up in the market. She stood in front of the long mirror in the bedroom and twisted from side to side, watching the dress swirl around the swell of her hips with satisfaction. If she couldn't seduce him in this outfit she never would!

Jessica wandered into the village, noticing with some satisfaction the admiring glances that she received on the way and took the path towards the pools which led to the stone circle. It was becoming even more humid now and she heard a rumble of thunder in the distance as the air started to discharge the static electricity that had been building up within the clouds. She pulled a torch from her shoulder bag as it was now almost completely dark. As she neared the split in the path that led under the torii to the stone circle she could see a faint flickering of light between the trees.

The circle was deserted but there were four oil lanterns on stands surrounding the altar in the centre where she had sat down with Sensi earlier in the day. There were small dishes of food set on a tray on the wooden platform that the altar rested upon and a jug with two goblets. There was also an incense stand which gave off a seductive aroma in the stillness of the night air. The altar itself was covered with several alpaca wool rugs and she felt the silky softness of the wool as she ran her hand over them. Her heart was racing, she had never realised that Raul was such a romantic; he had seemed so practical and slightly awkward in her company earlier that morning. How many other girls would be invited to such a majestic and mysterious setting on a first date? Jessica already knew that this was going to be a night that she would never forget.

Another rumble of thunder, this time a bit closer and the sky above the forest was momentarily lit up by a large flash as the gathering storm started to discharged it's pent up energy into the canopy below. A sudden gust of wind made the light from the lanterns flicker slightly behind their protective glass. Jessica saw Raul's figure entering the circle in the lightning's flash and she walked to meet him. They embraced, their lips meeting, reluctant to part whilst nature's orchestra provided its own backdrop of timpani as the thunder reverberated off the surrounding hills.

"I got your text but I never expected this" said Raul looking at the altar in amazement.

"My text?" said Jessica. "I didn't send you a text; I came because of your text."

They looked at each other in astonishment and then Jessica began to chuckle. "The minx! This is all Sensi's doing, she has set us both up."

Raul looked flushed and annoyed, "she shouldn't have done this Jessica; how will you ever forgive us." He was about to continue to protest when Jessica put a finger on his lips.

"She did this because she loves you Raul. Didn't you always say how much you trusted in Sensi's judgement? Let's trust her wisdom now. How many other sisters would go to these lengths out of love for their brother? Come; let's see what she has brought us."

They sat down and sampled the various dishes that Sensi had laid out before them like a sumptuous tapas. The jug contained one of Lumi's mead wines, although this one tasted very different to the one she had tasted in Lumi's home. It spread a warm honey glow through their bodies as they sampled it.

Jessica turned to Raul and grasping his hand she took him to the altar. She looked him seductively in the eyes as she slowly slipped out of her dress and lay down naked on her back. She became a living altar in female form, her womb now at the very centre of the circle. Raul looked down on this extraordinary beautiful young woman who was offering herself to his touch, her body highlighted in the frequent flashes of lightning that now seemed to have surrounded them.

Raul took off his clothes and lay above her, kissing her gently on her lips and her throat and tracing the lobes of her ears with his tongue. He cupped her firm young breasts, small and rounded and kissed the hardened nipples which were already responding to the rising arousal in Jessica's body. He moved down to her belly and kissed her again just above the small fan of hair leading to the little hood that nestled around the button head of her now engorged sex. She let out a groan of desire as his tongue flicked under the hood and then traced its way between her lips that were already beginning to part in anticipation and were glistening with desire.

Without warning Jessica suddenly grabbed hold of Raul and threw him down onto his back. She grasped his hard swollen member and in quick motion straddled him and guided him inside. There was a large crack above them and a deafening rumble of thunder as Jessica rode astride Raul. The wind had suddenly whipped up blowing her hair wildly behind her and torrential rain began to fall upon them as they made frantic love together. It was as if the great Goddess, herself was embracing their passion and desire and Jessica screamed into the storm as the sexual tension within her exploded into an intense orgasm that wracked her whole body. Raul's frantic movements underneath her told her that he was soon to join her. She rocked her hips above him drawing out his climax, the force of which physically lifted Jessica's body off the altar as his hips arched in ecstasy beneath her.

After the explosive nature of their first lovemaking, their second was much gentler as Raul lay above Jessica. The release of their first primeval surge of lust had now made room for the love that was developing between them to set a different tempo. Jessica's instincts were right, they would never forget this first wonderful night of lovemaking. The storm also judged the change of mood. The wind dropped and the rain ceased to fall on the naked bodies making love beneath the clearing night skies.

Much later, their passion spent, the two young lovers were enjoying the cool air of the night released by the passing of the storm. Jessica was sat on the edge of the wooden platform that supported the altar with Raul's head on her lap and she gently played with his hair. Her thoughts were now turning to the future with calm determination. Somehow the power of love, conscious love, would overcome the greed and anger of the world and although she had no idea how this was to be accomplished she knew her future was now inextricably joined to this purpose.

They heard a deep rumbling growl and a sleek powerful shape moved slowly into the circle which was still gently illuminated by the light of the lanterns. It slowly circled the altar and lay down before them a short distance from Jessica's feet. Raul started in momentary anxiety but Jessica just hushed him and placed a calming hand upon his forehead. All her instincts were telling her that they had nothing to fear. The horned god Cernunnos lay contentedly in the lap of the goddess Aradia and for this one night at least the Jaguar had come out of the shadows.

38772469R00152

Made in the USA
Charleston, SC
19 February 2015